D0209336

WILL

WILL

GRACE TIFFANY

𝕭

BERKLEY BOOKS, NEW YORK

𝐵

A Berkley Book
Published by The Berkley Publishing Group
A division of Penguin Group (USA) Inc.
375 Hudson Street
New York, New York 10014

This is an original publication of The Berkley Publishing Group.

Copyright © 2004 by Grace Tiffany
Book design by Kristin del Rosario
Cover design by Lesley Worrell
Cover art by Kinuko Craft

First Edition: May 2004

Library of Congress Cataloging-in-Publication Data

Tiffany, Grace, 1958–
    Will/Grace Tiffany.—1st ed.
        p. cm.
    ISBN 0-425-19596-1
    1. Shakespeare, William, 1564-1616—Fiction. 2. Great Britain—History—Elizabeth, 1558–1603—Fiction. 3. London (England)—History—16th century—Fiction. 4. Hathaway, Anne, 1556?–1623—Fiction. 5. Stratford-upon-Avon (England)—Fiction. 6. Authors' spouses—Fiction. 7. Married women—Fiction. 8. Dramatists—Fiction. 9. Theater—Fiction. I. Title.

PS3620.I45W55 2004
813'.54—dc22

                                                                        2003067219

Printed in the United States of America

10 9 8 7 6 5 4 3 2 1

For the Players

"Let my name, like Odysseus', be Nobody"

—JORGE LUIS BORGES

WILL

Grace Tiffany

Chapter One

GILBERT was good at Latin.

Schoolmaster Hunt's habit was to choose a passage from Pliny or Virgil and bid his pupils construe it line by line, boy by boy, starting with Ass Aspinall in the first row. Will would try to guess which line would fall to him, and desperately work to translate it before he heard the dread word: "Shakespeare?" But he could never tell with which side of the room Hunt would start as the construal snaked through the rows, and so usually his guess was worthless, and he was left, sweating, to improvise a translation of a line he had not yet read. Still, his inventions showed verve. "Great Caesar, hast thou fired the Dutch oven?" he would boldly bark. Or, "Like gush from a vomiting camel rushed the pea-green Tiber!" These answers pleased the boys, but not the master, a frail-looking recusant Catholic, who would advance down the rows to cuff Will on the back of the head.

Five days of the week, eight hours of the day, Will stood with the other boys in the airless schoolroom above the Guildhall, leaning on a wooden desk, copying phrases from a tedious Latin grammar and practicing declensions. *Singulariter, nominativo, hic, haec, hoc.* The grammar's author was a hated man named William Lyly, who dwelt in faraway London. Will imagined diabolical tortures for him, against the case that he one day met him on the street.

The boys had been alphabetized. Will stood in the rear row with Gilbert, knavish sibling, who rudely sniggered at Will's faltering tongue. By them stood Hamfist Sadler and Vinegar Tom Thompson. Two rows ahead was Rich Field, and behind Rich, Spiny Quiney. Will was the father of all the boys' nicknames. He toiled to make apt ones so that his schooltime might not be wasted. He favored names of two meanings. Hamfist had earned his for his terrible writing hand and his love of roast pig. Tom Thompson was "Vinegar" after a demon in which one of Will's aunts believed, and also after his breath, because his mother made him scrub his teeth with the stuff. Spiny Quiney had hair that stuck up in tufts when he took off his cap, and was so wastrel thin Will could count the joints in his backbone. Rich Field's name really *was* Rich Field. It had so many meanings in its own right that Will let it stand.

Will liked the rear row well. He had no trouble reading what the master scribbled on the large slate propped against the wall at the front of the room, and in the back it was easier to draw pictures, and not be seen. Hamfist Sadler could not master the ornate "secretary hand" two schoolmasters had tried to teach him, but he could sketch, and drew the best caricatures of Master Hunt. Paper was costly, and commonplace books were meant to be repositories of wise quotations from Greek and Roman authors, recorded for sober meditation, but those of Hamfist were filled with antic pictures, to which Will would supply captions. *I'LL BEET THEE SILLY WITH A CAT-O'-NINE TAILS!* Will would jot below the image of a crazed Hunt, eyes popping and mouth wide; or, *Shall I be the next POPE? thinx Master SIMONY Hunt,* under a sketch of Hunt looking beatific and self-satisfied, but sprouting horns. *Simony* was a word taught the boys by their old pedagogue, whom they'd called "Cock" Roche, and who'd disappeared forever from the schoolroom the day Will translated Virgil's famed line, "I sing of arms and the man," as "Do not, for God's love, call her Albert."

Before that sad occasion, Master Roche had explained that simony was a devilish practice performed in the unholy churches of the European continent. It concerned the sale of priestly offices for money. After rich men bought their clerical gowns and hats, Roche said, they sat in their French or Spanish churches and peddled what they claimed were spiritual favors, like prayers for the dead, to poor, gullible folk, taking their coin and imparting airy nothing in return. Will said this practice, indeed, was then much like schoolteaching, and received for that remark a horrible caning in front of the other boys. He had been glad to see Cock Roche go, and confessed to himself at times that Simon Hunt was more pleasant overall. Unbeknownst to the town fathers, Hunt would sometimes spice the boys' Latin diet with basic instruction in modern languages like French, and, when in one of his rare good humors, would lesson them in geography. The schoolmaster's mournful face would brighten as he spoke of foreign climates and customs, not only of European nations, but also of the Indies, Cathay, the far-off Antipodes, and strange lands across the Atlantic Sea. Aristotle, Master Hunt told them, had called those lands "torrid zones" and said they were uninhabitable. But Spanish explorers had since discovered thriving populations there, with flourishing towns, and it seemed Aristotle was *wrong.* The boys were shocked and delighted at these pedagogical heresies, and warmed slightly to Master Hunt when he spoke them.

Still, Simon Hunt was a schoolmaster, and needed an offensive nickname.

When Will suggested "Simony" it stuck.

Hunt, despite his good points, was widely known to be a member of the Unholy Church, and it seemed good to Will to suppose that he also aspired to be pope.

Pope. The word sounded well.

Some said the pope was a fire-breathing Antichrist who dressed in scarlet and had horns and seven heads. Schoolmaster Cock Roche had told of England's near escape from this monster in Rome. Less than twenty years before, when the land was spiritually benighted, many English folk had been fooled by the pope's dark powers into thinking he was their lord, was in fact God's representative on earth. Even England's last queen, Mary, now dead, had thought so. But now almost everyone knew that the new and much better queen, Mary's sister Elizabeth, was God's true agent, and that the pope was in fact the devil's kissing cousin. Still, Roche had told them, some English folk were yet deluded, and thought the pope was worth some smattering of awe. These folks were called Catholics, and to be one was to risk damnation.

When the boys from the godlier Protestant families tired of Latin lessons and Simon Hunt's thumps on their heads, they comforted themselves with the knowledge that the schoolmaster was Catholic, and, like all Catholics, would one day lie screaming in Hell.

It was sad that, since old Master Roche had belonged to the True English Church, he could not go there too.

WILL'S mother was once a Catholic. So it was horrifying—though wonderfully so—to hear one hot August morning in 1572 that the French had run riot in Paris on Saint Bartholomew's Day, hacking poor Protestants to death with axes and carving knives, burning their houses and shops, throwing Huguenot women and children into the Seine. When Queen Elizabeth heard of the massacre, she dressed all in black and unleashed her godliest preachers to rail against the papist threat. All Stratford, even the impious drunkards who lay abed on the Sabbath, had gone to Holy Trinity Church the next Sunday to hear their own puritanical rector blast Rome.

Even Catholics went.

Not to go would have implied pleased approval of the French murders.

Into one pew had squeezed the Shakespeares: Will and Gilbert, pushing and shoving one another; Will's mother, Mary Arden, an infant in her arms and her lips tight; Will's strong-armed father holding his small sister Joan on his lap. Next to and behind them sat Mary's seven sisters and their assorted husbands. Conspicuously absent had been one Arden man. Mary's rich cousin Edward had stayed home to observe mass in his usual way, with his odd old gardener who everyone knew was a Catholic priest.

His cousins were furious.

That afternoon a militant embassy of Arden women, trailed by a curious Will stuffing his face with bread and jam, visited and bearded their cousin at his manor. *How, Edward, canst thou dare to endanger thy family? Dost not know the risks of recusancy, most especially now? The Earl of Leicester's men are always in the town, asking whether this one or that one is Catholic; they seek sedition and they'll find what they want to find, no doubt of the matter. Now Edward Arden's name has been noted, thou'lt be fined, suspected . . .*

Will listened to the women's magpie chatter drifting across the garden, and to Uncle Edward barking back at his accusers. He himself wandered down the graveled pathways, peering at geometrically shaped plots of flowers. All was well ordered, and beautiful. Banks of lilies and full rosebushes cast their blended perfume on the breeze. Honeysuckle covered the walls, and through the windows carefully cut in the hedges by the gardener-priest wound sweetbriar and white-thorn. At the ends of the paths stood bowers of fruit trees whose branches intertwined. In the garden's center a marble statue of Mary raised her hands by a stone well.

Then he wandered inside, and discovered a new thing.

His uncle's library.

THE women were long gone and the sun was low in the sky. The boy lay inert on the library floor, behind a plush velvet settle, humming, eyes fixed on a book he held upright on his breast. It was a jam-smeared copy of the Roman poet Ovid's *Metamorphoses*. But it was not a Latin copy.

It was an English translation.

English! It smacked the ear; it rang; it sounded like what it meant. Like *weakened*. In Ovid, a youth was *weakened* by a nymph who pursued him. She knocked him into the water, and then he was fused with her forever, made *of a man but half a man*. And King Midas wished everything he touched might turn to gold, and so it had: the fruit he tried to eat, the bed he tried to lie in. When Midas's daughter ran, laughing, into his arms, he embraced her and turned her from a living girl to a block of solid, yellow metal. She came back to life in the end, but Midas had to wear ass's ears, ears, ears.

Ears was a very good word.

After the first day, Will's visits to the library continued. Uncle Edward let him take books into the garden. When Will's eyes grew bleary from reading he would rise and trail the old straw-hatted Jesuit around the bushes and plants and trees, watching him pluck the health-giving herbs like burnet and rosemary and mugwort, and listening to his half-mad babble about the endless cycle of birth, decay, death, and rebirth.

"Nature has a plot," the priest told Will. "A circular plot." The old man would touch the boy's hands to green ivy leaves or the petals of waxy red fumiter, saying, "Read. These are the pages of God's book."

"A circular book?"

"Geometry must be fathomed. Study it well. The circle, and the parabola, which stood on its end is the shape of a life." The priest made a *U* in the air with his finger, starting high, swooping low, then ending up again high.

"Yes, sir." Will had no idea what the old fool meant. Still, he thought himself apt to disparage the man's gardening. He pointed. "I think you are killing that tree."

"This?" The kneeling priest looked up. "I am not wounding this peach tree. Or rather, I wound it to heal it. I pierce it to let flow the sap that it may breathe. 'Tis a paradox. A confusion of contraries."

"Ah."

The mad priest squinted at Will. "Thine uncle's name is a paradox."

Will struck a debater's pose, right hand outstretched. "Explain."

The priest laughed. "*Arden* is Celtic. *Ard* is high and great, *den* is the low wooded valley. High and low, sky and earth, sun and darkness, spirit and clay, all coming together as one."

"Hmm. I am half Arden so half a paradox."

Again the priest laughed, and winked. "And so thou must puzzle thyself out."

Chapter Two

"IF *you do not love other people, what you do do doesn't bring you to Heaven. . . .*"

The gentle black-gowned rector was still preaching from Corinthians as Will crawled under pews to escape the narrow confines of Holy Trinity Church. "DOODOOdussent," he sang as he bounced through the woods. "DOODOOdussent, DOODOOdussent!" He tapped time on the trees with a stick. At the gate of the garden of Arden he rang his uncle's bell and was led by a simple-minded servant into the small chapel where the Arden household was worshipping. He knew he was not meant to be there, so, chameleonlike, he crept along the wall and crouched behind a rear pew, watching the backs of the family and servants who stood with their heads bowed.

The gardener-priest was transfigured.

He wore a white cassock in place of his kersey tunic and leggings, and raised a gold chalice skyward. Colored light streamed through the high glass windows of purple, yellow, blue, and red, and dappled the man's upturned face. Holy Trinity had once boasted such windows, Will's father had told him, but they'd been smashed by order of the Crown upon Elizabeth's accession. They were replaced by plain glass at the same time the town guild chapel's mural of devils, saints, and a rampant dragon and Saint George had been whitewashed and overlaid with the humble lettering of the Ten Commandments. All of that had happened before Will was born.

He had never seen anything so extravagant as the Arden chapel's windows.

He looked up at them in awe.

From his crouched position in back of the last chapel pew, he recognized the Prodigal Son, kneeling in ragged cloth at his joyful father's feet, and Adam and Eve in fig leaves, wending their way through Eden's gates past a white-robed angel with a flaming sword. The nearest window showed a vine heavily laden with grapes blown in purple glass, and underneath curved a long Latin sentence in the same shade of purple: *Alleluia, alleluia. Ego vos elegi de mundo, ut eatis et fructum afferatis, et fructus vester maneat.* Laboriously, he translated. *Alleluia. I have . . . elbowed? picked? you out of the world that you should . . . throw fruit? BEAR fruit, and that your fruit should stay.* He peeped at the priest. *"Ecce,"* the old man said, raising the host. *"Agnus Dei, ecce qui tollit peccata mundi."*

The Ardens and their servants gathered at the altar rail. Like baby sparrows they opened their mouths and received their crumbs of God.

"I saw you in the chapel," Uncle Edward said that afternoon in the library. "You do not hide as well as you think."

"I was not hiding," Will said brazenly. "I was watching the show."

"*Show!*" Edward knit his bushy brows and leaned toward his nephew, who had hidden his nose in *Canterbury Tales*. "The mass is not a play. 'Tis the change of bread and wine into the body and blood of Christ."

"The gardener's costume liked me well."

"That word is *vestments*. Are you a kind of idiot?"

"Yes, sir." Will turned a page. "I know not which kind."

"*Ha!*" Edward barked. "I am sure you made nothing of the Scripture because it was Latin. Corinthians, my lad. Let me see." He tapped his finger on his lip, thinking. "*The fire will try every man's work. If it is burned up, he himself may be saved, but only as one escaping through flames.*"

Will looked over at him. "What may *that* mean?"

"How would I know? I am no priest."

"Is't like the old Britons burning on their funeral pyres with their gold about them? *Eager for fame?*"

"Not very like."

"What are words *for,* uncle? To sound musical?"

"To tell truth." With that Edward turned back to his Greek translations.

Lying full-length and stomach-down on the floor, Will flipped Chaucer's pages and pondered. He had known his uncle's gardener was a priest. But now that he had met the wizened old digger, it boggled his mind that the man should have the power to turn wafers and claret into Christ Himself, or e'en the permission to try it. Once he had seen him step on a hornets' nest and leap a foot in the air yelping "*God's strossers!*" which meant *God's small clothes!* Would God entrust the handling of His Son to a man who spoke lightly of His smalls? And if He did, then to whom would He *deny* his authority? If an English elf like Will himself used the right words, could he not make the plain bread of life leap up and live?

" 'Twas a brave show," Will murmured to himself. Uncle Edward looked down at him, scowling ferociously.

"WAS'T not thee, sweeeeet William, last night, with thine ear to the floorboards and thine arse sticking skyward?" Gilbert asked pleasingly at supper. "When my aunts spoke of *private* things down in the parlor? It *seemed* to be thee. I nigh tripped o'er thee on my way to the jordan." At bedtime Gilbert spoke in exaggerated shock: "Will! What art doing in my parents' chamber? Art staring at that naked lass in the carving?"

Death to Gilbert, Will thought, in silent, brooding reply. *Death to Gilbert. He is a spy.* His younger brother spied on Will's own spying, then exposed him to view.

Will would have his revenge.

At night the two shared a bed. Before either slept, Gilbert would kick, and Will would kick back, and Gilbert would kick harder, and so on. It was a ritual, with verbal accompaniment:

"Scum. Changeling. No child of my mother."

"Whoreson, unlicked bear-whelp of chaos."

"Oh, William! Was it that you called my mother a whore just now?"

"You've the brains of a Cyclops! Slavish, sludge-mongering, false bat-shite!"

"What be true bat-shite?"

"Thou. I am wrong; th'art a piece of the true bat-shite."

"QUIET! YOU'LL HAVE MY BELT!" That from their father, with pounding, from the far side of the wall.

Uncle Edward's manor was a haven from these trivial conflicts. Will spent hours in the Glovery and hours in school, but when he could sneak away that was where he went. There pesky siblings never whined, and mothers did not speak sharply and raise hands to younger sons, stepping on the feet of elder ones as if they were not there. Fathers did not come home ale-sodden and shouting. At the Arden manor were solace and quiet and the library and the garden with the well and the statue of Mary.

And a man who liked what Will wrote.

For Will had resolved to tell his thoughts, and they took the form of a story. The tale took shape as he lay on his parents' bed, before its wondrous oaken headboard carved with a naked Adam and Eve and serpent in the Garden of Eden. In the shadow of the Garden in the evenings, he wrote a poem of the old Britons and their glorious doings, and how they ended. Burning on funeral pyres with all their gold about them. *Eager for fame.* On he scribbled, on his parents' bed, under a peach tree at Arden, or on the floor of his uncle's library. When he was done he shared his poem with his uncle. Edward applauded it, questioned him regarding it, read it aloud with him.

Then Gilbert found it hidden under their straw mattress.

Gilbert let it be known to their father that it was written on paper "borrowed" from John Shakespeare's own account books. Will spent the next four Thursday afternoons below the Market Cross, peddling gloves from his father's shop, to repay him.

Death to Gilbert.

Will kicked pebbles and brooded on his way to and from the schoolroom over the Guildhall. *Death to Gilbert.*

WILL was in Edward's library in his usual position, out of sight behind two chairs, on the day his schoolmaster appeared, holding his cap, and announcing he would soon be leaving Stratford for Rheims, in France, thanks to Edward's help. Will was sprawled on his back on the new Turkish rug with his neck against the wall, holding a book of woodcuts and peering at an image of a man and woman in water fused together like a tree, meant to signify something about marriage. The inscription was in Latin, and he did not bother with it. The woodcut itself drew his gaze. The picture was rough, but he could just see a small portion of the woman's buttocks as she clung passionately to the also-naked man.

Edward was arguing with his new son-in-law, an excited young fellow named Wallace Somerville, and had forgotten, as he often did, that Will was there. Somerville held a metal goblet from which he drank frequently, leaving drops of red wine on his moustache. But Will couldn't see this; his view was limited to the men's ankles and feet. He only half-listened to the argument, as he was looking for more woodcuts of naked people. He noted the temper of the discussion rather than its content: bitter and impulsive on Somerville's side, controlled and cautionary on Edward's. The talk concerned Mary Stuart, the Catholic queen of Scotland whom Queen Elizabeth kept confined in England. Somerville was saying something about Queen Mary's lineal connection to Queen Elizabeth's grandfather. The debate ended abruptly when a maidservant ushered Simon Hunt into the room. At the sound of his schoolmaster's voice, Will went very still. He had missed school that afternoon, and was sure Hunt had come to look for him.

Yet Master Hunt said nothing of Will. Instead he briefly shared the news of his coming departure for Rheims, gave thanks, and received blessings and letters from both Edward and Somerville. Will was so stunned to hear Master Hunt was bound for France that he sat upright, knocking his book to the floor. The room went dead quiet for a moment, and then his uncle called loudly, "Will!"

Trembling, Will stood up, straightening his wrinkled trunks and hose. He bowed awkwardly to Master Hunt, avoiding his eye. He was passing well scared. Often adults laughed when they discovered he had been quietly among them, absorbing their conversation, unbeknownst to them all. But these men were not laughing.

"What have you heard, you little boar-pig?" Somerville snapped.

"Shhh! My young cousin was reading, not spying," Edward said, though he looked worried. He frowned at Will. "Sirrah, this was private conversation. Thou shouldst have made thy presence known."

"Well, here I am," Will said lamely. "Behind these chairs." He fixed his gaze on the wall.

"Fear him not, Simon," Edward told the schoolmaster. "He's wise enough to say nothing of this."

Master Hunt looked doubtful, but nodded. "I'll say God buy thee, young William, to you, then, as well. I had forgot you were this good man's nephew. We'll meet in the schoolroom no more, you and I. You'll escape thy caning for this afternoon."

"I will give it to myself," Will said piously.

"Stow thy nonsense, boy. And may God watch over thee. It's clear to me that ye'll need His help."

"God buy ye, Master Hunt," Will said, confused. Had he chased *two* schoolmasters away? The thought made him feel sad, but powerful.

Godlike, in a small way.

Simon Hunt bowed and shook Uncle Edward's hand, and went through the door. Will gazed curiously after him. Indeed, he no longer looked the mournful Simony Hunt whom Hamfist Sadler had caricatured in his commonplace book. His step was light. For the first time, Will saw that the schoolmaster was a young man.

"Godspeed to him," said Somerville. "He's best out of this fractured land."

"Son, it grows late," Edward said. He looked tired as he sank into his chair. "Let's forget the fractured land for the nonce. My daughter will miss thee at home."

"I'll to her straight." Somerville bowed and took his leave.

"Though I know not why she married thee, rash dolt," Edward sighed after the door had closed. "I should ne'er have permitted it."

Will looked straight at his uncle. "Why Rheims, sir?"

"What do you know of the place?"

"That 'tis a haven for Catholics and spies of all sorts, and that the queen's men are busy there."

"*Ha!*" Edward gave his usual short laugh. "Thou hast been wiggling thine ears indeed. Listening to the Hathaway men in the market square, or some other wild-eyed godly folk. So Simon Hunt's a spy, is he? What valued intelligence d'ye think he's collected in your silly classroom, watching you punies pick your noses and snigger?" He shook his head. "Aye, the king of Spain would make much capital of that. No, Hunt's no spy, and that schoolroom's too small for his mind."

" 'Tis too small for anyone's mind."

Edward looked sharply at Will. "Didst thou avoid school today? Thou didst, I'll warrant. No matter, I suppose. You learn more here. But think not of minds. Master Hunt has something better than a mind. He's got Christian love."

"I felt his Christian love on the back of my head once. It left a knot."

"Yes. Christian love may hurt."

Will flopped down on the floor again, this time in front of the chairs. "What will the schoolmaster do in Rheims, sir nuncle?" he asked.

"Train for to be a Jesuit. He's a man of faith, he is. *Spy.*"

Edward spat out the window. "They've a seminary there, for English Catholics. I beg of thee—nay, I *command* thee, Will—say nothing until he's well embarked."

"Fear me not. I am outlandishly good with secrets."

"Hmmm."

"Be there not priests enough in France?"

Uncle Edward rose abruptly. His furred alderman's gown swung with his movement; he was bound for a meeting of the town council. He had been newly elected bailiff, the highest civic office in Stratford. "Yes, Will, there be priests enow in France," he said. "Half the refugees of England are there, along with France's own men. There are not cures for them all. But Master Hunt knows that, and he'll not stay in France, nor in Europe at all. He's going with a mission to the Americas, just above the Equator, to teach the savages there, and bring them to Christ. And I say, God bless him. I've given him a sum to help him on his travels, and Master Somerville has given as well."

Will popped his eyes and dropped his jaw theatrically, and his uncle laughed.

But truly, Will was astounded. Those lands in the torrid zones—did they exist, indeed? Simon Hunt's stories about the half-naked peoples there, with their intricate calendars and their human sacrifices, had seemed like fairy-tales. Yet Hunt was going to seek those folk, to live with them—to celebrate mass for them, placing consecrated wafers on their dark tongues! Or were their tongues pink, like those of the English?

Will shook his head.

A dream was becoming real.

IT was a good two months before another pedagogue was engaged to fill Hunt's position. The abruptness of the departures of two schoolmasters made candidates wary of the post, and eventually the councilmen had to raise the wage. At last a Welshman was hired. He was shaped like a pear, small on top and big at the base, and though he was from London he spoke like his Welsh parents. This interested Will, who when questioned would answer in a fair imitation. It sounded like mockery, though it was intended as tribute, and Will was outraged when one day he got caned for it.

"Murderous," said Rich Field the evening after the caning, as he and Will washed blood and fat from calfskins in the Fields' tannery. The guts of dead animals lay piled about them. "Murderous! Nought but Latin and caning and slaving."

"I want to run away to London," Will said.

"Thou canst not run. I tried and they caught me." Rich threw a bucket of water on the bloody floor. "What dost thou do when thou art murderous?"

"At times I steal a poppet from my sister and I fashion a noose for its neck. I hang it by a neighbor's window and pin a sign to its breast that says THEE! Then I knock hard on the window, and fly home. It gives me peace, and no harm is done."

The boys worked on in silence.

At length Rich asked, "What when Joan misseth her poppet?"

"I must make her a new one to stint her crying, else I am discovered."

Rich's father stuck his head into the tanning shed. "Home with you, Will! There is cutting for you there, says your da."

"Ah. Cutting. Work, work, work."

In minutes Will departed, his arms piled high with bloody skins.

GLOVERY, tannery, school, board, and bed.

Will longed to transmute his greasy world.

For years he'd collapsed on parlor floors or roads or riverbanks when struck by vivid impressions. From those base locations he had stared heavenward, musing, until prodded or kicked back into verticality. Now when he fell he had stolen paper in his pocket. In his uncle's garden he lay on his back, sharpening a swan's feather with a penknife, then unlidded a small ink-pot that he kept in the trunk of a tree. He turned on his stomach and glanced from the ground to the sky and back again. He looked at the world and he wrote.

For by now it was impossible for him to do one and not the other.

On his way home from Uncle Edward's manor he would go through the woods at the edge of the great Arden Forest. He was oft late for supper, and so he would run, past elm and ash and foxglove and the fernseed that his aunts said made children invisible. He felt colorless, magic, a goblin or sprite. He thought himself witched when the darkness fell and the tree branches reached like claws to grasp his sleeves, his trunks, and his hose, threatening to hold him for aye in the shadows, outside the pale, away from the human town. When he emerged, gasping, from the dark of the wood, he would find that pages of his poetry had slipped his grasp, now to lie moldering on the forest floor. Food for worms. *Death and damnation!* And he'd curse like a sailor all the way back to Henley Street.

But at home he was more quiet than ever, and Gilbert found it harder to bedevil him. At breakfast, dinner, and supper he would eat almost silently, while the clink of pewter mugs and the gabble of conversation eddied around him. He watched, and he heard. His brain was awash with noise. The paring of an apple, the trick of a maiden aunt's eye as a handsome swain passed the house, the carding of flax in the pungent barn, were all food, not for worms, but for words.

He had this trick: everything he touched turned to poetry.

But the trick left him always alone.

Chapter Three

IN the dark days after the cow fell on old Richard Hathaway, daughter Anne had been let to know by her brother, the farm's inheritor, that he'd no will to house her much longer. After all, he planned to marry soon. And so her gaze traveled. One who met it was a grey-eyed youth whose auburn thatch fell thick on his high forehead. Bare eighteen he looked, eyeing her in church from the pew at the side, thinking she never noted him. When she walked down the stone steps after the homily and the sacrament, her own hair, yellow and unmarried, spilled from under her black bonnet to end halfway down her back, and she held her straight nose high. The lad went goggle-eyed as he viewed her, and skittered sidewise from her path like a crab.

He made her laugh.

Her sisters could not guess why she chose him. His mother was thought to be Catholic. His father had lost most of the boy's mother's money and, what was more, drank. The boy himself was eight years her junior and entirely odd. Years before, he had been famous for lurking in lanes wearing half-made pairs of calfskin gloves, touching the world without touching it, muttering rhymes and slapping trees and lifting cats to look them sternly in the eye. He'd been seen more than once lying motionless, arms folded corpselike on his chest, next to this or that new-dug grave in Holy Trinity Churchyard. Anne's family lived in Shottery, miles from the scenes of these antics, which had abated once the lad's chin sprouted a tuft. Still, they'd heard the talk often enough.

Her family, Anne knew, thought her cracked herself, ever since she'd turned down the marriage pleas of a smitten Cambridge suitor, a Puritan sort, all ready to take his orders. But that one had put her too much in mind of her own father, *that strict godly man, might he rest in peace; a man in his prime, killed so untimely!* The Cambridge man, like her father, had cherished his Scripture most perilously. Perilously, that was, for her, since his most-cherished verse was one in Ephesians concerning a wife's subjection to her husband.

Yet she must marry.

The lad was there for the hooking.

She knew of his family, knew the men worked ceaselessly. She thought surely their business would prosper again, and that one so young would doubtless let her do as she would. In the end it was easy. She needed to do little more than smile at him on a Saturday as he stood peddling gloves below the Market Cross.

A walk was arranged.

"I am blunt," Anne said, as they threaded their way through the ash trees that wooded the town. The green Arden Forest would not stay put; it crept inward, threw spoors, and planted itself in the mercantile streets.

"Pleased to make thine acquaintance, Mistress Blunt. I, as you know, am called Will." Boldly, the grey-eyed youth took her arm. "May we walk by the river?"

She let herself be led. "I do not love you yet, but I find you friendly enough. I come with six marks, two silver spoons, a Geneva Bible, and a mare. I seek a mate."

Will laughed. "Fair thou art, as well as blunt," he said. "But I shall not be he."

Anne stopped, clutching her plain smock, and frowned. "Dost think thyself too good for a farmer's daughter because thy da makes gloves for gentlemen? I think it not fine to spend thy days slitting cows' throats and skinning off their hides. Look." She pointed. "Thou hast blood on thine arm."

Will twisted his sleeve out of sight. His voice remained mild, unoffended. "Rarely do I tanner's work now. My work is the stuff of romance. I cut and stitch and rub cheveril and dogs' skins with gum-dragon and cloves. And I plunge them all into vats of dye."

"Oh, very fine."

"Let us walk by the river," Will said again, guiding Anne toward the footpath. "Fair thou art, my mistress. And good enough for a Stratford man, but I will not stay a Stratford man and I am too young for a wife. Still, I would desire to find a beauteous spot at this swift flood's edge where we might blissfully disport ourselves in amorous encounter—"

Anne cuffed him on the chin, sending him hard against a tree.

"God's choppers!" Will said, and fingered his slight beard. "I said nothing amiss!"

"I know not *what* you said, but I liked not the sound of it."

"What call you this bashing of my face?"

"A taste of my bluntness."

Will looked delighted at this reply, and Anne laughed at that. He took her hand. "Look you, mistress, it is best that you know. I am not a fellow to serve your turn. I am bound for Oxford. I should have been there and nearly done, but my father— no matter. My uncle has pledged to support my efforts. And so me, to Oxford, and then to London and the court."

Anne rolled her blue eyes, which charmed Will further. "And what will'ee do *there?*" she said.

"I will be secretary to the son of my uncle."

"And what's he?"

"My uncle is a man of parts, and his son is a feather-capped popinjay in a silk cloak and an ear-ring and a rapier he wears for mere ornament. One of the New Men, as they say. He is also the undersecretary to Sir Francis Walsingham."

"And what's Sir Francis Walsingham?"

"A very great man. Secretary to the queen."

"Ah, then thou'lt be a secretary to a secretary to a secretary. Most fine."

Will frowned. "I see the word *fine* likes you well, Mistress Anne Hathaway. It is not that I wish to be fine."

Anne smiled prettily. "What, then?"

Will did not answer. Then he said, "A courtier may write things of his own invention. And others read and—praise it."

"And there is money for that?"

"Yes!" Will's face lit up again. "Much! One may know a patron whose pockets are lined with gold, which I mean most exactly. Cloth of gold, my cousin tells me. And gold *in* those gold pockets. Men pay for poetry."

Anne looked doubtful. "They pay for nothing, then. I ne'er have heard such matter."

Will smiled. "There are more things in heaven and earth than have met with *your* hearing, Mistress Anne."

"Heaven and earth, faugh. I thought you spoke of London!"

At this Will laughed long. Then he kissed her.

He was not the first to do that, or to do what he did soon after.

ANNE had meant to hook Will, but before her ear had drunk a hundred of his words it was she herself who was hooked. In the days and weeks after that first walk she found it hard to say him nay, though her hope of his pledging himself was ebbing, and she was doing her best to turn her eyes and thoughts to other swains.

Then came a week when she knew she had lost the power to choose.

"Do you doubt it's yours, Will?" she asked, standing by her gate at the Shottery farm.

"No," Will said, looking fair miserable. "I have stolen all your free hours. Else I *would* think it."

She raised her hand. "Should I cuff you as I did the first time?"

"Aye, and thou likest."

She dropped her arm. "Ah, Will, what can I do? Should I powder rue and fennel seed and drink it in a simple? It may kill me. It will most surely kill the babe."

Will winced. "Nay. I would not wish to kill the babe."

She looked at him narrowly, not fully liking his meaning, "As for I," she said, "I'd be *boiled* ere I'd do that."

THAT had been one year before, and now the loud-lunged babe lay yelling in Anne's arms or in this spot or that of the cramped Henley Street home while its mother bustled about her new duties. In the beginning Will thought it Hell's own polliwog, though in time he grew to like it after a fashion.

He and Anne slept in his parents' old wedding bed with its carved headboard, under the image of Adam and Eve and the fork-tongued snake. Their house was annexed to John Shakespeare's, and Anne had her own kitchen. She nailed a board on its wall and from the board she hung her cleaver, sieve, knives, graters, and pothooks. In the pantry she stored dried herbs and onions. In the mornings she opened the top half of her kitchen door and bid good morrow to the neighbors. She was happy enough.

Will did not go to university. Instead he found work as a pedagogue for the sons of a local squire. When Anne told Gilbert, he was beside himself with rage and envy. "My brother cannot Latin it!" Gilbert howled. "*I* can Latin it!" Anne winked and said, "Then Latin it, my boy! Let me hear a snatch or two from some old Roman." But Gilbert was too vexed for merriment.

Uncle Edward barked with laughter. "A good jest at Sir Thomas Lucy's expense," he told Will. "Ha! His boys will learn nothing, which will serve Lucy fittingly, bootlicking slave of Robert Dudley that he is." Dudley was the Earl of Leicester, the most powerful man in Warwickshire and a favorite of the queen.

"Have you met Robert Dudley, nuncle?" Will asked.

" 'Tis a vice to know him. He is an enemy of all Catholics, but he has no real religion himself, nor does Lucy, his fine follower. Lucy speaks all Puritan to please the earl and the earl speaks all Puritan to please the Parliament. Neither one would have a thing to say to one of the *real* godly folk." Edward cackled. "A pair of silk-stockinged fools! No clipped hair or Calvin's *Institutes* for the earl or his minion. I doubt Dudley or squirelet Lucy e'en know their *paternoster*, in Latin *or* English."

"They are not your friends."

"Friends! Both hate me because I say what I think. I fight their land enclosures and I won't join them in flattering the queen. Have at it, nephew! Teach them bad Latin!"

SIR Thomas Lucy's Latin was none too good itself, which was how Will convinced the squire he read the papistical tongue well.

When he baffled Lucy's sons with strange phrases like *habit has canto conifer,* and the boys told him the true grammar of it was *habent has caeno coenavi,* he called them saucy, pedantic wretches. On odd days he taught history by chasing the lads with a fire iron and yelling in bloodthirsty fashion. "In such manner," Will cried, prodding the youngest, yowling Lucy in the calf, "did the first Shakespeare win his name, fighting against the dog Richard the Third at Bosworth Field. He *shook* his *spear* in the hell-spawn's face!"

"Did it happen?" the older Lucy panted skeptically. He was halfway up-wall to the window, clinging to a curtain.

"*Yes!*" Will stabbed the iron at the boy's breeched legs. "Most assuredly, young sir!"

Will was dismissed from Sir Lucy's manor, but not before he'd perused each book in the squire's ample library, nor, sadly, before he'd left there a small work given him by his uncle on his nineteenth birthday. It was a Catholic spiritual testament inscribed *To W. S.* along with words in praise of *Mary, Heaven's Queen,* signed *Edward Arden.* It slipped from Will's pocket one day during his mad chase of a Lucy lad who especially needed a cuffing. It was years before he found it again, and before and after he did, he thought often of its loss, in guilt and in sorrow.

Will returned to work with his father and brothers in the Glovery. The money grew scarce, and Anne's mood was black. Will's was blacker. Now he dyed, cut, and stitched for ten hours each day and had little time to write in the evenings.

"Frivolity has cost me dear," he told Anne.

"It has cost me the hope of damask curtains and Holland bulbs for the garden," she said.

"A fond hope indeed." He sat scribbling at his flat table in the upstairs parlor.

Anne peered over his shoulder at the black marks she could

not read. She watched the bobbing quill. "Will you not talk with me instead?"

"Nay," he said amiably.

She sat herself on a stool, brushing floury hands on her smock. A strand of yellow hair escaped from her cap, and she pushed it back impatiently, leaving a smear of flour on her cheek. "Will," she said softly. "Dost blame me that you cannot be at university?"

"No," he lied, still scribbling.

Her voice grew sharp. " 'Twas hardly my doing, or not mine alone."

"I know," he said coolly. "A spark of wit still glows in my dye-drenched brain. I recall how babes are made."

"Ah, Will, now."

He did not answer. Little Susanna woke and cried in the neighbor room.

"The child, Nanny," Will said, still writing.

Sighing heavily, she went.

ON Saint George's Day of the next year, 1585, Anne watched through her kitchen window as Will came into the yard leading his father's mare. He'd been riding hard. His hat had blown off and his cheeks were red and wind-chapped, but around his eyes his face was ashy. Anne looked at him carefully as she nursed one of her new twins in the kitchen. He was tying the horse and speaking quickly to his father, who sat on a garden bench. The window was open an inch and she could hear Will's voice, low, tense, and fast, though she could not fathom his words. She heard John Shakespeare curse, and then saw John rise and walk quickly in the direction of the Bear Tavern.

Anne laid the baby in his cradle next to his sleeping sister. She went out to the garden, where Will was leaning against an ash tree, looking grim. He glanced at her, and said, "Wife, inside."

In the house he told her his uncle Edward Arden had been arrested by men belonging to the Earl of Leicester, Robert Dudley. Edward had been taken unarmed while falconing, and one of his birds had sorely pecked the eye and cheek of the red-haired earl's man who had pinned Edward's hands behind his back. "And with pinioned hands my uncle spurred his horse and raced down the hill," Will told Anne. "Though they caught him at the bottom. Three more earl's men were waiting there." His tone turned suddenly wondering. "I never saw such riding as Edward did."

"*What were you doing there?*" Anne shrieked.

"I?" Will looked surprised. "I was up in a tree some fifty yards off, composing a sonnet. The mare was tied back in the forest. I saw it all and could do nothing. 'Twas like a kind of play."

"Then none saw you."

Will looked at her coldly. "Nay," he said. "Fear not for *my* safety, wife."

Anne flushed with shame. But she felt relief all the same.

WITHIN the week local tavern news told all. Edward was charged with complicity in his wild son-in-law Wallace Somerville's plot to topple Queen Elizabeth from the throne. The hope had been to replace her with Mary, the imprisoned Scots queen. So the story ran. Few in Warwickshire thought Edward guilty of anything, but some proof had been offered against him, and Elizabeth's court of Star Chamber did not relent. Edward's failure to beg forgiveness for his papistry did not help his case. To the end he said what he thought. Through the short weeks of his imprisonment in the Tower of London he cried innocent, and wrote letters to everyone he knew. This only angered his Protestant enemies and the queen.

In the end they took his head.

Chapter Four

THREE years later the players came to town.

It was early summer and the fields were pink with gillyflowers. In the morning, in full view of Will, Gilbert asked Anne whether he might take her and Susanna and the little twins for a walk. *I think thy wife fine,* he seemed to be saying to Will. And she *was* fine, with her bright hair and her straight back and the mottled flush of her cheeks, her red and white; and the readiness of her laugh. Will hated his younger brother for watching her from the corners of his sly eyes. Yet he understood him, too.

Will stayed to cut skins in the Woolery. He had sliced his thumb and was cursing when his youngest brother, Edmund, put his head in the top of the door and bid him come before the town's entertainment was done entirely.

"Nay," Will said, not looking up, sucking his wound. He wrinkled his nose at the taste of the dye on his hand. *"Paugh!* No, Ned.

I've seen their foolish farces. They speak poetry abominably and the poetry itself is abominable."

"But these men play tragedy!" Edmund hopped from one leg to the other as though late for the privy. He was eight. "There will be killing, blood, guts, screaming, and revenge!"

"Worse yet. They will rant." But Will put down his cutting blade and looked thoughtful. "Revenge, say you?"

HE would have liked to stand at the edge of the crowd, but Edmund pulled him toward the rude wooden scaffold that the townsmen had thrown up in the Guildhall. The play was in progress. The brothers trod on the toes of an ample farmer, who glared from under his straw hat. They reached the front, within spitting range of a tall man who stood on the stage, dressed in a wizardly robe stitched with suns and moons and stars. The tall fellow was yelling bombastically.

"What's the argument?" Will whispered to a youth who stood by his elbow.

"And you cannot come at the start, you cannot expect to know it!" the youth replied. But in a moment Will recognized the tale. The tall spitting man was Doctor Faustus, who had sold his soul to the devil for the success of his black and magical art.

Edmund laughed loud and long at the scenes of buffoonery, most of which offered a purple-breeched clown who was clearly inventing his own lines whenever the urge overtook him. Will found the clown passing foolish, and irksome. The man who played Faustus was also dearly in love with the sound of his own voice, and within a quarter of an hour Will wanted to choke him, too. But the other players spoke well, and as for *what* they spoke, it was something entirely new. It had a bite and a rhythm that caught and held him and he felt, for God's love, the faintest flush of envy creep along his collarbone and up his neck as he heard it. The poetry was a wind-filled sail. But it was not only how but *what* the poetry said that made his heart beat fast.

"*Hell hath no limits, nor is circumscribed in one self place. But where we are is Hell,*" said a red-haired actor.

Hell not a place? A man might think it, but—*say* it? Before a crowd?

"Whose is the play?" Once more he addressed the rapt youth at his elbow.

"*Ssssttt!* I know not!"

"Look you, this crowd is all yelling and babes crying at the back of us. I know not why you'd stop *my* mouth for asking a thoughtful questi—"

"*SSSTTTTT!*"

There came a lag in the action, and some minutes passed. The crowd, feeling restless, began to throw nutshells and pieces of trash at the stage and shout for the return of damned Doctor Faustus, and where were the fireworks and devils to cart him to Hell? Suddenly, from behind a curtain the players had drawn between the scaffold and the wall came the purple-clad clown, this time wearing belled buskins on his legs and feet. He looked perturbed, but he mounted the stage manfully and held his hands out for quiet. "An interlude now!" he called. The crowd groaned and the clown's cap was knocked off his head by an apple core.

Will frowned.

But the clown took it well. He wheeled and staggered as though mortally wounded, dropped flat on his back, and then raised and dropped his arms and legs with a loud thump. In a trice he had somersaulted back to his feet while the crowd laughed. "A morris!" he called triumphantly, and started to dance while a piper piped and the watchers clapped. Will crept to the edge of the scaffold curtain and looked behind it.

The man who had been playing the demon Mephistophilis, the devil-tempter of Faustus, was stretched out on the floor unconscious. A small boy held a cold cloth to the back of the felled actor's head, and a costumed man held his wrist. The player who had been Helen of Troy, ear-ringed and bewigged and face-painted, was sitting alone on a trunk in apparent disgrace. That one's eyes caught Will's. "Can you devil it, sir?"

Will looked curiously at the apparition of Helen. "What's amiss?"

"All's amiss." The boy took off his Helen wig, revealing a crown of close-cropped ginger hair beneath. "I knocked Mephistophilis hard off the stair at his last exit."

"Why? 'Tis Faustus I would have knocked. Shut him up, perhaps—"

"I did not do it a'purpose!" the boy cried. "Now the truth of it is we're down to five men and we've no one to play Mephistophilis." He rose from the trunk, opened it, and handed Will a scroll. "D'ye see?"

Will unfurled the scroll. "This is much."

"Aye."

Will read in silence for several minutes. Then, rolling the paper back up, he said, "I ha't."

The clown jumped back through the curtain, out of breath. "What must we do, lads? Hath resurrection occurred?" He looked worriedly at the fallen actor, then curiously at Will.

Will told him, "I can speak your part of Mephistophilis."

The man snorted. "I can shoot butterflies out my arse."

"I've no doubt of *that.*"

Mephistophilis moaned, fluttered his eyes, and half-rose. Then he sank back to earth. He was wearing the robes of a Franciscan friar, and those lay flared about him on the ground. His hair was red, his left eye was patched, and his cheek was marked with an old scar. Will studied him carefully.

"Fellow, th'art holding Mephistophilis's scroll." The man who had been measuring the prostrate actor's pulse stood and approached Will. He was dressed in papal robes, and they swung with his movement. "E'en were you from London you could not know that part. The play's new."

"I've read it, and I'd speak it for you on your stage so you'd not lose your pennies and groats. I could devil it. My soul's black enough. But it's a small matter to me."

The crowd were moving toward the Guildhall's several doors, and the man's eyes flicked toward the departing folk in panic. Will tossed the scroll in the open trunk and turned to go, but the man grabbed his arm. "Well, it can get no worse than it is. Try it, scroll in hand if you like." An idea struck the man. "The scroll can stand for Faustus's bond with the devil."

"I do not think I need it," Will said. In any case, the boy-Helen had shut the trunk on the scroll.

The clown and the papal player quickly bustled Will into the friar's robe. Faustus poked his dark-bearded and anxious face around the scaffold, and the clown gestured him back on stage. "Go!" Other players followed. The ear-ringed boy took Will's hand. "This way, sir! Behind and below and up through the Hellmouth."

"What's thy name, sirrah?" Will asked, hurrying behind the young player.

"Felix Culpeper." The boy stood to the side and pointed. "That way. Go."

He felt the boy's hands shove his back and he fell down a step behind the scaffold, and then he was up and through and on the stage, looking at things from the other side. He saw a ring of gap-toothed country folk gaping in surprise at the sight of him. He stood stiffly before the Hell-mouth, and his eye's corner took in its pasteboards painted with orange flames. The players spoke around him, and then it was time. *Speak,* he commanded himself.

He spoke.

> *Was this the face that launched a thousand ships,*
> *And burnt the topless towers of Ilium?*

The play went on.

It seemed no time at all before the last scene, when fireworks exploded behind the stage and the watchers shrieked and jumped and red-suited devils with horns and tails swarmed up through the Hell-mouth to drag Faustus, screaming—*too loud,* Will thought— off to Hell. He saw the clown and the pope transformed to costumed devils, and even the small boy, who could not have been more than five, twirled a pointed red tail and shrieked and cavorted and put his pitchfork to Doctor Faustus's rear.

> *Fond worldling, now his heart blood dries with grief.*
> *His conscience kills it, and his labouring brain*
> *Begets a world of idle fantasies*
> *To overreach the devil.*

"NATE Field, stow the props." The clown wiped sweat from his upper body. His lower half was again encased in the purple breeches. Below the trunks he sported hose of a purple check, and for reasons mysterious he had donned his belled buskins again. His shirt was of yellow silk and his cap was topped with a long ostrich feather. From his ear a pearl ear-ring dangled.

The little boy made a face at him, but began collecting the properties that lay strewn behind the scaffold. Wooden pitchforks, a wand, a crown, a book.

"And you, sir."

Will was carefully folding the friar's robe. "What would ye, friend?"

"A drink of ale for a poor player."

Will looked up. "I think that poor player will be me. It would not offend me if you offered me a groat for my work."

Obediently, the clown fished in his pocket for a coin. He tossed it to Will. "Well conned and well done. We are grateful."

"I said a groat, sir."

The clown fished again. "Oh, frot me, I'll find it while we walk. I must wipe off this paint at the pump. Wouldst take a poor player to your tavern?"

Edmund raced around the dividing curtain, his face wild with excitement and envy. "Will! I could not see your face under that hood, but I knew by the voice it was you. How did you come to be up there?"

Will patted him on the shoulder. "I cannot truly say, Ned; neither how nor why. Run home now, and tell my wife I will be another hour. Or so."

Edmund was turning green. "But I want to go with—"

"Home. You are too young for taverns."

The first Mephistophilis had shown signs of revival, and the other players had carted him to a nearby house. Will walked with the jingling clown down Bridge Street toward the Bear Tavern, as citizens stared. The belled fellow bowed right and left as they proceeded. "So you're Will," he said. "A good omen, say the stars. I'm one too. Will Kempe is my name."

"Will Shakespeare." They stopped to clap hands, then continued.

"And where had you seen this play before now, to know it so well?" Kempe asked, as they reached the tavern and entered. "In Coventry? Oxford?"

"Nowhere." They sat. "I've been nowhere. The boy showed me the scroll. Now tell me, if you will, whose was the play?"

"It belongs to the great Christopher Marlowe, known as Kit to his inwards, among whom I count myself. Rather I should say it *did* once belong to Kit Marlowe, because now it belongs to us. Or rather I should say to the playhouse owner Philip Henslowe, who bought it, and a good purchase it was. It does challenge my skills to play in a tragic piece, but this one has good comedy, do you not think?"

"Hmmm."

The clown snapped his fingers. "Ale!"

"And cider," Will said. "That is for me."

"What you will. Will! What you will!" Kempe laughed.

Will smiled. "Would you credit it? I had heard that one before."

"A good jest may be twice-told, or thrice-told. Just as a dark play must not be overdark, lest our watchers squirm or, worse yet, snore."

"*You* exist to prevent that danger, I see."

Kempe looked at him suspiciously, suspecting mockery, but Will's face gave nothing away. The drinks arrived, and Kempe swigged his and continued. "Aye. I know what you wish to ask, and the answer is, yes, I do much of my jesting *extempore*, which is to say spontaneous, and to the jests this play of *Faustus* offers I am not loath to add a few well-chosen ones of my own making. And yes, I did indeed crack my head on the stage, all a'purpose, during my romp and dance. Why, have a look." He doffed his feathered cap and pointed at a small scratch on his right temple.

"Excellent impressive," Will said. "Luck that you did not share Mephistophilis's fate."

"He will revive. Now. What thought you of our play?"

"That—"

"You *were* privileged to see the sacrifice performance puts us to. Our work is arduous, and we must be well studied. The clown's part can ne'er be overstressed. Players must be all things. Even a player who excels at producing tears must learn to prompt laughter when laughter is called for. Plato said this."

"Plato said that play *writers* must be able to elicit both tears and laughter. He said nothing of players."

Kempe glared at Will. Briefly silenced, he took a fierce swig of ale. Then his face lightened. "So, ye love not players? What are ye, a Puritan? Since th'art Puritan, why wert thou at the play?"

"I've nought against—"

"What work do you do, when all's said and done?"

"Glovery." Will looked at his stained hand on the tabletop.

Kempe laughed. "Glovery and Plato?"

"I had notions of going to university. And to London after. I wished it fiercely."

"Ah. But no money."

"My father would have paid, in the end."

"They why did you not go?"

"The flesh intervened."

Kempe looked at him quizzically. "The flesh! There be flesh enow in London." He took a swallow of ale. "Families can be left, and fortunes made, in bigger towns."

"So speaks the childless man."

"And how would you know that?" Kempe squinted at Will, who squinted back, reflecting him. "Well, thou'rt right," Kempe conceded. "I've no children, and no wife."

"I'll not leave mine."

"Then go to London, make money, and send for them."

Will sat quiet, brooding. He rubbed the drops on the side of his mug.

"I would like some cold rabbit and quince jelly now," Kempe said.

"There's no food here."

"The shame of it! You've a groat—"

"In fact, I do not have a groat, yet."

"—but there's no food to be bought. Money is most curious. Has your wife money?"

"Her father had some, but she got little enough. And he's long gone."

"Corpsed?"

"Aye. A cow . . . An unfortunate tragedy of milking."

"The perils of the country."

"Aye."

"What *would* you have done in London?"

"A cousin at court meant to get me a place there. But he lost his own place amid some . . . sad family business." Will stared at the tabletop. "Gave his place up, I might say."

"You might be a player."

Will gave a short laugh.

"Why dost thou laugh? You did well enough today." Kempe tried vainly to catch a glimpse of himself in the leaded glass pane of the tavern window, and straightened his cap fussily. "A cool cod you are, at any rate. You've not been to university. No matter! You have read things."

"And once I wrote poetry." The sentence slipped out of its own will. He glanced quickly at Kempe, expecting a chuckle.

But Kempe did not laugh. He cocked an eyebrow instead. "Poetry of what?"

Will smiled, folded his arms, and leaned back against the tavern wall. "The last poem I wrote was of Venus and Adonis. A lusty goddess and the seduction of a hapless youth. But it has been years since I—"

"Is it actable?"

"I do not know or overmuch care what you mean. You are a great interrupter of other men's sentences."

"Look you." Kempe propped his silken elbows on the table and leaned forward for emphasis. His pearl ear-ring swung as he tapped the wet wood with a ringed forefinger. A pale green stone sparkled. "There is no profit," he said, "in a university degree." He looked challengingly at Will. "No profit!"

Will was amused. "You say?"

"London is full of university men, waving their diplomas and all out of work. Do you know what they do?"

"I know that you'll tell me."

"They write plays and sell them to us." Kempe sat back on his stool with a triumphant look. "I say a great thing to you, Shakespeare, and you sit and say nothing. You only put on odd faces. Marry, you might be a player indeed! You have no skills, but your memory terrifies me. Come and be one of us! You might make money that way."

"So I see," Will said, glancing pointedly at the clown's silk sleeve.

"Which is not to say," Kempe hastily added, "that we have any surplus of coin when we tramp the roads. 'Tis costly work, and country folk are stingy." He raised his tankard respectfully. "Saving thy presence."

"Then why do you tramp the roads?"

Kempe took a long swallow, then put his ale down hard upon the table. "Plague." He started to cross himself, then suppressed the motion. " 'Tis bad enough this year in London. The great clown Tarlton—ye've heard of him, Queen Elizabeth's fool?—he's dead, or dying. The city will not shut the theaters until the dead-count rises above fifty a week, but still, crowds are discouraged.

Crowds spread the pest. The horror of it!" He twisted his face into a frightening mask.

Will hoped Kempe would not begin to describe or, worse yet, act out the ravages of plague. "So playing's the thing," he said quickly.

"Aye," Kempe said, seeking a train of thought. "And at the Rose Theater we have the best plays and actors in the world. Edward Alleyn, that you saw today! Our Faustus!"

"A . . . phenomenon."

"The plays of Kit Marlowe! I will tell you straight, most of the university men cook rats for supper in their garrets, but not Master Marlowe, for he's our genius of the theater and he sells whatever he writes. Sells it for pounds. But there is only one of him."

"Ah."

"Find me in London and I'll get you spare work. We can put you on the scaffold when there is a horrid event like today's and we have no one else and have to take whomever we can get."

"I thank you, kind sir. Most flattered. But as you said, I've small playing skills."

"I said you had *no* playing skills." Kempe caught the tapster's eye and raised his hand once more. "So." He winked a blue eye at Will. "Get some."

Chapter Five

HE covered the distance to London in five days, walking south on the Watling road, a thousand-year-old Roman ribbon of dust and stone that stretched up to Northumbria. He slept in ditches using his pack for a pillow, keeping one eye open against highwaymen. He was full tired and sore and rag-bearded and filthy when he reached the mean cottages north of Bishopsgate. He thought himself no one, a spirit drawn by another's poetry. But instead of poetry he found talk of guns.

The war with Spain had London in a fever. He made his way to Fleet Street and found his old friend Rich Field, who had fled to London years before and now owned his own print shop. Field had a Huguenot wife who cooked Frenchified meals: cold soups whose names Will could not say and long, spiced bread ropes she called "priest stranglers." By day in their shop Will set type till his hands and face were black. By night he told Rich rollicking tales of his pedagogue days at the home of Sir Thomas Lucy. Though he chafed, on Rich's counsel he stayed clear of the playhouses.

The danger was not the plague, whose toll had lately dropped to ten deaths a week. It was the city guards who harvested lives, daily descending on theaters and taverns, rounding up masterless men for the war. Rumor was that Spanish gunboats threatened to sail up the Thames.

"We will win it without your sad soldiering, friend," Rich said, as he cranked his press handle. "Let folk panic. I will not. Read this broadside, if you will. Another victory for Francis Drake off the French coast. I say the Spanish will be hard put to breach our water-walled island."

Water-walled. " 'Tis good, Rich. Yet I do hear the Spaniards still have a few ships. Or a hundred."

"But the men cannot sail and are a crew of buggers besides."

"Ah. The Spanish vice."

"And they are mercenaries all. They cannot put hearts in a fight for their country when they hail from every rat-ridden province in the Mediterranean. Spanish Philip has no hope of beating down our true English army!"

"Our true English army was dragged from an alehouse and kicked into the drill-march at Mile End," said Will.

"Ah, Mile End! How the country lad flaunts his London geography!"

"And a wonder it is that I know it at all, when you'll not let me out of this hellish shop for a piss in the alley."

"Thou canst go for a piss in the alley. But let it be short."

Will made a bawdy gesture, and the two of them snorted like schoolboys.

*   *   *

QUEEN Elizabeth herself rode down to the sea, dressed in armor, a Protestant Joan of Arc. She appeared like a vision before the troops at Tilbury, and then sped north to safety. In the London streets Catholic King Philip was hanged in effigy, as was Elizabeth's older sister, Bloody Mary, though Mary was already well dead. Everyone wished that the battles be fought, if by some other fellow.

In a few weeks it was over.

By August the Spanish Armada was in shreds, its hundred ships battered to bits on the rocky coasts of Scotland and Ireland. Celts plundered the wrecks, and the dark-eyed survivors slipped into fields that dazzled them with greenness, never to sail south again. The church bells rang for days. Surely, here was the hand of God.

Will ventured forth to see a play.

He had studied Rich's printed maps of the city, and thought he knew it. But in its reality it baffled and buffeted and misled him more than once. It was mazelike and noisy and smelly and its lanes were narrow and dark. There were mishaps. On Wood Street a pail of slops narrowly missed his scuffed boots, and two passing fellows laughed, holding handkerchiefs and displaying their legs in tight hose of royal blue and orange tawny. "Best keep to the wall, plowman," one called over his shoulder. "Or hold to the fairway!" Will bowed with mock courtesy at their backs, his grey eyes smoldering. He saw they wore ornate capes and long-feathered bonnets, and that as they walked the hats' feathers bobbed as though they still graced the tails of live birds.

Will followed circuitous pathways shadowed by narrow wooden houses. Some of these houses leaned so close to each other that children played pat-a-cake across the lanes from the upper windows. He walked underneath them, enjoying their songs and splashing his boots through runnels of mud and horse foulings. He followed the sounds of waterbirds down steep, dark

Saint Dunstan's Hill, and then suddenly he blinked, for he stood under open sky and broad sunlight on Lower Thames Street, before the shining width of the river.

He saw and he heard and he sniffed. A breeze brought him the sea. Boatmen pounded their oars, crying *Westward ho!* and *Eastward ho!* He looked east, and immediately spied the grey and black stone of the Tower of London. Heart-chilled, he returned his gaze to the sunlit river. Ahead of him, on a waterside dock, a barrel-maker walked, a hammer at his belt and a canvas bag bursting with nails on his leather-clad back. "Cooper!" he cried. "Ha'ye any work for the cooper?"

Will threaded past fishmongers hawking eel and skate, down to the brown water's edge. After some chat with a boatman he hired a penny wherry and was rowed across, to Southwark. From the boat he could see what he felt sure was the Rose Theater. It was a thatch-roofed, white-walled polygon with a fluttering flag above it: clear weather, and a play today.

Once on shore he thanked the boatman and scrambled up the landing stairs to the top of the bank. There low buildings loured, crowded close on each other. He turned east and strode down a ditch-lined lane past ramshackle alehouses with red-latticed windows and notices for ales like Dragon's Breath and Father Whoreson and Left Leg, past the signboards of astrologers and piss-prophets and alchemists. He stopped short at the walls of Bedlam to stare at the madmen's noses stuck through the high barred windows, and their mouths that gibbered and spat. Then he walked on, past a white-painted tavern and stew whose sign said THE CARDINAL'S CAP. Six half-clad, painted whores lolled on benches outside. The women honked at him as he went, and he turned backwards, nodded, and doffed his cap. "Ladies." They cackled with laughter.

*   *   *

HE paid a penny to stand in the playhouse yard, a stinking round whose ground was knobbly with crushed hazelnuts. The air smelled of urine and sour, spilled ale. He came in with a crowd and keenly felt woolen elbows shoving, smelled onion breaths and animal decay, heard laughter and the murmurous rumble and hum of a thousand voices. Over the hum rang the orange-sellers' cries. He looked up. Above him, woven into the colored hangings that fronted the stage pillars, he recognized scenes from Greek myth. The Judgment of Paris. Hermaphroditus in his pond. He saw the painted balcony held up by strong pillars, and the steep, three-piled galleries. His eye traveled back down and swept the lower galleries, the recessed lords' rooms, whose curtained openings gave glimpses of damask cushions and feathered caps. He thought he heard refined, elegant laughter floating from behind those curtains. He tilted his head, wanting to gain a peep at the nobles inside.

From behind one of the velvet arrases sailed an empty ale-bottle, and it bounced at his feet.

The play began.

It was another by Christopher Marlowe, and Will himself had printed the bills for it, and given them to boys that ran out of door to stick them up on walls and fences all over the city. The ranting actor Edward Alleyn again played the main part, and this was hard to endure, but the language once more was rich and alive and Alleyn could not kill it with all his noise. Alleyn was Tamburlaine, mighty conqueror, and he strutted up and down the empty scaffold and filled it with visions of beauty and sounds and shapes of power. But it was not he who did so, but his shadow, the poet who had given him words to say.

Will's heart began to race as he listened, and he clenched his fists to slow it. When the stage briefly emptied between acts he looked at his palms, and saw that his nails had drawn blood.

The players returned after an interlude. Now battles raged on the scaffold, and a Catholic force was defeated. God favored the right. It was England and Spain all over again. So the audience thought, and cheered in its frenzy. Then a soldier stepped to the stage-front and cried his challenge. " 'Tis but the fortune of the wars, whose power is often THOUGHT a miracle!"

Silence fell on the playhouse. Then there was murmuring, and some snickers and guffaws from the wiser folk in the upper galleries. "Hang the playwright!" Will heard a man yell behind him, but when he turned he saw only a shifting sea of faces.

"HE is the talk of all in London who read, and many who don't," said Rich at supper that night. He spooned fish from a pastry coffin, and the crumbs caught in his ginger beard. He shook them out. "A poor craftsman's son, wouldst thou credit it? Some call him an atheist. I cannot say how he finds the courage to write such lines for the public."

"He dares." Will's grey eyes were hooded and intent. He sat at table with his face turned toward his lap, studying a book printed in Rich's shop. "He hath a wizardly wit. List. A king says, I swear by this my royal seat, and another fellow says, You may do well to kiss it then." Will laughed. "A dunce of a king, and kiss my royal seat to him! And the form of it all! Iambs, da da da da da da, but he turns it to conversation. The lines run like a magic bark o'er a waterfall. A richly laden bark."

"Some of his stage-verse is richly laden with heresy."

"His art excuses it." Will looked up. "And why should it be heresy to say Hell's inside us, or show a king who's a fool, or to propose that 'twas chance and not God that broke the Armada's back? Would not you and I say the same?"

Rich grimaced and shook his head. "In private? Perhaps. But before a crowd of thousands, with, it might be, a queen's privy councilman peering from his perch in a lord's room? I do not think we would."

Mistress Field, pouring ale, spoke sharply to her husband in French.

"What says she?" Will held up his hand courteously. *None, so please you.*

"That God surely strikes down the boats of all papist murderers, whatever a play may say."

Will chuckled and tapped the book in his hand. "This man Marlowe says otherwise. He dresses hard truths in soft poetry."

Rich looked at Will, who had turned his eyes back to the page. At length he said, "And that is what you would do yourself."

"What would I do?"

"Hide hard truths in poetry."

Will met his eye. "I see truths whate'er I look on. Some are hard and some are softer, and some of them are full contraries. Nothing but poetry can say them all at once, and it is my blessing or curse that I have the trick of it."

"So you would sell that trick."

"Yes! My brain would rot in a Glovery or this print shop— saving your presence."

Rich laughed.

"And yet I've a wife to keep, and children," said Will. "I would sell what I write for money, if I might do't without selling my soul."

Rich's smile was worldly-wise. "Then to the theaters you must go. A poet who writes only to be read may find his way to a nobleman's purse, but then he is a slave whose verse must please and praise. Go to the stage. The scum of the earth will pay to hear you, but there you can say anything." Rich pointed to the play in Will's hand. "So it seems."

Will read until midnight, then thought until dawn.

He thought of Anne's body on the day he had left her.

HER back, as she kneaded dough at the buttery bar, had spoken with dumb poetry. He could see she was crying, though she would not turn to answer when he said, "Kiss me, be kind." She shook off his hands when they touched her shoulders.

"You will join me there," he repeated for the tenth time. "I will profit and within the year you will come."

"Profit you may, but I will not come," she said. "My home is here."

"With my handsome brother."

At that she turned, but only to view him coldly and briefly. "I will not answer to thy fond jealousies," she said. "He does your work for you."

"Ah, does he?"

"I mean the work of *talking* to me. That is what he does."

Will picked up his little son and bounced him on his knee, humming.

"That one won't know you when you return," Anne said. "And that one." She pointed at their youngest daughter, who was dipping Susanna's doll head-first in a pot of molasses, to her twin brother's delight. "Can you not see *that* one will be trouble?"

"You will all be with me in the city—"

"To starve with you while you peddle stage-plays? I cannot make out how you think to make money with that. The clown said even the university men crowd each other for custom. So you *told* me. How can anyone *profit?*"

"One man does." Will kissed the little boy's neck, then rested his chin atop the child's small noggin and stared at the embers of the kitchen fire.

Anne sighed and shook her head, scattering tears. "And I cannot write. Not to speak to you or read what you would say to me."

WILL dreamed of her falling tears, and his sleep was fitful.

AT the church Will attended with the Fields the next morning, the flat-capped pastor told that plays were the cause of plague and all manner of human evil, and that players caused boys to dress as girls on the stage, which was an abomination unto the Lord. Considering this statement, Will walked in the afternoon in the yard of Saint Paul's Cathedral. But he soon forgot the pastor's homily, so goggle-eyed did he grow at the milling folk dressed in all manner of garb and gear and, especially, at the bookstalls. He leafed through pamphlets and quartos and tiny octavos and giant folios and wished he had money to buy. At the cathedral door plastered with bills, he stood for a time reading the *Si quis* notices. *If anyone seeks . . . a hooper, a carter, a wainwright . . .*

There were no requests for poets.

Three days into the week he was back at the Rose to hear Christopher Marlowe's *Tamburlaine* played again. He knew enough now to stay in the middle of the yard where there was less likelihood of being hit by missiles from the galleries, bottles or orange peels or dead cats. This time he mouthed lines with the players throughout.

At play's end he walked to London Bridge, to cross that way and save a penny. Kempe seemed to have no part in *Tamburlaine*, nor did young Felix Culpeper, who had first begged Will's help in Stratford. Will saw no profit in standing in wait to talk to Edward Alleyn or one of the other players, since though he had one time played on a stage with them, he had not met any of them after. He looked back once, to be sure Kempe had not appeared with the exiting players. Outside the tiring house that jutted from the back of the rounded theater he saw no Kempe but a gaggle of women, some in humble linsey-woolsey and others in sarcenet and velvet, surrounding tall Master Edward Alleyn. The actor stood on the steps, still wearing his cloth-of-gold cape and, *God save us,* his crown. "Fair gentles, we thank you for your custom!" Will could hear his stentorian rumble from the bankside, thirty yards away. Alleyn bowed with a flourish. The ladies fluttered and curtsied. Will turned back to his way, thinking, *Ah, the Apollo of Southwark.*

He reached the bridge. At its base watermills worked with a ceaseless, satanic clatter. The shops and houses on the bridgesides met at the top, and the way back to London was a dark, roofed tunnel. He paused at the Great Gateway before he went in. He took a breath, then forced himself to look up.

There they were. A row of half-rotted heads and skulls stood impaled on the gate-spikes. Below them were placards, and he passed over these with his eyes until he found the one that read:

EDWARD ARDEN

PAPIST AND TRAITOR OF WARWICKSHIRE

EXECUTED BY THE GRACE

OF OUR LADY QUEEN ELIZABETH, 1585

He looked at the yellow skull above the placard.

It was a monster and it had chased him for years, but from here it looked only a bleached bone, peering hollow-eyed into the air. He knew its only powers were those with which his mind had invested it, yet those were much. Careless of watchers, Will stared into the skull's eyeless sockets. He lifted his hands like Arden's old gardener-priest, and knit his brows in imitation of his uncle. "*Ha!*" he barked, in greeting and farewell and blessing and apology, and vague promise of revenge.

Chapter Six

A third time that week he stood outside the Rose. It was morning, and he was hat in hand at the door of the tiring house, eyeing the men who came for work and rehearsal. He recognized one from the acting of *Faustus* in Stratford and he stopped him and asked whether Will Kempe was playing today.

"He is playing at being sick," the man said. "Come a'Thursday. We act a comedy then, and he may well recover."

He came a fourth time, on Thursday. Kempe was there then, and cavorted bravely in a jester's cap and spangled yellow hose. But he slipped from the tiring house before Will could fight through the leaving crowd to speak to him. Will sighed and groaned in his soul, and fished a pebble from his boot.

When he did finally find the clown a week later it was not in the playhouse at all, but in an ill-lit tavern, much frequented by playing folk, called the Crippled Phoenix. On the strength of an overheard conversation he had gone there, and he saw the unmistakable clown in a corner, drinking happily, the ostrich plume on his hat bobbing with every swig. Kempe greeted him fondly, with a clap on his shoulders and back.

After this, they drank together at low places on odd nights, and Will took every occasion to press Kempe for spare playing work, the favor he'd promised in Stratford. The fee for this favor seemed to be the enduring of endless improbable tales, and that fee must, it also seemed, be paid well in advance of any service.

At a scarred wooden table in a crowded Southwark hole called the Dark Angel, Kempe pounded his own knee with frank hilarity. "And when he saw Phillips's head," he gasped, "he thought I'd killed the man!"

"Did he, aye?"

"Mark me! I say Phillips's head was stuck through a hole in the table! 'Twas all set to look like a magical speaking statued head of bronze, and there we were in practice of the scene when in walks Ned Alleyn! He starts. Leaps up fairly to hit his head on a roof-beam! Fearing foul play, d'ye see. But what followed was better! Jump upon Alleyn's start, Phillips cranes his neck round and says, 'G'day, Nedward! I'd ask for a sip of thy ale, but I've no stomach for it!' " Kempe shrieked with laughter. "*No stomach for it*, he said!"

Will laughed as much laugh as he could muster on this second hearing of the tale.

"Ah, ah." Kempe pulled an enormous green handkerchief from his pocket and wiped his eyes. "The splendid properties of our playhouse. We own trick tables, gentlemen's clothing, e'en the robes of cardinals—no good for any *but* players in this country now." He nodded sagely. "Canst thou believe we own Cardinal Wolsey's cap?"

"I believe you have *drunk* at the Cardinal's Cap, and there an end of it."

"Ah." Kempe looked a little chagrined. "You speak true. We do not own Cardinal Wolsey's cap. But we say we do, and who's to know that we lie? Now I must pluck a rose." He stood abruptly and sauntered out toward the alley.

Will eyed him, as did other drinkers. Kempe wore a bright blue doublet, slashed leg-of-mutton sleeves backed with yellow silk, and breeches of green fustian. His favorite pearl ear-ring hung from his earlobe, and on his head sat a velvet cap of orange tawny, to which he had, he'd told Will, himself affixed the feather, one so long it now brushed the faces of the patrons he passed, leaving them blinking and vexed.

Will rubbed his beard, thought of Anne and the children, and sighed.

A loud noise at the tavern entrance jerked him from his reverie. The door banged open, and in stumbled a youth. A serving maid shrieked and jumped out of his way, splashing ale onto a man's arm. Customers started and rose as the boy crashed forward and collapsed over a table. Will rose too, and craned his neck to look. Through a gap in the crowd he saw the unfortunate young man, who lay panting for breath on the tabletop. Gasps of shock went round the tavern. The youth's face was pallid, a ghastly white except for the livid red marks and blackish-green spots that dotted his neck and cheeks. His fingers curled and uncurled spasmodically. From his throat came a guttural groan.

" 'Tis plague!" a woman screamed. "His neck is rotten with buboes!"

The rush for the door began. Folk upended stools and knocked over tables, crowding each other in their haste for the windows and doors. With one arm a heavyset man crossed himself and with the other he pushed Will from his path. A toothless woman behind the man, who trod on Will's foot, held two fingers up as she passed him, guarding against the evil eye. Out from the scullery ran the tavern hostess, her eyes wide with terror and rage. *"Get 'im out!"* she yelled. *"Throw the wretch in the alley!"* But no one dared approach the dying youth. Instead the house was fast emptied.

Will stood by his overturned stool. He whispered, *"Jesu-MaryJoseph,"* half an oath, half a prayer, and took a step toward the boy.

At that moment the lad sat up. He seized a half-full tankard of beer, splashed it into his own face, and started to laugh. The sound was a deep chuckle that did not well suit his young looks, much less his marks of death. He rubbed his face with one sleeve—fine cambric, Will noted—and off came the ghoulish pallor, the greenish-black and red spots. Ruddy flesh shone beneath. The buboes were stage-paint. But who would plot such a jest?

"In, my masters!" the youth cried. At his word, two hooting, well-dressed gallants spilled into the nearly deserted tavern from the alleyway door. "Never a table at the Dark Angel, said ye?" the youth crowed from his tabletop. "I vowed we'd have the stinking place to ourselves."

"Damn ye, Kit Marlowe!" the hostess cried. "Empty my business, would ye? Give it the name of a plague house? *You* shog off! Women can sue as well as men!" She advanced threateningly toward the youth, a two-pronged skewer in hand.

Marlowe. Will blinked. *Marlowe the poet? Marlowe the playwright?* This was a *boy*, an imp, barely an inch over five feet tall. He looked no more than seventeen. Cleared of the greasepaint, his face was angelic, framed with a halo of silky, golden-brown hair. He was beardless, his neck slight in its cobweb collar. By the light of the flickering candles his eyes looked a deep, soft brown.

"Sweet Nell." Marlowe—if indeed it was he—laughed. With feline grace he jumped from the table and embraced the fat hostess, who stood some three inches taller than he. "Canst not *expel* us. Hast no more customers than we three! And that ghostly one, whate'er he be." He jerked a thumb at Will.

"I can expel *thee*." The hostess waved her fork in the air, but the venom had gone from her voice. "How wilt thou compensate me for this trick?"

"Amply! And so will we all!" He pulled out a leather purse, and from it shook gold coins on the table. "Pay thy share, lads!"

"Not I, Kit," called one of the men, a red-headed fellow who had righted a table and now sat at it, one arm thrown on a chair back and legs outstretched. He was thirtyish, garbed in a cloak and breeches of green velvet, and watered silk stockings. His flaming beard was barbered to a sharp point. Like the others, he wore an ear-ring. "I'm out at heels," he said petulantly. "I can pay for my drink, and no more. Besides, this was *thy* game."

"Aye, pay, Kit!" called the second man, taking his seat next to the first. " 'Twas thine own foolish notion. Th'art a twit, and no wit."

The hostess seized one of the gold coins and scanned it intently. "These are French."

"And is French gold not as good as English angels?" asked Marlowe.

"Blasphemer!" said the woman. But she bit the coin, and added, "It may be."

"Take my gold, then!" Marlowe threw out his arms extravagantly. He crossed the tavern floor and sat with his friends. "Take it all! And as more compensation, I'll pull this same trick at the Cardinal's Cap at street's end. I'll do it a'Thursday."

"Do it farther afield, mad ass," said the hostess. "And never in here again. Come, Elizabeth!" She gestured at the serving maid, who stood shaking with fear in the kitchen doorway. " 'Twas only a knavish jest. Best get these men some ale; they'll break the tables else."

Will Kempe poked his head through the front door, swearing. "Poxy Marlowe! I saw these rogues waiting in the alley. What a jest! Now you have met William the Second."

"Ah, he?" Marlowe said. They all looked at Will.

"One who thinks himself plague-proof," the red-bearded man said.

Kempe entered, and he joined the group and gestured Will over. "Master William Shakespeare, lately a glover, now a player. And Will, this be as you now know Master Christopher Marlowe, Kit to his inwards, author of plays, and this Tom Lodge, author of—"

"What have you," Lodge laughed. "Odd plays, odd prose, odd poems." Lodge was young, thick, and short. He rose and exchanged a brief bow with Will. Marlowe jumped up and bowed too, deeply, with a flourish. Close by, Marlowe looked older than seventeen; he might, in fact, be twenty-three or twenty-four. Will's own age.

The frightened serving girl reappeared, struggling with a tray of tankards. The men plucked them from her, each taking two, except for Will, who had nothing, and the still-seated red-haired man, who said, "I'll have sack." The girl scurried back into the nether regions of the house.

"Master Robert Greene," Kempe said, gesturing toward the red-bearded man. "A writer of—"

"High comedy in prose pamphlets. I am honored." Will held forth his hand. Greene stared at it, not rising. Then, indolently, he reached out his arm, and pressed Will's palm briefly. His grip was boneless and clammy. Will resisted the impulse to wipe his hand on his breeches when it was freed.

Now all four men stared at him as though he were an exhibit.

"Warwickshire man," Will said. "Lately a glover. Near seventy inches high, weighing eleven stone." This seemed not to be what was expected, so he added, "I have read and admired thy writings, good sirs. And I have heard and been most moved by thy plays, Master Marlowe."

Marlowe thanked him courteously, though he did not look well pleased.

"Our friend Kit is irked by praise," said Robert Greene.

"Ah, one might well be irked by praise from a man dressed in woolen worsted," Will said. "And I've even a stain on one collar, see here, and the other is frayed. Yet I know poetry."

Marlowe narrowed his eyes at him. He seemed on the point of reply, but Kempe forestalled him, saying, "Will is one of our newest players at the Rose."

"Now, that puts a strange face on the facts, Master Kempe," Will said.

Kempe ignored Will. "He is country fresh, from Stratford-upon-Avon."

"Evident by his *r*'s," Greene said.

"My *r*'s?" Will raised his brows at Greene. "Are they not as good as yours?"

Kempe scowled, and Greene made his face a mask of uncaring. Marlowe grinned slyly, and looked from Greene to Will and back again. "Well? Shall we have swords? Warwickshire Man, will you die in defense of your *r*'s? Or will you only sit and drink with us?"

Will laughed and pulled a stool to the table. "I will choose peace."

"Both players, sit! We will allow you to share a table with us, for once."

Kempe snorted. "*Allow* us! Well you might, Kit Marlowe, since we've got your plays *and* all the money they bring."

Marlowe laughed, and Greene frowned. His sack had been brought, and he sipped it languidly. The men talked of city gossip and of poetry. Will sat slightly pulled back, his chin on his fist.

"The play's the thing," Marlowe said suddenly, banging his glass on the table like a rambunctious boy. He pointed at Kempe. "Money lies therein, as this clownish fellow brags." He turned to Greene. "Thou must stop mocking it, Robin. You've profited from a play or two yourself. And what shame in it? The stage will host any form of writing, be it poetry, prose—"

"And if a verse be dangerous, why, 'tis a player who spoke it, and not thee," Will said.

Marlowe stopped short, then smiled, cold-eyed, at him. "Look you now," he said. "I do not *know* you—"

"I meant no offense."

Greene broke in. "You players are more than glad to speak our lines. Our words are jewels, and you pay us farthings for them. We give you the means to work. In return you pay us what would feed chickens, not men."

"*Buck-buck-buck!*" Kempe squawked happily. " 'Tis mere business. We serve a market."

Greene looked enraged, and Will stifled a laugh.

"Besides," Kempe added, " 'Tis not so bad for thee, getting thy money *before* the performance. What happens when thy poxy plays fail? 'Tis players out of pocket then, not playwrights."

"Why do authors not buy shares in a cry of players?" Will asked.

The three writers stared at him. Lodge looked baffled, Greene irked, and Marlowe amused.

"A *cry* of players?" Marlowe asked courteously. "Are players hounds, then?"

"Hounds whose quarry is poetry. But forgive my conceit, if it offends thee."

"It does insult to thee, not to me."

"Then all's well. But to return. If players and writers joined together—or if they were the same men, perhaps—"

"They are *not* the same men." Greene sat suddenly upright. "Poets are educated at university. Poets have wit and knowledge. Players, on the other hand, are excrementory dishlickers of learning."

"That's harsh," Kempe said.

" 'Tis true enough. You players learn lines by rote, and half the time you do not know what they mean. And the other half you spend adding lines of your own, destroying our work. I am speaking to *you.*"

Kempe was humming and examining his fingernails by the light of the candle.

"That is bad, I grant thee," Will said. Kempe frowned at him, but he went on, "Yet if the poets were the players, or shared stakes with the players, surely such offenses would—diminish. Why give birth to a play and then sell it away forever?"

"Do we, i'faith, need such leather-apron men in our guild? To advise us?" Greene appealed to the table at large. Marlowe regarded Greene coolly. Will did not look at Greene at all.

Kempe ended the silence. "One way I like thy notion, Will the Second. If playwrights had to please audiences for their bread and butter, as we do, they'd learn to applaud our additions. They'd see we put jests in to please the crowds and bring them back again. We add lines to save doomed plays."

"And hobbyhorse dances are the saving of tragedies?" Greene sneered.

"In point of fact, they often are. Heavy works need leavening."

Greene's face was turning as red as his beard.

"Now, Robin, do not quarrel with the clown," Marlowe said. He had been looking at Will curiously all this while. "What do you know of writing plays?" he asked.

"Aye, where hast thou studied?" Greene broke in. "Queen's College? Christ's?"

Will looked at him mildly. "I see how you prize your learning, fellow. You wear it stitched on your green sleeve. Much glory may it bring you! Yet knowledge can be found outside books, and books can be found outside universities. As for me, I studied in—"

"A place that encourages free thought, I doubt not," Marlowe said. "This would not be Oxford, or Cambridge."

Will smiled at him.

From his breast pocket Marlowe now removed a paper packet of brownish weed and a long-stemmed clay pipe. He crumbled some weed into the pipe bowl. Will watched the process with interest. "Give me thy tinderbox," Marlowe commanded Tom Lodge, who obliged him. Marlowe lit the pipe, and a harsh scent filled the air above the table. He drew, then leaned back and blew the smoke heavenward. "Ah. Virginia."

Greene waved smoke from his face. "It stinks," he said irritably. "Kit, thou lackst license to mock at universities. Myself can claim *magistri artium* from both Oxford *and* Cambridge. But you never completed your studies at the one."

"I grew restless." Marlowe blew smoke in Greene's direction, and Greene coughed. "And what matter? I obtained my degree, did I not?"

"Yes, how?" Tom Lodge asked. "What possessed the queen to command that honor on thy behalf?"

"I kissed her hard. She's a lusty wench."

Will looked warily over his shoulder. A few customers had straggled back in, but none were close enough to Marlowe to heed his babble. He looked again at the poet. Older than he'd first appeared, yes. But madly young to have been to university and then to have made such a success of himself in London.

"After all," Tom Lodge was saying in his soft voice, "Master Shakespeare speaks true. A university education is not the sole route to knowledge. Not every lad is born rich enough to receive one."

"Come not at me with thy 'I've rubbed shoulders with common sailors and what hast thou done' blither-blather." Marlowe blew smoke at Lodge. "*I* was a scholarship boy."

"And a less deserving scholarship boy I could not think of," Lodge said. "Thou didst drink and avoid the lectures."

"Conversation was as elevated in the taverns."

"*This* conversation is not," Greene said.

"Tom Lodge has been trained on the high seas," Marlowe said, with a sidelong glance at Will. "He has been to the Americas with Grenville."

"Say you so?" Will was thrilled. "Met you one Simon Hunt? A Jesuit pedagogue?"

"It is a large continent," Lodge said kindly. "I met Indians."

"Saw you the Popefish?" Marlowe interrupted.

"I saw no such thing."

"It was sketched in a traveler's account of his journeys. I bought the book in Paul's Yard. A sea creature with miter and staff! He dwells in the New World oceans and eats drowning Protestant sailors."

"Oh, yes, yes, the *Popefish*," Lodge said. "You talk an infinite deal of nothing, Kit. Most sailors are liars."

"Most *men* are liars," Marlowe said. "*All* men are liars. The Cretan Paradox."

"And the twelfth psalm," said Will.

Marlowe looked at him shrewdly. "So! Master Plague-Proof has at any rate read the Bible."

"With exceeding care."

"May it turn you holy. I had meant to say"—Marlowe turned back to Lodge—"a man need not be a sailor to be dishonest."

"Thou shouldst know," Robert Greene said.

"I was speaking to Master Shakespeare of my travels, rudes-bys," Lodge said to the others. "Now. The weather in Virginia we found hot, and the people naked."

"Women too?" Will asked.

"Aye, and they are brown."

"And they thought you gods." Marlowe put down his pipe and clapped his hands. "I would have had them to build me a temple and—"

"*Hsssttt, Kit!*" said Lodge. "You are something overloud."

Will glanced over his shoulder again. The alehouse was more crowded now. Kempe had fallen asleep with his head on the table. His plumed hat had fallen over his face, and its feather stirred with every snore. Will thought he should leave these fellows, but Marlowe's talk kept him nailed to his stool.

"The Indians were not fools," Lodge told Marlowe in a low voice. "We brought them disease, so they feared us." He drank some ale, then pushed the tankard from him. "*You* be a god, Kit. I've no taste for it."

"Nor I, in truth, Tom Lodge," Marlowe said, tapping out his pipe on the table. When its bowl was empty he hopped up and did a small jig. "This I pledge," he said, swiveling suddenly, his finger in the air. "In my commonwealth, none shall be *made* to kneel to anyone."

"Not e'en to God?" Lodge asked.

Marlowe laughed. "Ah, the Liberties!" he said. "The Southwark Liberties. Where a man can breathe without a license from's guild. A fine place, is it not? Full of whores and stews and pimps and bear-pits and stenches."

" 'Tis poxy and disgusting," said Greene, languid and petulant once more. "Why did ye bring us here, Kit? I prefer the Crippled Phoenix, near Westminster."

"Blessed are the Liberties!" Marlowe said. He raised his arms and adopted the zealous tone of a Puritan divine. *"For man is depraved, and his heart is DESperately wicked!"* He dropped his arms and his voice. "Passions will out. Grant us our bawdy houses and tobacco and dicing and plays in the suburbs, and here our vices will stay. So Saint Augustine would say. And let all remain clean in the City of God. *Ergo,* in chaste London. To which let us return, my fellows, while the boatmen are rowing. Rouse yon clown!"

Will shook Kempe's shoulder, as they all raked their pockets for coin. The hostess, magically reappearing, dropped the silver into her apron.

City of God. Will thought of the heads on London Bridge, and drew his finger over his own throat. Once more Marlowe looked at him strangely. Then he led them singing to the river.

Chapter Seven

THE next day Will came early to the door of the Rose Theater's tiring house, and for the first time walked through it, past a stout man with a gold-buttoned doublet and ringed fingers and thick orange hair that stood strangely upright as though he were permanently frightened. The man was busy marking entries in a ledger, but he stopped and glanced up to say, "Man, I am the owner of this house, and who art—"

But Will was well and nimbly on his way up a ladder, and did not answer.

He found Kempe stocking costumes in the upper room. He sat on a bench and looked pointedly at the clown.

"Ah, ah," Kempe groaned, throwing a lawyer's black gown to the floor. "To see thee renews the pains of last night's debauchery. Why art thou here? And how didst thou come past Henslowe?"

"I swallowed fernseed and am invisible."

"I'truth?" Kempe looked intrigued. "Yet *I* see thee, so how is—"

"Will Kempe, I come here to demand what is due me. Having boasted that I play with the men of the Earl of Worcester, or whatever fat lord you play for, you must now grant me the player's work you promised."

"Ah, but Will, 'tis not as neat a thing as that, for 'tis not I who choose—"

"But you shall get me the work."

Kempe chewed a fingernail, staring at Will in silence. "Well enough," he said at length. "I shall speak to Master Henslowe and some others. Meet me at six at the Cardinal's Cap."

"That I will." Will rose. "And can you tell me where I might find Felix Culpeper hereabouts?"

"Who would that be?"

"A boy. A little scrubby boy who played Helen in your *Faustus* in Stratford."

Kempe shook his head. "Nay. Henry Condell played Helen, and he is no boy. He hath a great hairy beard and had to shave it. There was no Felix."

"Well, thy memory's at fault. But mine is a terrifying instrument, as you said then, and on the strength of my memory you will argue my fitness for playing spare parts."

KEMPE got him work, though neither Kempe nor any other player he met could help him find or could even recall the boy Felix Culpeper, who had vanished into thin air. That was strange, but Will, who had only wanted to thank the lad for his lucky help, thought that boys came and went in the world and were often barely noted before they were lost to view. The city swallowed them, or something did.

*   *   *

HE took a room in Boot Street, near Bishopsgate, in the Liberties north of the Thames, just outside the city wall. His landlord was hard of hearing and addressed him as Philip Chanticleer, a name Will liked so did not bother to correct. The doorway of his house gave onto a noisy street, uncobbled and wet with churned mud and crowded with carts, but from his window on the other side he could see into a field spotted with red flowers. Below him lived a godly family of weavers, whose work was quiet but whose psalm-singing woke him at sunrise, coming up through the floor.

In the afternoons Will swept stages and fetched props and played small parts. He spent mornings learning the player's odd trade, which was all trades in one: fighting with soldiers' cast-off weapons, conning Latin terms to speak as a lawyer. He practiced the hand and head gestures that meant anger, doubt, warning, fear. Most of those gestures he knew, having spent weeks in playhouse yards watching the players' ways. He thought such stiff posturings foolish, but they were wanted and he did them.

He wore out his boots walking London. Fyefoot Lane, Distaff Street, Paternoster Row. He passed through the stink of the streets, his ears drinking the cries of the merchants selling Stratford wool and gold from the New World and Hackney turnips and Pimlico pudding pies. When he had the time he would wind through Paul's Walk at the great cathedral, and page through the books that he could not buy, and stare, sick-souled but big-eyed, at the black, lolling tongues of the hanged men in the yard.

So fortified with sound and sight and sense, he would come to a playhouse in the Liberties: the Rose in the south or the playing places north of the Thames, these being the Theater or the Curtain, or the yards of the Bel Savage or Cross Keys Inn. He would step on scaffolds on odd afternoons when players were sick. Whole scrolls of parts he swallowed, at a speed that astounded the men he met. He played lascivious lords and comic servants and, once, when every boy at the Rose was down with the quinsy, a ravished maid. He came for months, and among the actors he found much merriment and some good will, but still he counted no players other than Kempe as friends, since he was not given a place in a patron's company and did not rehearse with the men. Instead he took parts when suddenly asked, and stayed to hear plays when he wasn't. When he played, so wholly did he melt into his part that he left them no impression of himself at all.

When he did not play he took note when the audience laughed or the yardlings grew angry, and he heard what made the folk shriek and what mutter, and what drove them, yawning, from the houses when the plays were only half done. Afterwards he would go to his room and sit at his table and write.

Tragedies were simplest, but he would begin with the hardest thing.

A comedy must start with a breach, a dark thing, like a death. That must make a man flee from one place to another, from the city to the country, or from the country to the city. Once he was in the new place the plot might loosen. There should be many characters, much incident laxly tied, above all much merry and sweet-sounding discourse, and love must enter into it. At the end there should be forgiveness.

Then the man would go home.

MARLOWE paused by his door, took a key from a cord about his neck, and began to turn the lock. He stopped, finding that the door was open already. He pushed it inward. "Shouldst lock this," he said to someone in the room.

Will followed him in. The room was small, dim, and book-crowded. It held two stuffed shelves, and volumes were piled everywhere. A Saint Jerome's Bible. *Dialogues of Hermes Trismegistus.* An Italian work, *Il Principe,* by Niccolò Machiavelli. Crumpled papers were strewn on the floor, along with empty bottles and a few stained plates. A thin orange cat slunk along the frame of one of the two narrow bedsteads. The window was unshuttered but tiny, and admitted so little light that although it was still afternoon someone had lit two candles, which burned on a round table in a corner. On that table stood more books, an inkstand, a stale-looking hunk of brown bread, a stoup of wine, and a stack of new paper. A dark-haired man sat behind the stack. Hunched over, quill in hand, he wrote thoughtfully, stopping sometimes to dip his quill in the ink-pot or to tap the feather against his lips. He did not speak to Marlowe or even look up.

Will looked hungrily at the paper, and Marlowe noticed. "Take some of it," he said. "Your foul-papers are written on the backs of printers' old broadsheets and bills found in the street."

"They are," said Will. But he had seen the bending writer stiffen at Marlowe's offer, and he let the words pass as a jest. Doffing his cap, he approached a tall shelf and ran a finger across the spines of the quartos and folios. Gently, he pulled several out. "Some of these titles are on the Index," he murmured.

"That matters not in England most free."

"Forbidden by the Church to print or to read. Where did you get them?"

"France. From a brave printer in a place called Rheims. And the books were forbidden *there*, you may be sure of that." Marlowe locked the door. He unbelted his dagger and placed it gently on a stool. "Sweetheart, lie thou there."

"Less noise, may it please you," the writer said. He scratched something out.

Marlowe doffed his beaver hat and hurled it like a discus onto one of the beds. Will's cap was of plainer felt, and he stood holding it, still studying the book titles. "William Tyndale's Books of Moses," he said. "Do you worship God after all, then?" He cast a sidelong look at his host, who cocked an eyebrow and said, "Whom do you think I worship?"

"The great iamb." Will laughed softly, as if to himself. "I-amb that I-amb, saith Jehova."

Marlowe looked as though he would choke on envy, but he only said, "Thy jest is nine beats too long."

"Ah, such is the writerly counsel I seek, Master Marlowe. On, on."

"Our introductions first. Here, Master Kyd, is a friend named William Shakespeare. And Will, this scurrilous scribbler with the soiled cambric shirt is Thomas Kyd. He is another playwright to enrich thine acquaintance."

"And another Thomas," Will said, remembering Tom Lodge at the Dark Angel. He approached the table with a palm outstretched. Kyd half-rose and clasped it with one hand while he kept writing with his other.

The world is full of Thomases,
They never keep their promises
And poxy few of them doubt!

As he sang his ditty, Marlowe executed a few jig steps on the Oriental rug that covered most of the wood floor. Then he leapt, catlike, to the narrow bed, where he slouched next to his hat. The wood of the bedframe squeaked, and Kyd looked up with marked vexation. "Hast thought of becoming a balladeer, Kit?"

"There's cursed little in heaven and earth I've not thought of." Marlowe pulled out his long pipe and began to pinch tobacco into it.

"Well, Kit, I will be awake all night as it is, even without your noise and stink. The play's promised for tomorrow."

"*The* play?" Marlowe's tone was mock wonderment. "Is it, in truth, *the* play? The play of plays?"

"That the audience may judge." Kyd kept writing. "At any rate, you may expect Henslowe's men bursting in to cuff me about the ears tomorrow if it's not at the Rose by noon."

"Ah, *Henslowe's* men. First they're the Queen's Men, then Lord Worcester's, and now Henslowe's. Only one thing's certain of players. They're anyone's men but their own."

Kyd ignored him. Will heard, but his eyes went elsewhere. The room was a paradox: squalid and cramped, one table for two writers, but velvet draperies hung from the small window. And there was pure strangeness. An exotic waterpipe stood by a bed, its glass bowl muddy with use. Will's eyes rounded the walls and stopped where they had begun, at the crowded shelf of books before him. He turned from them, his fingers curling around his cap and his manuscript.

Meeting Marlowe outside the Theater in Shoreditch that morning, he had asked him to read a play. Weeks had passed since their encounter at the Dark Angel, and Marlowe had not at first known him, in the broad light of day and with traces of stage-powder whitening his cheeks. Marlowe had begun to deny him, but when Will pressed his remembrance Marlowe's brown eyes came alive and alert and he laughed loud and long for no clear reason. After that he had brought Will here.

"Let us have the poetry," Marlowe said now.

"Poetry is not the whole of it. There are prose patches and comic tricks drawn from the old Bible plays—"

He stopped. Marlowe was looking at him with amusement. "Should I read it, or dost thou prefer to describe it?" He blew a smoke-ring.

Will handed him the manuscript, which was indeed scribbled on the backs of printers' bills. "Read, so please you."

"*The Taming of the Shrew*. This has been played, you know," Marlowe said, glancing down at the sheaf of paper. He rose to seat himself across from Kyd. He blew more smoke-rings. Kyd sighed loudly and waved them from his face.

Will spoke just above a whisper. "It has not, sir. A play of like name has been played, but mine is different."

"Different how?"

"Should I describe it, or dost thou prefer to read it?"

Marlowe glanced up at him sardonically. "Well enough, then. It is different. I will see how. Why do you not say that it is better?"

"I'd be the more pleased were *you* to say that."

But Marlowe was already rapidly reading, and he did not respond. "Stay if you wish," he said absently.

"I'll walk. I've not dined yet and I saw an ordinary in the street."

"Their fowl pie is less rancid than their liver and onions."

AN hour later he was back, knocking softly on the door. "Who is't?" Marlowe's voice came, guarded.

"Will Shakespeare. Again."

Footsteps approached, and the latch was drawn. Tom Kyd let Will into the room and returned to his desk to resume his scribbling. *Scratch, scratch, scratch.* The two candles were burning low, and Marlowe's pipe sat cold on the table.

Marlowe sat motionless in his chair, gazing down at one of Will's pages. Will placed himself lightly on the edge of one of the beds, next to the beaver hat. He studied Marlowe's face, which wore a look of rare gravity.

After a minute Marlowe looked up. "Who taught you this?"

"What?"

"This." Marlowe held a page out and pointed at it. "Stichomythia between the lovers."

"Stick-o—what say you?"

"One-line exchanges, as in Greek—"

"Oh. The Greeks themselves. Sophocles."

"But you cannot read Greek."

"No. But I can see the shape."

"The *shape?*"

"Of the dialogue."

"The *shape.*" Marlowe shook his head. "If you could read Greek, you'd know that the tit-for-tat is for anger, not wooing. Tiresias and Oedipus do not woo each other. They curse each other."

Will frowned slightly. "I know the tale. I only thought that . . . *animus,* that *push* and *push,* might have something in it of *eros.* I thought it might lend itself to a wooing scene."

"Oh, you did."

"Aye."

"And who showed you *this?* Here. Breaking one line in three or four parts between characters." Will noticed that Kyd's pen had fallen silent. "Where learned you this?"

"From a play called *Tamburlaine.*" Will smiled.

"From *my* play? But I did not do it there."

"Yes, you did."

"Once, maybe. A few times, but not oft. And a line broken in half, but not into four parts!"

"A very good idea, I thought. Sped the interchange. Why not speed it more by dividing the line further? Keep the meter, quicken the pace. If the moment calls for it."

"And what moment calls for such a mad pace?"

"Well, not anger. The Greeks were wrong in this."

"*What?*"

"In their stick-o-what-is-it." Will played the country fool, though he remembered the Greek word. Seeing he was mocked,

Marlowe frowned and began to speak, but Will kept on. "Anger does not quicken the wit, it clouds it. So how can it quicken the speech? Nor does anger make a man and a woman more apt to listen to one another or to answer what is asked; no. Anger sends a fellow alone into his own thought and then all he can speak is a monologue about how he is right and the other fellow is wrong, or she is right and the other wrong or what have you. So anger is a 'stand back, let me say all' thing. Now, this back-and-forth, I can listen to you and outdo you with a better, this is for love and marriage."

Marlowe stared at him silently for a long moment. Then he said slowly, "I have no notion of what you mean."

Will leaned forward. "Let me say. Here is a woman, Kate, and a man, Petruchio. When they meet it does not take them long to find that they are the same, both clever ones. They can match each other word for word, jest for jest. So much in tandem do they think that they finish each other's thoughts, which is to say, each other's lines. It is wondrous, is't not?" Will had worked himself into a high pitch of excitement.

"If it's wondrous to you, what need you my say-so?" Marlowe asked.

"I call on you for a courtesy, to show you what I shall be presenting to the players."

He meant this as a jest, but saw right away he had made a mistake. Marlowe's face showed slight and injury. Will did what he could to allay the hurt. "But I do not speak seriously, Kit Marlowe. 'Twas an ill-made gibe, for which I ask pardon. I am a baby here, and you are a very great poet of the stage. It is generous of you to give counsel, and I sincerely seek it."

He could say it. All of it was true.

"Then list," Marlowe said. "First, it does not matter what folk might or might not do in life. Here you treat fictions on a stage, and their purpose is not to do what real folk might do but to make their watchers heed them."

"Ah. Well spoke."

"Stow. The next is that none of this fast talk would ever work because it depends on the players' skill. Men with barely an education—I speak of players—are not able to keep such a metrical pace while they are running all about the stage, as you have the man and woman doing here. And remember, your Kate will be a mere boy. How can he do such a task, and keep his rhythm?"

"But this is noth—" Will stopped again, seeing Marlowe's face. "These are excellent objections. But here is my answer. The verse itself will help them remember. They need only fall into its rhythm, and the lines will guide their movements and tell them when 'tis the other's turn. And they need not run here, as in the *commedia dell'arte*. Nothing so rough. They shall circle each other, like dancers."

"Dancers." Marlowe laughed shortly. "Dancers who dance at will, without lessons?"

"Well, certainly they'd need to *rehearse*, you apple-faced—pardon me."

Marlowe stared at him. His angelic countenance had gone dark with rage. They sat for a moment in a silence broken only by the suddenly renewed scratching of Kyd's quill.

Suddenly Marlowe let loose a stream of curses and knocked a book to the floor. He rose and turned on Will, who stood himself, thinking he might need to ward off a blow. But Marlowe only yelled. "Think you there's some magic in your rhymes? Think you that your lines can change actors from know-nothings to gentlemen? Or gods, perhaps? Just by the force of your will and the speaking of the lines?"

"I had not thought so far. I only—"

"Because I used to think as much," Marlowe interrupted, ignoring him. "And mark me well. Poetry changes no one. Heed the saying. You cannot make a silk purse from a sow's ear."

"*You* say that?" Will shook his head in disbelief. "I have seen three of your plays and every one urged such a transformation. A doctor makes himself a magician and a shepherd a conqueror, defying gods and kings, worshipping no one—"

"Not the same." Marlowe had calmed a little. He sat and lit his pipe again. "Those are sow's ears who make themselves into silk purses. Poetry does not do it for them. My will does not. *Their* will does it! And besides"—he shifted in his chair, and looked suddenly wary—"these my vaunting heroes are stage illusions. I have never claimed they act as men act, or should act."

This was not true. Will had heard him claim something like it, drunkenly, in the Dark Angel. But now Will said only, "Say on."

"Our word-art leaves actors untouched. Consider Ned Alleyn. Is he a Tamburlaine? My brave heroes have made him famous, but saying their words hasn't made *him* brave. Afraid of a mouse, is he! I challenged him to a sword-fight once, over his marring of a speech I wrote, and he—" Marlowe laughed at the memory.

Thomas Kyd laughed too, at something else, perhaps, his eyes fixed on his page. He mouthed dialogue.

"Thy point?" asked Will.

"Is this. You've written a play about a man who changes a woman into something better than she is. And in order to act it, the actors must be wiser than *they* are." Marlowe tossed the manuscript at Will, who caught it.

Will stood up abruptly. "Kit Marlowe, you are speaking to a player."

"But not a good one. I have seen you. You are lax at striking the tragic attitudes. I would not offend you—"

"I am not offended."

"It is clear that you would rather write than play." Marlowe sat brooding a moment, then said, "To gain a fair hearing for thy poetry, you must leave aside this interplay and write thy characters *speeches*. Then any player with a good memory can say them. Let them exchange monologues, not lines. The long one in thy play's second half, the husband who says, *My falcon now is sharp and passing empty*—that is good. And the woman's speech at the end. Keep those, and cast out the rest."

"I thank you," Will said pleasantly, and bowed.

Marlowe saw him to the door and closed it hard. Then he came back to the table and sat, drumming his fingers on the table, as Kyd wrote at a furious pace. "Dost thou know, there was a line or two in that man's work that I had said, in conversation," he said. "Months agone."

"He hath a good memory as well as a ready wit. But he knew courtesy. God knows where he learned it, with those up-country accents! I am sure he would take the line out if you objected."

"No need. I stole the page." Marlowe brandished a sheet of cheap paper crowded with spidery writing.

"Ah. Wise fellow."

Marlowe put the paper to the candleflame. In an instant it was ablaze. Kyd rose abruptly, cursing, and threw a half-glass of sack at the burning page. Then he crumpled the sodden mass and tossed it on the floor, where the cat jumped at it. "God's death, Kit, art mad?" He sat down, glaring at Marlowe.

Marlowe laughed. "How comes *The Spanish Tragedy?*"

"Well enough. But have a care, Kit. Some night ye'll destroy us both in this room. At times I doubt thy sanity."

Marlowe nodded. "Aye, quite so." He brooded another minute, then said, "A brain-wasting farce it was, of men and women a-marrying. Well. God keep Will Shakespeare from tragedy."

Chapter Eight

WILL resolved not to seek more advice. He went back to Kempe, whom he found practicing a morris dance on the Rose Theater stage, wearing bells tied by yarn to his fingers. He *thwocked* his manuscript on the boards before him. "I have written a play and I wish you and your friends to consider it, my Kempe."

"A *whole* play?" Kempe looked unhappy. "Will, our wont is to commission a work after we see a few scenes. And afterwards I con *my* part. I have never read a whole play and I do not think my eyes could stomach one. Wouldst read me *my* part?"

"Thou shalt be in the crowd's eye—or stomach, if you will—for the whole of the play."

Kempe brightened. "Ah! And will I dance?"

"You will sleep. From the middle of the first act on." Will raised his hands against Kempe's cry of rage. "But on stage, on stage! And ye may cut many a comic caper before you drowse, and after the play is done, as well." He leaned toward Kempe, tapped his manuscript, and repeated with emphasis, "*After* the play is done."

"I shall have a look." Kempe touched the papers with his green-jeweled finger. "And there will be a part for *thee* in a new tragedy, to go on our boards in a fortnight's time. We are owed the script today."

"By Thomas Kyd?"

"How knew you that? A great part for Alleyn, it has."

"Ah. Alleyn." Will nodded tiredly. "I shall be back tomorrow, then. You may show me my un-great part."

Yet as it turned out, it was the best part Will had yet been given. He rose through the trap in the middle of the stage as the ghost of a Spanish nobleman, and wore a clanking suit of armor that fully disguised him. For much of the play he viewed murder and mayhem from a recessed alcove of the stage, and listened intently to the speeches and to the fast dialogue that bounced between the Spanish princess and her ardent suitor.

Line answering line, tit for tat, a quickening pace, *sticho-mythia* . . .

When the play was done he strode clanking from the tiring house in a rare rage.

In the street he found he had forgotten to shed his armor, and had to return. "*I* was the first!" he muttered, throwing his greaves in a trunk. The other players in the room eyed him curiously.

"He listened, he listened, the thieving knave, but *I* was the first!"

"ANNE!" He burst through the front door, red from his journey and from pecuniary zeal. Henslowe, the be-ringed and shock-haired owner of the Rose Theater, had bought his comedy for two pounds, a day before the theaters had closed for the season of Lent. He'd rented a nag to ride home, and here he was, money in hand, to make good his long absence.

But all was silent. He looked in the Woolery, saw dyed skins laid on tables, ready for cutting, and smelled the pungent gum-dragon. The place was empty of folk.

But it was market day, of course.

He returned to the kitchen and laid his gold pieces on Anne's buttery bar. Then he went back to the workshop to cut.

An hour later, sweating from a cowskin's tough resistance, he heard the voices of children outside the window, and then Anne's merry laugh and Gilbert's low chuckle. He paused and looked out and saw them coming, and they seemed a family, well enough.

They entered through the kitchen. "What is this?" Anne said. "Who has left this?" Looking up she saw Will drying his arms and staring keenly at her from the doorway.

"It will pay for my board, and some warmer welcome, I hope," he said.

Susanna ran to him and hugged his knees, but the twins only stood staring. Judith clutched her mother's skirts, and Hamnet held Gilbert's hand.

"Brother," Will said.

Gilbert nodded.

That night Will lay with Anne in the Paradise bed. With one hand he clasped his wife's, and with the other he traced, above and behind him, the carved image of the Tree of Knowledge. He felt the body of the serpent, coiled around the trunk, half-hidden under the wooden leaves.

IN the morning he was awake before she was, shriveled and naked and rummaging through his traveling trunk in the wan light of dawn. She told him it was the Sabbath and to come back to bed until church, but he told her nay, there was gold to be made, more gold to be made. He brought out some scribbled-on papers and a corked ink-pot and a quill.

Stretched out shivery bare on the floor, he began to write.

HE was six weeks at home, and in that time he ate pastry and Lenten eel pie and put on the flesh he had lost in London and some besides. When he spoke at supper board he spoke of playing, and his parents regarded him bemusedly. He and Gilbert avoided each other entirely. His youngest children played with his boot-laces as he scribbled at his table. As for Anne, by the end of the Lenten season she had come close to forgiving him for not visiting them in half a year.

It was Christmastide, she said, that had hurt them the most, for at Christmas there were singing and good cheer and games inside the house, though the Church now forbade the Yule Log in the town, and what did he think his children thought of the empty place at table?

He reminded her that he had sent a fine substitute, namely a note for the money he'd earned by playing parts at the Queen's Christmas Revels, not a task to be turned down, with gold flowing like water from the hands of nobles to humble players who bright-ened their feasting. To say nothing of the sight of a thousand candles lighting a room and a hundred courtiers off-capping when the queen entered with her train, a hundred men kneeling in three-piled velvet and peascod doublets stuffed so thick with pad-ding they could barely stand up again. And the curtsying ladies with their silks and their pearls and their hair tinted red to look like their great sovereign. And then the queen herself, with a flam-ing wig, it was clearly a wig, and a dress of silver weave and a collar standing high behind her head like the shell of a giant oyster.

"What good does it do me," asked Anne, "if I cannot see it too?"

"I will turn it all to poetry and the poetry to money."

"Ah, is't so easy, then?"

"Aye, Nanny." Will had begun to think that it was. "I say I will put it on a stage. I will put *you* on a stage, though you may not know yourself when I do. All things known may be said in a play, and where I have sold one play I may sell another. As for kings and queens, they will say what I will them to say. I will show them all a mirror. I will show them what they are."

"Will, art mad?" Anne said sharply. "Hast forgot thine uncle's fate? Thou mayst think of the rest of us when writing thy rash words."

"I will never forget him," Will said, his grey eyes dark. "But poetry can never be rash. And in the end 'tis not a playwright who speaks the poetry. Nay, not even a player."

"Who, then?"

"A character. Which is to say an illusion. Which is to say no one."

EASTER came and went. Anne had no wish to drag her three children to a bare room in London, and anyway the thing was not reasonable yet. But she was wounded to the heart that he did not ask it of her. From the front window of their house she watched him disappear in a cloud of road dust, and when he was gone she felt too desolate to cry. Behind her Hamnet fell from a stool and started to yell. She turned and picked him up and dusted him off.

"All's well, little man, all's well," she said, and held him tight.

Chapter Nine

WILL came back into London with another play and sold it too, but it was not performed, nor the other one either, and he schooled himself to a wait.

Marlowe was friendlier now, and hailed him when they passed in the tiring houses or crossed paths in the taverns. Once, as Will was plodding dustily down Cheapside, the gold-emblazoned door of a fine coach opened and there was Marlowe, legs jauntily crossed, sitting next to two stiff-ruffed men in scalloped doublets and velvet capes who wore chains of office about their necks. Will got in and rode at a tortuous pace for two blocks. He found that the fatter of the lords was Francis Bacon and the lean one, who wore a soldier's beard cut like the ace of spades, and whose eyes were a startling sea-green, was Sir Walter Raleigh, the New World explorer.

Sir Walter was attempting to prove that he was an alchemist in reverse. While the alchemist turned base metals into gold, Sir Walter took gold hacked from the mines of the Indian savages and turned it into base metals, such as silver to pay off his debts, cast iron to turn into cannons, and lead for balls to fire at the Armada. Will thought this a clever conceit, but said nothing, and the lords showed little interest in him until Sir Francis asked whether the women of the country matched those of the city in beauty. Will replied that he could not judge, since he had never seen a London woman's face below the paint. That produced a laugh from Bacon and Raleigh as well as Marlowe, and Sir Walter asked if Will had a wife as witty as he. "She is not so witty as myself, my lord," Will said, "but the quickness of her tongue might put any red-haired queen to shame, and as for her beauty—"

Though Raleigh and Marlowe smiled, Francis Bacon seemed glad to put Will out at the corner of Gutter Lane. Marlowe gave him a parting wink. The whole business left Will wondering why a poet—even one as famous as Kit—would be asked to share carriage space with the greatest noblemen in the land.

"WORD has gone round of thy jest in the carriage," Kempe said to Will soon after. "Wit is well, but it is not well thought on to practice it everyplace!"

"Aye, clown." Will sat in the shade of an elm tree outside the Rose tiring house, scribbling on the back of a broadside that read THE PLAY OF FRIAR BACON AND FRIAR BUNGAY, BY MASTER ROBERT GREENE. "I full lost my head in the presence of such grandeur." He looked up. "Hast a part for me today?"

"No part today. But I tell you friendly, Will, Kit Marlowe's company has made you rash. He has some color for his mad bibble-babble, but you have none, and should not speak so freely."

"Ah, yes." Will wiggled his brows. "Marlowe has angels' protection. Is't not so, friend?"

"I do not know all." Kempe looked as though he regretted having spoken. "I hear rumors. But have a care, Will."

WILL did not discuss spying with Marlowe. When they met in the players' haunts, they spoke on other themes, finding much to say about poetry and the demerits of Edward Alleyn, the Rose's great tragic actor.

"But I thought *you* thought him fine!" Will said.

"Brave gestures he has, and a voice that cannot be matched. But there can be too much. He ruins my plays, most especially *Faustus*. My Faustus." Marlowe's voice caressed the name. "Dear Faustus, possessed, as I am, by *libido sciendi*, the lust of the mind."

They were seated in the Crippled Phoenix in Westminster, over cider, tobacco, and ale. Marlowe leaned close to Will, arching his golden brows. Holding his pipe off to one side, he said, "Dost know, my upland friend, that the mind is more sinful than the body? It seeks for never-ending delight, the eternal stimulus of knowledge. Thus its lusts exceedeth the short vehemence of"— he made a bawdy thrusting motion—"carnal pleasures." He leaned back in his chair and drew on his pipe. "And its punishment is proportionally worse."

Will laughed. "I thought *Doctor Faustus* a moral tale. You make it sound lascivious. And I thought you favored ambition and the *libido*—oh, whatever it was you said. I have small Latin, ye know; mayhop we could spake of hogs, aye, and farrrmin—"

"Enough!" Marlowe said. "You have your jest."

A shadow fell over the table, and Will looked up. An elegant man stood by them, looking at Marlowe as though begging recognition. He was of middle age and wore fine courtier's silks that were, all the same, something threadbare. His expression was melancholy, but he looked disposed to sit. "Greetings, Kit," he said.

Marlowe squinted at him through a cloud of his own smoke. *"O unfortunate Endymion. Why are not thy fortunes as great as thy deserts?"*

"Why indeed," the man said, and took a stool. "You are lacking some of your fellows. Where is Wit-Without-Money?"

"Robin Greene, in his garments of goose-turd hue, walketh with sprightly step to the bower of his fair mistress." Marlowe made a gagging noise. "And you, sir? How go things at court? Do you still storm the golden-haired earl for patronage?"

"Nay," the man said, looking pained. "The Earl of Southampton has declined my suit."

"And thy lovely collection of boys, how do they?"

The man looked at Marlowe with distaste. "They do well. I do not call them lovely, but they are disciplined players. At any rate I am writing something else now, and it will earn the favor of the queen if nothing else does." His face lightened a little. "You have heard of Martin Mar-Prelate, as he calls himself."

"Heard of him! I have read his merry papers. A Puritan mocking the bishops, with his back-room hidden printing press! Says whatever he thinks. Says it most wittily."

The man scowled. "His jests are scurrilous."

"So are the bishops," said Marlowe. "The Bishop of Winchester owns three-fourths of the brothels in Southwark. He makes a fair profit from sin! We revere him, of course. But what's it to us if another mock him as a whited sepulchre?"

"Wilt speak lower?" the man said pleadingly. "I'll not heed thine irreverences, Kit Marlowe. They may pass, since you lent me some paper—even though it did belong to thy bedmate. As for Martin Mar-Prelate, he has lent me no paper, and his mockeries will *not* stand. He may hide like a fox, but they will find out who he is and gut and *skin* him like a fox."

Will winced.

"A pox on all dissenters!" the man said, and gulped a swallow of ale from an untouched glass by his elbow. As it happened, it was Will's. "Out on the whole crowd of them, Anabaptists and Ranters and Family of Love!"

"May a man not be a Puritan, then?"

The man paused, glass half to his mouth, and looked at Will for the first time. His gaze was cool and level. "An Englishman may be Catholic, True Protestant, or even rabble-rousing Puritan if he wills. The queen ensures liberty of conscience in religion to every man."

Will's gaze matched his. "So long as that man keep his thoughts to himself."

Marlowe laughed and clapped. The other man looked vexed, and said, "Some thoughts are dangerous." He turned back to Marlowe. "Now, Kit, this new task may interest you. That same Bishop of Winchester, Thomas Cooper—"

"Ha'ye any work for the cooper?" Marlowe sang.

The man shook his head impatiently. "As I say, the Bishop of Winchester will not be mocked. He seeks authors to answer the Mar-Prelate's japes, and he pays gold. I am one who has taken his offer. I can mock a mocker." He finished Will's glass and waved a hand in the air for the drawer, while with his other he pulled a sheaf of papers from a leather bag. He placed the papers before Marlowe. "See. Here is the butt of my humor, their godly meetings where all recite Bible and sway and sing psalms. 'Geneva jigs,' I call their gatherings."

Marlowe scanned the papers, smiling.

"Have you attended them?" asked Will.

The man looked at him in surprise. "Attend their assemblies, sir? Nay, not I. What would I do in their dingy upper rooms where the men and women howl out of tune and then all fly out the windows like crickets to escape the Crown's officers!"

"The godly weavers below my room sing sweetly," Will said. "And, my witty master, crickets don't fly."

Marlowe laughed again, his gaze still on the writings before him. The man frowned thoughtfully. "Is it a metaphor?" he said.

"No. A fact," said Will.

"This fellow is from the country, John," Marlowe said, looking up. "But it is I who am the rustic, for I have not presented him. He is my friend Master William Shakespeare, who carries about his own scribbly foul-papers wherever he walks, and is, by his talk now, a Puritan himself and at work on a new translation of Saint Paul's letter to the Ephesians. He is offended by our conversation."

"No," said Will.

"Will, I present Master John Lyly, a distinguished playwright. He is the author of *Endymion.* And *Midas,* the play with the ass's ears." Marlowe reached across the table and pulled Will's ears. Will stood abruptly, brushing his hands away. "Ah, don't beat me with your piebald hands, Shake-a-spear," Marlowe said. "I know you have read Master Lyly's *Midas.*"

"I have, and something else as well." Will's tone was grim. "*Lyly.* Was it thee who composed a Latin grammar for boys? Taught in the schools in country and town?"

"Not I," Lyly said. "That was my grandfather's doing."

Will relaxed his fist. " 'Tis well," he said. "Well for thee. And now my own work calls me. Sirs, I take my leave." He bowed and left the tavern.

"Odd fish," Lyly said, looking after him.

"We are all odd fish," Marlowe said, and signaled for a new tankard.

THREE days later Will found Marlowe in the same room in the Crippled Phoenix, mincing across the floor and waving a scarf for the entertainment of a group of out-at-elbows wits that included

Tom Kyd and Robert Greene. The men sat crowded together at a table littered with empty glasses as Marlowe paraded before them.

"I wore an exthellent gold jerkin that day, very fine, and thtockings of gold weave," Marlowe lisped. He wore a look of foppish complacency as he pranced. "It looked motht well as I danthed the morrith in *The Thpanish Tragedy*. 'Tith thought by thum that a gay danth hinderth the playing of murder, but tush, I thay. Tush."

"Will Kempe to the life!" a watcher yelled, and they all laughed and clapped.

"Do Ned Alleyn."

Marlowe turned, frowning, in the direction of the voice. It came from Will, who was not laughing with the others. He stood leaning against the doorway with his arms folded.

"Alleyn, then." Marlowe jumped onto a table with one motion. He struck a pose, one arm held high.

"Up there with thine arm raised thou comest near to his height, thou shrimpkin!" Kyd teased.

"*Silence!*" Marlowe thundered, his voice suddenly deep. The watchers started. "I have dispatched him!" Marlowe contorted his face horribly. "*Dooo-ooown* he doth fall! With speed, cut his heart out, and give it to *meeee!!*" He grabbed a pastry knife from the tabletop and stabbed wildly into the air.

The men spat ale in their hilarity and clapped, but for Will, who said, "Not that. Give us Alleyn botching thine *own* verse."

A look of disgust came over Marlowe's face, and he dropped to the floor. " 'Tis enough that I hear him butcher my numbers in the playhouses. I'll imitate that King Herod no more."

Kyd rose. "Masters, I must quit thy company. Kit owes me for a game of bowls. Let him pay for my drink."

Marlowe's face lengthened in comical woe. "*Alas, I am a*

scholar. How should I have gold? All that I have is but my stipend from the king, which is no sooner received than it is spent."

"Is that from a new play? Stipend from the queen, *you* mean. I've small pence at present." Kyd shrugged himself into his cape and raised a hand. "Anon. I must go."

"And I." Robert Greene pulled a jeweled oval timepiece from his pocket, consulted it, then snapped it shut and stroked his pointed beard. "My mistress will rail at me if I tarry."

"Henpecked," said Marlowe. "Buck buck."

Greene made an impatient gesture and turned to go.

"Thy money?" Marlowe asked.

"Ah." Greene turned back. "I'm short now. Tomorrow I'll pay."

"If thou needst to sell thy fine timepiece to do it, thou wilt," said Marlowe, smiling. His voice was edged.

"Fear me not. Five of the clock, at the Dark Angel."

The rest of the group dispersed, and Marlowe sat smoking. Rain pelted the windows, and the room's interior looked as dark as night. Will took a seat next to him. "You would like to be rid of Ned Alleyn," he said.

They gazed at one another in silence for a moment. Marlowe said, "He brings in custom. He causes my verse to be celebrated."

"It is your verse that causes him to be celebrated."

Marlowe scrutinized his face carefully. "You are sure."

"Yes."

"Ah. Then so it is." Marlowe nodded almost gratefully, then frowned, remembering their subject. *Alleyn.* "Even so, there is nothing to be done about him."

"Something can be done. What would you give to have our King Herod swear off the playing of Faustus, forever?"

"You could not. The part suits him like a fine fitted glove."

"Nay. I know something of gloves, Kit. Tamburlaine is his part.

I can fright him from the playing of Faustus forever. Do you know that when he draws the chalk circle on stage to summon Mephistophilis, he shakes? He thinks he may summon the real devil."

"It is not only he who thinks it."

"But he thinks it more than most."

"What would you do, Will Shakespeare?"

"What would you give me?"

Marlowe looked about him to share the absurdity with fellows, but the room was empty save for the two of them. He shrugged. "Three pound."

"Done." Will offered his hand and Marlowe took it, but he still protested, "I cannot credit your scheme until I know it."

"And you cannot know it until it is well performed."

"You would do this for money?"

"For money and in the service of poetry."

SO it was that four days later at the Bel Savage Inn Edward Alleyn looked up, in his final scene as the devils cavorted about him, to see an apparition that he ever after swore was a real devil, come finally to cart him to Hell. It was dressed all in black and its ghostly face could barely be seen in the shadow of its fearsome hood. It glided softly across the stage, amid the dancing devils, and whispered something in his ear that sent him howling off stage through the Hell-mouth, to snatch off his necromantical robe and sit quivering like a rabbit in the tiring house behind.

WILL was still wiping white powder from his face when he came in the Knavish Loon on Rotherhithe Street, to be greeted by a Marlowe who howled with glee. "Marry, I saw it all!" Kit yelled. "Hell's a manner of thinking, and you sent him there! I will stand you five glasses."

"Three pound will be excellent." Will dropped to his chair, perspiring from his hard run.

"I was in the house behind!" Marlowe leaned forward, hardly able to speak for laughter. "They are all in a mad babble and Alleyn was frothing at the mouth. He swears he will play no more!"

"He turns Puritan."

"*Is* one. A Ranter!"

Will laughed. "Good! Good!"

"But *what!*" Kit leaned back and looked at Will admiringly. "*What* didst thou say to him?"

"May I drink from that tankard?"

"Ah, the sober Stratfordian will have ale. What was it you said?"

Will drank a long draught and wiped his mouth. "Something about the particular evils of pride and playwright-gouging."

"Ah, very good! Very good! But I cannot credit that he did not know you!"

"I knew he would not, e'en did he peer below my hood. He has stood thirty times on a stage with me and he does not hail me when he passes me in the street. *So swollen with a self-conceit—*"

"A very good line."

"I thank you. I had it from a weed-puffing dwarf, one graceless enough to steal a page from another man's play."

"I—"

"Nay, nay. No words. Our victory o'er Alleyn makes all good. I cannot believe His Rant-ship will leave the stage as he swears, but he will surely leave *Faustus,* and another and a better will play the part. And what's more, his *acting* may grow better."

"How so?"

Will smiled merrily and signaled for a drink. "I have a notion that a player might act terror best when he has once been terrified."

Marlowe looked puzzled, then thoughtful.

The crowd from the Southwark theaters were coming into the Loon, some of them abuzz with the story of the odd-looking devil and Alleyn's mad dash for the tiring house. Among them came Thomas Kyd and Thomas Lodge, on fire to share the news and laughing the harder to find that Shakespeare and Marlowe already knew it, and to hear the real truth of the thing. More folk sat at their table, and drinks were bought, and after a while faces blended and blurred.

Robert Greene had come in and said they should visit the Cardinal's Cap and see the doxies, and they all rose and spilled forth into the rain-soaked street. Will heard a voice singing and recognized it as his own. They went in the white house marked by the painted red cardinal's cap that looked like a phallus. His friends sat him on a stool and removed his hat and pulled at his ear, stretching it. "My ass's ears," Will said, laughing and feebly brushing them away. He sang all the drinking catches he could remember, and his fellows joined in the choruses.

> *And let me the canakin clink, clink;*
> *And let me the canakin clink.*
> *Your breeches cost but half a crown,*
> *'Tis pride that pulls the country down. WHOOP!*

After a while a blowsy and painted woman came down the stair and sat on Will's lap. Her hair was the color of Anne's, and he caressed it. She was half-dressed, in a petticoat and an unlaced bodice. Will pulled at her stays and her heavy breasts tumbled out. Robert Greene pulled the woman to him and kissed her, and then there was shouting and the crack of fist on bone and Greene lay on the floor cursing and Marlowe and Lodge were pulling Will up and off him, and Will's hand was bloodied. A trio of women threw him out the door. He fell against the outside wall, muttering, "Hell's—a manner—of drinking."

Singing spilled from the brothel's open window. *"O drunken madness wrought by wine and ruts of filthy freaks!"* he mumbled, including himself among the party so addressed.

He shut his eyes briefly.

And suddenly, by a strange metamorphosis, he felt he was not William Shakespeare, dye-stained glover from Stratford, but a dissolute scholar, Lucifer-proud of his learning, hating the low world that drew him to whore his talents. *Greene.* Will sighed. *Poor Greene! A pardon to be begged from the man, but not now, not . . .* His earlobe throbbed, and he raised a hand to it. His fingers encountered a tiny hoop. *What . . . ?* He looked at his hand and saw it bright with his own fresh blood, next to the dried blood from Greene's nose. *They have branded me with an ear-ring,* he thought as he rested against the wall. *I am one of them now.*

COLD mud splattered his cheek and his lids shot up. He looked to the side, blear-eyed. A cart was rolling by, its wheels splashing through puddles, its rainy panels gilded by the evening sun that had finally come out at its setting. A half-naked man stood in the cart, his hands tied at his back and his chest striped with lashes. There were rage and despair on his face. A rabble of folk ran behind the cart, idle men and women and starveling children, yelling, "A hanging! To Tyburn! To Tyburn!"

Will pulled himself up and staggered after the crowd. "What's he done?" he said thickly to a woman.

She turned. "Traitor spoke ill of the queen!" she yelled with the thrill of it. "He called her a bitch, and was heard. *'The queen is a bitch and the Earl of Leicester's whore!'* "

Will grabbed her dress. "Have you not now said it too?"

A look of terror froze her face. She shook him off and scurried away, stopping to bend and pick up a handful of mud that she threw at the man in the cart. Then she vanished down an alley.

Will turned and was sick, then straightened and was dizzy. He grabbed his head and counted to ten and afterwards felt more sober, though still sick. He thought of the skull-studded Hell-mouth of the bridge, through which he must pass. "I had forgot my purpose," he whispered. "God forgive it, I had forgot me."

He put a hand to his belt, and found his purse gone. Its strings had been cut by someone as he lay. He swore. No boat for him, and the bridge indeed. Unsteadily, he began the walk.

Chapter Ten

ANOTHER year.

It was Saint David's Day, the cold first of March, and a hundred loud, drunken Welshmen paraded down Paul's Walk, wearing leeks in their caps and singing incomprehensibly. A smell of cheap burning paper and glue came, breeze-borne, from the far side of Paul's Yard. There the Bishop of Winchester stood on a scaffold before a crowd, speechifying and casting the pamphlets of Martin Mar-Prelate into a public bonfire, one by one. The black smoke wafted east, making some of the Welsh marchers cough.

Will heard and smelled it all, but paid small notice. He was standing at the east entrance of the cathedral, reading a bill that was plastered to the wide church door.

Tomorrow beinge Thursdaie shall be seen at the Beargardin on the banckside a great Mach played by the gamstirs of Henslowe, who hath chalenged all comers what soever to play v dogges at the single beare for v pounds and also to wearie a bull dead at the stage and for your better content shall have pleasant sport with the horse and ape and whiping of the blind beare.

"Right pleasant sport, and well spelled," he murmured. He glanced left, then right. With a quick motion he tore the bill from the door. The paper's back was broad and blank, and he smiled at it. Quickly he rolled it and stuffed it inside his jerkin. Then he melted into the crowd of Welsh drunks. *"Dirthin day David!"* he sang as he marched, batting smoke with his right hand and pressing the paper tight against his body with his left.

TWO weeks later he met Kempe's bloodshot blue eye across a battered table in the clown's Southwark rooms. Kempe was not feigning illness today. His throat was wrapped in a wet rag, and he paused every minute or two to douse it with a foul-smelling mixture of chopped oysters, eggs, and garlic.

"Faugh," Will said, wrinkling his nose. "I pity the man or boy who plays opposite thee this afternoon."

Kempe shook his head. "Louder," he said hoarsely. "Both ears be clogged."

Will spoke loud and slow. "Then how will you know your cues?"

Kempe smiled proudly and tapped his head. "I have committed them to memory."

No sense could be made of this remark. Will shook his head, then pointed to the sheaf of scrappy, variously sized papers, thickly covered with his own spidery scrawl, that lay bound with twine next to the gargle on the table. "Will he buy them?" he asked.

Kempe looked alarmed. "I cannot speak overmuch of Henslowe's plans, or of anything," he croaked. "I am resting my instrument."

"Thine instrument? What care I for thy tool?"

Kempe shook his head violently. "My *voice*. Now, to your question. Three plays. A cycle of histories. 'Tis untried matter; dull stuff, you know, Will, and another thing." He coughed. " 'Tis a risk."

"Say on."

"I will speak plain. Your monarchs are rotten tyrants."

Will waited.

Kempe sighed. "Yes, Henslowe will buy them. He likes the murders; likes the blood. He rubs his hands and says the thing will bring custom."

"More so than my comedies, which he has chosen never to stage."

The clown shifted nervously in his chair. "Well, I know nothing of that," he said, and coughed. "My part is only—"

"Conduit, go-between, panderer of play-pages."

"Just so."

There was something odd in the rabbity look that came over Kempe's face whenever the subject of Will's plays arose. Will stared hard at the clown in the hopes of inspiring a frank revelation of where Henslowe had buried his comedies, and why.

But Kempe only sneezed, a right shower of garlic. Then he pointed at the plays on the table. "These your histories he has offered to buy, at a pound per play, but I tell you truly it would not be wise to sell them without some . . . alterations."

"I thought you never read whole plays."

"I took an interest in these, and I did so, for once. Now, the monarchs—I warn you." He blew his nose on his silk handkerchief. "Offend anyone before you offend the queen! And these *will* offend her. She is bound, and her Revels Master is bound, to see her own image in any staged English king. You must present them all awash in good fame. Make them heroes, not weaklings or knaves. Your Henry Six and Edward Four seem almost human. That is to be avoided."

"If not human, what?"

"Apollo. Better, Christ. The Revels Master—"

"Revels Master." Will's voice was contemptuous. "He wears the title of a carnival king. A misnomer for a puritanical functionary who cares only to quash merriment and ban plays."

"But he can do it. He'd ban the Puritans if he could." Kempe coughed, gargled, and spat on the floor.

"Ah, God!" said Will, looking at the stained planks.

"Pardon for that. Anyway, I speak true. The Revels Master hates all rowdies, including those mad pastors who preach to the folk out of door on the corners of streets. I've seen the Revels Master in his black robe, hanging about the crowd-edges and frowning. I can almost hear his thought. He is the queen's own man, and he waits to pounce on the pastor who would say a word against her policies. And he might as well arrest those pastors as us, for the reverend godly are players too, with their jumping and rantings, and such names as they have! 'Pastor Thomas Playfair,' and 'Pastor Zealous Praisegod,' I tell you, Will, these are not real names—"

"Peace, clown," Will laughed. "You speak a rare wisdom—rare for thee—but you roughen your voice. I cannot play your part this afternoon if you turn mute; I am patching another man's play for a pound."

"Patch thine own play," Kempe croaked sullenly.

"I'll not. Let my plays stand. I thank thee for thy care, but my kings are mere shadows of the past, and I need the money. If Master Henslowe will stage them, there is no more to be said."

But Henslowe did not stage them, that year or the next. Will took the money and sent the bulk of it to Anne, and went home to Stratford at Christmas and Lent, and came hopefully back to

London. Yet time went by and he did not hear his poetry spoken on any London scaffold. He himself spoke others' lines on many of them, and was paid more and more as he grew more practiced, but his own plays were gone into a void.

"IT does not *matter*," Marlowe said again. "You were paid. You stood to gain no more money from them, in any case."

Will glowered and tapped his long fingers on the burn-scarred table in Marlowe's room. "So says the genius of the English stage, whose poetry is trumpeted by every celebrated player."

"Yes, the abominable players as well as the good. But to speak of the good, I like the man Burbage who plays Faustus now. I still honor you for ridding me of Alleyn. *Why* does he play?"

"Alleyn wants to be loved," said Will. "Your new Faustus knows he is loved. He wants to be believed."

"And he is. He is a wonder. A worthy heir to his father, who built the first playhouse we have. The Theater." Marlowe laughed. "Dull name."

" 'Twas the only such place at the time. What should he have called it?"

"The Cunny House."

"Ah."

"It is a ramshackle place now." Marlowe twirled an ivory toothpick he had bought in Cheapside that day. His doublet was blue and his collar was lace. "My plays do better at the Rose."

"Ah, so we speak of thee again," said Will, whose collar was not lace. "By the rood, I ought to have known."

"By the *rood!* By the *rood!* Oh, excellent. Are you a knight of the Crusades?"

"I showed you of whom I am writing now. And if I write of their times I must think in their speech. Like a dyer's hand, subdued to what it works in." Will stared pensively at his own stained palm.

A spasm of jealousy passed over Marlowe's face. It was a quick contortion, there and gone. He said only, sweetly, "You speak in iambics."

HENSLOWE, the king of custom south of the Thames, the sultan of stews and the bard of bear-baits, was so rich he could buy plays and let them gather dust on a shelf. He bought plays so that others would not. He bought plays that were not great plays, that were not Marlowe's plays, or even Robert Greene's. Surplus plays, middling plays, in order to have something new on hand if he wished it. And if he did not wish it, then the plays were his all the same, and there was nothing to be done about it.

Will threw down his quill and took to the road with the players.

They left at sunset on May Day, walking north through Bishopsgate and down Blomfield Street to the wide western road. There the houses grew few and the poles still stood high in the fields, with breeze-blown streamers rippling from them in colors of red and green and blue, and at the end of each strand a merry dancing youth.

AT that same hour Marlowe sat perched on a rail by the bookstalls in Paul's Yard, evading the eye of a cleric he'd known at Cambridge, avidly scanning Hakluyt's *Voyages and Navigations*. His silky hair, charged with static, fanned his angel's face, whose chin was barely touched with down.

The fourth of November we went on shore to a town of the Negroes. . . . It was of about two hundred houses. . . . Our men at their departure set the town on fire, and it was burnt in a quarter of an hour, the houses being covered with reed and straw.

Marlowe laughed, and replaced the book in the stall. The flat-capped Cambridge reverend looked over at him, but Kit was already dancing away, through the runagates and pickpockets, past the curbers, cozeners, clapperdudgeons, and clergymen who haunted the gullible.

Tom Kyd waited at the entrance to Bread Street. "Anything new to read?" he asked.

"English voyagers' tales. *Veni, vidi, vici.*"

"Lies."

"Not this, I think." Marlowe hummed for a moment, then chanted in a sing-song voice,

> *I will confute those blind geographers*
> *That make a triple region in the world,*
> *Excluding regions which I mean to trace,*
> *And with this pen reduce them to a map,*
> *Calling the provinces, cities, and towns*
> *After my name.*

"Ha, that's good," Kyd said. "You'd have made a better Tamburlaine than Ned Alleyn."

"Queen Elizabeth would have made a better Tamburlaine than Ned Alleyn." As he said it Marlowe thought in surprise, *Yes, she would have.* The queen and her men. Like Tamburlaine, they swallowed lands to make an empire. From Ireland to Africa to Virginia . . . *Our men at their departure set the town on fire.* This was an age of ornate and brutal power. A conqueror might elegantly inscribe his name, or hers, on the clean pages of other men's simplicity. Might burn their towns to the ground. *I am that I am*, England says. *Nothing else is.*

The men walked in silence as far as the Strand. "I'm dining with Alleyn and Henslowe," Kyd said. "Wilt come?"

"In Southwark?"

"Cardinal's Cap."

"Nay. I'll to home."

The new play burned in his mind like a sparked thatch roof. *Out. Write it out.* There was one thing to say, and a thousand ways to say it. The will to power, the thousand masks the self wore as it rose above other selves. And to write was to *show* the self-will at the heart of all things that happened. The way of the powerful was not to redeem, not to save, not to carry Christ or spread love or govern wisely or well, but only to make the world reflect their names.

And *their* world would reflect *his* name.

Not the old name, the shoemaker's name, from back in the old town of Canterbury. Pounding hobnails into boots on a wooden last, cobbling and mending soles. Where was the rhyme in that? The leather strap to buff and sometimes to hit, the disappointed father's eyes: not a trade, not the Church, but *poetry.*

Kit had recited the first book of *The Iliad* in Greek at the age of nine, standing in front of the prefect at the King's School, and his father had said to him, *Yes, lad, but thou knowest the Greeks were sodomites.* The other parents laughed and the pupils laughed and the tutors had blanched but smiled. Because after all the town hired the tutors, paid them well to teach its sons, to give them Latin and a swift, heart-tearing glimpse of Aegean beauty before clasping Roman manacles on their thin wrists, saying here, copy these contracts, these accounts. Or pound these nails, marry that wench, fold this cloth, for the rest of your life.

No. Not the old name of Marlowe in the old town of Canterbury but the name made new in the new town, new world of London. Here he did magic, was Merlin. Mended not soles but his soul, remade his soul by letting it breathe. He'd the freedom to make a new self and the time to do it, and the money to pay for it. And the labor was light. The shrouded eyes of the bulky lord and his hushed voice saying, *Write down what you hear. Write down what he says—and men can be made to say things. The queen will be grateful.*

Yes. Grateful.

Especially if he followed the man with the sea-green eyes and the soldier's beard and the New World lust and wrote down whatever he said.

And the rest of the time for poetry. The labor was light, and the laborer was worthy of his hire.

Kit mounted the stairs to his little room and lit one candle. A blank page shimmered in front of him like a bay. He parted its surface like an English ship. He wrote.

> *The sight of London to my exil'd eyes*
> *Is as Elysium to a new-come soul:*
> *Not that I love the city or the men.*

For hours he built colossal selves in speeches. A new history play for Henslowe. Better than Tom Lodge's last play, with its sedate reverence for the monarchy. Better than anything yet heard. Kit liked this, liked ripping the Christian masks from the faces of Europe's rulers with his iambical claws. The Machiavellians, the self-worshippers, exposed themselves on his stage. Living outrageously and loud, then dying the same way.

And his own task was the same as any tragic hero's, if it came to that. To live one way, and then to die well. The *ars moriendi,* the art of dying. To die as one had lived, only more so. That was the thing.

At nightfall he lit a pipe and went to the ordinary two streets east. Kyd was doubtless roistering in Southwark, with Henslowe, who always did business in the stews. Kyd, peddling his new revenge play; gloomy ghosts and Senecan murder. Kit smiled with mixed affection and scorn. Kyd could write only one kind of play.

And then he remembered a late night's drunk when Kyd, leering as he gnawed on an end of dried stockfish in the bed where he lay, had said that same thing of him. Of *him*.

Kit shook his head once, hard, to clear it of the memory.

"Threepence," said the girl, handing him a paper of tobacco. Blue eyes sought his, but his returning gaze was brief, uninterested. He could play this game, and sometimes did, but tonight was too busy to disappoint, to court attentions he would later spurn.

Dark evening on the walk back, mother night, few stars. *At my nativity the front of Heaven was full of fiery shapes.* I. My.

But who had written that?

Not he, but the other. On some foul-paper pages, street-scraps, the backs of playbills and bear-baiting broadsides. Dialogue. Interruptions, quick, quick. Living, breathing. First one would speak, and then another, fluid, hot liquid, fire meeting fire. And the one who wrote it: pale, quiet, high-browed, eyes grey like the cloud-shrouded sea. Glover and son of a glover. Gloves. Wearing them, you touched and did not touch. That one touched, and did not touch. Listened. His eyes were the color of nothing. They threw back the light that played on their surface, like the ocean reflected the sky. A stoup of ale would stand a long time, untasted, before him. His arms would be folded, himself quiet and cold, like a fish in the depths of the sea.

Marlowe climbed the stairs to his room. Kyd was there, drunk.

"Did he stick you with the scot?" Marlowe asked.

"Aye; two shillings. He always does. But he'll take my play."

"I never pay it."

"I know not how you 'scape. But mark, Kit, he'll take my play."

"Good." Marlowe threw off his damp shirt, thinking, *I never pay the reckoning. But Henslowe's paid by me all the same; Henslowe has his profit of me. And I need give him only a few more plays, enough to write my name with an ink that cannot fade. An ink that cannot be o'erwritten.*

But later he lay in the dark, again recalling the lines the other had shown him. Scratches made by a dye-stained hand. *This will be long in the writing, but I have made a start,* he had said. Then that son of a glover had shown him his proud creation—*an imitation, of course,* he'd said in his courteous way. The character was a Welsh wizard of two centuries gone by, an ambitious, vaunting soul, a Tamburlaine, a Faustus, a Merlin, who cried with terrible power,

> *At my nativity*
> *The front of Heav'n was full of fiery shapes*
> *Of burning cressets, and at my birth*
> *The frame and huge foundation of the earth*
> *Shaked like a coward!*

Then he had pointed to the new thing, the terrible thing. The next lines. A knight, a lounging Northumbrian soldier, who spat a peach pit onto the stage and then answered the wizard, mildly, *Why, so it would have done at the same season if your mother's cat had but kittened.*

Kit knotted his fists in fury. A *prose* reply. A jesting challenge that shrank the wizard's speech like a square of leather, and made the audience laugh at it!

Two speakers. Two voices. Two *truths*.

And the play burst into a new dimension, and shook the foundation of the earth.

Kyd stirred. "Where are you . . . ?" His voice was slurred with drowse and drink.

"Nowhere. I cannot sleep."

Lighting a taper, Marlowe returned to his desk, where he wrote frantically, desperately, until the sky was as grey as the other one's eyes.

Chapter Eleven

THEY walked seventeen miles a day and played six days a week. With a cart and a nag and a drum and a banner they trooped through Guildford to Winchester to Dunster and the sea, and then back to Wells. They trudged across Salisbury Plain, where the Druids' stones cast their long shadows in the distance. They were eight men and boys in all, and most were veterans: Will and Augustine Phillips and Thomas Pope and Will Kempe and three young apprentices. And a new man who moved all watchers to tears and awe and left the crowd pitching groats and sometimes gold into the players' passed hats, swearing that Ned Alleyn was toppled, toppled indeed, and Tamburlaine newly born on the scaffold.

Richard Burbage was his name.

He was twenty-two and six feet tall and built like the carpenter he was. His locks were a dark chestnut, and he scorned to dye them black like Ned Alleyn's, but like Alleyn he grew them long and, like most of the players, he wore a bare hoop of an ear-ring that glinted under his cap. His costumes fit him like cheveril gloves. After a play was played he would stand half-hidden by the curtain to the left of the scaffold and take off his shirt and wipe his face with it, and the sighing of women could be heard from the clock-towers to the city walls.

The players walked in the blistering sun and the healing rain, and stopped in big towns and small hamlets. They saw that English time was magical, for the clock of Amesbury struck ten on their leaving, and three hours' walk brought them to Salisbury, where the town clock was chiming half past twelve.

Will played his parts, sometimes five in one play, in inns and great houses and guildhalls and town squares. At the mansions, food and beds were added to the players' wage. In the small towns they played for pennies, slept in the grass under tents, and ate cold meat and bread.

After six westering weeks they turned north to Bath, west again to Bristol, and then east toward Fairford and Bibury. Midsummer night found them at the grand Midlands estate of the Earl of Oxford, a man much famed as a dabbler in magic and a patron of poets, and one who claimed to love all players.

The sumptuousness of his manor humbled them, though they refused to show their awe. Their bows and off-cappings were courteous, but not servile, and it was only covertly that their eyes widened at the long oaken beams in the ceilings, the majestic fireplace in which four of them could easily have been roasted on spits. They trod lightly on the Turkish floor-coverings, walking from room to room to room. Velvet drapes shrouded the tall windows of leaded glass, and plush-cushioned settles and wine-bearing tables were scattered everywhere. On the walls Will saw oil portraits of richly attired earls of days past and their ladies. Silk-clad men and women who might have been their twins crowded past the paintings, taking seats to watch the players' comedy.

It went well, and when it ended jewels sparkled on clapping hands. As always, the applause was loudest for Burbage. Behind the curtain for the last act, Will had sat, listening hard to him. His voice was low music, its cadences controlled, its passion perfect.

When all was over Will joined the rest in a bow and he gripped Burbage's hand so tightly that the young man looked at him in surprise.

"What is't, Will?" the actor whispered as they slipped with the others into a rear chamber, given to them by the earl for dressing.

"You speak Nothing well," Will said.

Burbage frowned. "I speak *nothing* well?"

"It is praise, but it hardly bears explaining."

A servant in green livery appeared to tell them that the earl would be pleased if the players would join them for wine and revelry in another chamber. The men looked at each other skeptically, and sent the boys to their beds, but Augustine Phillips murmured to them that they could not refuse, though their apparel was scarcely fit for such company, so the servant departed with their acceptance.

"Perhaps they will give us some cast-off clothes?" Kempe said hopefully.

Will laughed. "Perhaps they will give us some cast-off money. As for clothes, they must take us as we are."

In fact, Will and the others were able to dress featly in brocade and velvet taken from their costume trunk. When they entered the chamber where the oboe and lute were played and the lords and ladies danced, it seemed to Will and Burbage that their host, the lover of players, was startled at their perfect bows and, still more, at their courteous speech.

"What matter if we learned it for the stage?" Burbage murmured to Will from the corner of his mouth.

Two glittering ladies came toward them, stepping sprightly and giggling, their kohl-rimmed eyes ardent above their jeweled fans. Burbage was their quarry. "Hold, here is luck," he whispered. "There are two."

But Will could not answer.

He was staring at a gentlewoman who sat alone on a carved bench by a window. Her hair, partly dressed with combs in front, fell free in back, in the unmarried style, so that yellow curls rippled past her shoulders. She held herself straight, in a gown of deep blue fronted with a stiff, lace-trimmed velvet stomacher. Her earrings were sapphire, and as she turned to catch Will's glance they sparkled in the candlelight.

So Anne might have looked, had she been a lord's daughter.

He breathed deeply, and returned the woman's unblinking gaze.

Then she smiled at him, and for a moment he thought his heart would stop.

"*Hem.*"

He looked down. At his side stood a youthful person, capped and liveried like a servant boy, though one glance at the figure's hip-handed bow and saucy, impish face told him that this "lad" was a girl.

"You gaze at my mistress, sir." She made her voice comically gruff. "She desires acquaintance."

Will looked back at the seated woman, and nodded.

The costumed girl led him across the room, past couples who danced the stately French *pavane*, to the golden-haired beauty's side. "Here is one most smitten with thine eyes," the boy-girl said to the lady, in a clear voice that she forgot to roughen. Catching herself, she dropped her pitch an octave, and turned to Will. "Thy name, sir player?"

"William Shakespeare." Will doffed his cap and bowed. When he raised his head he saw that the seated woman's eyes were as merry and bold and blue as Anne's. She was covering her smile with one gloved hand, and holding the other out for him to kiss, in the French fashion. He took the hand, then dropped it quickly, as though it had stung him. "You are—" he said, and blushed in confusion. "You are not—"

The liveried boy-girl burst into laughter. "Here's one who won't be fooled, my dear," she said. "Thou must uncover."

"Uncover what? These curls are my own, Bessie." The voice that came from the golden-haired woman was masculine and amused. Now Will, looking closely at the face, could see the very faint shadow of beard on the upper lip, and its overcaking with powder. Disconcerted, he put his hands in his pockets, then took them out again and placed them behind his back.

"Pardon our merriment, good Master Shakespeare," Bessie said in her own bell-like voice. "My dear friend is something of a player himself."

"That's of no moment to me, milady," Will said, scratching his head and looking desperately about him for Burbage. He could just see the back of Richard's head amid the high, stiff ruffs of the half-dozen ladies surrounding him. Will looked back at the transvestite pair. "Milady and milord, I should say."

"But how did you know me so soon?" the young man asked. "Is my face-paint awry?"

"Thy face is perfection," said Will, fixing his gaze on the gowned young man's shoulder. "Yet a man's hand is not a woman's, even masked in a kidskin glove."

"I will leave you two players, and dance with mine uncle." Bessie skipped to the middle of the hall. There she coyly took the arm of their host, a tall, skull-faced man who was conversing earnestly with Will Kempe, whilst Kempe enviously regarded the man's lace and pearl cuffs. Will followed the girl with his eyes.

"Bessie likes to go as a boy," said the young man.

"She does not convince."

"Not as much as I do in my woman's tires?"

Will looked at the youth, who was smiling widely. The boy raised a fan that hung from a gold chain at his waist, and waved it briskly toward his face, so that his curls flew back. Then he fanned Will's face, and laughed. "It pleases me to do this!"

Will looked wonderingly at him.

"You think me a simpleton." With the fan the youth pointed to his bench. "*Will* you sit, William? My name, though you do not ask, is Henry." He let the fan drop, then briskly stripped off his gloves and threw them to the floor. "Warm, those."

"Most unladylike, that gesture, sir, and most cruel to thy costly gloves." Will stooped and retrieved the pair. "Although, if I may say it, these are not well made."

"Take them! Ah, the pity of it. I can never lady it for long, though I study Bessie's movements. She is excellent merry, though she is the great dull earl's niece. Hast thou met the great dull earl?"

Will sat next to the youth, pocketing the gloves. "We bowed before him at the start of the play and on entrance to this . . . festivity. But as for meeting—"

"May God spare you the trouble. He will force you to listen to his sonnets, and they are most vile."

"Ah." Will watched the young man smooth his petticoat. "Thy gown fits thee well, young sir."

"An old one of the earl's lady. She had no bosom to speak of. I think it is better on me than on her."

"And is it thy wont to lady it?"

"A recent amusement. I grow restless in the country. 'Twould shock thee, how far I have gone in a lady's gown. Even danced, a thing not as easy as it looks."

"I do not think it looks easy."

"None have guessed me as quickly as you did. Or perhaps you knew me from the first? In your playing, men dress as women every day."

"Aye, they do."

"So you thought me a man-woman and hoped for some—dalliance?"

Will frowned and shifted on the bench. "I did not. Milord."

"Ah. Then you did not find me seemly."

"Seemly you are," Will said. "But my tastes do not run that way." Will pulled at his ruff, which felt suddenly stiff and uncomfortable.

The young man crossed his legs in a mannish way under his gown. "I shame you. The jest has gone too far. Let us talk of thy playing. You spoke the verse well."

"I thank you, milord."

"No milording. Let us talk man to man, and be friends. Art a poet yourself?"

Will looked at him in surprise. "Why would you say so, sir?"

"*Sir* is forbidden."

Will laughed. "Then why, fair not-lady, would you say so?"

"Because of the wincing you did as you stood on the stage, when the clown spoke out of rhythm."

"*Did* I do so?" Will smiled sadly. "My playing is not of the best."

"But your poetry? I am sure you have some. Show it me. I have read all the sonnets my friends have written. Do you have any about you?"

"Poetry in a pocket?" Will laughed. "No, though I sometimes do carry it there."

"I would pay you for it if you did. Would that offend you?"

"No. Sir."

"*Sir* is for—"

"No, milady."

"*Henry* I should be to you."

LONG before sunrise, as the cloudy-headed players loaded their cart, Will placed a folded paper in the hand of a servant who stood at the door of the manor. "With my respects to the elegant young man of the golden hair, whose name is Henry," he said. "Written on such trash as I could find among our playing scrolls." The servant bowed.

Kempe, splendid in new kidskin gloves, looked at Will strangely. "Henry?" he said. "He with whom you spoke last night. Do you have any notion who he is?"

"A mad-brained boy, but he amused me."

"He is Henry Wriothesley, the Earl of Southampton. Bare eighteen years old and flabbergastingly rich. The most sought-for patron in England."

"Such was my guess," Will said.

THEY walked east for an hour until a storm blew up and drenched them. Then they sat under a spreading oak tree, and huddled together, all seeking the driest spots. Burbage said he was sick to the death of being chased by dogs and pissed on by the gods and threatened by rock-throwing Puritans, and that after they played for the Earl of Leicester it would be time to go home. Will said that was all to the good, but he would not play for Robert Dudley, the Earl of Leicester, not for ten pounds, not for twenty gold angels, not for the throne of England. Not even if all he need do was play the senex and hobble with a cane for a quarter of an hour and then keel over and die on the earl's marble floor.

A great dispute broke forth, in which some called Will traitor, and others confessed that, as Will said, playing for Sir Robert Dudley had not been in their plans when they left London. The invitation had come to them by messenger the night before at the Earl of Oxford's home in Oxfordshire. Yet none thought it right that Will should put them in danger of losing such an excellent wage as this other earl was like to pay them, *and more silks may come our way too,* said Kempe.

But Will said no and that they might play as they liked and what they liked, and if they could find no play they could play without him, then they were not players at all. Then he took his money and shouldered his pack and bid them goodbye, saying this dispute was now played out, and he would see them anon in London.

They forgave him, because the eight of them had walked side by side on the roads for weeks, and by now they were a family.

HE walked north on the muddy road, and the rain soaked his hat. He veered and took a drier path through a wood. After an hour the rain stopped. The sun came out from behind a cloud and its early rays shone in a checkered pattern on the forest floor. The path widened and Will emerged from the trees.

Before him lay Oxford.

It was tall-towered and studded with stone churches that shone in the morning sun and grew bigger as he walked. He passed through the city gates and saw Magdalen Tower. The streets were already thronged with gowned, gabbling, book-bearing youths whose arguments drifted past him in snatches of English and Latin. They jabbered and quarreled about this or that master and Erasmus and Duns Scotus and Aristotle, Aristotle, Aristotle. Listening, his heart beat with gladness as it broke with lost promise.

As he walked he gazed above and all about him at the high doors of the colleges, Balliol, Exeter, Lincoln, Oriel, Queen's. Past the brook of human voices that babbled at his shoulder he heard the cuckoo-echoing, bell-swarmed, lark-charmed, roof-racked murmur of the town.

After he passed out of the city he turned. More deeply than he had before Queen Elizabeth, he bowed.

Chapter Twelve

HE walked the whole day and slept by the roadside, then woke at dawn, ate bread and a rind of cheese, drank dark river water, grimaced and spat, rose, and walked on. By late afternoon he was on Banbury Road. When he came to the river he threw his last bread-crust to a greedy swan, then crossed Clopton Bridge.

Footsore, he limped to Henley Street.

His father was sitting on a bench in his garden, smoking a long pipe. Will laughed, peering over the hedge. "I had not thought that vice could travel so far north."

John Shakespeare stood slowly and stared at his son. He puffed in silence as Will dropped his pack, leapt the hedge, and bowed grandly before him. "Father."

"Those not let by their wives to drink must do something," John said, and put down his pipe to kiss Will.

★   ★   ★

HIS children were like someone else's children. Hamnet and Judith were thin as weeds and tall for their years, and pretty Susanna verged on plumpness. All three of them sat and watched as he wrote in the parlor, nine-year-old Susanna in her prim cap, chattering merrily, Hamnet grave and shy, Judith staring at him and his pages with a frank and bold curiosity that was almost frightening. After a while one after the other would clamber onto his lap, and he would read to them from his plays.

He seemed, when he wrote, to take no note of the children, but Anne would see him pause for long minutes to watch them through the open doorway as they played in the garden or street. At those times his face was crossed with longing and love. Hamnet most drew his gaze. The boy was flaxen-haired like his sister and mother, and slow of speech. At meals Will would coax him, singing "diddle diddle dobbin," but Hamnet would only smile faintly, and lick his spoon. He lived in his twin sister's world, and she saw nothing amiss in him. But to Will he seemed melancholy and awash in strange fancies that kept his eye trained on the windowglass or the dust-motes that floated in sunlight. His hands made strange gestures, and now and again he would shriek.

To Anne father and son seemed a pair, with the difference that Will was writing something.

For her part, Anne did her best to stay quiet in the kitchen or the bedroom, sewing her caps, sweeping the floor, salting the stew, wanting to talk to Will but wanting more to punish him with her silence. But he did not hear her keeping mum, so it was no good chastisement.

Time slipped by him as he wrote, and he could not tell how valiantly she was holding her tongue. It cramped her far more than it pained him, so in two days' time she gave it up, and let spill forth the collected news of half a year. Will seemed not to listen, and so she began to spin nonsense, thinking, *Surely I am a ghost and will vanish into thin air.*

And finally she grew quiet again.

But Will listened to her. Deep in the night when she thought he was sleeping, he would grab her waist so she started, and say, "So dear sister Joan is a werewolf? And Susanna shall marry King Philip of Spain?"

So the ice between them melted, if not the frost.

ONE day he was gone for hours with the mare. When he returned he did not sit down at his table to write, but went up to their bedroom and closed the door hard. When she mounted the stair an hour later with a candle, thinking him asleep, she found him staring at the thatched ceiling with one arm resting against the oaken headboard of their bed. His fingers traced the serpent's shape on the carved scene of Paradise.

"Where didst thou ride today?" she asked.

He said nothing.

She put her candle down and took off her kirtle and smock, feeling shy, as though she were undressing before a stranger. She felt his eyes watching her, but when she blew out the candle and lay down next to him in the moonlight he did not turn, but looked again at the ceiling.

After a moment he said, "The house is closed up, and the garden is overgrown."

"Where?" she asked, only to hear his voice, because she could guess the answer.

"Arden Manor."

The next day he told her he was returning to London.

She had known he would go, but the suddenness of it shocked her, and she turned and said bitterly, "*What* hast thou there?"

"Work," he said, through a mouthful of barley bread. He sat alone at their table.

"Work. Work that is jeered at in the streets of our town. You be a *player.*"

"It pays more and more, Anne." She would not make him angry.

"You have met someone," she said, half-fearfully, half-accusingly.

"Nay," he said. He felt as though he was lying when he said it, but he did not know why.

She put a hand on her hip. "You have told me you disdain half the parts that you speak. You say it angers you to be on a scaffold parroting others' words when your own are ringing in your head."

"You listen well, Anne," he said admiringly.

"Two can listen." She threw down her dishclout, sank to the floor, and put her head in her hands.

He regarded her with amusement. "I believe thou couldst be a player too. Wilt come with me?"

She looked up at him. "Is it a jest?"

"In part."

"Which part?"

He hesitated.

Tears filled her eyes. "Thou dost not want me there, sweet William." She stood and crossed to the front window. From the street came the yells of the children, Hamnet and Judith and Susanna and young Edmund, their uncle, who was still only a boy. "If thou didst desire it, thou couldst write plays here as well as there," she said softly.

"That I could not." He came forward and touched her shoulder. "I live alone. I play and I write. I do not know night and day, only the times of playing and the times of talking about playing. I speak with those who, when I have learned the secret of it all, will play my work. I do not know what *stops* it." He pulled his ear in vexation, then dropped his hand and sighed. "And there is something more. Do you want to know it?"

She said nothing.

"I will tell it. I went to London to say things I saw and kept within me, to say them in the only way it is possible for me to say what I think and feel, and earn a hearing, and leave with my life. But here is the rub. In the end it will not be me who says what I write, or not only me. I must give my words to others."

"Then give them to others."

"But I find that I do not only want the thing said. What I would say, I would have said *rightly*. With beauty. I *will* have it said with beauty. I will have players speak it well."

She looked at him, and saw that his eyes had gone hard. But when he caught her tearful gaze, they softened, and he looked at her pleadingly. "I cannot do any of it here. This matters, Anne. Do you not think so?"

She shook her head. "I think the world matters, not your stage."

THAT afternoon he stood in the Woolery, mending his boots and muttering a line of verse as he stared out the window. So intent was he on his poetry that it took him a full minute to note what he saw.

It was Gilbert, who had not directed ten words to him since his homecoming. Gilbert was not doing anything much, only bending to look at the lilies that sprouted from their neighbor's garden. Anne bent with him, listening as Will's brother tipped his mouth close to her ear and spoke at some length. She was smiling.

So.

* * *

"YOU are thick with Gilbert," he said that night to her in bed.

He had waited all day, savoring the simple sentence in his head. He had meant to shock her with his powers of sight. But Anne did not flap. As quick as a shot came her answer. "He that is giddy thinks the world turns round."

"And this means?"

"Your soul is charged with guilt, and so your head is crammed with fancies."

"A nice round iambic, something too long in meter. A fourteener, with a limp hanging tail of a suffix."

"*What* folly! Shut thy mouth. Boy."

"As for the truth of your claim, that is something else again. Guilty I may be, but of what crime, you do not know."

"You would be in London. *That* I know."

"When my wife's heart is absent, dost thou wonder at my leaving?"

Her back was already to him, but she gave her shoulders an angry shake to make plain her remoteness. Then she put her pillow over her head.

The next morning he arranged a bargain with a neighbor. He would take the man's horse to London and sell it there, and send back the money. He rode the nag back to Henley Street. As he stood before his house, fastening his pack to its saddle, the shutters of the upstairs parlor flew open and out popped Anne's head like a jack-of-the-clock. She called down to him like a fishmonger's wife, not heeding who heard her, but what she said was no fishwife's railing:

"Ah, th'art wise, Will Shakespeare. Thou hast *dreamed* my heart's absence, to give some excuse to thine own!"

Then she slammed the shutters tight against his wit.

She was only half-right, but he gave her the last word.

Chapter Thirteen

WILL entered the George Tavern, an alehouse north of the Thames, lightly gripping the promptbook he had stolen earlier that day from the Rose Theater tiring house. To force a locked window with an iron bar had proved easy before sunrise, as he'd guessed it would. No player stirred before seven, and though Philip Henslowe was there, face-down on his ledger with his ringed hands hanging, he'd only snored as Will stepped lightly by him bearing the bundle.

Kempe was seated with Edward Alleyn at the back of the common room, smacking his lips over oysters. He hailed Will, who was already halfway to their table, saying, "Good noontide, clown. And good Master Alleyn! Your accustomed haunt, the George, is't not?"

Alleyn sat on a corner stool, arms folded, scanning the room for folk as notable as he. He flicked his eyes leftward to Kempe. "Who is this fellow?" he asked.

"Ah—friend Edward." Kempe was looking nervously at the book in Will's hands. "This be Master William Shakespeare, a sometime play—"

"Wright." Will bowed. "And player. We have played on a stage together, sir."

Alleyn gave his head a toss and stayed seated. His unlikely jet-black hair bounced on his shoulders. His eyebrows were dyed black as well.

Without waiting to be asked, Will took a stool next to Kempe, who was excellent in mauve trunk hose, a cloak embroidered with Spanish curlicues, and a high-crowned yellow hat fronted with what looked like duck-feathers. His doublet was deep purple, and he wore gold-rimmed spectacles that framed rose-tinted discs of glass. On his right hand sparkled the emerald that had so dazzled Will when first he'd seen it in Stratford, though he'd long since seen it was paste.

Kempe said, "We toast our new patron. We are not just the Admiral's Men now, but also the men of Lord Strange."

"A good patron for thee."

"Ah, now, Will. Where didst thou—"

"And what are your doings of late, my masters?" Will said, placing the promptbook on the table.

"Hast been buried in the countryside." Kempe chewed and stared at the book. "All London knows of our doings. With Dick Burbage on the road—"

Alleyn winced at the name.

"—we played for a time for his father, at the Theater, until Master Edward Alleyn, here, adopted the notion that he was not being paid his worth. Edward told old James Burbage he'd complain of it to the Lord Admiral, and old Burbage said he might complain to the queen herself, but he himself would not be gouged by a speechifying tailor's dummy. Then the old man went after Edward in the street with a broom, so Edward betook himself quite readily to his heels—I am sorry, Ned, but you did—and the rest of us ran with him. And so we are back at the Rose, and now Dick Burbage is home at the Theater. Some of us—not all"—Kempe glanced at Alleyn—"are angling for Dick to join us south of the river, but he stays loyal to his da-da."

"He does not wish to share a stage with me," Alleyn said abruptly.

"Few would." Will's voice was bland.

"Oyster, Will?" Kempe proffered him the trencher.

"I have no time for oysters, thank thee, friend. I come on business, and my business is with Master Alleyn." With a woolen sleeve Will wiped a coat of dust from the promptbook cover. "It concerns my plays of *Henry the Sixth,* bound together here."

Kempe gave a squawk.

"Masters, be not dismayed by this book's antique appearance—befitting, perhaps, three plays of olden days. They have moldered"—Kempe leaned to stare at the promptbook and Will shoved him back with an elbow—"for two years in a storeroom. Methinks they stopped a draft that came through a chink in the wall. Useful things."

"Let me see." Alleyn leaned forward curiously. "Marlowe has a history play now—"

"Yes, and it does most well at James Burbage's Theater," Will said smoothly. "A shame Henslowe could not meet his price for it. Still, I understand Richard Burbage is perfect as King Edward the Second."

Alleyn's face purpled. He grabbed a glass and took a fast swig of ale. "Edward the Second is a good part," he said. "Yet I need it not."

"You need it not because *here* you have double glory. A part of a warrior, and then a part of another king. Here, in the first play, a conquering hero, Talbot! A valiant arm against the French papists during the days of Joan of Arc."

"But Will." Kempe spoke up. "We were all papists during—"

"Hsst. And in the third play, King Henry the Sixth. A good king, a saintly king, a king with many long speeches. View this one, Master Alleyn! If I do say it, Marlowe's play's a dishclout to these three. And here's further advantage. The play will not end when it ends. It goes on! The first part a'Tuesday, the second part a'Wednesday, the third part a'Thursday." With rare intensity, Will pounded his fist three times on the table. "The groundlings will come back and *back.*" He sat back, flushed. "I have done."

Alleyn was not looking at him but reading a marked passage, mouthing the words with growing interest. Kempe looked troubled, but said nothing. Will avoided Kempe's look, and sampled an oyster.

At length Alleyn looked up, eyes glowing. "Henslowe would buy these, I think."

"*Would* buy these?" Will stood up. "Would you credit that he already has?"

THE plays went smoothly in their rehearsals, which began within an hour of the muffled, closed-door debate between Alleyn and Henslowe. Alleyn, now Henslowe's son-in-law, punctuated each of his arguments with *Dear Father.*

The first play was played to a fourth of a house, for who was William Shakespeare? The next day the house was half-full, and the third day, by the time the third play was about to begin, the yard was so well packed that the hazelnut vendors had to walk with their sacks held high over their heads. Will himself had two parts in each play, and so was in the Rose to watch and listen and, at times, cringe as the Ranter spoke his verse. The experience diminished his very great thrill at the sound of his poetry on the stage.

In rehearsal in the plays' second week, Alleyn bayed his sufferings to the painted Heavens. *"My crown is in my heart, not on my head!"* He threw his arms wide, dropped to his knees, closed his eyes, and let fly an agonized scream.

"Hear me now." Unable to stop himself, Will popped from the stool where he'd been crouched behind the inner-stage curtain. The players on stage stared at him in amazement. Alleyn opened a cold eye. "So please you, Master Alleyn, if I may say it, in all courtesy, King Henry Six is not—Tamburlaine."

All went silent, even the boys sweeping the yard.

"He is, do you see, a private man with a library. He wishes only to—go his own way, to bother no one, but he is pummeled by politics and now beset in the wild by these villains, who will arrest him and take him away to the Tower." Will pointed behind Alleyn at two bemused-looking players. "Master Alleyn, if you could—so please you—think not on thy playing of Tamburlaine, but recall a time when thou wert, perhaps, unjustly beset by ruffians—"

"Such as when old Burbage chased you down Golding Lane with the broom," Kempe called helpfully from stage-side.

Alleyn jumped to his feet angrily and shook out his cloak. "I need no poet's instruction on playing. Thou hast done thy part; let us do ours. Mind thy sphere. Marry, what art thou?"

"A player as well as a poet, good sir, and I am bold to say that a fellow may improve his playing if he endeavors to feel what his character doth. Had you once known guiltless suffering, been attacked for no reason, then—"

"This you advise is not *acting,* but some—" Alleyn tugged at his hair. "*Aaaggghhh!!!* Some strange stuff, some private madness of thine own. *I* know how to play a king! Enough on this; we have three plays in all; *let us get on.*"

THAT night, as Alleyn was leaving the Knavish Loon, the wind whipping his long, black cape, he felt himself suddenly grabbed from behind. He lost his footing, and was thrown to the muddy earth by a fellow two-thirds his size, who pummeled him hard in the ribs for half a minute as Alleyn sobbed and whimpered, "Why do you use me thus?" He held up his purse of gold coins to the attacker, but the man only took it and hurled it at the gutter, contemptuously, it seemed, and disappeared down an alley.

The next day the last play went on, despite Alleyn's bruises and eloquent, pained descriptions of the six knaves who'd robbed him on Rotherhithe Street. Will listened with only half an ear as he donned stage-armor, rubbing his sore knuckles as he waited with the rest for his cue.

Alleyn, it was said after, had never played a king's sorrows so feelingly.

HENRY *the Sixth* played for three full weeks, an amazement and a phenomenon. Twenty-five hundred a day came, standing outside the walls in the morning, jostling to get a place on a bench or in the yard, tinkers and sailors and whores and lords and tapsters and wives and apprentices scanting work for the day, as Will had prophesied. In haste Henslowe dug Will's two comedies from the bottom of a pile of scripts, and within the month those were on the Rose's stage too. Will had been nothing, and now he was a repertory.

But his plays were not his anymore.

No law would let him lay claim to them. Beyond his new fame he earned nothing from their playing but the meager fee of a player. *"The first thing we do, let's kill all the lawyers!"* he howled with true fury at the robed law students, fresh from the Inns of Court and crowded into the Rose's lower galleries. They jumped to their feet and howled back, *"Die, rebel!"* They cheered when the defiant peasant he played was beheaded, and when a canvas ball painted crudely, too crudely, with his own features was held aloft on a pike.

That night Will dreamed of his uncle's skull baking on London Bridge. The bony sconce turned and winked at him, and then it became a canvas ball and bounced across the scaffold of the Rose. He woke with a jolt, then sat up. "Haunt me not, uncle," he said. "I have done thy ghost some justice, and there'll be more, and money, to follow."

Then the plague struck again.

BY autumn the carts were rattling thrice daily down the main streets, pulling bodies from the cross-marked houses. The naked dead lay piled six deep on the carts, their flesh discolored with leprous scabs and greenish-black and red sores. Some were half-rotted. The carters wore two pairs of gloves and held handkerchiefs to their mouths as they handled the dead and then drove them a mile outside the city walls. There they dumped the corpses into deep pits and sprinkled lime and shoveled dirt over them.

Will heard the plague-cart bell and went to his window on Boot Street to watch the wagon's slow progress. He heard a tapping on his door below.

It was Kempe, holding a perfumed handkerchief to his nose. "A word with thee?"

"One."

Upstairs, Kempe sat on Will's mattress, where he shifted uncomfortably and kicked at dust-rounds on the floor. "We are all made fellows by plague-death," he said, by way of launching a parley.

"Not so," Will said coldly. He sat at his desk and picked up his quill. "The poor die and the nobles flee the city. They are safe in their manors."

"And you?"

"I cannot catch it."

"You are Bedlam mad."

Will looked up. "And this you have come to tell me?"

"Nay. I come to ask you to come with us. We players have our own means; we can flee to the country as well as the rich men can. Thou canst act in thine own play." Kempe leaned forward. "Dost thou not like the saying of thine own lines?"

"I do. But I like not to hear others butcher them, and I cannot pound Ned Alleyn into thoughtfulness every night."

Kempe looked puzzled. "Pound him?"

Will sighed and put down his pen. "Go, clown. I have no interest in thy Strange Admiral's Men."

"*Strange's* Admiral's Men. Lord Strange."

"I care not."

"Then stay and catch plague. But I must tell you—" Kempe took a deep breath. "I have come to beg pardon of thee. Whatever Kit did, thou art my fast friend, and so . . ."

Will looked hard at him. "What mean you, whatever Kit did?"

Kempe looked uncertain. "I thought . . . thought you had some inkling. You had seemed to forswear his company."

"I have never forsworn him. I have had no time for him, or any man. Since I came back to London this time, my sole aim has been to see my plays staged. An endeavor you have not helped me in." Will pointed his quill accusingly at Kempe. "*Friend!* From my first coming here I have had to do all myself."

"But Will, I am speaking of that!" Kempe jumped up in his agitation. "I'faith, I am sorry I did not tell you. I am sorry I did not stand against Kit, but I. . . . It did go to my head, the first time he and the poet-wits bought me drink in the Loon. A mere player, you know." He glanced in the small flawed glass that hung on Will's wall and laughed sadly. "I was his inward."

"Excepting Tom Lodge they are all sad sacks; I could see it at the first. Kit is different, he is . . . himself. But what of it? What has he done?"

Kempe sank back onto Will's mattress. " 'Twas three years ago he did it. He gave Henslowe a goodly sum not to show thy plays to the players. Until you came to me and Alleyn at the George, not one of the men save me had ever seen any of them. I do not think Henslowe even marked the purchases in his ledger."

Will was quiet, gripping his quill tightly and staring at the clown.

"I should have told you."

Will said nothing.

"You will want to know why Kit did so."

"No. I can guess it."

Kempe plowed on anyway. "He loved thee not and wished thee gone. Once in the Crippled Phoenix I heard him tell Robin Greene that in a year or two thou wouldst throw down thy pen and go back to Warwickshire."

"Throw it down? Nay, I will throw it farther." Will hurled his quill at Kempe's head. It bounced from the man's ruddy cheek and left a blotch. "Accursed, poxy *knave* of a clown!"

"Spare me!" Kempe wiped his face with his handkerchief, holding one pleading hand out dramatically. "I have asked thy forgiveness and as a Christian you must—"

"Ah, a pastor now! Tell me my Christian duty!" Will shoved back his chair and walked to the window. He looked down at the street. The death cart was long gone and now all was silent as the grave, but emptier. He calmed his breathing. After a long moment he said, "I must speak to him. Be it soon or late, I must."

"Well." Kempe put his chin on his hands. "Thou'lt need to catch him 'twixt battles. He has been arrested thrice in the last four months for fighting in the street. Last week he was caught playing cards under a mirror at the Dark Angel, fleecing one of his cronies bare." He chortled, then sighed. "You know him. He will go off like a stage-devil sparkler, one moment laughing, the next in a rage because someone said something wrong about poetry. Poetry is all he cares for."

"Yes." Will turned and faced Kempe, nodding. "His own. Mark. If you see him, tell him he may stay on his guard."

"Ah, God," Kempe said. "Do not mention my name! I have only sought not to be hooked into Kit's affairs." He picked at the ends of straw that poked through Will's mattress, and frowned worriedly. "A poor playwright in a miserable room, yet rich enow to bribe Henslowe. He has no money from his family, sure. His da's a shoemaker in Canterbury."

"He's a damned spy for the queen and she pays him."

Kempe stopped picking. "Who told you this?"

"Hints have dropped on me here and there. You are not the only one with long ears, clown. But I make better use of the things I hear."

"Well, let's leave all this, Will. Come to the country with us."

"Nay." Will reseated himself, pulling at his ringed earlobe thoughtfully. The anger had gone from his voice. "I've plays to write."

"But wilt thou grant me thy forgiveness?"

Will glanced over at the clown and saw him fully. Ink-stained cheek, pea-green doublet, yellow shoes with pointed tips. "With all my heart," he said gently. "Thou hast done ten minutes' penance on that hairshirt of a bed, which may serve us for a mercy stool. Now go, clownkin."

Kempe rose happily. "And thou'lt sell us more plays?"

"Ah." Will pulled a fresh quill from his drawer and inked it. "That is a different question."

A week passed and the church bells tolled and he barely rose from his chair. Up to use the jordan, or to search for more paper, all the while muttering words as though they were spells against the pest. Once a day to an ordinary for bread or stew, then back through the streets, passing men and women who glanced at each other with frightened eyes or not at all. He heard without hearing the death-rattle of the carts. He climbed up the stairs and wrote to the sounds of the weavers below. Through the floor came their looms' shuttle and clack, mixed with the sweet, mournful notes of their psalm-singing. Against his tabletop Will beat a hand to their rhythms, murmuring. *"Thou common friend that's without faith or love."* When the play was done he sat back in his chair, sweat-stale all over and his shirt stained with ink. *Now I will go home.*

He had washed and was packing his things when the knock came. A letter. Fine parchment, and a gold wax seal. An *H* intertwined with a *W* and a coat of arms. He broke it open.

Henry Wriothesley, Earl of Southampton, is pleased to ask Master William Shakespeare to winter with him at his manor Titchfield in Hampshire. A welcome is assured.

Will read the letter several times, then put it aside.

He bound his new play with twine and tossed it into his traveling trunk, on the top of his clothes. He stood for a moment gazing down, regarding his meager wardrobe. Then he closed the lid, strapped the trunk to his back, and descended the stairs to Boot Street. Outside, he stood for a minute looking north, to Bishopsgate and the Warwickshire road. Then he turned south.

He crossed the river into Southwark and passed the bear-pits and the Rose Theater, now flagless and deserted. He knew he was miles from the sea, but he walked toward it.

He was passing the Tower of London across the river when he heard the crowd. Leaving Tooley Street, he saw it.

There were hundreds of them, all cheering. Men, women, and children waved in mad joy, crowding together, heedless of the plague danger, calling out. In their midst a great procession retreated slowly from Lambeth Road, moving southward as he was. Will put his hand to his forehead and narrowed his eyes against the strong evening sun, squinting to see full clearly the person he already knew rode in front.

She sat her horse like a man. Her cloth-of-gold gown billowed behind her, covering the palfrey's white flanks, so that from a distance she seemed a magical beast, a female centaur. Her hair shone bright red and her hands glinted with real emeralds as she saluted the people who flocked near for a glimpse of her.

The queen was fleeing the plague.

From the shadows cast by the close-packed house walls, Will watched her ride by, his face bent into a look that was half-hateful and half-admiring. That look did not slip from his face until Elizabeth was lost from view and only her traces remained: cartload on cartload of luggage rumbling through Southwark, and scores of horsed retainers, all silk-clad and satiny.

When the dust of their passage settled, Will followed in their wake.

BACK in the city, Kit Marlowe sat naked in a metal tub, his head turbaned in a towel. Tom Kyd poured warm water brought from the tavern below over Marlowe's shoulder blades and down his spine.

" 'Tis not plague, I hope," Kyd murmured.

"Nay," Marlowe said wearily. "An autumn chill."

"Thou knowest best what ailest thee." Gently, Kyd sponged the little man's back. After a moment he added, "There is room for an infinitude of playwrights in London. If the theaters re-open—"

"They will."

"Then fret not." Kyd poured more water into the tub. "He's not thou."

"Not yet," Marlowe said.

Chapter Fourteen

"SHALL I compare thee to a summer's day?"

" 'Twould please my mother endlessly, but I think the conceit something worn."

" 'Tis, but I can do something with it for the right amount of money."

"Name the sum."

"Ten pounds six for this in a batch of twelve, the other sonnets to be framed as, to wit, an exhortation to marry, produce beauteous offspring, *et cetera*, as specified by said mother; all poems subject to your satisfaction."

"And hers."

"Yes. The money—in gold—to be sent by horsed courier to my wife in Henley Street, Stratford-upon-Avon, upon completion of the work."

"Done."

Will proffered a hand to shake, but Henry Wriothesley only laughed at it. "Will you not learn that we do not clap hands here?"

WILL had presented himself at the stupendous granite mansion of Titchfield almost two months before, dusty with travel and in bad need of barbering. With a bluntness that bordered on discourtesy, he told the handsome and perfumed young earl that he knew he was wanted as a poet, and a poet he would be. But only for a fair amount of money and only while the plague held the theaters closed in London, and during his stay there must be no milording or knee-bending or off-capping or other such forms of flattery—

"Am I permitted to flatter *thee?*" the earl had asked, delighted by the comedy of it. "Or to off-cap in *thy* presence?"

"If that is your desire, I would not deny it. I know how role-play delights you."

Henry asked him how a commoner dared to speak so to an earl, and Will answered quite seriously that he had been invited to do so at their last meeting, in Oxfordshire, which he begged the earl to recall. Had he not thought Lord Wriothesley's request that he call him by his Christian name an honest one, he would not be here at all. Henry laughed, and then Will laughed, and then Henry called for a servant to show Will his spacious chamber.

The room had velvet bed-hangings and crisp lawn sheets and a view of a garden path where peacocks strolled. But Will's glance at all these things was brief, because it was caught by the sheen of a polished oaken table on which lay two reams of fine parchment paper.

Now winter was approaching and the plague had abated in London, yet he was still here. He was caught by the beauteous greenswards of Titchfield, and the sea-breezes he had so rarely smelled, that now blew in through his window at night. He was fascinated by the glittering, ever-shifting groups of lords and ladies that floated through the manor's rooms.

And the money was excellent good.

Some nights he did not write, but danced the galliard and the *pavane* in the huge feasting chamber. To the amusement of Henry, he taught others the new Continental dances, the *volta*, and the *coranto*, in which the men leapt high in the air in time to the quick beat of a drum. Henry's fine guests did not know these dances yet, but Will did, because players learned everything first.

Some days he shot at the archery butts and whacked horsehair-filled balls in the French game of tennis. He was good at this. In each taut sphere he saw Gilbert's mocking face speeding toward him.

Ah, sweet William! Milord!

THWOCK!! *That for thee, Bertie!*

Ah, Will, was't thee, jumping like a leapfrog in the grand hall t'other night? Cavorting with men who looked like ladies? Was't thee, scummy son of a glover?

THWOCK!! *That for thee!*

ON Will's third day at the estate he had stood alone in Henry's large library, laboring to read a Latin translation of Plato's myth of the androgyne. Half-man, half-woman, until Zeus split these beings with a thunderbolt. He read slowly. *Love is born into every human being; it tries to make one out of two and heal the wound of human nature.*

"Master Shakespeare."

Will turned hastily. "Milady countess." He bowed.

Henry's mother gestured him toward the settle. It was only midday, but already she was majestically attired as though for evening, in a sarcenet gown and a velvet headdress. "I will come to the point," she said. "Henry must marry."

"The earl is young," Will murmured.

"Nineteen is not too young to marry. Since his father is dead, I must be Henry's guide, his guardian. I have a match in mind for him."

"And I am to rhyme him into enthusiasm."

The countess looked at him in surprise. "Henry said this? He has guessed this?"

"Nay, madam. He has no inkling, as far as I can tell. He asked me here because I pleased him with a sonnet I wrote at our first acquaintance. He says nothing to me of his marrying."

"No. He would not." The countess adjusted her headdress impatiently. "He lacks gravity. He dreams of sailing off to fight against Spain with the Earl of Essex, while he prances here, with his friends and his . . . sports of all kinds. He fills his home with silken butterflies." She looked hard at Will. "My son has beauty and wealth and is sought after by many."

This was much. "Madam, my coat is woven wool, not silk. And thy son has sought *my* company. 'Twas not the reverse." This was mostly true.

She folded her arms. "So thou hast come for the splendor and the fine meals, *gratis.*"

He shook his head. "Not *gratis.* But I will eat a fine meal when it is offered."

She smiled. "I see why Henry chose you. He finds simpering as tedious as I do. And you are right. You give rhymes for your board, though I know not what to make of them. Are you not a stage poet?" She stared at him accusingly, but he nodded with no change of his courteous expression. "And your other poems? A mature woman seducing a boy?"

"A goddess. Venus and Adonis."

"Yes, and then the other. Tarquin raping Lucrece! Not subjects to incline a young man toward sober marriage."

Will stood looking pleasantly at her, the Plato still open in his hand. "Lady, I noted a likeness of Tarquin and Lucrece on a painted pillar in thine own great hall," he said. "Half-naked, both of them."

"Quick you are. But 'tis not my great hall. This house is Henry's, and I am a dowager-visitor. I am new married to a count who lives elsewhere, and when I stay here it is by my son's invitation. I do not choose Henry's frescoes. Still," she added, frowning thoughtfully, "I am not entirely without influence over my son. And part of my influence lies in knowing who may influence him more." She looked pointedly at Will.

WILL had told Henry of this talk with the countess, saying he felt unable to write any poems to fulfill such orders, yet was unwilling to court the countess's daily anger by refusing to comply with her wishes. Perhaps he should go. Yet Henry was so amused by it all that the thing became a game to them both, and so in spite of himself Will set to work. He did not do it for the countess, but for Henry, whose effect on him was curious.

His eyes were drawn to the young earl in envy and fascination. Henry was handsome in men's attire of lace and cloth-of-gold and velvet trunks, yet Will could never erase from his mind his first image of him, a serene, bold-eyed beauty in woman's dress. It was partly the earl's amazing hair that sustained this illusion. His tresses were six inches longer than even Edward Alleyn's or Richard Burbage's. Since his form was not greatly tall, like Alleyn's, or square-shouldered and muscular, like Burbage's, but of average height for a man, and slim, when he sat serenely reading or spellbound by an entertainment, he often seemed woman indeed.

But when he stood or moved the spell was broken. Not only

were his hands large, his gestures were entirely masculine. And he was strong, as could be seen not only in his tennis play but in his more serious sport with rapier and sword, and in his horsemanship. But what caught at Will's heart—besides the money that ran from Henry's hands like water—were the things that Henry said.

"I cannot help your missing your children," Henry told him abruptly one day.

The two were strolling down the cloister that fronted the Southampton mansion. To their left lay sculpted gardens, middled with a maze of evergreen bushes. On the stone wall to their right hung woven tapestries. Narcissus, gazing at his reflection in a clear pond, near the nymph Echo, whose hands stretched longingly toward the lovely boy. The bull Zeus chasing Europa. Hermaphroditus, stuck in a pond. Will had studied these images with fascination his first week at the mansion, but did not regard them now. He was taken aback at Henry's comment, and he stopped short on the flagstone walk. "Why say you this?"

Henry shook his golden head, smiling. " 'Tis the only concern of your sonnets."

"My *excellent* sonnets, you mean."

"Children, children, children! *You had a father, let your son say so. Unlooked on die, unless thou get a son.* These are *your* matters, not mine."

Will began walking again, slowly. At length he said, "I have said nought of my children to you, dear Henry."

"But your poems say you have them. Or wish to."

"I have a son, who is in his eighth year." Will strolled gravely, head held down meditatively and hands behind his back.

"No daughters?"

"Ah, yes. Two daughters."

"But they do not matter."

"I said no such thing."

"Yes. You did. Ah, look! That bird, circling." Henry pointed. "They have gone falconing beyond the copse, though we lack hills for it here."

Will squinted up at the wide-winged bird, who suddenly dived from view. Instinctively he put his hand before his face.

Henry looked at him with interest. "Does the bird make you think of a poem?"

"No." Will dropped his hand to his belt. "Of a thing I saw once. But no matter."

"No matter. Daughters matter not, falcons matter not. What of another matter? The queen? Your face contorts in an odd mingle of awe and disdain whenever she is mentioned."

Will darted a look of irritation at Henry. "Why do you scrutinize me?"

"Are you the only man who can scrutinize? I will not be a mere occasion for your poetry. I have eyes; I can see you when you look at me, and you interest me. What has our royal mother done to you?"

"To me? She does not know who I am!"

"And that insults you."

"Jesus God!" Will sat on a stone bench and folded his arms. "Let us speak of poetry!"

Henry sat next to him, crossed a blue-velvet breeched leg over the other, and tapped his silver-buckled shoe. Will gave his head a shake to empty it of thoughts of angling for that shoe and its fellow, then sending both to Kempe as a Christmas gift.

"Let us first speak of our sins," Henry said. "What is the worst thing you have ever done?"

Will's laugh was short and humorless. "I lost a book once."

"Not quite murder, is it?"

"Not quite." He looked hard at his friend. "May we speak of verse?"

"Of a certainty," Henry agreed. "Let us speak of the satire you would write against the queen."

Again Will laughed grimly, and pointed up. "I would sooner jump from yon battlements."

"Others have dared to criticize her."

"And others have ended with their heads on pikes, and excellent views of the River Thames."

"Because she is a tyrant."

Will looked sidewise at Henry, whose eyes were candid, wide, and smiling.

He thought, *Spy*.

He rose quickly, and Henry followed suit. "I am not what you think," Henry said, apology in his voice. "Not one of her agents. The jest was unseemly. List, Will." He laid a hand on Will's arm. "I have grown up in households where men sweated over a misplaced word or a knee bent a moment too late. You are a man of a wider world, and I thought you and I could speak freely. But you have little reason to trust me."

He sounded suddenly boyish, younger even than he was. He gripped Will's shoulder. "Forgive me, Will. I offer only friendship."

Meeting his eye, Will felt a stunning surge of affection for him, and at the same time, a great heart's pain.

"What is't?" Henry asked worriedly.

Embarrassed, Will looked down. "Thy pardon," he said. "I . . . was betrayed by one who called himself friend."

THAT night he said nearly nothing as the Wriothesleys and their guests chattered, seated at the sumptuous board loaded with broiled sturgeon, roast pheasant, currant pie, four puddings, gooseberry fool, and French and Rhenish wines.

"Regard this," Henry said, holding up a thing that looked like a tiny hay-fork. He proceeded to stab at his food with it, and the rest could do nothing but laugh at him behind their spoons. At the end of the meal a liveried servant brought in a cold dish from Italy that Henry proudly called "iced cream" and that splattered in his face when he prodded it with his hay-fork. The stuff melted within the minute, but he pronounced it a marvelous delectation.

Afterwards the guests went to dance, but Henry and Will stayed to talk at table. After a time Henry threw a morsel of sturgeon to his cat, Drake, and then both men rose and walked out into the chill air, across the castle drawbridge.

"So." Will smiled in the torchlight. "Do my sonnets persuade thee to marry?"

Henry laughed. "Nay. I will not marry until I must."

"Ah."

"It will not be poems that persuade me, or the need to pass on this great earldom which has stood for, oh, some forty years."

"So few?"

"We are rank upstarts." Henry poured his wine in the moat, scattering goldfish. "This palace! Built this very century. Made to look old."

"By whom?"

"My grandfather. A low commoner. A civil servant, but one with the cleverness to side with Henry the Eighth in his great matter. An earldom and a parcel of lands, all for voting *yea* in Parliament, *yea* for divorce from Spanish Katherine. And money to build a stone horror. Had you not wondered at its ugliness?"

Will looked at the *faux* Gothic walls and the moat, and said nothing.

"You will never trust me enough to speak your mind fully. Well, be wise. 'Let us speak of poetry,' as you say. My mother disdains your poems, all of them."

"She found the story of Lucrece's rape too fleshly."

"Yet she read it from start to finish."

Will laughed.

"And the sonnets disturb her." Henry paused. They stood on the bridge, looking not at each other, but at their two torchlit images in the water. "I have not shown her the first one."

"Which?"

"That you wrote me in Oxfordshire. *A woman's face, with Nature's own hand painted, hast thou, the master-mistress of my passion.* It moved me more than the others."

"It was a jest, Henry! A mere . . ." Will stopped. Even in the partial light he could see the hurt on Henry's face.

He reached out in confusion, wanting to touch the earl. But the young man stepped away from him, bowing formally. "The hour grows late, poet," he said stiffly. "Until the morrow." Then he turned and walked quickly inside, leaving Will alone with his reflection.

Chapter Fifteen

THAT night Will lay alone with a crowd.

His brain was peopled with a thousand living thoughts and faces and forms, and these whispered to him. With his eyes shut tight against the darkness, he felt their cold breath on his skin. He heard their tongues' rustling rumor.

Henry loves thee, they said. *Thou lovest Henry.*

And he knew the rumor as truth.

He had come to love Henry as he'd loved no one since Anne. Squeezing his eyes tighter, he summoned Anne's image, trying to conjure her shade into the bed where he sprawled, his head on a fine goose-down pillow. Her face came, lovely in its frame of loose yellow hair. But her eyes were Henry's eyes, and as he reached to touch her cheek her face became Henry's. Not Henry's face as he had first seen it, eyebrows plucked and skin powdered and rouged for a humorous charade. He saw Henry's face as it was, and it was like Anne's face: bare, smooth, and candid, offering Will his own reflection in its honest gaze.

He turned restlessly on the smooth lawn sheets.

My tastes do not run that way.

Henry was an odd creature, a charming friend and a glorious beauty. But he was, when all was said and done, a man. Will willed himself to imagine the world of men and women as viewed by wide-eyed Henry himself, who erected no barriers to desire. Into his mind floated a sentence from a book Henry had given him. *Nothing that is human is foreign to me.*

Then, suspending reason, suspending manly disgust, suspending his very breathing, Will opened the last and farthest flood-gate of his thought. He imagined Henry in the bed beside him.

He imagined the earl's caress.

And his heart and his flesh responded, alive on the instant.

In the sweet flood of passion that engulfed him, he feared he might drown.

Yet while a tide of amorous fancy tugged and pulled him, reason held him fettered. He allowed it to bind him, and to speak louder and louder. It told him—and he knew it spoke true—that did he not tame with a pen this new and horrifying self-knowledge, did he treat boundless passion as a world and not the dream of a world, his real world would disappear. He saw himself at sea in a universe where the men and boys with whom he supped and worked and clapped hands in bargains became beautiful, not in their rough friendship, but in their limbs, their skin, their eyes.

That way lay madness, a realm of ungovernable chaos.

With an act of will so violent it near stopped his heart, he opened his eyes.

The flames had died to embers in the fireplace, and he rose into air so cold it puckered his skin into goosebumps. He pulled on his rough woolen breeches, lit a candle, sat at his table, and picked up a quill.

IN the weeks that followed Will avoided the earl's company. He stayed shut in his chamber, trapped by a welter of passions. Sorrow and regret, shame, longing, and confusion, and nothing to be done with the whole mingle-mangle, he was sure, but to bleed precious ink on the costly paper on the heavy table in the elegant room. He wrote what he was paid to write and what he would have written without being paid. He delivered the sonnets to Henry, saying, "These lines, and my heart's love in friendship, I am able to give thee." He thought, *I am sorry it can be no more.*

Henry gazed at him, understanding, and took the poems.

In the days afterwards there was silence between them, not cold or angry, but weighty and charged, like the wet, heavy air of the seaside before a storm.

Henry traveled to London for a week, leaving Will in Southampton.

The weather had grown full chill. At night Will opened the window to let the rush of cold air blow out the candles on his table. He rocked back and forth on his heels on the floor of the rich chamber, shivering in the sea-wind, hearing the breeze rustle the bed-hangings. He gripped his head and thought, *Art cold tonight, Anne?* When he climbed into bed he hugged the bolster in loneliness, and wondered why he did not leave this place and go home to his family, or back to his work in London.

It came to him as he lay that there was no escape from sin.

To deliver himself from chaos, he buried his passion in poems: in sonnets that spoke of love and promised what he had determined not to perform. Still, while those poems freed his own heart, they could do nothing but tangle Henry's further. Verse was his speech and his release and his only tool of penance. Yet verse was the knife that deepened his friend's wound. What sickened him most was that he had taken Henry's money. And another thing plagued him. Late at night, when his candles sputtered and the letters doubled on the parchment before him and he sought refuge from words in dark, silent sleep, his body tormented him. It stiffened and bucked against his will and cried out for the touch of another. Lust raged like the hectic in his blood.

JUDGING himself a very Marlowe in both perverseness and treachery, Will walked into the evergreen maze on the grounds of the estate, thinking of Henry, seeking the maze's center. After several false starts and turns he came to an open clearing with a marble bench and a dry fountain at its middle. A woman sat on the bench, reading. She looked up like a startled deer to see him standing there. He himself held two books.

They regarded one another in silence. He became conscious that his figure was not entirely fashionable, though he knew it was helped by the cambric ruff and watered silk stockings he wore, an early gift from Henry. By her garb, the woman on the bench looked to have come straight from the courts of Italy. Her dark-purple gown was of fine wool, and her cape and hood a rare and costly black, as were her well-cut gloves. In her startled shyness, she seemed younger than she had at first sight. She had sensual features: full lips, a heart-shaped chin. Her skin was olive-toned, and what he saw of her hair was dark, and dressed with an ivory comb.

"You are the poet." Her voice was accented.

He bowed, said his name, and asked for hers.

"I am Emilia Lanyer," she said. "I have come for Advent and Christmas Revels. Sir Henry has been so kind."

In the softening of her lips and voice when she said the earl's name, Will saw his own heart reflected. "If I may." He sat next to her. "This, then, is your revels? To read alone on a bench?" She looked down in shame, and he felt guilty for having caused her discomfort. "I jest, lady," he said. "As you see"—he pointed at his books—"it is revels enough for your servant."

"My—servant?"

"Myself, lady. What read you?"

Shyly, she showed him a book of sonnets by a poet whose chief skill, Will thought, was to rhyme *love* with *dove*.

"Well." He looked doubtfully at its cover. "I say all books are good." He showed her his own. "Here I have Montaigne's *Essais*, which I cannot read much of, given me by our host, with a fine dedication. And this, Homer; *The Odyssey*, in the Greek. I cannot read this one at all."

"Cannot?" She frowned in puzzlement. "Then why should you . . . ?"

"Carry it? As a token, a prop, a thing befitting the part I play in this place. These books imply learning and suggest wisdom."

Her laugh changed her face, showing its youthfulness. "But there is none here to see!"

"Ah, th'art wrong." He smiled. "*Thou* art here."

SHE was twenty-four, the daughter of an Italian silk merchant who had brought her to London when she was nineteen. She had worked in her father's shop until a lord had seen her there and kindly gotten her a place at court. Within a year that lord had also kindly gotten her with child. He had then been so gracious as to get her a husband among the Italian musicians who played for Elizabeth, but that husband was not inclined toward women, and Emilia was not inclined toward children. So she allowed her son to be raised by royal nursemaids and her husband to play his lute while she traveled among the country estates of friends.

Much of this history Will stitched together from her fragmented confessions, made in broken English as they walked on the cold, graveled pathways of the estate or sat in Henry's library. He shunned archery and dancing to talk with her, to ask her questions about the southern land from which she had come. She preferred talk about the English court, and the fine houses and dress and pleasures of the gentry, by whom she was entranced. She adored cloth-of-gold; and amorous exchanges of glances; and gowns, petticoats, and caps; and diamond-encrusted viziers and fans. She loved the customs of the court, though she was shy of them because of her faulty English. She spoke of stately dances and royal processions and ornate love poems delivered on silver platters to disdainful ladies.

He, too, was drawn by the nobles and their fashions, though his interest remained that of the observer. Unlike her, he had never wished or thought it possible to be one of them. He did his best to turn the talk to Italy. "You have seen the *commedia dell'arte?*" he asked her.

She shuddered. "Crude, yes. No—poetry. Just—fall down, audience laughs. English plays are better."

"Yet have we our clowns and our farts, dear lady."

She giggled. "And murders and revenge. All done by Italians in the English plays. Is no English murder?"

"You have not seen *my* plays."

"I would wish it," she said very seriously.

This warmed him. "When I write a play of revenge, I shall set it in England. Or in icy Norway or cold Denmark," he promised.

He began to think again of the stage.

SHE was silent one day, and he asked her why.

She pointed to the paper before her, and the poem on it, written in Will's hand.

"This sonnet likes you not?"

She shook her head.

"Not as much as the one I wrote for *you?*"

She shook her head again, smiling shyly.

"Why? Our host cared much for it."

"You write against money-lending and the—the—"

"Charging of interest. But 'tis a mere conceit."

She looked puzzled.

"A figure of speech, lady. Why should it trouble you?"

"My father practice this in Verona."

"Usury? Why chose he such a business?"

She was silent for so long that his patience was tried, and he picked up a pen to write. Then he heard her say quietly, "He did not choose."

He paused in his writing. "Ah."

He raised his eyes. She met them with her own, which were frightened. They were cloudy oceans and black desert skies, and nothing like the sun.

FOR three days she kept distant from him, as Henry had done for weeks. On the third night snow came and covered the flat ground outside his window. In the morning he walked in the whiteness for hours, until his fingers grew numb. A weak winter sun peered down at him. He heard only the cawing of ravens. At length he entered the house and came to the library.

She was there, glancing through an illustrated book of devotions. She looked up at him once, then nervously down.

He closed the door. "Art made Christian yet, by that book?"

She closed the book and went to the window. "By God, you mock me," she said.

"Mock you?" He came behind her, and spoke quietly. "Because you are a Jew?"

Her back stiffened. He put his hands on her shoulders. "Lady, can you not see it's all one to me?"

She turned to meet his lips.

LATER he lay at her side, feeling light and empty and thinking of nothing. When she woke they lay looking at one another, until the quiet unnerved him and he felt he would sink in her black eyes, which threatened some infinite silence. So to say something he asked her how it was that her eyes were like soft velvet. She pointed to a bottle of belladonna that stood on a table. He rose and poured it in the jordan and asked her whether she did not know it was poison and would ruin her sight. She grew angry and told him it was no such thing and that at court she had learned many recipes for beauty and to stay the progress of aging. When he came back to the bed, she touched his forehead and told him that bear's grease and onion would slow loss of hair, and he took her hand away from him and kissed her again to stop her folly, or to stop himself from hearing it.

They returned to the maze and sat where they had first spoken, on the marble bench that was now cold and wet. She told him she had seen a play in London where a man played a Jew who cackled like a devil and killed a convent full of nuns with poisoned oatmeal. Will told her he had seen it too and that he knew its author, indeed had once called him friend, and that he thought his tragic speeches sublime but his comedy less than artful. He tried to make her talk about Jewishness and its teachings, but all she would say was there was much in it about asking questions. He said that was good and right moral, but she rose impatiently and said that she was a Christian now and no Jewess. Then she swept into a passageway in the maze and Will was a long time looking for her, and in the end gave up and found his way out.

The next day he learned that she had changed her plan and gone back to court to join her husband for Christmastide.

ANNE'S letters, dictated to his sister Joan and then sent south, lay unopened in his desk. He read them now. News, wit, and chatter. He replaced them in a drawer. He could not go home. He could not face Anne till he'd fathomed the meaning of what he had done with Emilia.

Anne had said public dancing was forbidden in Stratford now. But at Southampton there were music and plays, and on Saint Stephen's Day costumed servants carried the earl into the great hall. He wore a parti-colored coxcomb and carried a tin scepter and declared himself the Lord of Misrule.

They reveled and ate. Roast boar, stuffed goose, rabbit pie, capons, swan, ten kinds of bread, peas with onions and peppercorns, spiced olives, leek pie, cakes and sweetmeats, sweet potatoes from far-off America. Wines and forks and iced cream.

On a side table stood a pasteboard ship, decked with flags and streamers and guns made of hollow plant stems. Lords and ladies shrieked in glee as servants lit flaming raisins in the stem-mouths. " 'Tis Drake's own vessel!" a woman cried. Next to the ship lay a molded pastry stag with antlers of marzipan. Henry rose and pierced it with a butter-knife, and blood-red claret flowed forth. He filled a glass and handed it to Will.

Will stared broodingly at it for a moment, then downed it most basely, in two gulps, and joined the revelry.

IN a sodden dream he walked toward a manger that blazed with white light. The face of the child in it shone so that it hurt to look on him. Yet he advanced, at the back of a choir of angels whose own faces, he saw dimly, were those of his playhouse fellows, Will Kempe and Dick Burbage and Kit Marlowe and Ned

Alleyn and even shock-haired Philip Henslowe, and dozens of boys tottering on tall chopines. Will himself was dressed as one of the Three Kings, with a crown fashioned from an iron cookpot. It kept slipping over his brows, and he was ashamed. Yet he sang with the rest:

> *Omnes clericuli*
> *Pariter pueri,*
> *Cantent ut angeli,*
> *Ad venisti mundo,*
> *Laudes tibi fundo.*
> *Ideo Gloria*
> *In excelsis Deo.*

With joy he felt the Latin stream from his throat, in perfect declensions. But the words fled from him as his shoulder was roughly shaken and a voice said, "Will. Will!"

He opened his eyes.

He was in a soft chair in a room neighboring the banqueting hall. On the floor at his side lay an empty bottle of Rhenish. Henry was shaking him. "Will! You have slept through the entertainment, though players came from London. Thine own play, and done in thine honor, but all's one. There is one would speak with you. Go to the kitchens."

Will sat on a stool in the kitchens, his elbows on the table before him and his hands pressed tightly to his forehead. Across from him clown Kempe smacked his lips over his own Rhenish, but Will would not look at it, or him. "What news, patch," he said dully.

"In Southwark and Billingsgate some knave has been cutting folks' heads off, and leaving behind their bodies for the thirdboroughs to find. And this be new." Kempe tossed a pamphlet under Will's nose.

Will picked it up. *Greene's Groatsworth of Wit.* "What is't? Robin Greene?"

"An address to all poet-playwrights. I have marked the page." Will turned to the place.

Yes, trust not the players. For there is an upstart crow, beautified with our feathers, that supposes he is as well able to bombast out a blank verse as the best of you, and being an absolute JOHANNES FACTO-TUM, is in his own conceit the only Shake-scene in a country.

"Makes a brave show of his Latin." Will tossed the pamphlet back to Kempe and clutched his head with his hands again. "I never did beg his pardon for knocking his pate at the Cardinal's Cap. My mistake, I see. Now I warrant I must kill him."

"You cannot. He is dead already."

Will lifted his head. "Ah?"

"A pitiful tale, fit for the stage. Died of the French malady, alone in his lodgings in Holborn, writing, writing, writing. Grieving for the wife he'd abandoned, railing at the mistress who'd poxed him. Dead at thirty-four." Kempe savored a swallow, then held his glass suspended in air and looked perplexedly at Will. "Can you credit this happening to a man?"

Feeling his gut roil, Will shoved his stool away from the table and stood. For a moment he swayed and then he stumbled toward a slops bucket and was loudly sick in it.

Kempe placidly refilled his glass from the bottle on the table. Will returned and sat down again, groaning. "Enough. Enough. I will go home for a time."

"What wilt thou do about Greene's trash pamphlet?"

"Let it lie."

"Let it *lie!* A fair jest! Something to eat here, is there?"

Will looked balefully at him.

"No. Well, let me see. What more to tell? John Lyly is in troubles for writing against the Puritans. He put them in a play and then Henslowe's men played it before the queen. She liked it not, for all his crafty planning. Wise queen! There are more Puritans in Parliament than e'er before; she cannot praise too much mocking of them. Master Lyly is disgraced."

"Did you act in the play?"

Kempe regarded his nails, which today were polished with a clear sheen. " 'Twas a pity, but I was ill with sore throat that day."

"Hm."

"Marlowe is friends with Henslowe again, and writes a new play. *Richard the Third.*"

Will stood up, toppling his stool. *"What?"* He steadied himself, grabbing his head with one hand and the table-edge with the other. "Ah, God in Heaven."

Kempe looked at him in surprise. "What is't? Hast thou written such a play?"

"A *donkey* would know I had meant to! Richard of Gloucester speaks at the end of *Henry the Sixth* about the evil he will do. He's a century dead! Where would he do his evil if not on the stage? And who would write it if not me?"

Kempe raised his eyebrows and said nothing.

Will righted his stool and sank back onto it. He stared blankly at Kempe. "The wit," he whispered. "The devilish craft of him!"

"Marry, thou lookst like a clubbed sheep. If *you* have such a play, sell it to us."

"I have *not* such a play. I was busy with a comedy before I left London. My *Richard Three* is in my head."

Kempe shrugged. "Then we will stage Marlowe's."

Chapter Sixteen

SO he did not go home. He was still at Titchfield when Emilia returned after Twelfth Night, surprising him. That night she lay in his bed, staring at the rain-pelted window. He sat, breeched and shirtless and barefoot, on the chair at his table, and regarded her soberly.

She looked at him. "What is thy thought?"

"I pity you," he said, "for your marriage."

She looked angry, and he knew he had stepped wrong with her. *Marriage* was a word she liked not. But he knew no honest words that would soothe her, so he said nothing as she rose and started to dress. "Why do you not love your son?" he asked her suddenly.

She turned to face him, her eyes like coals. "You think of nothing but children."

"It is that I—write of children now. Two of them. Left alone and lost and destroyed."

"Writing is all you think of."

He opened his mouth to say to her, *Lady, fair you are, but there be no man or woman who can rightly claim what belongs to another.* But he shut it without speaking. Whatever came from his lips could only make matters worse. When the door shut behind her he cursed himself for their pointless sin. She was no Henry. He had sought depth beneath her first silence, but the silence had yielded to endless chat about the court, the hunt, amorous sonnets hidden in velvet sleeves, the cut of a Spanish cloak. He was only a mask of words to her, and to him she was not the boundless mystery or the bottomless peace her dark eyes had seemed to promise. In the end he had wished her as English as Henry, or Anne.

He knew her for a will-o'-the-wisp.

But he still desired her.

HEDGEHOG. Bunch-backed spider. Toad.

Will rose from his table and stood before the pier-glass that hung by his bed. The glass was defective, and gave back a distorted image of a lumpen face. He worsened the image, contorting his features, twisting his body.

Adulterer.

He broke loose from the glass and limped heavily about the room. Then he stood in the middle of the floor, hunched and sneering. He breathed heavily.

After a minute of this he sat down to write.

I.

He had finished the rest. Now he had the beginning. Richard of Gloucester's first speech. *I.*

Not Marlowe's "I." Not *I can, I will.* The other "I." *I am alone. I am shut out. I am abandoned. I am denied. I am not king. I am not loved. I am deformed, unfinished, sent before my time into this breathing world, scarce half made up, and that so lamely and unfashionable that dogs bark at me as I halt by them.*

I am nothing.

He was binding the pages with a cord when he saw them together.

They stood in the carriageway. Beyond them was the white, snow-covered sward, before them the frozen moat. All was framed by the square of the window. He leaned toward the glass, and it fogged with his breath. He rubbed it with his hand, and peered. Henry was raising Emilia to the saddle of a horse, his hands around her waist, and as he seated her sideways she clung to his arms, leaned down, and brushed his forehead with hers. They laughed.

His stomach clenched like a fist, and he turned away.

He had never asked her what her friendship with Henry was. Now he felt no need to. He had sensed from the start her fondness for the earl, though in his growing lust for her he'd come to forget it. Now he remembered. So she had not returned to see him. With a passion inferior to his own, she had come to see the one all came to see, the golden one, who casually scattered his charm among all smitten gazers. *A woman's face, with Nature's own hand painted. Which steals men's eyes, and women's souls amazeth.*

Will clenched his real fist.

She had idled her time with him when Henry was hawking and making merry with other friends. She had not cared for him at all.

That night his pen was not idle. He used all his paper and finally ripped the page of dedication from the volume of Montaigne given him by Henry, and wrote on its back. By midnight Emilia lived in half a hundred lines of verse, as the whore of a hundred men, an easy glove, going off and on at any man's pleasure. *On and off?* No. *Off and on.* She was a bay where all men rode. She was rank and fulsome and so bad she was barely oathable.

He retired when the moon was low and lay staring at darkness, wondering whether she had poxed him and he was bound for the quicksilver and the sweating tubs. When he finally slept, he dreamed he stood in the middle of a stage by the trap leading down to the cellarage. From somewhere he smelled smoke. The trap opened slowly, and there in the dark was the leering face of dead Robin Greene, half-decayed, its chin sprouting a beard red and pointed as ever. Then Greene's face was the face of the carved serpent on the bedstead at home in Henley Street, and the snake was crawling out of the wood with its tongue flicking. It hovered before him and stared at him with grey Shakespeare eyes.

HE walked north through the frozen countryside and drank water and cider for hard pissing, to clear out disease and protect him and his wife from the pox he was sure he had. It took him a day to travel ten miles, so oft did he stop, and then he rented a nag at Winchester. At Guildford the nag went lame and he waited another day at an inn for a coach. When it came it was a ramshackle thing, a roofed cart whose steerage was all awry, and he and the three other men who rode in it piled forth every eight miles to shoulder it out of a ditch. They were pulled by two horses, a black and a white.

In the cart he bumped along next to a black-gowned priest whose nose was deep in a Testament. Out the man's pocket peeped an octavo copy of Augustine's *Confessions*. Will was partly minded to snatch the octavo and blithely read, and almost did it, but his other will prevailed, and then the cart wheel hit a great frozen ridge in the road and priest and all were thrown to the wall. The *Confessions* slipped from view below the hem of the priestly pocket, and it was a missed opportunity.

Will began to compose a tragic monologue.

The priest abandoned his reading of Romans and introduced himself to Will. His name was Lenten Puzzle. He asked Will where he was going and where he had been, and Will said he was going to London and had been to Hell. Master Puzzle laughed and asked him why he had gone *there,* and Will said he had gone to sully his ten years of virtue by breaking the Seventh Commandment, and had stayed until he'd discovered why he had done so.

"And found thee thy motive?"

"A necessary and governable chaos," he said. "Fitter than the other." He gave a hollow, ghostly laugh. "Ah, yes. A lamentable sin, but far, far safer than the other."

The priest frowned in bafflement. Will noted the man's confusion with only part of his thought while with the rest of his mind he took himself away, and went word-casting on an imaginary London stage. The bent carriage wheel jolted each time it turned, and he aligned himself with its rhythm, tapping his fingers on the hard but resonant wooden seat.

"You must go to thy church," said the priest at length, "and confess thyself before the congregation."

For an instant the half of Will who heard was tempted by the thought: to stand and openly name what was broken, nevermore to hide wounds in plays! But the song in his head held him. He said, "My good sir priest, I do not think I will."

"Give o'er your will. How else can God help thee to virtue?"

"Ay, there's the rub. I do not think God can."

Chapter Seventeen

WHEN Mary Arden was a young wife her baby died, and then her next baby died, and so when her son William was born, in a plague year when the babes were dying up and down the street, she thought he would follow the rest to Eternity. She kept believing this, despite the healthy yells of rage that came from the cradle where she had placed him, having decided not to hold or nurse him, because what would be the good? In time his screeches brought his father from the Woolery to say, *Mary, the bairn is hungry, and why do you sit spinning and humming?* In the end John himself had to give the boy cow's milk and pap with a cup and a spoon.

William persisted in living throughout his whole childhood, surprising his mother into making the sign of the cross whenever she rounded a corner and saw him there. Her madness passed, but she could never quite credit his realness. When they went by each other in house or yard she looked at him askance and fearfully. More than once, before she thought he could understand her, she put up two fingers to vex his evil eye, and told him, only half-jesting, that he was a changeling, no son of hers, and furthermore plague-proof. She was soon busy with her next children, and so Will learned to take care of himself by watching what others did. When he got older and showed little interest in girls of his own age, yet cast longing gazes on women full mature, his mother thought she knew why, and was not surprised when he obligated himself to marry such a one.

Anne Hathaway knew all this history, the spoken and the merely hinted-at. But she also knew there was more to her and Will than that. So she tried not to let her heart be hurt when townsfolk looked at her pityingly, and whispered, not quite shy of her hearing, that young Will Shakespeare had liked the taste of a woman of twenty-six, but found one of thirty-six full stale.

Still, the pitying and the whispers wore on her.

Folk had talked from the first, when she came a new bride from the church at Temple Grafton, bearing before her a belly that showed all who looked—and they looked—how needful her marriage had been. She had met their eyes boldly then, and was apt to stare them down still, but that was harder now, when she lived without a man's embrace to comfort her at home. To chat and tangle eyes with Will's handsome young brother was pleasant enough, but she did not do it because it was pleasant. For her it was a means to show whoever watched that she need not lack a man's attentions if she wanted them. She had tolerated Will's leaving, but hated the glances of neighbors in Holy Trinity Church on Sundays, when his absence from the Shakespeare pew seemed to tell everyone that he did not love his wife. When plague closed the theaters in London and Will came not home, but went to Southampton to write poetry for a lord, and then went straight back to the city, she became sure her neighbors were right.

Five years in London, and his love was stone cold.

She began to plan her life without him.

In her mind she made a bitter bargain. He would send her money and she would raise his children and never publicly shame him. He would do what he did in London, and she would do what she liked at home. He would come home at Lent, or at other times when the work was not plentiful in the great city. That was certain, because of his children. He would come most of all for Hamnet, of the shy smile and the odd gestures; Hamnet, whom he adored and would pull into his lap and sing foolish rhymes to and teach to fight with sticks in the yard. Hamnet, whom he would stop writing to stare at most lovingly when the lad tussled in the garden with his bold-eyed, wild-haired twin.

He would come home for Hamnet, but not for her.

AFTER leaving Southampton, Will was not thinking of Anne or her troubles at all, or even of his beloved Hamnet. He was caught in a race. His opponent was an angel-faced fellow, not a child, if he looked like one. This foe carried a quill in his pocket to quicken his pace.

And Will feared he himself might already be outrun.

So he sat in the George Tavern, drumming his fingers with the fright of that notion, and rose only when he saw the Burbages, Richard and his brother Cuthbert, coming in off the street. Richard asked for a mustard steak with onions and the barmaid brought it and leaned far over the table as she placed it before him, so that the tops of her breasts well nigh brushed the actor's face. Cuthbert rolled his eyes at Will. Richard pinched the maid's bottom as she left the table. He said to the men, "Thou seest my constant temptation."

"Lead us not into," Will said impatiently, drumming his fingers again.

Cuthbert plucked a hot half-onion from his brother's steak, blew on it, popped it into his mouth, and said, chewing, "What of Will's play?" He looked at Will. "Dick would not speak to me of it until we sat with you. But he told me its title, and I know that Kit Marlowe is finishing such a play for Henslowe, to open at the Rose."

Finishing. Will stopped his fingers. He said quietly, "Mine is done. It can be played next week at the Theater. *If* the part is to Dick's liking."

They both looked at Dick, who sat calmly cutting his steak. Cuthbert took out his knife to shave off a piece for himself. "What, then, Dick?"

Dick chewed in silence. "Henslowe," he finally said. "He grows rich even in plague times. Usury. Lending money at interest, sending his roaring boys to pummel the folk who don't pay, even when they be his own actors who cannot earn because of plague closings."

"A delicate fellow," Will said.

"Nothing stops his own earning. *Adversity is a toad who wears a jewel in his head,* he says. But it cannot be his line; 'tis too rich. Marlowe's, it must be."

Will glowered at him and said nothing.

Richard noticed Will's frown, but pretended not to. "I have heard Henslowe thinks Marlowe's *Richard the Third* will make him Midas-rich. He thinks to scant comedy now, and play only tragedies."

"Woe for Kempe."

"Aye, Will, woe for the clown. *Mene, mene, tekel, and parsin.* Kempe's days are numbered at Henslowe's Rose. Now they will play the noblest art there, the art of Sophocles and Aeschylus and Seneca."

"Well, a crowd of Aristotelians are they," Will said, pushing his chair back. "Henslowe and the noble art. Bear-baiting, cock-fighting, and Ned Alleyn hollering."

"Ah, I've roused him. Sit again, Will."

"I will not. I've let you read my play. Now buy it or I'll go my ways."

Richard squinted up at him. "I mean to say that Henslowe gives *blood*. There's little blood in *thy* play. Only one beheading, if I counted aright."

"Aye, there's little blood. There's a poxy great number of words, though, and if thou desirest to reach the scaffold before Ned Alleyn thou wouldst be well advised to stop jawing it and start learning them."

Cuthbert guffawed as Richard wiped his mouth. Richard's face stayed unexpressive. He swallowed some ale and held a hand up for the bill. "Six pounds it shall be," he said to Will, as the lovesick serving wench scurried toward them, adjusting her bodice. "The first speech will be the making of me. Six pounds."

Cuthbert's knife clattered to the floor.

"AYE, thou art master of our purse, and I know it," Richard said to his brother an hour later. They had left Will at his door pocketing gold pieces, and now walked north, toward Shoreditch and the Theater. "I know thy duty well. But allow me for this. We have given only four pounds now. Two in a week, if he cuts the lines that offend."

"He did not seem well inclined to do that, brother, and—"

"He must. And 'tis as I said. A war betwixt the Rose and the Theater, betwixt *Richard the Thirds*, betwixt William Shakespeare and Christopher Marlowe—can anything be better than this? It will bring more money than we have ever seen."

"And on this supposition you have let him jew us out of six pound?"

"I would not say that word again before him. You saw his look when you did; he did not like it, and he might peddle his next plays elsewhere. Henslowe would buy them."

"Ah, Henslowe would do what he could to undercut us. But Will said he would sell nought to Henslowe anymore."

"Things may change."

"And what if Marlowe's *Richard the Third* reaches the stage before ours, after all? What will become of our money then?"

"We will still bring in great custom. We must keep this man. You do not know him. I have seen him mutter to himself on the road between Bath and Bristol, and then put five scenes onto cast-off paper at the supper board, never stopping. Done in an hour, and 'tis not journey-work. All finished and perfect. No one else offers plays full-fleshed. The rest give us bones, and we must guess how they will come off when they are finally done."

"We must guess how *this* will come off, on the scaffold."

"I have read it," Richard said, tightly gripping his new manuscript. He quickened his pace. "I do not need to guess. I know."

CUTHBERT'S mood improved at the practicing of the play the next day. "Do it again!" he called from the Theater's yard, and his brother obliged him by throwing his arm heavenward as he stood at the center of the stage. He began in mock-quavery voice.

> *Come, cousin, canst thou quake, and change thy color,*
> *Murder thy breath in middle of a word,*
> *And then begin again, and stop again,*
> *As if thou wert distraught and mad with terror?*

Another player, cackling and fustian-clad, threw up his arm in like manner, and answered.

Tut, I can counterfeit the deep tragedian,
Speak, and look back, and pry on every side,
Tremble and start at wagging of a straw!

"Ah, good, good." Cuthbert turned to Will, laughing. "A kick at Ned Alleyn's arse, and Alleyn will know it."

"He will not," said Will, who was watching Richard's movements intently and jotting notes on his script. "He is too vain to know it." He smiled. "But Kit will know."

THREE nights later, in a tavern near Fleet Street, Will saw Marlowe.

He had vowed to challenge him when next they met. The urge had ebbed—if Marlowe was traitorous, were not all men traitors? Was he not one too?—and now his anger melted completely, resolving itself into shock.

The man was greatly changed. His angel's face looked bloated and pale; his hair was unkempt, and his cambric shirt disheveled. He was drunk, and seated at a corner table, laughing loudly with a group of sword-belted men whose weapons did not look ornamental. Will knew none of them. Tom Kyd was not there.

Will paid for his meal. As he turned toward the door he found Marlowe suddenly right in front of him, separated from him only by an empty table. Kit had risen to address a toothless, foul-smelling man who sat dicing under a tavern window. Will paused, looking at the pair, and Kit raised his eyes and saw him. The mocking smile slid from Kit's face, and he stared at Will expressionless. Will stared back, and both stood frozen, each a Gorgon transfixing the other.

Then Marlowe's mouth curved upward in his sardonic grin once more. He bowed deeply to Will, who nodded briefly in return. "Yon goes the swan of Avon!" Kit called, in a voice that rang through the tavern. "The Seneca of England! The Marlowe of Shoreditch!" The laughter of Marlowe's friends followed Will as he pushed toward the door, not answering.

"NO one is his friend," Richard Burbage said the next day. He and Will were seated with their part-scrolls on the boards of the Theater stage, scribbling and underlining. "He is odd; has always been. People entertain him, and he thinks he owes them nothing. Even his dearest companion, Tom Kyd."

"Kyd was not there last night." Will crossed out a line.

"Of course he was not." Burbage looked hard at Will. "You did not know?"

"What?"

"He is in Bridewell."

Will looked up from his script, frowning. "Jailed? Why?"

"For a thing Marlowe did. A libel of some kind was pinned on a door. The Lord Mayor's Men sought its writer among their customary suspects. Kyd had ousted Marlowe from his lodgings at last, but too late to escape the knock on the door, and now Kyd's deep in. The Lord Mayor's Men found a host of banned books and some writings saying God was not God. Now Kyd must explain the matter."

"How know you this?"

"My father has a friend on the queen's privy council."

"The *queen*'s been told?"

"Aye, 'tis a most dire matter."

"But the queen—"

"I know what is said of the queen paying Marlowe to spy, but this is . . . The paper said things she cannot excuse for him. And Kyd was tortured and said it was Kit's and that Kit had said worse things, that the apostles were idiots and Joseph a cuckold and that the sacrament were best shared in a tobacco pipe."

Will could not laugh at this. "Then why does Kyd lie jailed while Kit walks about London?"

"I do not know. Someone protects Marlowe. He is free and merry."

"He's neither free *nor* merry. His betrayals are a snake twisting his guts and they eat him."

"How can you know? I will speak of this no more. I care more about walking free in my own skin, and so you will cut these lines." Burbage prodded Will's script with a forefinger.

"Nay."

Burbage withdrew his finger. "Then you lose two pounds, and *I* will cut them. The play is mine."

Will looked blackly at him. "The lines speak of King Edward's bastardy. Richard of Gloucester alleges it for strategy—"

"Aye, very good strategy for Richard of Gloucester, and very bad strategy for us. Since Queen Bess came to the throne every enemy she has has cast illegitimacy upon her."

"Queen Elizabeth is not in my play."

"Fool! She will see herself in it. When she hears the lines, or hears *of* them, she will hear a papist voice telling her she cannot be queen because her father's true wife was Katherine of Aragon when she was begot, and because her mother Anne Boleyn was a whore."

Will dropped his scroll on the stage and got to his feet. "Keep thy two pounds and do as thou wilt."

But the next day he patched the play, cursing all the while, after he heard how butchered the scene sounded with its lines rudely ripped out. And he cursed Burbage for owning the play.

He sent the two pounds home to Anne.

THE Lord Mayor's Men were pounding on his door, but he was behind them on the stairs and they could not see him. One of them had red hair and a scarred face and was saying that William Shakespeare was a Catholic and a bastard. *He has no real mother,* the red-haired man said.

The pounding ceased, and Will sat up, suddenly awake. It was dark, and he was alone in his room. He heard nothing, then the sound of gravel tossed against his window. Naked, he went to the casement and looked down into the street. The night sky was crossed with clouds. Below he could see only a cloak-shrouded figure. "Let me in!" it called in a distraught whisper.

Will inhaled sharply. *"Kit?"*

"Nay." The man struck a flint, and looked up piteously. His ringstone of green paste sparkled with a sickly sheen. " 'Tis only me."

KEMPE sat in the room's single chair, while Will leaned on his mattress. In the light of a half-spent taper Will looked closely at the clown, who was trembling and the color of ash. Kempe took off his colored hat and with it mopped his forehead. A chill breeze blew through the open casement, ruffling the papers on Will's desk. Will rose to place a book on the papers. "What, then?"

"Marlowe's dead."

Will paused. "Ah." He sank back on his bedstead, hands covering his mouth. "Ah," he said. "Ah."

Kempe stared at him nervously. He seemed on the verge of weeping.

"Calm thyself," Will said, taking his hands from his mouth. *"You* are not dead."

"Ah, but if they find me—"

"For what? What has happened? How did Kit die?"

"In a quarrel at Deptford. Not far from Southwark. He had drunk with three rogues in a room and two quarreled o'er the reckoning. Kit was trying to sleep, and he full lost his temper at the noise and struck one. The man struck back and Kit got stabbed. The rogue bent his hand back so Kit stabbed himself. In the eye."

Will winced.

"That is what the other rogue told me. Kit died where he fell, in the moment."

"That is good, at least," said Will, staring out of the window at the black sky. "When was it?"

"Three hours past."

"Three! How came you to know of it, then, and to speak to this man?"

"I was there."

Will turned to him, amazed. *"You!"*

Kempe straightened one of his sleeves, looking indignant, and a little restored. "I as well as another man may be present at a brawl," he said haughtily.

"Then tell more."

At this Kempe cowered and shrank back in his chair again. "I had only got there, and went in, to see Kit laid on a bench. They had not covered him. Christ protect me from another such sight!"

"That sign you are making means nought to Christ. But keep thy hand up if it comforts thee. I would hear why Kit asked thee there, if ask thee he did. What gave he thee?"

Kempe raised his eyebrows in surprise, then moved his hand, fingers set to ward off the evil eye, so it stood between his own face and Will's. "How canst thou guess he gave me anything? Marry, thou art magical!"

Will looked at him hard. Sighing, Kempe dropped his hand and said, "He gave me nothing. He *meant* to give me his play. His *Richard the Third.*"

Will's back stiffened, though his face did not change.

"He could not keep it in his room," Kempe said. "He knew

the place might be searched, and said if the play was found they would have him in Bridewell because of what he had written in it about the queen."

"*They.* Who?"

"I do not know. But I was to hide it—"

"Because none would search *thy* rooms for matter of treason or heresy."

Kempe looked a jot wounded. "Well," he said. "Thou'rt right in thy guess, I think. But I ne'er got the play, and I know not where it is, and I came back to London hid in a clothier's cart."

"Good. Good for thee, Kempe."

Kempe stared at the low-burning taper. "All said he was marked to die young."

Will rose and went to the window again.

"What dost thou see?" Kempe asked, peering from the chair.

The breeze had died, and the curtain at Will's shoulder now hung like a windless sail. When Will spoke his voice was a thin whisper. It sounded ghostly and dead. "I see him, as first I did, friend. Choking on a table and rotten with plague sores."

Chapter Eighteen

CHRISTOPHER "Kit" Marlowe, aged twenty-nine, was buried with scant ceremony in a Deptford churchyard. At the funeral two richly clad queen's officers kept eyes up during the praying, darting their glances here and there to spy out who had come.

Will saw them, and pulled down his hat.

After the psalm was sung he slipped away.

On the walk back he passed the corpse of a dog that someone had flung in a ditch. The thing was crawling with maggots. He stopped to study it, then resumed his walk, absorbed by inward recitation.

> *All things do change. But nothing sure doth perish.*
> *Then vouch thou safe to tell*
> *(O gentle Thetis) how the loss that on our own kind befell*
> *May now recovered be, and help us*
> *To repair the world.*

At the Rose Theater all was hung in black bunting, and Will thought at first that this must be for Marlowe, their bright fallen star. But Kempe came forth to greet him and said no, it was only Henslowe's new scheme, a black stage-set for tragedy. The Admiral's Men would find some tragedy or other to play this afternoon, and no, none had a copy of Marlowe's *Richard* here, not even a set of unfinished foul-papers, and Kit was already forgotten.

Though not by Kempe. The clown was splendidly mournful in a sable doublet starred with aquamarine buttons and a dark-blue feathered cap sewn with false black pearls. His eyes looked fitly desolate. Still, Will guessed his melancholy manner owed as much to the Rose's black bunting as to Marlowe's death. There would likely be no part for him in the afternoon's tragedy, whate'er the play might be.

"Our patron's been beheaded," Kempe called sadly after Will, as he walked toward the bankside wherries.

Will turned to look at him. "Strange!"

"Aye. Strange." Kempe drew a black silk napkin from a fold of his codpiece and dabbed at his eyes. "Much hugger-muggery. First Marlowe killed, and then jump upon that, Lord Strange robbed of life. Found headless in an upper room of the Cardinal's Cap."

Will frowned. "Art inventing this tale, Kempe?"

"Nay." Kempe came down the path toward Will, and lowered his voice. "Lord Strange had fallen afoul of the Earl of Oxford over something touching on business with us, and had come to the Cardinal's Cap to meet Henslowe to 'discuss the dispute.' That is what he said. Then late last night someone took his head off. They knew him by the warts on his thumb. Now the Lord Admiral is our only patron. God preserve *his* head. 'Tis tragedy all around, Will, a hard world."

Will looked carefully at him, then said gently, "I think, clown-kin, thou shouldst take to thy bed for the day."

INSTEAD Kempe took a comforting glass with Will at the Dark Angel, and made many toasts to dead Kit Marlowe. When Will finally emerged from the tavern, leaving Kempe still there, it had started to rain, and he could not get past a crowd that surrounded the Clink, a street away from the Rose. He saw guards hauling a grey, gaunt man from the prison while watchers jeered and threw stones and rotten fruit at them all, both prisoner and guards. The prisoner showed blackened teeth in a snarl or perhaps a smile as an orange peel struck his face. Will knew better than to ask anyone who he was. Most of the onlookers would not know his crime or anything more than that he was being carted away to be hanged. Still, Will had heard something the night before that gave him an inkling of the fellow's identity.

He watched the man go into his cart and be roped to the metal rings on its insides. A horsed man wearing dark robes and a lawyer's flat cap forced his way through the folk. Will saw something familiar in the cast of his face. The cart was moving and the horseman kept his mount abreast of it, reaching over heads to clasp the prisoner's hand and shouting something that sounded like "Courage!" The prisoner nodded at him and showed his jail-blackened teeth again, and Will saw that his look was indeed a smile, a show of indifference to the peltings of the crowd.

The lawyer kept on at the cart's side, keeping the man's hand clasped in his. At the same time he managed his frightened stallion, keeping it calm amid the pushing and yelling.

Will had seen such horsemanship only once before in his life.

The bridge was too crowded to walk on, and it was thirty more minutes before he could get a boat for the north side of the river. As he finally climbed into an empty wherry he saw that same lawyer at the top of the bank, handing the reins of his horse to a man near the dock, and knew that the mount he had ridden so well was not even his own. The lawyer slid down the bank and looked questioningly at Will and the boat, saying "Northward?" Will nodded, and they climbed in together.

He was strong-faced and in his middle thirties, and as he sat he was deeply absorbed in the papers he had drawn from the inside of his cloak, but not so deeply that Will's stare did not unnerve him. The man looked up and met Will's cool grey eyes and asked, "What is't, fellow? Do I have something on my face?"

"Thy father's nose. Adam Arden, is't not?"

The man looked surprised. "So 'tis, but I had not thought me so famous that a thin-faced ghost such as thee should know me." He frowned in puzzlement. "Art not a player?"

"I am your cousin. Mary Arden's son, they say, though my mother calls me changeling."

"God's eyes!" The man folded his papers and held out his hand. "I thought you an elf, too. The sneaking hiding boy in my father's library, and now a London playwright. My hand, cousin. Why dost thou still stare?"

Will laughed. "I remember thee in a silken cloak and a peacock-blue doublet and tight hose, not in a sober gown. Look." He touched his ear. "I have thine ear-ring now."

"Oh." Adam pulled his own ear self-consciously. "I'd win no cases did I still wear that."

NORTH of the Thames, in a plain house near Milford Street, they chose a table far from the other patrons. Adam ordered canary wine, bread, and soup. "Barley soup," he said, polishing his spoon. "I eat it because it likes me well, but it puts me in mind of a tale. A man I knew when in Walsingham's service once passed me in Gray's Inn, as I ate, and told me that had I learned to bow before the queen's secretary, I'd not have to eat thin soup."

"And you said—"

"That had he learned to eat thin soup, he'd not have to bow before the queen's secretary. *Ha!*"

Will smiled at the sound of that laugh, but his eyes stayed sober. "We did not know what became of you after Edward's trial," he said.

Adam paused with his spoon halfway to his mouth, and put it down again. " 'After my father's trial?' " he said slowly. " 'Twas no trial. So I told my master Walsingham, in front of the queen, no less."

"That, we knew."

"And I am sure you also know that I shouted at the Privy Council in Star Chamber and ruined all my future chances at court."

"And mine!" Will laughed. " 'Twas luck for thee that they let thee away with thy head."

"Luck, yes. Luck that our queen hated Walsingham and liked to see him shouted at. Well, I entered Gray's Inn. I chose law. It hath made a new man of me. I joined the English Church, as I had to, but I argue for Catholic recusants pushed out of a living or a life because they said what they thought."

"You defend not only recusants, but Puritans."

"And anyone else in the world who asks, but how would you know?"

"The Puritans are not let to speak, but they themselves would stop everyone else's mouth if they could."

"Not all of them. Why do you tie me to Puritans?"

"It was Martin Mar-Prelate, was't not? Coming out of the Clink?"

"Ah." Adam sat back, stroking his beard. "Thou wert in the crowd this morning."

"Not by choice."

"Yes. It was Martin Mar-Prelate the bishop-mocker." Adam leaned forward and spoke low. "Ferreted out with his printing press, by the queen's ministers in Scotland. As we sit comfortable here, he's hanging dead at Saint Thomas Watering. Condemned for slander and heresy by Star Chamber. A case I could not win."

"It is the heretics who build the gibbets, not those who hang from them. Thou wert brave to fight for the man."

"He mocked a twisted justice and then fell prey to it. But do you know"—Adam wagged a finger at Will—"his dangerous jests were no more than might be heard any day in a Southwark play-house."

Will shifted in his chair and scanned the room, which was almost empty. His head ached from lack of sleep. Into his mind came a picture of Marlowe, spouting his heresies at the Dark Angel. Then dead on a bench in Deptford.

"*Thou hast appointed justices of peace, to call poor men before them about matters they were not able to answer!*" his cousin was saying. "*Moreover, thou hast put them in prison, and because they could not read, thou hast hanged them!*" Adam laughed softly and sipped his soup. "That is good. I saw your play of Henry the Sixth, cousin Shakespeare. Though, God be praised, with the wild wig you wore, I'd never have guessed you were the speaker. Now I can see—"

"A fifteenth-century English rebel was the speaker," Will corrected. "I only played the part."

"Oh, aye." Adam winked. "*Ha!*"

"But the two things are not the same," Will said, as emphatically as he could while still whispering. "Mayhap I think the thing the rebel says. Mayhap I do not. *He* says it, not I. And they hang him. Do I think it right that they hang him? Who may guess? It is not I who speaks, but the play, and the play is poetry, and poetry is many-sided."

"Ah, so many words from a quiet one!" Adam said. "What is't about me that opens thy mouth?"

Will fell silent immediately, and Adam sipped his soup. He winked at Will, who at last said sullenly, "I say only that there is safety in poetry's doubleness."

"In that safety lies your peril." Adam shook out his handkerchief and wiped his beard. "If no one knows what you are saying, you may as well say nothing."

Will frowned. "Nay. I will say everything."

"You will get lost in the manner of the saying of it and care that it sounds well and that you are applauded. Now, plays like me well. I like when I am told by my yelling cousin from the stage that all lawyers should be killed. But still I say that a playwright or a player stands to lose himself in words, as a hand's true color may get lost in glover's dye." He pointed to Will's hand.

Will muttered, "I had thought of such a conceit, before thee."

Adam barked *"Ha!"* as though he had won a point at shovelboard. "Dost see? You will think only of conceits, and care not a jot for what is human, real, and true."

"Pray do not point your finger at me, sir," said Will. "You understand me not. On my living stage I will say *all* the truths."

"All the truths?" Adam tugged his beard and frowned, looking bushy browed and suddenly fierce. "Jesting Pilate, do you say there are *many* truths?"

"You yourself say the same, when you defend men's rights to speak their minds. You say there is not one truth!"

Adam slammed his hand on the table so hard that his soup sloshed and spilled. "Of a surety, there is *one truth!* God knows it!" he roared, forgetting all secrecy. "But why in the devil's name should some fat queen's secretary or bulb-nosed, red-hatted bishop tell me or any of us what it is?"

WILL came back to Shoreditch that afternoon looking as though he had seen a ghost.

Amid the buzz at the Theater, the actors were excitedly chattering about Marlowe's death, as well as the beheading of Lord Strange. Still, despite these two lively horrors, many of the players seemed dour. Their great new play had no rival now. There was no spur to prick the sides of their achievement.

Will paid Cuthbert Burbage his shilling for a missed rehearsal, crossed the stage, seized the promptbook of *Richard the Third* from its hook on the tiring-house wall, and began to write in its pages.

"Nay, nay!" Dick Burbage approached him from behind. " 'Tis not thine; we'll have no more changes!"

"You'll have this." Will jabbed his pencil at the new lines, waving the book before Burbage's beard. "Four lines!"

Burbage read, shaking his head. "No. King Richard defending a good man's execution? King Richard saying the man plotted against his crown? King Richard lying? This touches Elizabeth, and 'tis I who will have to say it!"

"Do it, Dick Burbage. Do it, and I swear to you that in exchange, one day, I will write you the greatest tragic part that ever was, is, or will be on any stage of the world."

"*You! You!* What canting rot. You are nobody."

"Here, give it. Give me!" They struggled ridiculously over Will's pencil. In a second Burbage had it and was holding Will at arm's length against the wall while with the other he blacked out the new lines. Will fell to the ground and tried to bite Burbage's leg. Burbage yelled and kicked at him, but Will held on until another player ran to separate them.

"God's death!" Will howled at Burbage, his arms pinned behind his back by the other actor. "He is Richard the Third! Our English monster! Will you have him pick flowers and dance the morris? Will we have Will Kempe play him?"

"Leave off my shin, forever! You have bruised it!"

" 'Twill sweeten thy limp! King! King! King!"

A canvas ball whacked Will in the back of the head, and he fell to the tiring-house floorboards, stunned. He heard the sound of many running feet and then the whoops of a chased boy outside the Theater walls. He glanced dizzily at the ball that had come to rest against the wall, and saw it was crudely painted with his own features.

"Foul mirror," he said, rubbing his head and sitting up. He put the ball on his lap and regarded it closely. "This will not serve. This should not be. This cannot be Hastings' head in our play. Dick?"

But Burbage was gone in the chase for the boy, who in minutes was brought back kicking and yelling and was forced to submit to a cuffing. Will waited patiently for the drubbing to end and then approached the lad, holding the ball. "Where got you this, puny?" he asked.

"Beg pardon of thine elder!" yelled a player from the yard.

The boy bowed and then straightened, green-eyed and glowering and rubbing a sore shoulder. "With slavish submission I beg pardon for this vilest of accidents."

Burbage, now blunting a rapier with wax, looked a warning at the boy.

"But where had you this?" Will said, brandishing the ball. "We had thrown them out with the slops after *Henry Six* was first played to the finish."

"They be fair enough for football," the boy said, bouncing back and forth from foot to foot. "Give me."

Will frowned.

"Sir."

Will tossed him the ball. "Nathan Field, you would do better to learn the part of Lady Anne. We can send you back to Henslowe along with a list of everything you stole from the Rose."

"A list, but not the properties. Those you would keep." Nathan smirked. "I know you masters." Will made a threatening move toward him, and Nathan held up his hands. "Sir."

NATHAN Field was a runaway, and no relation to Will's friend the printer. His father, John Field, was a well-known London divine who raged from his Puritan pulpit against the evils of stage-play, and lived what he preached. He never touched the money Nathan earned on the stage, though the boy's wages were his by right. Philip Henslowe had pocketed most of them, and Nate knew it. It had given him good reason to slip from the Rose to the Theater. Now Cuthbert Burbage kept the boy's earnings in trust, and what he doled out Nathan spent on ale and tobacco, though he was only ten. When he could, he sneaked back to the Rose to steal props, thinking them no more than his due from Henslowe.

In the end the vile camp-ball he had taken, repainted, had to serve as Lord Hastings' lopped head in *Richard the Third,* and this vexed Will. Yet he won one victory: despite his fears of spies in the lords' rooms, Burbage agreed to say the added lines, because, on consideration, he did like how they sounded. So, from behind an open stage door Will watched Burbage twist his body into the likeness of the deformed duke. He listened to the smooth tongue drip the sweet poison of Richard of Gloucester, and silently mouthed his words where he stood.

I. Alone. I.

The players thought they played in a void because Marlowe

was not there to give his blank-verse answer. But the people of London went mad over the play. Week after week they filled the house when it was performed and cheered it, and their money fattened the Burbages.

Will stayed thin. He sat in the Theater's tiring room and stared at the promptbook of *Richard the Third* and began to see in it only a thing that should be his and was his no longer. It yielded him no more profit than six pounds, already spent. The boys in the tiring house made him think of Hamnet. The thoughts of Hamnet turned to thoughts of Anne. And the thoughts of Anne made him think of the money he must give her to pay for his guiltiness.

So in the days he collected shillings for part-playing and in the nights he returned to his rooms to write. Now he did not write for beauty or to beat back Marlowe's brave pen or to say the many truths that he thought.

Now he wrote for money.

After some weeks, on a November day, feeling light as a spilled wineskin, he gathered his papers and walked down Fish Street to the river. Yellow leaves hung from the boughs of the bankside trees. He paid a penny to the ferryman and crossed to Southwark to strike a deal with Philip Henslowe.

Chapter Nineteen

THE stout man's hand checked the angle of the cap that perched on his orange uprush of hair. A ruby shone from the cap's crown, and beneath the stone hung his face, round, thick-skinned, and goggle-eyed.

He was a toad with a jewel in his head.

"Your play was partly made by another man, I have heard." The man speared a hunk of pinkish meat and chewed meditatively. "The poet George Peele, is't?"

Will shrugged. He sat on his stool with arms folded, an untouched glass of ale before him. "It was mostly mine. Peele gave his pages to me for five tankards at the Crippled Phoenix, and now 'tis all mine."

"And you would keep it so." Henslowe pointed his knife at Will. "For us, a license to play, but not to own. Yet there is none such."

"I know me a lawyer would make me one."

The toadish man looked briefly leftward. In minutes the owner of the Knavish Loon was by him, bending, servile in his leather jacket with crystal buttons, his wool stockings and plain worsted garters. "A fresh capon, Master Henslowe?"

"Aye." Henslowe put down his knife to rub the emerald pendant that hung from his ear halfway to his ruff. Then he rubbed his chin. "And you will supply ghosts. Dismemberings."

"A tongue cut out—"

"Has been done."

"—*and* the ravishment of a fair maid."

"Ah, good! Played before the audience? Not reported by messenger?"

"Ne'er shown on the stage till now."

Henslowe extended a greasy hand. "Done, for eight pounds."

IT was a waking nightmare. The behind-stage smelled like a butcher's shop, with buckets of sheep's blood and guts standing by the doors. In the trees behind the tiring house the boys filled pigs' bladders with the stuff. On stage, the players poked the bladders with rapiers, squeezed them under their armpits, soaked their shirts with reddish liquid, bled over their silks and onto the stage until they slipped and slid on their entrances.

"JesuMaryJoseph." Will stood, wide-eyed, behind the Rose's middle-stage curtain, but he was not watching the carnage on the scaffold. He was watching the audience. After an hour he turned abruptly and left through the tiring-house rear. He walked toward London Bridge, past the shallow pit where, behind a low wall, three snapping dogs were madding a huge bear. The howls of the beasts blended with the shrieks of the Beargarden crowd and the yells of the folk at the Rose, and those noises were joined by the hoots and gibbering of the Bedlamites in the mad-folks' jail close behind. Will walked faster and faster and finally he broke into a run.

He stopped under the Great Gate. Against his will, as it seemed, he lifted his head, which felt pulled by the eyeless gaze above him. *There. Still there.* His uncle's skull grinned down at him, chapless and whitey yellow.

"Forgive me, Nuncle," he said.

AT supper at Richard Burbage's house he was told he would have much ado explaining himself for the treachery of selling to Henslowe. But he said little in his own defense. He had already decided to think of the deal no more, and besides was distracted by the back-and-forth between Burbage and his wife as the actor tried vainly to send her to her kitchen and keep her there. It was *meddling hag* and *proud-chested jackanapes* until Will's fingers itched for a quill. Burbage and Cuthbert, their moods already foul, grew irked at his silence. The Theater had been less than half-full that afternoon, and Cuthbert thought it proof their repertory was stale. As for Burbage, he had played Richard Three for full near three hours before that small crowd; puff-faced for more than two of them because Lady Anne had spit in his eye with tobacco juice in the second scene. Nathan Field had played the innocent after, saying the script was ambiguous. Will, who danced in late, had roared with laughter at that, which put Burbage in a fury. Now not even his fair wife would bless him with the kind sympathy owed a player of his stature.

"Do not Ned Alleyn it, Dick," Will said. "As for my *Titus Andronicus*, I have it still in my keeping owing to my cousin's lawyerly ways. But I will not rent it to you. It made *me* fainty. I know you would not stoop so low as to play in it."

"You stooped so low as to write it."

"I will do what I must to make money."

"Sell thy soul?" Cuthbert asked.

"What know you of souls, money box?" Will looked at him shrewdly. "Have you one? Mine is tarred and beshitted, but I have only sold a small part of it. I would keep the rest for my future need, but my plays in your keeping are yielding me nothing. I may have to kiss new arses."

Bess Burbage hooted from the scullery, but Burbage glared at Will. "Would you have us *give* you a share in the Theater, that you might reap fresh gold at every playing of your plays? Three hundred pound might buy a third. Did you share in the cost of its building?"

"I know *thou* didst not. Thy dada built it and then gave all to the two sweet boylets." This brought the brothers to their feet, shouting, so Will left the house hastily, while at his back Cuthbert cursed him for a *poor player, hardly visible on stage.* "Yet I come cheap!" was Will's response, as he slammed the front door hard.

He was sorry for that on his walk home. Money matters were not what most curdled his heart. What soured him was a thing he could not say to Burbage or to any man of the theater. He could barely speak it to himself, yet he could not avoid knowing.

Marlowe was dead.

Without Kit's breath to his sail, how could he write true tragedy?

He walked all night, skirting ruts of hardened mud from Holywell Street to Cheapside to Old Bailey and down to the Thames, turning north only to avoid coming close to the grey walls of the Tower. In the darkest part of the night, he prayed.

That I might be granted a rival.

When the sun rose he was still walking. He turned into the Strand. He heard an oath, and looked up as a sprinkling of mortar flakes fell on his sleeve. Above him on a scaffold a tall, dark, and very thin workman strove to balance a teetering tray of bricks with one hand. With the other he pressed a trowel on the half-built wall before him, trying to steady himself, but as the bricks tipped he dropped the trowel and grabbed the tray with both hands, too late, and then bricks followed trowel to the ground, just missing Will's shoulder.

"Deus et omni diaboli! Istum laborem odi!" the man swore. His black eyes were popping, and his face was dark with wrath.

Will knelt, retrieved the trowel, and replaced it on the wall. The workman nodded thanks as he gathered the bricks, still spluttering curses in perfect Latin.

Even to Will, he seemed odd.

HE rented a horse, and went home to Stratford for a time, and poured out his difficulties to Anne, who he knew understood them well, although she did her best to be cool and feign not listening. Her brave intent to give him a long show of indifference collapsed at his first jest, which was something foolish on the order of *Nanny nonny wears not tawny for her sides are grown too brawny*. The song was most unflattering, but try as she did she could not forbear laughing at it, and at the antic look of his face when he sang it.

She had not seen him for more than a year, and he had changed. He had turned thirty and his hair was thinning, though his face was still smooth as a youth's. She herself was fatter, but he did not care and so she did not either.

This visit he spent his days playing with his children. That joyed his heart, though it saddened him that Hamnet looked sometimes ghostly pale, and lay abed now and then, smitten with odd ailments, despite Anne's remedies of rose hips and boiled eucalyptus and oil of poppy. Gilbert read to the boy and this angered Will, but he would not show it, since it made the child happy.

When Hamnet felt well enough, Will taught him to sword-fight with sticks in the yard. Judith, his twin, mocked each parry and thrust, and to Will's dismay, she executed them far better than her brother.

What Hamnet liked better than fighting were the fairy stories Will spun. Seated by the fire and surrounded by Susanna and Hamnet and Judith and his sister Joan and his young brother Edmund, fourteen but still mad for fancy, Will would tell tales each night. Gilbert, who might be in the house for supper, would lurk and glare and try not to listen, and finally depart loudly to do work in the Woolery. When Will was last home Anne had done her best to spur his jealousy by nestling close to Gilbert in the garden. Now she and Gilbert both did their best not to look at one another. Will saw it, and thought it meant more than any of the rest of it had.

But he let it lie.

"MY quill is dry." Will sat with his legs stretched before the kitchen fire, his boots wet from the mud of the Arden woods. His arms were folded, and his face was a mask of exaggerated melancholy.

Anne glanced at him impishly, but to tease him she withheld the bawdy retort he so clearly expected. "Dry, is't? Then thou dost not see what is before thy face." She turned to face him. "Thou dost not heed what thou hearest all day, e'en when I see thy hands itch to run from it and turn it to ink-scratches. If thou must go back to that church of damnation and hollowness—"

"I take this phrase to mean *playhouse.*"

"If thou must go to that pit of nothing, put *life* in it, not sheep's blood and death!"

"Ah."

He had written comedy before. To do so was not dignified or Marlowe-like, but it was profitable. Yet this time he would do something new.

YOUNG Nathan Field, sitting cross-legged on the Theater's scaffold, looked up from the foul-copy script, his hard eyes wet with passion.

"Nay." Will lifted the book from him and clapped it shut. "Thou shalt *not* play Beatrice. None of you shall. I only came to show you what cannot be had for six pounds."

"I am not your enemy!" Field shouted with rage. "Sir."

"Nay. *You* are not." Will looked pointedly at Cuthbert Burbage, who had read the script over the boy's shoulder and was now frowning deeply at Will.

"You are stark, raving mad," Dick Burbage said coming on from the tiring house. "We will sign no crafty lawyer's contract that lets us play this play once and then lets you go peddle it at the Rose the day after! Henslowe may be tripped—once—but the Burbages will not."

"Then the Burbages may hang, and I will read my *Love's Labour's Won* for my private enjoyment."

"Then best rename it *Much Ado about Nothing*," Cuthbert said, and laughed scornfully. "And what will you do for money?"

"I will earn it by my poor playing, hardly visible on stage."

"What wouldst thou have us do, Shakespeare?" Dick followed him into the Shoreditch street, whining. "We are men of business. We buy plays, and then we play them for *our* profit. We owe creditors! We cannot grant shares in our playhouse *gratis*! Canst thou not see our view of the matter?"

"My curse"—Will turned, sighing, to look at him—"is that I can."

★   ★   ★

THAT night Will sat long at his desk, staring at the moonlit chimney pots of the roofs across the street. Finally he sighed heavily, inked his quill, and wrote a page. He folded and sealed it, scribbled a name on its outside, then stared out again at the chimney pots.

Within a week he had his answer, carried by a fellow in livery so fine it brought stares from the working folk of Saint Helen's, Bishopsgate, where now he dwelt. Will unfolded the parchment and read.

> *Here is what you request and the sum paid me by the printer Richard Field for your poems. The longer ones only. I will not sell thy sonnets.*
>
> *Do not write to thank me. I have joined our great general Essex and shall be sailing with him off the coast of Spain to thump Iberian heads. A thousand ruffed Spaniards resemble a thousand John the Baptists, is't not so? Goggle-eyed on their starched lace platters. We may hope for good things from this Essex later. I will say no more.*
>
> In continued love,
Henry Wriothesley

Chapter Twenty

ON the third morning of Will's newly bought partnership with the Burbages, Richard Burbage had to stop his grey-bearded father from lunging at their playwright with a sharp wooden sword while Will coolly instructed all the players to forget "hands-up" for fear and "the cackling laugh" for villainy, and only *remember who they were*.

The next day Will persuaded the Burbages that shares must be sold to *more* players, if their players were to care *who they were*. Besides, he said, the new money could pay a carpenter to tighten the benches so that Richard did not have to hammer by moonlight at the close of each day. When Cuthbert, scoffing, told him no players could be found who had such money, Will said he knew of one. And though he was loath to include him because of his scene-stealing ways there was no other answer; his new play needed a clown.

To their great surprise, they found Kempe in the Fleet.

For a groat the warden let the three of them into the sprawling Southwark prison. They were led up windowless stairways and past cells packed with grumbling caught pickpockets, and through dark passages smelling of unemptied jordans, decaying food, and sweat. Snatches of bawdy songs, curses, and a few groans smote their ears. At the end of a hall the turnkey stopped and gestured. On a bench in a small cell sat the clown, barely recognizable in a torn undergarment and faded green breeches. He peered at the faces that looked in at him through the grate.

"And what are you clapped in for, fellow?" Richard asked.

"Holla, lads," Kempe said, and came to the grate. "A morsel? Aught? I almost faint for food."

Will gave him some bread.

" 'Twas a foolish thing," Kempe said through his mouthful. "A cloth-of-gold garment. I looked excellent well in it in the part of Fortunatus, and I thought, what is the harm if I wear the coat to the Knavish Loon for a tankard? Alleyn does it, and Henslowe himself wears a furred robe on occasion."

"Yes."

"But the beaks had me before I'd finished my third draught. Posing as one above my station, said the magistrate! Now, here I sit. Henslowe won't free me." The clown's face looked pained. "Says he does not need me now. So a boy told me."

"But what of thy money, Kempe?"

"Thine ear." Will leaned closer, and Kempe whispered, " 'Tis much, and 'tis in a bag in my straw-tick mattress. I have told no one. It would be enough."

"We will pay your way out and you will get your gold yourself," Will said. "We know a better place for it than a straw-tick mattress."

That same evening Cuthbert dropped Kempe's gold pieces into a strongbox.

"There is another who should have the sum we seek," Will shouted to Richard, trying hard not to wince as Kempe—dancing nimbly across the stage and waving a scarf—added loud, unscripted comments to his Dogberry speeches.

"What?" Richard said fearfully, cupping his ear. "Who? You will mar all with your selections!"

"Nay. This one is Gabriel Spencer."

"I know him." Richard stepped closer. "Red hair. A scar-face. Gap-toothed, and a good comic villain. He plays for us often, but I ne'er thought to offer him a share. Why think you he has money?"

"If he does not he ought to."

Richard looked carefully at Will. "What do you know of him? Is he a runaway lord's son?"

"Not that."

"I had heard he spent time in Warwickshire."

"He did. I will sound him if you agree."

SPENCER'S scars were thick, yet lay all on one side of his face. He had one good, blue eye, and the left was sewn shut. "I know your name," he told Will, who had bought him a meal of mutton in the George.

"Ah. And what is it?"

"William Shakespeare, of course." Spencer looked at him strangely. "Do you not know your own name? I knew it in Warwickshire. 'Tis where I hail from."

"Ah, indeed. Did service for the Earl of Leicester, did you not? Until a falcon ruined your fine face in the service of your duty. A trivial arrest of a trivial Warwickshire gentleman whom Robert Dudley wanted out of the way, but the trivial man's bird took offense at it. A strange happening."

Spencer stopped chewing, and stared greenly at Will.

"No work serving a lord after that, not with a scarred face," Will said. "Best to come to London and play for a living. Play that you were not a foul tool of a lord."

"Who are you?" Spencer whispered.

Will shook his head and relaxed his dark scowl. "I am sorry for this game. I will tell you who I am. My uncle was Edward Arden."

"Oh." Spencer breathed out a long sigh, and pushed back his stool. "And you guessed my part in his arrest. I cannot tell how, but no matter." He stood. "I regret the part I played in his ruin, though that will mean little to you."

"It means something."

"I earned more gold than I'd ever seen, working for Leicester, but I would not do it again. And now I'll seek new employ, or change my name. I am sure you have brought me here to tell me I am found out and to spoil my chances to play for the Burbages."

"For *me* and the Burbages. And if that was my plan I might have launched it long ago. I have known you for years. You played Mephistophilis in Stratford once, and fell on your head. I played a fifth of your part for you. Did Will Kempe never tell you it was me?"

Spencer stared at Will in wonder. "Nay!"

"Forgetful and distracted clown! Kempe, not thee. But sit down. I have brought you here not to deny you work, but to demand your money. All of it, all the gold you got for arresting my uncle. It will buy you a share and a home in our theater, and then I will give you lines to say. Evil Don John's lines, for a start, in our new comedy. You will have ample chance to do penance for your crime in our church of hollowness."

Spencer looked puzzled.

"Our stage."

Spencer grinned.

*   *   *

SPENCER joined them, and without Cuthbert knowing how it happened, Will was persuading them all to sell shares to still more players, good players, players stolen away from Henslowe's Rose, at sums those players could manage. And to hire apprentices.

And so they grew to a fellowship.

Thomas Pope, old and dignified, the best to play bishops and justices. Clown Kempe with his flaring green trunks and belled buskins, and Spencer with his villainous, gap-toothed leer. John Heminge, a green-grocer, who sold vegetables from a cart in the morning, and dodged them on a stage in the afternoon. Fire-eyed young William Sly, come smoldering from the Rose like a red-hot coal, unwilling longer to share a stage with *clot-headed, self-glorious Ned Alleyn!* Rough-voiced Will, who played ghosts and old men and fed them all their daily poetry. Cuthbert Burbage, secret, silent sharer, hunched in a back room over his box of gold. Bold, green-eyed Nate Field and three other boys, their hair chopped short for the wigs of Lady Anne, of Beatrice, of Julia and Silvia. Augustine Phillips, high-voiced and perfect in the gestures of old queens and matrons.

And Richard Burbage, who could do anything.

The Lord Chamberlain himself stood as their patron, and Will took them all as his family.

A band of brothers.

Now he needed no Marlowe to spur him to writing a play. The players' passion gave him his fire. And so he was writing again, a new tragedy, but a different sort of one, with lightning shafts of comedy sparking the whole. Not a man's tragedy. Not Edward Alleyn baying at the moon, nor even Richard Burbage twisting his mouth in lonely malice. A woman's tragedy. Nay, not even that. A girl's!

Which was to say, a boy's.

*   *   *

"WILL you have done calling me mad?" he asked Burbage. They were in Rich Field's print shop, and Will's old schoolfriend was handing him a newly made promptbook. Will held it to his nose and sniffed the fresh ink.

"Dog, I tell you a youth could not carry this part, to say nothing of a boy of ten," Burbage said, as they paid and left the shop. "If we *will* do it, we must have someone older. One of our younger men shall play Juliet."

Will made a rude sound. "One of our younger men with a gravel voice and a fuzz on his lip? I do not think it."

"Then one of our older boys! But not *him!*"

"He did well enough as Lady Anne."

"For twenty minutes he did, and then he was off in the tiring house, stuffing himself with pastries."

"Tobacco juice, was't not?" Will tapped the corner of his eye. "Stow thee."

"He will do it or none will."

Burbage grabbed Will by the elbow and turned him to face him. "You have a share in thy plays, Will. 'Tis more than thou hadst before. But you do not own the whole of them."

"Forgive me, Dick." Will patted Burbage's strong arm. "I know it. I speak too surely. Marry, now let me go, I beg. I will show you why I say as I do."

The play needed finishing first, and that night Will wrote late. The sky was lightening into grey when he came to the speech he had left for last. *But soft! What light comes through the window there?* He stared at the paper, frowning. A sudden gust of wind lifted his papers and blew them about the room. He rose with an oath and replaced them, anchoring them with the ink-pot. But his last-written line was already smudged and unreadable. He tried again, scribbling in the space above it. *But soft! What light through yonder window breaks?*

Then his quill did not stop until he was done.

"NO placards saying VERONA, held by boys. *You* tell the audience where you are."

"How?"

"Romeo finds the poison *in Mantua, here.* He says it. It will always be thus. We trust to the dialogue for everything."

Nathan Field, on the balcony, brushed a foot on its floorboards like a nervous colt. "When, Master Shakespeare?"

"Now. Say whatever you have."

Nathan moved to the rail. His voice was low, but Will heard its resonance and knew it could be heard from the back benches and the upper galleries of the playhouse.

> *Come, civil night,*
> *Thou sober-suited matron all in black,*
> *And learn me how to lose a winning match,*
> *Play'd for a pair of stainless maidenhoods.*
> *Hood my unmann'd blood, bating in my cheeks,*
> *With thy black mantle, till strange love grow bold,*
> *Think true love acted simple modesty.*

Will opened his mouth to prompt him, but Nate had already raised his arms, and his voice. The speech found shape as he spoke it, and grew warmer, line by line, growing in intensity. His rhythm and pitch remained perfect.

> *Come, night, come, Romeo, come, thou day in night,*
> *For thou wilt lie upon the wings of night,*

Whiter than new snow upon a raven's back.
Come, gentle night, come, loving, black-brow'd night!
Give me my Romeo, and when I shall die,
Take him and cut him out in little stars,
And he will make the face of heav'n so fine
That all the world will be in love with night
And pay no worship to the garish sun.

Nathan dropped his arms.

There was no sound in the house but breathing. Then a slow, hard clapping came from the far reaches of the yard, and all the men turned to look.

Bess Burbage had come with the dinner, and stood with tears on her face, applauding.

FROM then on, the sharers made fewer questions of Will's choices. Only Burbage stayed guarded, as he said the brunt of the lines and stood most to be blamed if a thing gave offense. So when Will turned back to historical tragedy Burbage was afeard.

"Truly, you will erase Marlowe's name with these histories," he said, carefully scanning the new script for dangerous matter.

"Well erased." Contempt fired the voice of the speaker who interrupted. He was lean and darkly handsome, and lay sprawled on a bench in the rear of the George Tavern, where they had been lent a room to drink and to work. "*Well* erased," the young man said again. "Christopher Marlowe. A writer of spectacular trash. A bogeyman Jew boiling in a cauldron! Savage farce."

Will glanced at him with raised eyebrows. "*The Jew of Malta* was a great play, William Sly. You cannot find fault in its poetry."

Sly frowned. "Poetry is not all that matters."

"I do not say so. But poetry excuses many a moral fault."

"Think you so?" Sly looked angrily at him.

Will's returning glance was mild and curious. He had praised Marlowe to Sly earlier, and told him Mercutio of *Romeo and Juliet* was Marlowe brought to life again. After, Will played Mercutio to Sly's Tybalt, an odd choice for Will, who usually lurked in minor parts. But this time he danced in the center, playing the nimble, half-mad jester, railing until he lay gasping on a bench, run through by Tybalt's sword. Sly had attacked him with real malice, slapping the flat of his sword hard against Will's arm so the skin reddened and rose in a painful welt. Along with this injury, Will had borne Kempe's peevish complaint that *he* had not gotten to play merry Mercutio, but only the servant Peter, and that to make it worse the men had voted most cruelly against a morris dance at play's end.

Now Kempe was sulking in his rooms back in Southwark and Sly was frowning here in the George, and Will knew nought that he had done to deserve any of it.

"Nay," Burbage said suddenly, looking up from his reading. "Nay, Will. Not this."

"What, Dick?" Will yanked his eyes from Sly's hot gaze. "Will you join my accusers?"

"I know only that I would not be accused myself, of treason. I will not play a monarch who is knocked off the English throne by a strong soldier."

"Why?"

"Do not play the fool, Will." Burbage dropped the offending pages on a bench. "All in London know General Essex is out of England, sailing by the Spanish coast and reaping victories and glory, and that he is no friend of Elizabeth! *She* knows it."

"Is't not enough that the parish priest railed at my *Romeo and Juliet*? A 'monstrous bellows to blow up carnal passions,' said he. Yet I have done nothing. I *am* nothing, I am only a poet. Must I be attacked by mine own?"

"The priest railed at *our* play. Not *thy* play. And we are used to the Puritans' rantings." Richard raised a finger in front of Will's face. "Another matter. Remember that the greeting in church is *Peace* be with you, not *Peas* be with you. A thing as small as that can wreak you a fine of sixpence."

"Oh, tush and tilly valley."

"In any case the parish pastors are one thing. The queen is another. If the Revels Master approves this part, the age of miracles is not past. At any rate, you will not make me say it."

"Well enough, Dick," Will said, gathering up his papers. "I ask one thing only. Take home with thee the scene of Richard Two's deposition and read o'er the lines." He handed the pages back to Burbage. Sly watched the transaction, his dark, alert face curious. Will went from the room, calling back over his shoulder, "Read with thy wife, if thou wilt."

The next morning a knock woke Will, and he came blear-eyed to his door.

Burbage stood there, wild-eyed and unkempt, clutching the pages covered with Will's inky scrawl. "A pox on thee," he swore. "A villainous pox and a murrain plague thy rest!"

"I take this to mean you will do it."

"Damn thee to Hell! I will."

SLY'S voice stabbed through the curtain, sounding as sharp and cold as his eyes looked hot. He was Bolingbroke, the strong soldier, presiding over the medieval parliament. *"Are you contented to resign the crown?"*

"Aye. No. No. Aye." Burbage wept in confusion. *"For I must nothing be!"*

Will moved farther behind the stage curtain, smiling in the darkness as he listened.

For I must nothing be.

Chapter Twenty-one

"*GOD'S death!*"

Facing the window, Queen Elizabeth looked headless to her councilman. He saw only the back of the tall, shell-shaped collar that fanned upward from her silver dress.

She turned suddenly, repeating, *"God's death!"*

Viewed from this point, the pearl-studded collar surrounded her aging face like a nimbus. Francis Bacon's knees shook, partly with fear of her, but mostly with gout. He prayed that she might sit, so he could.

" 'Tis like that other play, by the dead one, where the Scythian shepherd plays catch with a crown—"

"*Tamburlaine*, Your Majesty." Bacon's voice was like silk. "Penned by our false friend—"

"But this is worse. This is an *English* king! What means that man by it?"

"Earlier in the scene a bishop warns *against* the transfer of the crown," Bacon said. " 'Tis nothing plain that the playwright wishes the audience to approve of the staged happenings."

"Stow you," the queen said crudely. "Stow thy careful *reading* of the play, thou slithering garden pest. In the *playhouse* I will warrant they approve those happenings!" She sat down at the council table and adjusted her huge, stiff farthingale of blue brocade. Exhaling with relief, Bacon sat at the table's far end. Elizabeth fixed him with her gimlet eyes. "What will we do?"

"Arrest him," Bacon said without hesitation.

Elizabeth's eyes narrowed. "I am not sure I trust your judgment, Sir Francis. My wisdom says do *not* arrest him, yet."

"Ah, your wisdom speaks well," Bacon said smoothly. "This man writes plays in cycles, and this cycle is not yet complete. We may leave him some rope. See what he does next."

"Aye." Elizabeth nodded broodingly. "Leave him some rope to hang himself."

Chapter Twenty-two

"FORTUNE blessed us that time."

"Aye, Richard." Thomas Pope, the eldest of the Lord Chamberlain's Men, agreed. "Let's hope there is no more to be heard of the matter."

"Beyond the censoring of the king's uncrowning from the printed—"

The door to the tiring house opened wide, fell from its hinges, and crashed to the floor. "*Pox!*" The men looked up to see Will, late as usual, standing in the rain in the open doorway. His clothes were mud-spattered and the papers he bore looked damp. "I did not wish the thing printed in any case, John Heminge," he said, shaking water from his hat. He shot a cold look at Cuthbert.

"We put it to the vote," Burbage said, shrugging. "You did not refuse your portion of the money it brought."

"Why should I have? And may we now repair this playhouse? Every third board on the scaffold is rotten." Will sat himself on the floor with the other players. They watched as he arranged a stack of closely overwritten papers before him. Next to it he placed a bound packet of scrolls. "No more of the rotten playhouse or the rotten printed *Richard Two*. I bring the *next* plays in the cycle, worked and reworked over years, I will say. I copied the part-scrolls for all. Burbage now is King Henry Four, and—ay, it burns me!" He blew on his hand. "A very *hot* new part for hot William Sly. Our moment is—"

"Not now."

Will threw Richard Burbage a surprised look. "Why not, pray? Henslowe made *Henry Six* come hard, part *one* and *two* and *three*, all in a week and then back to the start for the next. It garnered him hundreds three years ago." Will began to look glassy eyed. "*Hundreds*, it garnered him—"

"And you want your hundreds, and so does my brother, but there is something in this business that makes me skittish. Afeard." Richard looked questioningly at Will, as though Will could banish his unease, or explain it.

But it was Sly who spoke. "Dick is wise, fellows. I saw the queen's face as I sat on my throne." He rubbed his beard, still trim in its soldier's cut. "There we sat, I on my tin chair, she on her gold one, facing each other across the palace floor. When I seized King Richard's crown she gave me a look that froze my blood. 'Twas all I could do not to leap off the chair and say, 'Majesty, 'tis only our play, believe none of us! I am not Henry Bolingbroke, but plain William Sly! Usurping and murdering in jest!' "

Will laughed heartily.

" 'Tis no laughing matter." Sly scowled at him. "You make us your pawns. 'Twas I who bore that queen's stare, while you cowered behind the curtain."

"*Cowered?*" Will half-rose, not laughing now. Kempe, at his left, pulled him back to the floor, cautioning, "Enough, now, friend. There is remedy for this hullabaloo."

"What remedy?" asked Pope.

"A simple one." Kempe smiled widely. "Will must only go back to his room and write us a sweet comedy that will make our queen laugh and be flattered. With a dance and a fat part for me."

Will stared at the circle of men, who looked roundly pleased with the notion.

"So." He gathered up his papers and stood. "And when should this sweet play be done?"

"Ah." Cuthbert coughed. "Thursday next?"

Again he could not go home for Christmastide.

"ONLY a madman could find statecraft in this." Richard Burbage nodded his head approvingly, scanning his scroll for the twentieth time.

Will had provided a script in less than the time allotted, building on a thing he'd begun in Stratford, for his children. He was pale and hungry from six days of constant writing, spent locked up in his room. His right hand was dry from salt-water soaking, and it ached. Still, he found the spirit to smile at Burbage. "Do not be too sure," he said. "Some wise fellow from university might make Bottom the weaver the very figure of the English citizen, hard-working and borne down by vile oppression."

"E'en *magistri artium* could not be so foolish," said Kempe, trying on a dogskin ass's head. "They might as well say the elf-goddess is Queen Elizabeth!"

The players laughed long and hard.

CHRISTMAS was the occasion, Richmond Palace the place, and the Revels Office paid for all: the painted scene of the castle tower, the tinsel and taffeta robes for the fairies, even the donkey's head. In the grand chamber at the royal court, Will took care to look past his dancing pixies and the quarreling maidens, played by Nate Field and their new boy, Sander Cooke, a penniless urchin Burbage had found begging in the street. His ears drank their shouted verse insults—*back and forth, back and forth*—and the laughter that greeted each line. But his gaze was fixed on the queen.

She sat at the hall's far end on a raised throne, and because the assembled courtiers gave her their constant covert, nervous glances—*Doth she laugh? May we laugh?*—Will knew her for what she was, a rival show. Yet he was caught by her, and let himself breathe only when he saw her expression was pure delight. It had been no sure question, whether the queen would be happy to-night. She might have been restless, or even enraged. The issue had not been staged crownings, but staged clownings.

Which was to say, Will Kempe.

All crowds adored Kempe. In the public playhouses the yard gifted him with roars of laughter for doing no more than appearing on stage, grinning his lopsided grin and shaking his belled buskins. But the players feared him mightily. Despite Dick's and Will's constant warnings, he still took all opportunities to add lines of his own, not only to his speeches, but to those of other players. The men and boys preparing to enter the stage or already on it never knew what unscripted sally would confuse their cues, for when Kempe hooked a laugh he saw no reason not to angle for another one. And so he did, with an odd word like "Pickle!" or a spontaneous jig or a sudden, shouted declaration that he had on no small clothes, and would the yardlings like a view of his rosy red arse? Will had written the part of Bottom the weaver for Kempe alone, thinking here was a role big enough to accommodate any folly the clown might utter—even in front of the queen. But he sweated still.

And yet, for a mystery, on this night Kempe was a charmed thing. Finally given the freedom to speak as he would, the clown said what he was told to say, and no more. As Bottom, transformed to an ass by the fairies and then turned back into himself, Kempe was buffoonish, outrageous, riotous, and extravagant.

He was perfect.

When all was ended and Will readying himself for the changing chamber, he felt the hair on the back of his neck prickle. He turned to see the queen herself, approaching with two of her councilmen in tow. Still dressed in the shimmering robes of Oberon, he bowed deeply.

"The delightful work of thine own hand, I am told, Master Shakespeare," she said.

"My part was airy nothing, Your Majesty," he murmured. Then he raised his head and looked into her face.

She was sixty-two years old and slightly bent, and her teeth were black. She wore a red peruke whose falseness had been obvious even from the far side of the room where the players played. Her perfume was overpowering, and her face a parti-colored wonder: blue eyes rimmed with kohl, lips reddened with fucus, skin painted with white lead, cheeks dotted with ochre. Her breath smelled like an open grave. But her eyes were alive, eagle-sharp, and cunning beyond measure.

He felt an odd desire to spit in her face and then fall at her feet.

"I like thy comedies better than thine histories," she said with a sly smile, and shook her finger.

THE players had gone to stow props on the barge at the dock, and the makeshift tiring room off the grand hall was empty save for William Sly. Sly stood still in his tights, rolling and tying the last part-scrolls. He glanced briefly at Will, and nodded. Will stowed the parts in the bag. Next to him Sly stripped off his tights with a quick motion, then turned to the wall to don strossers and plain woolen breeches. *Uncommon modesty,* Will almost said, but something stayed his tongue. Looking carefully away from Sly, he doffed his elf-robe and put on his own woolen trunks, hose, and shirt.

"What of it?" Sly said softly behind him, as they left the room for the back exit to the river dock.

"I have no notion what you mean."

Sly caught Will's arm. "What *of* it?"

Will shrugged off Sly's arm and kept walking, but he glanced back at him and smiled. "Come, player. The boatman will leave us. I care nothing for your circumcised tool."

"And a good thing, because it is meant for women and not for you."

Will laughed. "And if you be a Jew—"

"A *converso.* My true name is Sanchez. My parents fled the Inquisition, but I was born here in London, and I am as good a member of the English Church as you."

"You are not a very good one, then. I miss two Sunday services a month to sleep. The fines grow costly, and still I do it." Will stopped and looked hard at Sly. "Do you fear me? If I care what you are, it is only because things interest me." His eyes clouded. "I knew a Jewess once . . ."

"Good for thee, Shakespeare. Get on." Sly pushed his shoulder and they walked again, passing through a high wooden door into the freezing night air. Palace guards stood to either side, and ahead of them Burbage, Augustine Phillips, and John Heminge strapped a bale of costumes to a flat boat. Burbage spotted Will and Sly and gestured impatiently. *Come help!* But Will stopped Sly again, before their voices could reach the guards' hearing.

"Wait," he said softly. "I have heard there are rituals, here in the city—"

"When we boil Christian babies and drink their blood?" Sly scoffed, blowing on his hands, then rubbing them impatiently in the cold. "And you would spy through the window, would you not?"

"I am not an idiot. My play of the Jew was meant to mock such wrong—"

"If your play of the Jew was meant to mock such wrong notions you would not have let a monster play the Jew."

Will frowned. "Gabriel Spencer is not a monster."

"Red-haired, one-eyed, scar-faced—"

"He is not handsome like you. I grant that."

Sly laughed. "*Hath not a Jew eyes?* And he only had one! The audience laughed."

Will's face burned, though in the dark Sly could not see it. "That was not intended," Will said. "Not foreseen."

Chapter Twenty-three

IT was nearly dawn when Will reached his room, but he lay awake for another hour, tossing. The moon shone full through his window. In his mind he tried to replace Sly's remembered glare with the picture of Kempe's face. In time he was successful, and lost himself in images of the clown hee-hawing, cavorting on the floor of the palace hall, shaking his donkey's ears. And he saw the queen's mouth, gaping with black laughter, as the clown said:

> I have had a dream, past the wit of man to say what dream
> it was. . . .
> It shall be called Bottom's Dream, because it hath no bottom.

Will blinked his eyes, and saw Elizabeth's face, close to his own. *I like thy comedy better than thine histories.* And it came to him, how he would thwart her. "I take thy meaning," he muttered to his mattress. "Yet thou shalt have histories enow. I will give thee a big fat sweet pill of comedy to swallow, but thou shalt not escape my histories."

When next he went home to Stratford he took with him the full text of *A Midsummer Night's Dream,* stuffed deep in the bottom of his saddlebag. "For the children," he told Anne.

"YOU know what I am after with you." With a foot Will banged shut the lid of a costume trunk, then sat on it.

"Do I need to know?"

"It would help us if you knew. So know that you are not wholly bad, and that your friend the prince is not wholly good. You are drunk and dishonest, but in the end it is royalty who has ruined you, not the other way around."

John Lowin, their newest sharer, knit his forehead in a puzzled frown. "How?"

"By making you believe a king could love commoners."

"I am no commoner in this play. I am a knight."

"But a common one, as knights do go. A dirty one."

Lowin sat back in his chair and loosened his doublet, sighing. "Marry, I may not need your padding. I have been downing roast capons and cream cakes since Christmas."

"Good! Now, the prince is at odds with his father, but he desires greatly to please him. His father has been much absent—"

Lowin wrinkled his forehead. "Our script makes the king complain that the *prince* is much absent." Lowin leaned over to tap Will's arm. "Will?"

"What is't?" Will turned his gaze from the window to Lowin. "The prince, as I say, uses you as a tool. He will swallow you and then spew you forth in our last scene."

"Oh, disgusting."

"Aye."

Lowin sat frowning.

"What is the matter?" Will asked.

"This is a part that might go to Kempe. I like not to nettle the cl—"

"No," Will said quickly and firmly. "Not him. I cannot trust him in a part of this magnitude."

Lowin nodded. "Well." He half-rose, then paused. "Why do you name me for a Puritan?"

"You will have a kind of popular zeal."

Lowin smirked. "Oh, I will, sir. I will indeed."

ON the twentieth of April, 1596, *Henry the Fourth* was mounted on the stage of the rented Swan Theater in Southwark. On April twenty-fifth, amid an explosion of public complaining, the Lord Chamberlain's Men pulled it from the stage.

"Marry, I *told* you, you *cannot* call the man Oldcastle," Burbage said to Will in vexation, over a meal of onion and venison stew in the George. "John Oldcastle's been near canonized by the Puritans. An English knight who defied the pope! If they honored saints, they'd have made him one. We cannot present him as a fat, thieving drunkard!"

"But this is a different Oldcastle," Will said through his mouthful of bread. "This one *is* a fat, thieving drunkard."

"*Will.* Will you tell that to the man's descendants? They are wealthy. They will have us shut down. Further, none of us will do it. Kempe is angry already since we did not ask him to play the fat knight and he says he will not go back to jail for such as thee."

"Well enough, well enough." Will put down his knife. "I cannot fight with a quinsy pale mammety wimpet such as *you*—"

"A *what,* say you?"

"—all of my days. Name the fat knight as you like. No! Wait."

Will narrowed his eyes. "The knight is a false king. A false king, but a true master of the revels—not one such as the present spoilsport, who censors our every other line before it reaches the audience. Our knight is a *jolly* king of the revels with a false scepter, a false staff. Call him *that.*"

Burbage frowned. "I never understand thee. Call him *what?*"

BEHIND a curtain at Greenwich Palace in late May, Will handed out the long scrolls. "O'erlook them once more, brothers. Dick, King Henry Four. John Heminge, Prince Hal. Welsh wizard, me, of a certainty. And Sly—where art thou? Here. The noble Hotspur. Fight, fight, and *pluck bright honor from the pale-faced moon!*"

Sly snatched his part. "Marry, I know the role," he said with ritual sullenness. But his eyes were busy on the script.

"Now I will cower behind the curtain, and let us begin." Will made his voice bold before the men, but when out of their sight and hearing behind the stretched tarpaulin, he whispered a prayer. *"Great I-amb, let her laugh at it."*

He had reason to fear.

He knew that Burbage, for all his worries about the queen and the censors and bishops and nobles and lords and Puritans, on stage could not fail to stress the subtlest, most dangerous nuances of the words. It was not Will's poetry Dick feared, but his own voice saying it. Will pitied him.

But there was nothing to be done about it.

Now Burbage held all their safeties in his hand as, there in the royal hall, he began to speak of how he, King Henry the Fourth, had compassed the crown. Not with lineal right. Not even with strength and valor.

With a show.

The men would tell their children, "This is he!"
Others would say, "Where? Which is Bolingbroke?"
And then I stole all courtesy from heaven,
And dressed myself in such humility
That I did pluck allegiance from men's hearts
Loud shouts and salutations from their mouths
Even in the presence of the crownéd king.

Widening his eyes, looking excitedly about him, Burbage played the common folk even as he described them. As he told his princely son what the prince had to know: *how to secure a throne.*

From his perch behind the curtain Will looked at the queen, whose eagle eyes were trained on Burbage. He knew Burbage felt her eyes, but Burbage did not quake or throttle his wind.

She was good, the queen.

But Burbage was the greatest actor in the world.

AFTER the scene Burbage was furious. He approached Will in the neighbor room where the players scurried to change, and addressed him in a fierce whisper. "Did you *note* her? Does she not think you meant *her?* Exiled to the Tower by her sister Mary? Now earning our loves bowing and waving on a once-a-year royal progress?"

"But I said nothing against such progresses. The shows are bonny. They please people, and they also please me."

Burbage crushed his crown in his hand, and immediately set to straightening it, muttering, "I should have stopped it. I should—"

"Dick!" Will grabbed his shoulders. "You are King Richard the Third and King Henry Four but you are *not* the king of this company. And you may think me a fool, but 'twas not for nothing that I put our fat Falstaff next. List." A gale of laughter swept over them from the hall. "List!"

"Is *she* laughing?"

Will peered through the door, then looked back at him, exuberant. "She howls with it!"

YET there were rough waters still to come. The queen congratulated him afterwards, and praised Sir John Falstaff especially. But as Will smiled and bowed, she put a barbed question: "What meant you, Master Shakespeare, by King Henry's lines? About public opinion smoothing the way to the crown?"

"Your Majesty." Will's answer was prepared. "I drew on Plutarch's *Life of Pericles of Athens* for the king's speech. 'Tis not, in essence, mine." He bowed again. His Welsh wizard's robes swept the marble floor with a satisfying swish, and he bowed still another time.

"Ah," said the queen craftily. "You drew on the Latin?"

"North's translation, Majesty. My Latin, I fear, is not up to the learned standard set by our gracious queen." He was enjoying himself very much. He bowed a fourth time.

"Indeed," said Elizabeth, looking at him with adder's eyes. "I shall search out the reference. In the Latin." She turned, then looked back at him suddenly. "And I have a command. Write a whole play of fat Falstaff! He deserves a comedy. Make him fall in love!"

Will stood with a frozen grin. This time Burbage had to prod him to bow.

John Lowin approached from behind, discreetly pulling a pillow from under his doublet. "What think you of that?" he murmured.

"I think it's poxed," Will said. "I'm done with Falstaff."

"Oh, no, you are not." Burbage joined Lowin in a theatrical laugh, hollow, cackly, and villainous. "It seems you are not, Welsh wizard."

But Will paid small attention, for his eye had been snagged by a scene unfolding across the room.

Covered in red and gold, Elizabeth was moving, heavily attended, toward a doorway wide enough to accommodate three farthingales. Near the door stood a lone, silk-clad gentleman, his blond locks reaching past his shoulders, his chin hidden behind a bushy "Cádiz" beard, worn longish, in the style London men had favored since Essex's great victory over that Spanish city. The gentleman knelt and bowed.

The queen ignored him.

As she disappeared through the door, head high and eyes set forward, a murmur swept the watching courtiers. It died away as in twos and threes they rushed to follow the queen. The kneeling man stayed as he was until her train was well departed. Then he jumped to his feet, smiled, turned, and bowed deeply to Will. *"When in disgrace with Fortune and men's eyes . . ."*

Will's robe billowed behind as he ran to him.

Chapter Twenty-four

WHEN Henry freed himself from Will's embrace he was laughing. Will's own face was contorted, and he was blinking as fast as he could, but he conquered himself, and not a tear fell. "O friend that I have not deserved—" he began.

Henry held up his hand. "I think it best for me to make my way from these palace rooms. You saw what just passed. And for thee it might be best to go back to thy fellows."

"I will walk with thee," Will said, and they went hastily through the now almost empty hall to the echoing corridors beyond.

Henry told him of the queen's quarrel with him. A foolish matter, a drunken game of cards that went on too long in her presence chamber, with Sir Walter Raleigh a party to it. This added to the trouble, as Raleigh was a man the queen liked not. The Squire of Attendance had ordered them all to leave and Henry had hit the fellow. "A bad-brained idea. I have been *rusticated.*"

He smiled grimly. "Sent back to the country, for my ill behavior. I arranged these revels to regain her good graces. I cannot say the scheme played out as I hoped."

"Had I known 'twas your doing, I'd have written a frothier play. *Henry Four* has probably plunged you in deeper trouble." Will darted a glance at Henry's Cádiz beard. "Thy soldiering with Essex, in the Azores—"

"A masterful man. One with brave visions of . . . you shall meet him, one day."

Will looked thoughtful. "I have heard of these visions. Paying common soldiers what gentlemen get? Perhaps it is dangerous to know him."

"Ah, well." Henry smiled. "Dangers must be brooked in the service of truth. And Essex represents a certain truth that his soldiers find—marry, they find it bracing, and so do I, but I can speak no more of the matter in the queen's very palace." He spoke low. "I have at any rate another secret to hide from the queen."

Queen's soldiers lined the doorways they now passed. Will put a hand on Henry's arm until they were clear and past the final portal, and outside at the start of a tree-lined path to the river. There they stopped, shaded and half-hidden by poplars and elms. The day was cloudy, and torches lit the upper rooms from whence they had come. Looking back, Will could see Kempe in a glittering suit of woven silver stitched with a hundred tiny mirrors. Light bounced from the clown as he and another player pranced past the open windows with sticks in their hands and hobbyhorses tacked to their middles, playing at Christians and Moors. The cheers and laughter of the courtiers drifted down on the wind.

"Thy pied clown." Henry gestured briefly toward the windows. "He makes trouble."

"I know it."

" 'Twas he who fetched thee out of my house, with his Siren

tales of the playhouses, though you pretended something else made you go."

"Ah—yes."

"I let your half-cooked fancy stand, Will. It gave you license to do what you wanted; to go back to London. I will not waste breath telling you there was nought between me and the lady Emilia, because you know it already." He shook his shaggy blond head. "Beloved poet, you blow fantasies into life! You build them from a stray look, a thin gesture, from airy—"

Will stopped him with an embarrassed wave of his hand. "I cannot help it. Forgive me."

"There's nought to forgive, but I fear for you. Out of nothing you dream reasons to flee those who . . . care for you. You may do it again, to your peril."

A breeze stirred Will's wizard robe. He had forgotten he wore it, and now laughed half-heartedly, glancing at his sleeve.

Henry looked closely at him. "You wish to know where she is, but I—"

"Pray do not tell me," Will said quickly.

"Friend, I could not if I would. She read your sonnets and then she, too, left Titchfield. I do not know for whence. And the sonnets—"

"Methought you came off well in them," Will said lightly. He still looked askance, toward the river, and then at the trees, not meeting Henry's candid and too-lovely blue eyes.

"My own secret does not interest you, I see."

"Ah." Now Will looked at him sideways, curious. "It does. Tell it me."

"I have gotten the lady Elizabeth Vernon with child and must marry her."

For a moment Will was speechless with mingled jealousy and shock and relief.

"Bessie," he finally said. "Bessie. At the Earl of Oxford's manor, in cap and breeches."

"Nay, right here in her bed in the palace, and as for her gear, she wore nothing at all. Does my news surprise you?"

"A little. A . . . touch. I did not think you—"

"Had the will to put a woman to the squeak? This despite your fond fancies of me and your dark lady. A fine jest, Will! Wise you are, but you do not know all about everyone. Now this thing has happened, and my mother is sanguine, but you know our queen does not like such—events—among her ladies-in-waiting." Henry smiled. " 'Tis an odd thing. I have known Bessie since childhood, and suddenly I find I would die for her. Is't not strange?"

"This is called love."

"And soon I shall test what you wrote for me in your poems, of the blessings of children."

"Yes! May you have a son! A son is the greatest of gifts. Let me see, mine is—" Will rubbed his brow perplexedly. "He is ten, or eleven—"

"Son, daughter, I care not. Ah, Will! Love—can you even begin to describe it?"

"Yes, I can. A little more than begin, I think."

They walked to the river, where the earl's private boat waited. His plan, Henry said, was to wed Bessie and flee to France until the queen's displeasure abated, and until Essex returned to England. "But I can speak no more of Essex," he cautioned.

"I think you can speak of little else but Essex, and Bessie," said Will. "But I will turn the tiller of your dangerous discourse. You bade me not thank you. But thank you I will, and never can according to your deserts, for—"

The boatman pushed off just then at the earl's signal, and Henry waved his cap at Will. "Enough," he cried. "Repay me by showing England *truth* on thy stage." From the middle of the Thames he cupped his hands to add, "As you did today!"

"I am not as sure as you what a single truth might be," Will murmured, bowing to him from the shore. He turned to walk back to the palace. As he did, Hamnet's pale face flitted, mothlike, through his mind, and was gone. He stopped, tapping his finger on the bark of an elm tree in brief distraction. *Ten, or eleven?*

AS the weather grew hotter the plague began to return. With news of the deaths of families came equally horrid news of the beheader, still loose in London and leaving trunks of bodies in odd places, from taverns to gentlemen's houses.

So the rumor ran.

"We will take to the road," Burbage told Will. "I long to see the Oxford youth who has your picture in miniature on his wall. 'Sweet Master Shakespeare,' you are called there, in honor of *Romeo and Juliet.*"

"So I got into university after all," said Will.

But the sharers voted to take the low road, south to Maidstone and Canterbury and Dover and Hastings. So they tramped eastward, Will rising each morning to view the folk of each new town, and coming back when packing for the new day's walk was well underway. One Sunday in Dover he heard a pastor preach against players, and when he came back to camp he asked Burbage why the Ancient Greeks had a sacred playing festival but the English did not.

Dick said nothing, but Kempe said that Will's question brought another to mind, which was, why was Will not to be found when tents were being folded and stowed? Will asked Kempe whether that was the question rhetorical or the taunt base, and Kempe said Will might take it as he would. Will said he'd not take it at all from such a clown, and said further that he knew Kempe had been doing his gargle again because his breath smelled like old Saturn's sweaty socks. And had he mentioned, friendly in Kempe's ear, that he'd been an inch from killing him last night, for his snoring? At that Kempe offered to grace Will's buttocks with a sharp jingling shoe, and blows nearly flew, but all was forgotten when Burbage said the promptbook for *Richard the Third* was not to be found.

Nathan Field was told to go look for the book in the wagon among the parts, where he'd stowed them. Field gave the masters a blank look and asked what meant they, where *he'd* stowed them? Then they all erupted in a frenzy of searching and tore apart the hampers, scattering props and playbooks, but no one could find the play.

"The stars last night warned of a mishap," said Kempe, who had taken to reading astrology and muttering at the moon as they walked. But the rest of the men said nay, and Will said that the stars knew nothing. "An odd thing for you to claim," said Kempe, "since we have all heard otherwise in a play called *Romeo and Juliet.*" At this Will called the clown a pied ninny and an airy-headed nitwit who could never grasp that a play was a play. Again they were ready to jump at each other, full fiercer than before, but Burbage and Augustine Phillips held them apart, reminding them that the parts were in *London* and this play was promised in *Hastings* and their memories could not be trusted without a prompt-text. They needed a script for *Richard the Third.*

In the end they could think of nothing else but for Will to ride in the wagon and write the play again, from start to finish. The players yelled out their lines to him, back and forth, as they remembered them, and Will corrected them and scribbled it all down and changed the lines when he saw fit, while Kempe grumbled that Will would do anything for a ride in the wagon.

So the play was rewritten. Yet their troubles went on. When they reached Hastings they found another group of players had come there before them, calling themselves William Shakespeare's Men, and claiming as patron one Sir Gamaliel Ratsey. As they entered the town the imposters were staging a vile version of *A Midsummer Night's Dream* in the market square. The Lord Chamberlain's Men watched it, aghast. Kempe was outraged at their knavish Bottom and the lines the villainous player was so bold as to add to Will's script, which was not, in truth, Will's script at all. It took an afternoon of wrangling with the town council to get the false players run out on a rail, and by then half the Lord Chamberlain's Men were ill with a flux caught from eating green grapes on the road. The sickness brought their strength to four, two of them only boys, and since Burbage was down and none but he could play King Richard, the play they at last presented was a strange one indeed.

" 'Twas much like a Greek tragedy," Kempe told the sick players after. "Messengers racing on to report what had been said offstage. And always the same messengers." He bit into a peach, and offered the rest to Burbage, who lay moaning by a bush and ignored him.

"*Oedipus Rex, sans* Oedipus," groaned Will.

"Very like! It began well, with my speech to Hastings—Nate played Hastings, wearing the highest chopines, you know—*Methinks I have just now heard Richard of Gloucester complaining that the winter of our discontent was made glorious summer by this son of York,* and so on. Methinks I got all of it in. Next, Lady Anne—Nate again, to be sure—concluded all on her own that Richard might not be such a trout, though he did kill her husband, and that peradventure she'd ask him for his ring—"

"I beg thee, no more," Will gasped, clutching his abdomen.

They recovered, and were on their way back to London the

next day. Kempe was good friends with Will again, and walked with him to Bishopsgate. Along the way Will opened the letters that had come to the Theater in his absence. Kempe chattered happily, waving his orange tawny sleeves in pure delight that the plague numbers had stayed low and the Theater had not had to close while they were on the road. So the players who had braved London had made them money at home while they made money away.

"Full houses, Old Burbage said, e'en with no Dick on stage!" Kempe crowed. "We may dine on roast pheasant this week, if we like! What's the matter?"

Will was standing stock still in the middle of Shoreditch High Street, gazing blankly at a paper in his hand. Kempe gripped his shoulder. "Will?"

"My son," Will said. "My son is dead."

Chapter Twenty-five

TREES, hills, and roadside inns slipped past like an endless painting, viewed from the corner of an eye. The sun was bright, though thin scrolls of papery cloud hung in the sky. The grainfields were green. Lodged in the corner of a roadside birch a hiveful of wasps lay sleeping in their grey, fragile cage. Dully Will wondered and sneered at his mind, that went on with its busy observations while his heart lay crushed and still. He hated the wasps, hated the irksome light, hated the day, hated himself. . . .

He had no need for haste. The boy was buried. His horse's hooves thudded on the sun-baked thoroughfare, rhythmically, numbingly.

My son. My sun. My son.

HE came into the house in the late afternoon. He passed through the kitchen and into the empty parlor, where he stood for a moment, looking at the shafts of sun that lit the clean wood floor, and the dust-motes that swam in the light. He took off his cap and rubbed his hair, which was damp from the sweat of summer riding.

The stair creaked, and he looked up.

For a moment he did not know her. She was thin and drawn, and her hair was more tightly bound under her cap than ever he'd seen it. But that was not it. What was new was the look on her face. He had seen her affectionate, peeved, ardent, laughing, furious. But never before had he seen Anne look at him with indifference.

As though he were strange, and did not belong to her.

It undid him, and he turned away.

His father entered from the Woolery, limping on a bad leg. "Ah, son," he said. Will went to his embrace. Crying, John held him, and Will's body shook with sobs. But the sobs were dry.

A drowning it was, the letters had said. Anne had little to add to what Will's sister Joan had written. A mad midnight game with his twin sister. They had swum in the Avon, risen high and fast-rushing with the summer rains. The boy had gone under, and had not come up.

"And Judith?"

Anne knew he was not asking whether the girl's body had been harmed. She gestured toward the window, the one close to the buttery bar in the kitchen where they both sat.

Will leaned to pull the curtain. He saw Judith at the edge of their garden, crouched like a boy on the ground, her knees jutting from under her smock. Strands of unruly hair poked from her untied cap. She was listlessly scratching a stick into the soft soil. He watched her for several minutes, until she suddenly looked toward him, seeming to feel his stare. But when their eyes met she quickly let hers fall, back to the earth she was digging.

"Our neighbors will see her." Will's mother, Mary Arden, had come into the room from the parlor, bearing some fresh-baked bread, made for Anne by one of the Arden sisters. "My gossips—"

"I will let her be, madam." Anne's voice was sharp.

Mary drew in her breath, but said nothing. She put down the loaf and left, as Anne nodded thanks.

Will let the window curtain fall.

HE visited his son's small grave every day of a stay that stretched out for weeks. Some days he rode his horse to the boarded Arden manor, and once he dropped over a wall, now thickly overgrown with honeysuckle vines, into the ruined garden. For an hour he weeded and pruned branches. The statue of Mary still stood by the well, her hands palm up, asking Heaven for blessing; her feet poised as though she might any moment step to the ground from her stone base. Will glanced at her from time to time, and wondered what it had been like to be her, and have a son come back to life.

When rain started to fall he climbed back over the wall and went home.

The next morning he left the house early and came back with two clumps of honeysuckle. He put one clump in a bowl on Anne's kitchen table, tucked the second in his shirt, and left the house again. As he rounded the corner he heard the front window open. Anne put her head out. "Will."

He came to the ledge. Her eyes were gentle. She put her hand to his cheek.

"So you know me?" he said softly.

She gave him a faint smile. He took her hand and squeezed it, then kissed it lightly and walked into the street.

Within a quarter of an hour he was in Holy Trinity Churchyard. When he came close to Hamnet's grave, he was surprised to see that the plot was marked already this morning, graced with three cut lilies. He knelt down, placing his own spray of flowers on the mound, and looked curiously at the lilies. They had been cut with garden shears. He stood suddenly, sensing eyes watching him, and looked to his left. The shape of a man was moving away from the graveyard through the trees and down to the river.

He watched the spot where he'd seen him for a long time after he disappeared.

He did not go home, but rode again through the forest, sometimes dismounting to walk, sometimes stopping by streams or, once, by the river to rest, but always thinking. After dark fell he came home and mounted the stairs to his bedroom. He closed the door hard behind him.

Anne was fetching her nightcap from the cherrywood chest where she kept her clothes. She paused with the cap in her hand and looked at him, startled.

"Thou art perfect without me, art not, Anne Hathaway?" he said, with quiet fury.

Fear crossed her face, but she said calmly, "Explain thyself."

"He chops wood for thee and hunts game for thee and keeps thee company in the nights too, I would guess."

She sat on the bed and folded her arms. Stubbornly silent, she met his gaze.

"Ah, she will say nothing. I will say for her. He drinks all his money and cannot get a wife, and why should he? Since you are so glad as to—"

"Now you are cruel. I will not say you are cuckolded, but you would deserve it if you were."

"So. This is the game."

"Do you deny it?"

He said nothing, staring at her with an unfathomable look in his grey eyes. Then suddenly those eyes darkened, and he slapped his hand hard against the bed. She drew herself back in alarm, her nightgown white against the dark wood of the headboard, the carved Eden.

"I have sinned. In my loneliness I have sinned. But to be a cuckold in mine own house?" he hissed, leaning close to her. "To pay mourning duties for a son who may not be mine *own?*"

"What matter any of that, now he is gone? All of us loved him!"

She was weeping now, and he grabbed her shoulders. "Tears are a woman's weapon meant to blind my eyes, but I can see. I see the pair of you, paddling palms and pinching fingers. I have seen it for years. Even in this house of mourning I have seen it!"

"You are mad with grief, and so you accuse me," she sobbed, hardly able to talk. "I could accuse you—I have lost two children, one dead and one with a heart destroyed, and for *you* they are gone—"

"What mean you by this dodge?" he said angrily, shaking her. "*I* am to blame for this horror?"

She shook her head in agony. "God must help me. I cannot live blaming you, but I do." Her voice turned suddenly pleading. "Will, cast not thine anger at me. Can we speak of this—"

"So you dodge me with your riddling talk. My son is dead. There is nought more to be said of my son. I am speaking of you and my brother. Should I prove to you which of us is your husband?" He pressed hard against her, knocking the bedside candlestand to the floor, crushing her lungs. "Should I do that?"

"No!" She pushed at him violently, and he released her quickly, saying, "Ah. You do not want me, then."

She lay still, her head against the pillow, crying softly now. "You—twist—everything from its proper—shape."

He banged the door shut and went fast down the stairs. In his rush in the dark he did not see the slim figure pressed against the wall outside the bedroom. The child was wide-eyed and shaking with fear. Cautiously, she opened the door her father had slammed, and peeked inside the room. One candle still burned in the window, above the cradle that had once held her, that had held her sister once, and her brother, but had stood empty at the foot of her parents' bed for years. She was terrified at the strange sound of her mother's sobs, as Anne lay on the huge oaken bed with her face to the wall. The girl stood for a moment, frozen. Then Anne turned, drying her tears with her sleeve, and held out her hand. Softly she said, "Susanna."

BEFORE two more days had passed Will was saddling the horse he had bought in London for the journey to Stratford. Now he readied it for his return. He had kissed his sleeping daughters and bidden farewell to his parents, and now he put the bread and cold mutton and cheese Anne had given him into his saddlebags, and filled a skin with water, telling her he knew brooks to stop at on the way *home*. At the door to their house he gave her all the money he had, except what he needed for the journey. He clasped her stiffly for a moment and she made a motion to hold him, but she arrested it after the merest touch, and let her arms fall back to her apron. She looked at him as she had looked at him on the day he came weeks ago, as though she had heard of him, but did not know him.

Will kissed her cheek and made his face into a mask of pleasantness. He mounted his horse, and bade the neighbors good morrow and farewell as he rode down Henley Street. Then he rounded a corner and was gone.

Anne stood looking after him until she heard Gilbert's step close behind her. Without turning she reached back to him and clasped his hand.

Chapter Twenty-six

THE priest of Saint Saviour's Church was snuffing the high altar candles in the chancel when he heard a cough, and turned. At the corner of the transept stood a hooded man, barely visible in the dusky light that filtered through the high windows. "A word with you, sir priest." The man's voice was rough.

The priest left the last high candle burning. "What dost thou wish, my friend?"

"The rite of confession."

The priest frowned. After a moment he said, "It is not . . . well regarded."

The man was silent.

"It is a Romish practice. I am none of the precise godly, who think we do not hate Rome enough. But all of Her Majesty's subjects must hate Rome—"

"I do not." The voice was now a ghostly whisper. "Not Rome or Wittenberg or Geneva. I only want to confess my sins."

"The General Confession—"

"My sins are specific."

"We might speak face-to-face."

"No." The answer was quick. "I would not be seen."

The priest looked carefully around. There was no one else in the church. "Well enough," he said. "Follow."

At the far edge of the transept stood a dusty confessional. The priest seated himself inside with a rustle of skirts, and pulled the screen. The altar candle did not throw its beams this far, and the booth was dark.

The man entered and knelt beside the screen. "I have never confessed and I do not know the words," he said.

"That does not matter. I offer no sacrament. Only tell me what you would say."

"I have sinned."

"What have you done?"

"The act of darkness and the sin of Cain."

The priest shifted nervously. "Let us take each sin in turn, so please you, and less poetry in the telling of them. We will start with the last. You have killed your brother?"

"Nay, not him. *That* would be nothing."

"Well, hardly noth—"

"I have killed my uncle and my son."

The priest drew in his breath. "Those are grievous crimes. How is it that you walk free?"

"The violence was done by executioners and by nature. The negligence was mine."

The priest exhaled. "When by our faults we hasten others' destruction, our souls are sore charged. But God, to whom violence and murder were done, forgives all, including His murderers. You must pray and seek His grace and His solace." The priest paused. "And the—act of darkness?"

"Adultery, sir. With a particular lady, and occasional whores since."

"Ah. That you must first confess to your wife."

"But she guesses it, I am sure. And I think she is doing it too."

"Then tell *her* to come to me. Friend—" The priest's voice had grown exasperated. "Do you, i'truth, want the rite of confession?"

"I wish to lay down my burden."

"Then, reminding you that I am not Christ, I will tell you what Christ tells the fallen. Go, and sin no more."

They said the Our Father together. The priest gave him no penance.

HE bought Anne the biggest house in Stratford. He had money enough, and Anne was glad to accept this visible mark of her marriedness. She was as rich as a gentlewoman now. When she moved to New Place with her daughters she scrubbed the house up and down and sent to Coventry for damask curtains and oak furnishings. From Henley Street she transported her Paradise bed with its image of threatened Eden. She bought some sheep and began to raise wool.

Gilbert came to her after his hours in the Woolery. He worked in the garden in the evenings and when it was dark he drank ale and wine on the new settle in the parlor. He tried not to spill his ales, but when he grew blear-eyed he did spill them, and Anne railed at him like a wife.

WILL visited at Lent, when the playhouses closed for six weeks. He came home to find his new parlor filled with Anne's gossips and an Oxford swain who thought he might court Susanna. Will invited the youth to return in five years. Yet Susanna, he saw, was beginning to look full womanly and wise, not just in her form but in her eyes, which seemed more than fourteen. She looked at her father with a pity he tried to misunderstand.

Judith was in Coventry, in the house of a sister of Anne's.

Gilbert stayed in Henley Street that season.

For three days Will kept distance from Anne, writing behind a closed door in his new, spacious study. He slept there at night.

At the end of the week he looked at the leaded glass windows that gave from the study into the garden. The candle burned behind him, and he saw his image multiplied by the diamond panes, sent back to him thirtyfold. For a minute he gazed at his selves.

Then he blew out the taper and went up the stairs to knock on his wife's door.

She opened it a crack and peered at him.

He gazed at her somberly.

"Hast come to visit thy whore?" she asked.

"Aye."

She grew hot. "Ne'er was I—" She broke off suddenly, and sighed. "Ah, come thou in."

The day after Easter he was gone.

That afternoon Susanna came to her mother in the garden. Rain was starting to fall in fat drops, but Anne still bent, furiously weeding a patch of earth where the new Holland bulbs were beginning to grow. "These tulips are worth gold," she said, throwing crabgrass in a basket. "I'll not have them choked."

"Madam." Susanna knelt by her side. "I am old enough to know now."

"To know what, girl?" She clucked her tongue in disgust. "But look ye, this bulb's turned black and never sprouted. A bane and a murrain! I'll be dragged by horses ere I'll buy another time from—"

"*Mama.* I am saying I am old enough to know of what happened last summer, when—the night you and my—and my—"

"Father."

"When you quarreled. And you said it was not a thing for me to ask, but I am a woman last month, and have had a suitor already, and so—"

"Your parentage is nought to be ashamed of." Anne glanced at her daughter, smiling wryly. "Though you came into this world something unlooked for, I am married to your father."

Susanna let her breath out slowly. Then she said, "And the tw—and Judith?"

"He is Judith's father too."

She kept weeding, and Susanna stayed still, watching her. After a moment Anne said, "Do not only sit there idling. Help me, if you must plague me with questions." Her tone was gentler than her words.

Susanna tugged at a blade of coarse grass, which broke off in her hand. "He thinks you have betrayed him," she said, a question in her voice.

Anne stopped troweling grass then, and looked Susanna in the face. "Let us speak it, then, once, and no more. Last summer you heard what you should not have. But since you cannot cease to dwell on it, I will tell you thy father dreams what suits his fancy, and I do what suits my life. Thine uncle and I are fast friends, and if we have come near to sin in the past, the thing was—avoided."

Anne's cheeks grew hot at the memory of the Christmas Night in Henley Street when, merry with wine and lonely for Will's body in bed beside her, she had gone in the dark to the room where Gilbert slept. Soused with ale, he had kissed and caressed her, then called her the name of a woman in the town. At that she'd pulled back from him, and within a minute he had gone to sleep. She'd crept back to her bed taking care not to wake her children, and the next day Gilbert had smiled jovially at her at his late breakfast, clearly remembering none of it.

"My own brother Hathaway cares little for me, Susanna," she

said now. "Nor did he ever, much. He wants lands and money, and once feared he might have to keep me on my father's farm. I have a kinder brother now. And a brother's love is a precious—" She stopped, seeing Susanna's look. "What is't, girl?"

Her daughter wiped her eyes. "I am sorry for Judith."

"Ah." Anne was quiet, watching the girl's face. When Susanna composed herself, Anne said, "There is love between Gilbert and me, but not of the sort thou fearest."

"Doth my father know this now?" Susanna said. "Doth he—"

Anne quieted her with a gesture. "Doth he know?" She rose, dusting her apron. Her face was sad. "He does not wish to know," she said. "He must blame me for something. When he faces himself, he sees things he cannot bear." She held her hand out to her daughter, helping her to rise. "He thinks he is something horrible. So he looks at himself askance, as though he were someone else."

WILL boarded a coach bound from Stratford to London, thinking he might write while journeying. But the carriage bounced violently, and so tight-packed was he among four other passengers that to wield a pen was impossible. After the wagon wheel had thrice crashed into a ditch, sending ink flying from his jar to his face, Will bundled his gear into his bag and sat still, composing in his head. That exercise was cut short when, twenty miles south of Oxford, the coach was stopped and robbed by a masked highwayman. The knave wore military scarves about his neck. He was a lover of verse, and finding Will's ink, pen, and play-draft in his bag, he praised him as a poet, and asked his name.

"Herod," said Will.

The highwayman laughed. "Well answered. Dost know, thou resemblest William Shakespeare, though thou hast fewer hairs on thy head. Thou couldst play him! I met Master Shakespeare himself last summer. He was on the road to Hastings with his actors, bound to play *A Midsummer Night's Dream*. I gave him some coin and my patronage. Sir Gamaliel Ratsey am I. A self-knighting. Come. The timepiece, fellow."

Will gave him his gold chronometer, listening as the man justified the theft because of his service at Cádiz. "I climbed o'er the sides of the men-o'-war, fighting sword to sword!" he bragged. "Was accounted a hero! But they did not pay us common soldiers. Gentles alone got stipends and booty. Brave Essex wished to reward us, but the pay ne'er reached us. Now I rob gentry, and give the money to the poor. Which is to say, to me. I have written a poem of it, an heroic amatory lyric. It begins, *Come live with me and be my love, and I'll not smite thee with my glove . . .*"

When the man finally freed the passengers and their driver, they were less frightened than dulled by the tedium of it all. Will slept the rest of the way to London.

HE paced back and forth between the pillars of the rented stage of the Curtain, where they'd played since Thomas Pope dropped through one of the Theater's floorboards during an afternoon performance of *A Midsummer Night's Dream*.

Burbage barked at a young actor. "Do not tug at your ear when you stand at attention. You are still visible even when you are not talking. And cease putting your back to the crowd and playing to the lords' rooms, lad. I don't care that they have more money."

" 'Tis that they've *paid* more, Master Burb—"

" 'Tis that you fear the stinkards' fruit. But you'll get it worse if you slight those in the yard."

Ignoring them, Will paced and said, "Hmm."

Sweating in shirtsleeves, Burbage swore an oath, then commissioned a boy to bring him a wet rag. Behind him, against the stage wall, stood a flag emblazoned with the English royal crest still used by Queen Elizabeth. Along with a rampant lion it included the French *fleur-de-lis,* as though to picture a conquest was all that was needed to bring one into being. The boy brought the rag, and Burbage pushed back his metal beaver and mopped his face. He leaned on his wooden pike. "What, now, Will?"

"There is a thing missing from the scene." Will tapped his forehead.

"Great King Henry hath given his speech before Agincourt. All that is left is valiant fighting with our ragged swords, and you to gloss all when you speak between the acts."

Will still paced, tapping his brow.

" 'Tis well as it is, man. This will buy us some sufferance of thine other histories. Elizabeth cannot complain of this. Here is a bold English monarch, all-praised and perfect."

"His soul is sore-charged with ancient sin. He thinks himself guilty of murder."

"Well, he is not." Burbage threw his beaver to the floor. "He is not guilty of murder. Only *you* could think so. We must get on with it."

"Aye, we must," said Sly. He and Heminge knelt on the floor. They were feigning to be French prisoners, and Will had tied their hands behind their backs. "This rope chafes," said Heminge, "and these boards are not sanded."

"He has killed all the English boys," Will said.

"The *French* have killed all the boys," Burbage said.

"He has killed all the English boys. He brought them to the battle."

"Very good. He has killed all the English boys. May we rehearse?"

"Do you think the queen will not see that he has killed all the English boys?"

"I think she will not. And that is as we wish it."

"Damn his chivalry, then. Have him kill his French prisoners, too."

Chapter Twenty-seven

THEY were all horrified, but they played the scene as he wanted it. And it turned out they need not have worried that anyone would question Burbage's prisoner-killing king, or think him a churl. It was all in the history books—a sure defense—though Will knew the queen knew that printing was one thing, and staging another. Still, with England all hot for a new war with Spain, no yardlings could fail to cheer Harry Five's rage against any Catholic enemy.

Though good Harry had been Catholic himself, as Kempe noted in puzzlement.

Again the soldiers drilled at Mile End, holding their pikes high and marching in spondee rhythm, *left-right, left-right*. Chains were drawn across city lanes to stop women from rioting when their husbands and sons were dragged off to war. Yet the riots did not even begin to happen, and the hubbub came to little. A play, a crowd streaming from the theater into the street and yelling for

England and Saint George, an archbishop on the steps of Saint Paul's praying loudly for Protestant victory. Then word of another of Essex's bold triumphs off the Spanish coast, won with his sea dogs, Walter Raleigh and the exiled earl Henry Wriothesley, fighting by his side.

The Spanish were beaten back once more, for a decade had not healed its navy from the wounds inflicted in '88.

The tinkers and coopers and lawyers and printers went back to their business, and the queen, not a fool, saw that a playwright who hated her had once more eluded her grasp.

"I always think," she told Francis Bacon, "that Master Shakespeare hovers just out of my sight, and whispers a thing to me beneath his breath. Yet I cannot arrest him for saying what I cannot hear."

"Yes, you can," Bacon said.

"Ah, but if *my* wit can find no clear treason in the plays he writes, there is little danger that lesser minds will do so. Is that not what you meant to say, my fine flatterer?"

"Yes, Majesty," Bacon said hastily. "That was it."

NONE, it seemed, could find fault with the play of King Henry the Fifth.

And yet one did.

He was a giant of a fellow, pop-eyed, copper-skinned, large-handed, and young, and he had strong views he did not fear to share. These were, to wit: that most women were whores, that all courtiers were fools, and that bad poets should be struck with an axe.

Not that he thought Will a bad poet.

He believed Will's work would come to something, in the end.

And yet, what sort of a vile, ill-considered, and full lazy notion were it to send a Chorus onto a stage not once, not twice, not thrice, but *six times* to beg the foul crowd to imagine they saw a battle they didn't see, and heard a battle they didn't hear? "And that *three full years* have passed in two poxy goddamned Christ-be-crying minutes—"

" 'Tis only a play, Ben," Will told him mildly, over their glass-littered table at the Mermaid Tavern.

"Balls!"

He had come to them two years before, fallen from the grace of the lordly patrons, since a play partly of his making had run afoul of the Crown. He himself could not fathom what offense the good monarch had found in the silk-and-velvet-clad players with dog-ears and dog-noses who responded to calls of "Bacon!" and panted after a red-haired queen, trying to sniff under her far-thingale. After all, *his* queen was *not* named Elizabeth. And yet, a mere two days after his play was first played, he found himself on a hard bench in Marshalsea Prison, while each playhouse in London made haste to disclaim all knowledge of him, and begged the Privy Council not to close it forever.

That turmoil passed, and he was let out of jail with only a fine. Yet his money was gone, and he needed to sell something else.

When Will saw him walking, grubby papers in hand, toward the tavern table where he and three other Lord Chamberlain's Men drank, he knew right away that, strange though it were, he had known the man before; had retrieved for him a dropped trowel in the Strand where the tall, skinny fellow was laying mortar and cursing the work roundly in Latin.

Ben Jonson did not remember him. But now he made himself known full better to Will, sitting down at his ease and telling them all that his play was complete. *And* correctly written; when the

Latin was bad it was that the characters were fools; and the Lord Chamberlain's Bitches would take it and play it as it was or be damned to Satan's sulfur-pitchy Hell.

Will fell in love with him immediately.

After that day the two wasted odd evenings grog-pounding—Will on hard cider—at the Boar's Head or the Mermaid in Bread Street or the Crippled Phoenix, or in the Knavish Loon in Southwark, near where Will now lived. Both men brought their goose-quills and ink-pots and papers and Ben bragged of the boys' companies who played his work and would do as he told them much quicker than would the Lord Chamberlain's Sluts. And he tried with words to pummel Will into writing more prose into his plays. "Folk do not strut about, versifying," he said, leaning threateningly toward Will, one dark eye a-squint, his matted forearms sticking three inches out beyond his ink-stained cuffs. "Write language such as men *do* speak!"

"I do, on each day of the week." Will swigged and looked thoughtful. "*And* women."

"You twist proper word orders to make a thought fit your poxy meter."

"When rhythm doth guide them, the players speak feater."

"*Aaacchh!!*"

WILL had known Jonson a year when their friendship was tried sorely.

There had been earlier tests. Will had turned the thing into a jest when Jonson called Kempe—to his face—a sawdust-filled, dressed tailor's-dummy from Paul's Yard. He'd let pass Jonson's ridicule of the gentleman's rank he'd purchased for his father, John Shakespeare. He had even borne it patiently when Jonson named Kit Marlowe a frenzy-brained-romantic-dead-atheist-sodomite whose fair face should be melting in Hell, and mocked Marlowe's lines in a loud falsetto that rang through the Swan Theater's tiring house:

> *Ah, fair Zenocrate! divine Zenocrate!*
> *Fair is too foul an epithet for thee!*

But when Will's red-haired, scarred friend Gabriel Spencer lay dead in Saint Martin's Fields, pierced by Jonson's sword, his one good eye closed forever, Will was hard put not to come after Jonson with a rapier himself. What stopped him was that Jonson was shut up safe in Newgate Prison.

And that Jonson owed them a play.

Indeed, on the strength of the play-promise, Ben made so bold as to write Will and his fellows to ask them to bail him out. Kempe found this surprising, since, as he said, they all, save Will, had liked Spencer much more than they liked Monsieur Arrogance. Even though poor Gabriel had left them for Lord Pembroke's Men, he had gone with their good wishes.

Only Will consented to visit Jonson.

"SPENCER! *Mala bestia!* He could not keep from slandering me, behind my back and again to my face!" Ben sat next to a lit candle on the floor of his cell. Around him lay freshly penned letters, ink drying on their parchment surfaces. These all contained poems: *To Lucy, Countess of Bedford; To Her Majesty Queen Elizabeth.* Will picked one up and read it, and found it full of compliment, of expressions of high regard, so beauteously phrased it astonished him, as he noted the dank and dripping walls of the cell in which they had been composed, and the dank and dripping face of the poet who'd penned them.

"Ho, jailer!" Ben wiped the wine from his chin. "Will, knavish

Spencer called me a base hypocrite, in that I mocked sycophants and court-climbing courtiers on the stage. He said that in my out-stage verse I *was* such a bootlicker! What cause had he to care? Here, blow on this paper, Will. Ho! Turnkey!"

A surly jailer appeared at the door. "More sausage, if it please you, and e'en if it does not," Ben said. "And a white pudding. I'll see you well paid, key-turner, when these letters are answered. I have composed court masques and have friends among the great. And bring wine."

The jailer left, muttering, "Stupid sot," a taunt Ben chose to ignore.

"Will, we were strolling the bankside and all afloat with wine, and before I knew it we had quarreled most seriously," he said, with faint remorse. "Had he *had* front teeth, I would have been content to knock them out. But somehow it came to a duel. I cannot well remember who challenged whom, but the fight was a fair one."

" 'Tis done, Ben. Poor Gabriel has paid the price."

"And so have I!" Jonson held up his hand. It was branded with a livid *T*. Tyburn Jail, where they'd punished him. "It hurt most foul. What think you?"

"That you, at the least, are alive."

"Ah, yes. Well, I might not have been."

Will nodded sadly. "We might lend money to free thee, but let the Countess of Bedford answer thee first."

"I will. I thank you."

Will looked again at the letters. "If you can write this matter in here, you can write us the promised play."

"You speak true," Jonson said, his head down. He had returned to his scribbling. But when Will got up to go, he said, "Marry, why wouldst thou leave me so soon?"

"We both are busy."

Ben frowned, and muttered, *"Bu-sy,"* as though he knew not the word.

"Tempis fugit, then, if you will have it Latinly. I write plays too, do you know it? My time is scarce. Perhaps I will write a scene where drunk fools quarrel and blood is spilt and none can remember why because it was all so surpassingly stupid."

"Ah, but I *do* remember why." Jonson squinted and pointed his quill at a sketch Will held in his hand. "What is that?"

Will showed him the coat-of-arms the London Heralds' College had lately sketched for the Shakespeares. He fully expected Jonson's scoffing response.

"Ah, you and Kit Marlowe, cut of the same cloth. From tradesmen to gentlemen." Ben snorted. *"I* was a soldier and a bricklayer, *and* a player once, but I will not buy gentility. I went not to university because I could read books well enough where I was." He looked at Will challengingly. "And so I am bold to say that I remain what I am!"

"I take your meaning," Will said. "Indeed, I find you as right as can be."

Ben's face fell. "You'll not argue, then?" A crafty look came into his eyes, and he said, "But can you *explain* my meaning, to my full satisfaction?"

Will felt pity for him, alone in his cell without discussants. He held the coat-of-arms sketch closer to Ben's eyes. "Here's matter for a quarrel, Ben! What thinkest thou?"

Ben squinted harder in the dim light. "What is't? A falcon rampant? And the motto. *Non sans droict."* He smiled broadly. *"Not without right.* 'Tis passing defensive. Turnkey! The sausage!" His smile grew broader. *"Not without mustard!"*

THIS time Ben was let go when he showed the magistrates he knew Latin. That erudition gave him, as an educated man, the right not to be killed. Straightaway after, he was back peddling poems to the nobles, and plays to lower-born fellows like Henslowe and Burbage. Matters were frosty for a time between him and the Lord Chamberlain's Men, but they bought his comedies because Ben's plays made crowds flock to the playhouses, where all fell off their benches and held their guts with the pain of laughing.

Will forgave Ben for Spencer. He had to, in order to be friends with him, and he had to be friends with him in order to read what Ben wrote and listen to what he said. These things he desired most fervently to do, because he was thrilled at how Jonson refused to seek safety in poetry. Not only did he write *prose* for the stage, he sought to print his plays, with prefaces signed with his own name saying just what he meant by them, and damning as fools those who did not understand. And since his meanings were often displeasing to the powerful, Ben was always skating on the thin ice-edge of the law.

A paradox, was Ben.

When he came to court or wrote poems for his patrons he could play—for money—the arch-sycophant. Ben knew it. It was his sore point, the one Gabriel Spencer had probed to his peril. But Will knew that in the other London universe, the fluid world of the stage, Ben was no hypocrite, no shape-shifting Proteus. In the houses where players daily metamorphosed into new forms, into wizards and beasts and monsters and fairies, Ben stood solid.

He had an unmistakable human shape.

Chapter Twenty-eight

"MEN," said Burbage. "Brother sharers!" The buzz in his parlor diminished, then faded completely. "Our public playhouse is no longer usable and the landowner claims its title. The private house my father bought before he died cannot open by order of the city council, who hate all players and will not brook our presence in any fine part of town. To make things worse for our coffers, a promptbook of a comedy has been stolen and printed, and now we cannot sell it, yet others may perform it. *Henry the Fifth* has brought us noble returns and been duly insulted by Ben Jonson, which helped spread its fame. But the two hundred pounds it has put in our bank cannot build us a theater."

"If we despair of Blackfriars ever opening, marry, let us sell the place and get the money that way," said Augustine Phillips.

"No," Will said firmly. They all looked at him. "We may open the roofed playhouse someday, and we have money from renting it now. It will bring us returns in the end."

"What, then?" said William Sly. "Where do we act? Shall we shuffle like beggars from playhouse to playhouse for another five years? Do we throw all our money away?"

"Let us throw *none* of it away, least of all what Old Burbage spent to build the Theater," Will said.

"Had James Burbage bought the land he built it on, 'twould have done us some good," Kempe said. Stroking the newly waxed tips of his moustaches, he feigned not to see the scowls of the Burbages, alert to any failure of reverence toward their father. "Had he bought the land he built it on, we could go and seize the lumber. Whate'er's not full rotten."

Richard Burbage opened his mouth wide for a round chastisement in full tragic voice, but Will spoke first, and quickly. "A pox on the boggy land! The *lumber* is ours, so we'll take it and build with it new. 'Twill save us a flat hundred pounds."

John Lowin stared at him. "Take the lumber, on land we are not let to walk on? And how think you to do this in broad daylight?"

Will smiled at him. "I ne'er said a word about daylight."

IT was a cloudy, cold night when the twelve black-clad men and boys stole onto the Theater grounds. They did not bother to cut the chain the landowner had set round the place, but simply stepped over it, pulling the sledges that bore their ropes and hammers and chisels and saws. *An auspicious night for dark ventures,* Kempe had said, consulting his almanac, and he'd proved right. It was three days into Christmastide, and holiday revels had tempted the groundsman to beer or to bed. The players were alone in Shoreditch.

It was Burbage who showed them all how best to knock out the remaining good wood, crawling under the stage into the Hell of the cellarage, numbering planks with charcoal, pulling the nails, then aiming a well-placed blow at the corners of each board. For hours they worked like devils. Benches and pillars, wall-planks and flooring were piled onto carts and driven down the hill to the river. By the grey dawn nothing remained in the forbidden field but a clutter of useless boards and a torn curtain-cloth.

The hired bargemen and carters left the lumber piled on a bought lot in Maiden Lane, Southwark. By eight of the clock all the men and boys save Will and Burbage had gone home to bed. But those two stayed, circling the stacked boards and rubbing their hands and singing and laughing like their new neighbors, the Bedlamites. Finally the man they had been waiting for appeared. "Ho!" came his angry cry. Philip Henslowe, red-faced, stood next to a city guard at the edge of their lot. "I know you fellows! What do you here?"

Will and Burbage bowed in unison, like trained twins. "A fine Christmas season to you, Master Henslowe," said Burbage.

"What be this monstrous ruin you have deposited near my property? It defaces the ground, and you sully the peace!"

"It graces the ground," sang Will. Burbage joined him in the song. "It graces the ground, it graces the ground, it graces the ground!"

"We are to be friends with you, Philip Henslowe!" called Burbage, breaking out of the catch. "You and your Lenten-faced Admiral's Men. We are to be neighbors to the stinking Rose! Here thou seest the start of the sweetest playhouse on the south Thames shore." He and Will began to dance a sailor's jig, and returned to their song. "It graces the ground, it graces the ground!"

Henslowe's face had gone from red to purple. Now it turned white. He looked about him for the guard's assistance, but that truncheoned one had gone down to the Cardinal's Cap for a Christmas grog. So he turned back to the jigging men, letting fly at them with *frotting dogs* and *poxy stinking whores* and other such terms of the fairground, and throwing clods of earth in his rage, though those fell far short of the two celebrants.

In the street behind him, four men pulled a growling caged bear toward one of Master Henslowe's pits, and a trio of singing inebriates spilled out of a stew at the Maid Lane corner. A woman's shrill voice shouted curses after the drunkards, and a door banged.

"We sully the peace, we sully the peace!" chanted Will and Burbage, still jigging it past the piled boards, now spicing the dance with some steps from the morris, and then going back to the jig, four steps forward, four back, linking elbows to turn, keeping time well, though not footing as featly as Kempe could have done.

Henslowe threw his hands skyward, a gesture old James Burbage would have well approved, signifying Despair.

THE new playhouse took twenty-two weeks to build. The work would have gone slower and cost more than it did, but on rainy days the players came to join the builders in planing boards and fitting joists and planting oaken staves between struts. With mortice and tenon they fitted the lime-soaked wood-pieces to make the playhouse the old Theater's shape, but bigger. They drew together tie-beams and huge rafters and wall-plates and then raised the house-frame with ropes onto its brick foundation. A watching crowd cheered as wall after wall went up. Finally there stood a rounded polygon of eighteen separate bays, stretching a hundred feet wide over the warming spring ground.

Then the men nailed the oaken laths to the supporting staves for the theater's out-wall, and plasterers filled the square gaps between with white clay. Inside the frame there was hammering for sixteen hours a day, and the stairways and gallery benches grew, and carved balusters were fitted into the flooring. At the last, the men and boys climbed like monkeys up ladders to the upper scaffolding, nailing the roof-beams and covering them with thatch. When the players worked, they handed along the sedge and waterweed roofing in bundles. At the base near the river Kempe pulled them from barges, handing them to Sander Cooke and Nate Field and the other boys, who ran with the bundles to Thomas Pope by the ladder. Pope handed them up to Lowin on the third rung, who gave them to Phillips and Sly and Will and Heminge and the new sharer Henry Condell in the middle, and so on up the ladder to Burbage, who laid the thatch on the roof-boards. No boy was let on a ladder after young Robert Gough, halfway up, let go hands to catch a ball thrown by Nathan Field, and toppled and broke his leg on the ground.

In June it was done. They stood on the stage with their arms linked. To their left and their right stood live ash trees, twenty feet apart, thrusting through the stage built around them, growing straight out of the Southwark soil. To save money and to flatter Will's fancy, the builders had not cut the two trees, but had used them as stage posts. Now from above where the men and boys stood came a rustling of leaves in the wind. They looked up to see the trees' tops waving over the thatch, and the painted Heavens on the roof that stretched between the ashes and above the balcony that jutted from the stage-rear.

Then they looked down at the strong, smooth floorboards. As one they jumped, and heard the echoes from the hollow Hell below.

It was a world, and they had made it.

They called it the Globe.

THEY would beard the Admiral's Men with a tragedy. Richard Burbage as old Roman Brutus; William Sly as Cassius, with his lean and hungry look. Henry Condell as Mark Antony, and Augustine Phillips as doomed Caesar, dying most pig's-bloodily on the stage-boards. They would steal the audience from Alleyn at the Rose on the very first day of their opening.

Borrowing Henslowe's idea, they draped their theater in black. Will strictly counseled them all to deep solemnity, informing them that ancient Rome was not as merry a place as England. Yet they were wreathed in smiles. They were all strong and fit from pounding boards and porting thatch and now they rose early with lights in their eyes, feeling like gods, and spat and shouted and brooded and growled on the wide new stage of the Globe.

So they were all merry, but for the one whose business it was to be merry.

"Be there no part for me, Will?" The clown's voice was plaintive.

Will sighed. "There is no foolery here. But of course there is a part for thee, Kempe. Thou art Cinna the poet."

"What doth he do?"

"He is beaten and stabbed by the Roman rabble." Will handed Kempe a scroll, and Kempe looked at it morosely.

The playhouse was packed to the roof an hour before the start of the play, and the gatherers at the door had to turn folk away. Foreseeing some mayhem, the sharers had hired ten burly ex-soldiers to act as guards and escort disappointed apprentices and law students from the grounds before the word *riot* entered their heads.

When the first players appeared, a deafening roar greeted them, and they could not be heard for a full minute. The hoots and applause reverberated from the circular walls of the house, and for some moments the actors thought it was not going to stop. When Will suddenly entered through a stage door the noise grew louder, feeding upon itself, and the hired players looked nervously at him, and each other, fearing to be plum-pounded victims of the watchers' frenzy. But Will walked to the lip of the stage and raised his hands, and the audience suddenly calmed, like rough seas before a wizard's spell. Then Will bowed, and in his rough voice thanked the gentles for their patronage.

The play went on then, its audience well settled. The men's and boys' voices rang so loud in the new structure that the players surprised themselves, and could hardly forbear starting at their own resonant and solemn speeches. And even with the place filled with thousands, the meanest customer could hear them from the back of the yard or the galleries. After their first near-riot the watchers did not scream and drown out the players. They listened.

The play bettered hope. The hired men who were Roman citizens garbled a line or two, but not so any but Will could note it. Caesar and Brutus and Cassius were splendid, and the boys did well, even the new one, who'd replaced Robert Gough. The new lad was pale and thin and rudely kept his cap jammed low on his head at mealtimes. Yet he spoke lively as Brutus's slave, though with such a Midlands drawl that Kempe laughed out loud when he heard him, reminded of Will as he'd sounded his first years in London.

Will did not laugh. He listened.

The crowd cheered the boys as well as the men, especially Nate Field stabbing his thigh as Portia, Brutus's wise wife, shut from the plottings of the men, the conspirators, the brothers. Left behind by a husband who went far away; left to make her life as she could, on her own; or in sadness to end it.

Behind the curtain, Will held his head to calm his beating mind.

When Caesar collapsed from his stab-wounds the folk did not howl, but fell silent, and so they were able to hear *Et tu, Brute?*, his wondrous line. Speechless the crowd was again, and full reverent, at the last scene, when Condell stood over the fallen body of Burbage. Of Brutus, the noblest Roman of them all.

And then the applause came like thunder.

In the tiring house Will clasped hands with Burbage. "I redeemed them!"

"What?" said Burbage excitedly. He was wiping the sweat from his face with a rag.

"They came in like animals and they go out like folk who are thinking."

"Ah. Didst *hear* them? Crying as one, gasping as one, and all in my hands when I spoke, every moment!"

Cuthbert joined them, holding a paper. *"Three thousand one hundred seventy-six!* Canst thou *dream* the money we'll have in from this one day?"

"They go out all sober and chastened and—hsst." Will frowned. "What is that?"

The musicians had begun playing. They were not piping the somber song requested for the audience exit, but a merry, fast-paced moresco.

Will's face darkened. "He would *not,*" he hissed. He bolted from the tiring house onto the scaffold and then stopped there, immobilized by rage.

In the center of the stage Will Kempe was dancing the morris, wearing a wig, earrings, and a woman's kirtle that flared out as he spun, revealing his hairy legs, which were clad in yellow stockings. Those who had left the playhouse had come back in, and the whole audience was bellowing with laughter and clapping in time to the music.

For three heartbeats Will stood stony and statuelike, his eyes locked on this new Gorgon. Then he shook off the spell and went back through the curtain and into the tiring house. As he passed the store-room, he saw through the crack of its door the bent figure of Nathan Field, studying lines from the book of the new comedy. Nate looked quickly up to meet Will's tragic eyes, and his own went wide, seeing the master's pale anger. He straightened and dropped or knocked something to the floor. Then he came into the passage and called after Will, who had gone back into the tiring room, seeking Burbage.

"Master Shakespeare! Master! A word with you."

"HE must go." In the end it was Burbage who said it.

They sat in a circle on the Globe stage the next morning. With their hair cut short as Romans' from the prior day's performance, they seemed a band of senators, hunched in conspiracy. Save Kempe, all the sharers were present. Nathan Field sat a little apart from their group.

The men's faces were stiff and unhappy, but no one argued with Burbage.

"Certain it is that there's no place for him here," said William Sly. "He does not get the parts he wants, and he mars those he gets, with foolish lines of his own making, and dance steps."

" 'Tis more than that," Burbage said. "Nathan came to Will last night, and—"

"Let him say," Will said. " 'Tis why he is brought here."

Nathan looked skittish and wolfish and wary. "I thought the masters should know that 'twas Kempe who stole *The Merry Wives of Windsor* two years ago, and sold it for profit."

The partners murmured, and Sly said, "How came you by this intelligence? And it shall be *Master* Kempe to you, sirrah. Do you know what you say?"

"Of a certainty, *Master* Sly." Nathan looked back at the frowning actor and did not blink. "I was told it yesterday by a Pembroke's boy, who also said why the cl—why Master Kempe chose that play. He thought he'd be let to play Falstaff if he brought it to another company."

"Yes," said Will, nodding. "Yes."

"Doth this sort with thy judgment of the clown, Will?" Sly asked. "Eleven years thou hast known him. Hath he ever betrayed thy trust?"

Will said nothing for a moment, awash as he was in memories of plays hard-penned on the backs of broadsides and paper scraps and sold, with high hope, to Henslowe. Scripts dropped into a black pit at the Rose Theater, where Kempe danced gaily and daily through other men's plays.

At last he said, sighing, "Yes."

Kempe came half an hour later, as he'd been asked to do, calling "What's the meeting, good Trojans? Are you *all* here early?" He came smiling on stage from the yard, shaking off raindrops, clad in yellow and lavender and a hat crowned with a plume. His grin faded when he saw their faces.

He denied the theft, though he did not shrink from defending his jig at the end of *Julius Caesar*.

"Here we are *brethren*," Will angrily told him. Kempe replied, with some heat, that if they were brothers then he was the ragtag runt of the litter who got pushed off the bitch's tit though he'd put up his share like the rest of them. And what sin was it, he might ask, to shine on a stage at the end of a dark play with a dance and merry music that lightened the hearts of folk in spring when the birds sang in the trees? "Poor penny-paying folk falsely made all tear-stained and dour by some heavy dull Roman speeches—"

"Get out, clown." Will's face was calm, but his voice held black fury. He stood rigid, half a stage from Kempe, hugging the promptbook of *Julius Caesar* to his chest as though clasping a beloved woman, or a child. *"Go."*

Kempe paled a little. He turned and walked to the inner-stage curtain. But once there he turned suddenly back, and faced the circle of men, and Nate Field. The clown's blue eyes held tears, and he wiped them away with his hand. On his finger he still wore his bilious green paste emerald. His face was mottled, red and white.

"And *you*, Shakespeare!" he cried. "*You shall repent of it!* You *brothers* wish no true clown. Marry, *you* wish a crying jester like that hangdog of a Robert Armin from Lord Chandos's Men. One who may please the learned, but never the folk. *Thou shalt rue this day.* Bottom's Dream shall perish with me. In place of it, take this nightmare!" He took a deep breath and howled: "Will Shakespeare, may thy tragedies founder on comedy, and thy comedies collapse into tragedy! May all thy plays be a—a—mingle-mangle, and *may no folk e'er agree on their morals!*"

He wheeled and disappeared through the curtain. They heard his pointy-tipped shoes flapping on the passageway, the slam of a door, and then silence.

A muffled sound came from Will's left, and he turned his head. Nathan Field sat sniggering, his head half-buried in his arms. "Forgive me, my masters," he gasped, raising his chin. "Master Kempe is full comical, e'en when he's in a wroth."

Chapter Twenty-nine

" 'TIS a high price you ask," the little man said nervously.

"And a high profit we promise." Burbage pointed to the open ledger in the lap of his brother, who sat on a stool before the tiring-room mirror. "You are free to examine our books."

"There is no need. Thy company's fame is known, and thy name reputed honest."

"Honesty is our rule," said John Lowin gruffly.

"In any case," said Burbage, "it is not ourselves who stand to benefit from your investment."

"Except as your presence will grace our stage," Will said quietly.

"Yes," Burbage said. "What I mean to say is that the money you pay for your share will go to the man from whom you bought it."

"The man I replace," said the little man.

Burbage nodded. "Our former clown."

* * *

FROM the first day they practiced *Twelfth Night*, Will could see Robert Armin was what he had wanted for years. Quiet in the world, on the scaffold he sprang to life and was wit incarnate, prettily saying his jests—*Will's* jests—in quick rhythm. Never once as they rehearsed did he throw in a broad wink at an imaginary crowd, or jingle his cap and bells for the sheer pleasure of the noise. His pleasure was in poetry, and he was good at that, too. He was not given to extemporizing, except in a manner that Will and the rest of them could well forgive. For on that first morning they saw him do a new thing on the stage.

When John Lowin forgot a line of his character, Sir Toby Belch, Armin quick made a jest that followed snugly from the last line he'd been given, and also hinted at what Sir Toby was meant to say next. So without pause or help from the prompter, Lowin remembered, and the scene went on unbroken and even livelier than before. Will was stunned, even envious, and wanted at first to put Armin's invention into the script. But he did not, since he knew Armin's quick line of poetry had had life and purpose in that stage moment alone, though the hearers were only the players themselves.

In the intervals between practiced scenes Armin sat himself with the musicians, playing a mournful tabor that sorted strangely with his comical jester's garb. Yet his music perfectly framed the bittersweet songs Will had written for his sad new comedy. The pleasures of Armin were almost enough to make them forget the dark words Kempe had hurled at them, and the look on the clown's tearful face when he'd last exited their stage.

CAME the day of the first performance of the first comedy at the Globe.

Will walked from the rooms in Green Dragon Court where

he'd lived for two years, having forsaken Bishopsgate for South-wark. He came past the Rose and Henslowe's bear-pit, where a wooly beast named Sackerson growled at him from a cage. Up from the shore climbed a giggling flock of fine-dressed folk. They looked out of place on the Bankside, yet Will knew what they were: gallants and ladies come to pay to view the comical Bedlam mad.

Chaos ruled on the stage and in the tiring house, though that was as usual. The players' wives sat stitching an inner-stage curtain, since none of those cloths stayed whole for a week at a time; and four different scenes played themselves loudly out as actors rehearsed at the scaffold's four corners. The crowd of folk had already begun to sneak in and make a Bedlam of their own with hoots and hollers and the tossing about of what looked to be the corpse of a polecat. But then there came silence and shock and new upheaval when it was heard that brave, bold Nathan Field was proved, at sixteen, a man at last, with his voice badly cracked.

He could not play.

They had no Viola, no girl merrily mourning her lost twin brother, no beating heart for their play. Sander Cooke could not do it, for he played Olivia, and Robert Gough lay miserable in a bed in the house of John Heminge, unable to walk on his leg for a month and ignorant, anyway, of all *Twelfth Night*'s lines. "And so it begins." Will sat on the stage with his head in his hands. "*May thy comedies collapse into tragedy.* He'll be revenged on the whole pack of us, and now it begins."

Words flew around him, and then he heard the clear bell of the new boy's voice, the boy who'd played Brutus's servant, speaking quiet and nervous, but sure. He looked up, and the boy was near to him, bits of straw-colored hair sticking out from under his hat. He stood by Dick, saying, *Master Burbage, I can do it, I can say Viola's lines,* and it seemed to Will that he could see the boy's heart pounding fast under his shirt and his skin. No one spoke then, while Will looked hard at him, until it seemed in the silence Will could *hear* the lad's heart, though it might have been his own, beating hard in his ears. The lad breathed quick and studied the floor. After a long moment Will said, "I'm sorry, boy. No."

Then he rose and walked into the tiring house.

HE had known who she was from the start, of course; on the first day this weedy one with the low-pulled hat had said *Called you, my lord?* on the scaffold in *Julius Caesar*. "Called you, my lord?" she had said, and bowed with a playful solemnity that was hers and Hamnet's alone. His eyes had widened in disbelief as he listened at the curtain, but he could not deny what he heard and saw.

Then close on the heels of astonishment had come pity and understanding. It was as though he could look in her ragged, cropped head past her nervous eyes to the self of her, and know all: the desperate sorrow that had called her from home, the nameless shame she bore. He was moved, imagining the wild hope and valor that had led her to make herself new, to hide herself God knew where and study oaths and casual shrugs and spitting, and practice as hard as she must have done to be able to boy it so frighteningly well.

And then, at the last, to seek her redemption through speaking on a stage.

It touched him, too, that so fierce was her yearning to say his verse that she'd come to believe the incredible: that a man such as he—less a man, after all, than a bodiless eye—would not know his own daughter.

On the first day *Caesar* was played, after Henry Condell had been duly stabbed and left to die on the Globe's Senate floor, Will had abandoned his close listening and gone to Condell, who was busy dousing himself with Thames water to clear off the pig's blood. Will asked him to house the new boy, and for him and his wife to take care in his keeping, since the lad seemed from his voice to be country-bred, not wise in the ways of London. Condell first looked surprised, and a little dismayed, since shows of special regard for a boy were discouraged among the players. But it came to him—Will saw it come to him—that Will had lost such a country son not three years before. Condell understood, or thought he did. So the boy was well housed. And late that night, after Kempe's dancing catastrophe and Nate's revelation and the hours of conference Will held with Burbage, Will had written fast to Anne's sister in Coventry, saying all's well, Judith's whereabouts are known, and do not, pray, *do not* send word to my wife that she has slipped your safe care and is gone.

Now for two weeks he had watched the girl come to life on his stage.

Just this morning he'd learned that the letter to Judith's aunt had not been well sent. The carter who'd planned to travel as far north as Coventry had fallen afoul of spring mud short of Oxford. Two axles broken, and a horse back to London, with a *Here is your letter, Master Shakespeare, for bringing in the week to come, if it still matters then.* It horrified Will to recognize that Anne must now surely know of her daughter's flight, and would fear that a second child of her body was dead. He thought with dread of the last letter he'd had from sister Joan. It lay yet unopened in his strongbox, and he left it sealed there, closing his eyes against the thought of the pain it must contain. For he could not do anything about it. *Twelfth Night* was today. Viola would speak, and Judith would have one last, bold triumph as Fabian the servant boy. They needed her, and she needed them, and after the play—*after* the play—he would pack her home.

So he'd thought. But then Nathan's voice had gone wild,

stranding all of them like shipless sailors. With unthinkable courage his daughter had dared his gaze, standing two feet from him with her face dropped down, saying low and sure in Hamnet's voice, *I know the lines.* In that instant he knew that she did, and could do it.

But he himself had felt the great drunk of a crowd's applause, had known it for more than a decade.

And he feared that if she played this part, she would never be glad to go home.

The door to the store-room opened. Burbage stood there, wild-eyed. "Will," he said. "Why are you lying in the dust of the floor? What mean you by this? A play's to be played."

"It cannot be *Twelfth Night.*"

"Marry, it must be. We've no other comedy well practiced, and this crowd did not come for a history or a tragedy; they're stuffed to the gills with the Admiral's Men's fare." He cocked his head to the left. "Hear them."

Through the door spilled a ruckus of laughter and song, pouring from the now-full yard and the benches, across the stage, into the tiring house. "The house is as crammed as it's been any playing day these two weeks past. As full as it was the day we opened! It's half past the hour." A rhythmic clapping began as he spoke, and grew in volume.

"Give them *Julius*—"

"We need not, Will." Robert Armin now stood in the door behind Burbage. "The boy knows the lines; he can do Viola."

"Nay."

Burbage jerked Will to his feet and shook him. "Why do you naysay? We've giv'n him the test this past quarter-hour. He gets everything right. John Rice may say Fabian."

"Methinks she could not carry it."

"She?"

"I mean, the boy."

"What matters Shakespeare's let-alone?" The cool voice came from past Armin's shoulder. Will looked up to see the dark face of William Sly, who now stood in the passageway with his arms folded. "His vote is one in ten."

Will looked at him evenly. "True enough."

A boy rushed to the door bearing Orsino's ducal robe. Burbage shrugged himself into it, not taking his eyes off Will. "As the matter lies we will play it, Will. But of course we crave thy blessing."

"Master Shakespeare," Armin said softly. He jingled his jester's staff gently, and smiled in wry sadness. "The play must be played."

Will looked at him, and his eyes held a grief so bottomless that Armin stood stock-still with wonder. But Will's voice was detached and dry. "What you will," he said. "Play the play."

SO he sat in the inner-stage space, by the newly stitched curtain, holding the book of *Twelfth Night* like a priest might hold a chalice. He himself knew the lines by heart, but he kept the book there as she spoke on the stage, and turned each page quietly, holding her afloat with the strength of his mind, willing her with all his heart and soul not to fail. She was Viola, the girl with the drowned twin, the lass whom love redeemed long before her brother's fanciful resurrection in the play's last act. And she was speaking the lines as though they belonged to her.

They were nearing the end of the play when Will turned a page and went still.

A loose paper lay in the promptbook. On it, quickly set down, as it seemed, were the lines of Viola and Sir Andrew Aguecheek and Fool Feste that filled that page of the book. The lines had been copied, in a hand that was not Kempe's hand. Will knew Kempe's hand well. This hand was a boy's scrawl, and Will recognized it. He had seen it here and there, most memorably on the renewed apprentice's contract the sharers had lately signed with Nathan Field.

In a moment the separate awarenesses met. The furtive look of Nate Field in the store-room two weeks past, as he'd looked up to see Will look at *him* leaning over the promptbook. The sound on the floor: a dropped pencil or quill. And here was the telltale paper, left by Nathan in haste as, fearing discovery, he had hurried out to deflect Will's suspicion and tar Kempe with a slander.

The *wit* of the boy! Quicksilver, like Kit Marlowe. To have known in an instant that the masters, and Will most of all, were full frenzied by anger at Kempe for his flouting of all the tragic decorums! And now Kempe was gone, and Nate Field had taken his gear half an hour ago and fled the playhouse, unwilling to brook the sound of a lead comic part said by anyone but himself— least of all by an unknown boy who'd not been with them three full weeks. Gone, too, since doubtless he knew his ruse could not stay undiscovered for long.

Wise you are, but you do not know all about everyone. Henry Wriothesley's voice rang in Will's mind, and he winced.

Kempe was innocent.

Nathan Field sold their plays.

Without knowing it Will had risen to his feet. The promptbook lay on the floor. Then his ears pricked at the sound of a thing gone awry on the stage, a rhythm disrupted, and he heard, to his dismay, Armin speaking lines Will had not written. They were Armin's own lines, made up in the moment and said urgently, proddingly, because Viola was not saying hers. Judith, on stage, had gone silent—shaken, perhaps, by the bump of the book he'd let fall to the floor. Her face was white. He had woken her from her stage-dream, and she suddenly saw all too clearly where she was. She stared at him, stricken. *Daughter,* he thought in fierce pain.

As they stood eye to eye, the world of the Globe threatened to split apart and send the pair of them hurtling into the raw, mute truth of things. He saw himself and his daughter falling, silent and grief-struck, thinking of Hamnet, thinking of death. He hated the speechless agony on her face—*Hamnet's face*—and he feared beyond all things their unworded grief. So he spoke, and gave her her line.

And the play went on.

WHEN it ended it still had not ended. It was time then for his arch-performance, although to watch and describe, not to play, had always been his stronger suit. He knew he must feign he had not known her till that terrible moment she'd lost her lines. He could not trust her silence. She was only fourteen and might blab, and he'd never earn Anne's forgiveness if his wife found he had *let* their daughter play on the stage. He knew not how he would have made the thing good to Anne's sister in Coventry, had his letter arrived at her house. He'd have spun some sticky lies about where the girl had been and how he knew it and why he had not told Anne. But none of that mattered now. His letter had *not* arrived, and now the thing was to share the whole family's shock and wrath—indeed, to begin it—by showing his daughter an anger he did not feel.

At least, not toward her.

"Vile, detested, cursed kite and insolent wretch!" At the edge of the river he caught her, but she slipped from his grasp and scrambled up a tree. Now she hung just out of reach, stretched along a branch eight feet above the ground. He pelted her with dirt-clods. "Thou *thwart disnatured torment! Disease! Plague-sore! Embos-*

séd carbuncle!" Crouching low, he grabbed a handful of mire and flung it. *"Thou egg!"*

"Da!" Judith kicked helplessly at the well-aimed clods. "Da! 'Tis I!"

"I know!" he yelled.

Though in truth he'd begun to forget who she was, and to see in her place Nathan Field, as in a dream where a person melts magically into some other self. As on the stage. *"Dwarfish thief!"* He threw harder, and she yelped. "Frot me, it hurts, Da!"

"What said you? *WHAT?!?* Stow thee now! I will wring thy paltry irreverent clown-hating play-stealing *neck* for what you did to us!"

"I do not hate clowns!"

"Silence, thou thieving, knavish boy! *Fraud!"*

What finally roused him from his malevolent fancy was Judith's own body. Raising her hands to fend off a handful of flying mud, she fell off her branch hard atop him, so he found himself holding her up. They both sat down hard on the bankside then, and she collapsed on his chest, weeping. He held her as she cried, and his own body shook with the force of her sobs. But his own sobs were dry.

On their walk to his lodgings he stopped at a tavern, and gave a new letter to a rider who left that same night for the north.

That evening Judith relieved her heart and burdened his with the story Anne had kept from him. Hamnet's death was a mishap that came from the child's longing for his father. The twins played a game the night of his drowning, spun out of fancies of fairies and lines from the play he'd left them. *A Midsummer Night's Dream.* They'd cast a fatal river spell to conjure their father home. He had not heard of this, for Anne had been merciful even amid her grief and her anger. Yet the story confirmed the guilt he had somehow known he bore.

Hamnet's drowning was no one's fault.

Which was to say, it was Will's.

Only spun tales of horror could soften the grief of such true heartbreak. So he and his daughter traded ghost stories until, late at night, they started, relieved by a sudden knock on the door. It swung open, and in tumbled a trio of variously aged fellows. The skinny first of them removed his cap, showing hair that stuck up in pointy tufts.

"Spiny Quiney!" Will shouted.

His old, thin schoolfriend's curious train were Spiny's ten-year-old son and Will's gangly nineteen-year-old brother, Edmund. Edmund soon made it known that he full intended to sleep in Will's bed, or at least on the floor, and to stay in London forever, and be a player himself. As for Spiny Quiney, he'd be pleased with a ten-pound loan—now that the urgent message they'd brought was moot, as Will's daughter was clearly found and could be sent back with them to relieve her mother's grieving heart.

Within two days they all—save Will—were bound north for Stratford.

WILL walked long on the bankside, and thought of the playhouse boys.

The day before, he'd told his fellows what he'd guessed of Nate Field. Afterwards Sly and Burbage had gone forth to hunt the lad. But John Rice found Nathan first in a bankside ordinary, and from Rice, Nate gathered that he must lie low. Rice swore to the men he'd not meant to warn him, a true tale, most likely, but still, Nate had guessed what was what.

"Do not punish him," Will said to the gathered, glowering sharers at the Globe. His own wrath had passed, or been strangely played out of him. "We're well rid of Nate Field. Let's be glad on it."

"We'll hold his money," Cuthbert growled.

"Aye, we can do that."

"What of Kempe?" This, gently, from Armin, the sole man of them guiltless of sin against the clown.

"I went to his lodgings," Will said quietly. "He is packed up and gone."

They all looked at each other, and none of them had anything to say.

In that same dialogue with the men Will shrugged his shoulders at the strange disappearance of the new boy, he who had done so surpassingly well as Viola. He looked all ignorance, saying only that *new* new boys were needed, full needed; that boys nowadays came and went and could hardly be trusted, fie, fie. From the corner of his eye he saw young Sander Cooke stocking props and pretending not to listen. The lad's face was all bliss; Will could almost see Sander's visions of his own reedy self as Juliet, Portia, and Beatrice.

He smiled faintly now as he walked by the river, remembering Sander's face, and thinking of Judith's as he'd last seen it through the slats of a miserable Stratford-bound coach. She had smiled at him broadly, and blown him a kiss.

Her eyes had been clear and alive.

Chapter Thirty

IN the year 1600, eighteen died of the smallpox in Stratford, and twelve of consumption. Fifteen women perished in childbirth, and nineteen of both sexes were done in by typhus, scurvy, vomiting, or distraction. Twenty-four bled to death. One died of fright, and three from grief. The other forty-two lay down and did not get up anymore because they were tired. Of these last, John Shakespeare was one.

Will stood against a January wind in Holy Trinity Churchyard, halfway between his son's grave and his father's. He was still tired from his watch at John's bedside two nights before. "Age claws me in his clutch," the old man had said. "Forgive me, my eldest. Many's the time I hit thee without mercy or thy deserving. Being sodden with drink—"

"I forgave thee. Besides, you gave it up."

"I know not how. God helped me, I suppose. I hope you need

never find out how it is. Best you should not serve as town conner."

"Town conner?"

"My first office, and I was proud on't. But ale-tasting was the ruin of me. It gave me a thirst for Mad Dog and Huffcap. I'd shun it for years, but I'd always come back, and then it was darkness and devils everywhere. I was"—he sighed—"bailiff once, you know. . . ."

"I know, sir."

"William." His father paused for breath. "The plays. Can you fellows not do as they did before?" He bent his old mouth in a grin. "God in a flaxen beard, and three woolen yards for the Red Sea?"

Will smiled faintly. "Nay."

"Why not, my boy?"

"To show God on stage is now forbidden. As you know."

"But that's not why."

"No."

"God in a flaxen beard?"

"No."

John Shakespeare blew out a long sigh, nodding the while. He closed his eyes.

As Will rose, cap in hand, to leave the room, his father's eyes opened once more. "Shun the office of conner," he pled weakly. "Let them not make you conner."

"I swear it."

THE house at Henley Street was filled with neighbors whom Will barely knew anymore, except by sight. His mother was abed upstairs, and Anne, smooth as an orange, was cutting bread in her old kitchen, and saying nothing to him. In the parlor Gilbert spoke of wool matters. Will wandered from room to room like a ghost. "Anne," he said finally, catching her by an elbow on her third passage between kitchen and parlor. "Cease disdaining me for Judith's folly. She is unscarred by what she did last spring, and in any case she did it without my knowing."

"Ah, did she, then?" Anne's gaze was ice-blue.

"What dost thou think?"

She shook her head impatiently. "Speak na' more of this. I am not angry for Judith. Her spirit mends, and I care not how, so long as it doth."

"Then what?" He dropped his voice low and laid a hand on her arm. "Thy miscarrying?"

She stared at him long and hard. "How knew you of it?" she asked.

"From Judith."

"Ah. Well, it was not the first time. She did not know *that*. Though it should be the last. I am sure of it." Her voice was not bitter, but matter-of-fact.

He swallowed hard, and blinked. "Nanny. Why did you not tell me?"

"Who would be accused of whoredom a second time? I needed no husband counting months on his fingers."

He frowned faintly.

She sighed. "Though my heart breaks at it, I could not blame thee for that loss. 'Twas none of *thy* fault, and what sense would there be? If you will know, 'tis a thing Gilbert showed me. Forgot in a desk in this house." She plucked a creased paper from her bodice and gave it to Will. Her voice became cold. "You should not be so heedless, husband."

By the worn edges of the paper's creases it looked to have been scrutinized often. Anne did him the grace of not watching as he scanned it. She went to serve claret in the parlor, leaving

Will leaning against the doorjamb, his mouth drawn tight and his eyes fixed on his poem.

GILBERT was chopping wood in the yard when he heard the kitchen door shut and hard bootsteps crunching on snow. "Curse all sneaking villainous common brothers, without faith or love," came the voice. "No *true* brother—"

Gilbert turned toward the advancing figure, and stared for a moment in scorn. "Faith and love! What mean you? What care you for faith and love? Thou hast thy gentleman's crest, and that is enough, 'tis not?"

Will stopped in front of him and gave a harsh laugh. "I care nothing for that. That was our father's thing, to flatter his Shakespeare fancy. But you!" He held the sonnet aloft.

"Ah, that. *Then will I swear beauty herself is black, and all they foul that thy complexion lack.* Fine lines, though by their argument thine own wife is foul. Thou wert proud of the conceit, else you'd not have copied it out for yourself to keep once you'd given it to—whoe'er you gave it to." Gilbert wiped his cold, reddish nose. "Blame your stinking vanity if my sister Anne read of it."

"I do blame my stinking vanity. I blame you too. Not least because I know my wife *could* not read of it, and that you read it *to* her."

Gilbert grinned, showing teeth that were browned from winebibbing. His once-handsome face was mottled with broken veins in his nose and cheeks, and his eyes were bleared. "You know her little," he said in dismissal. "She reads some now. *I* taught her. We have time enow together."

"Do ye, i'truth?" Will folded his arms. "Or is it a boast made for hate of me? Thou dislikest me out of envy, and thine envy comes from thy sodden nothingness. Marry, why dost thou feed on my life?"

Gilbert turned sullenly back to the block, and gave the wood-chunk a vicious chop. But his arm was unsteady from claret, and the stroke was not neat. The axe fell slantwise and splintered the wood.

"Hand me the tool," Will said.

"Nay, brother," Gilbert laughed. "I be not such a fool as to—"

"Idiot. Put it down, then."

"I will put it down in thy pate."

"Stop thy schoolboy blatherings. I would you would face me."

Gilbert dropped the axe and kicked it behind the woodpile. He looked at Will. "What, then? Why shouldst thou insult me?"

" 'Tis you who gives occasion for it."

"With my great fail in faith and love. Where wert *thy* faith and love when thou madest mews and sheep's eyes at thy black whore?"

On instinct Will tightened his fists, but he kept his hands to his sides. "What's that to thee, unless it be that thou lovest my *wife*? You would have her, would you not?"

" 'Tis brotherly love."

"Hast had her?"

"*That* thou'lt not know."

Will's fist hit his face then, but all Gilbert saw was a flash of light, and then the opal sky high above him. He groaned and sat groggily up in the snow, his glove to his nose. When he took the glove away it was covered with blood. He pushed himself to his feet and looked about him for his brother, to rail or to laugh at him, or to hit him back, but a door had banged shut and Gilbert was alone.

Two days later Will rode back to London.

He found there he'd a second funeral to attend.

*   *   *

KEMPE had left his lodgings in Southwark after the Lord Chamberlain's Men hurled him from their midst. Will sought him fruitlessly in the riverside haunts. He was gone.

Yet Kempe had not left in despair, as they all soon learned, but in high hopes of earning his share's worth and more, from a daring enterprise of his own. He'd vowed to London's Lord Mayor that he'd dance all the way to Norwich in nine days for thus many pounds, and had done so, leaving London at eight of the clock one morning with his scarves whirling and his belled buskins flying. An enormous crowd saw him go, and the folk of town and country came out to cheer him all along the way, and add to his moneys. So heartened was he by the success of this Nine Days' Wonder that he boasted he'd dance over the Alps to Rome. He left to begin the mad journey before Cuthbert Burbage could find him and return what the company owed him. The dance through the Alps was bravely assayed, yet it did not run smooth. In Geneva the grave sons of Church Reformers came out by the hundreds to pelt him with hard bits of Communion biscuit, as though to prove it was only bread and could well be used to attack a dancing clown. And their aim was good. Kempe got sorely bruised. So the Bankside story ran.

Kempe abandoned his dance and returned to London, where he had to give back all the stake his supporters had put down for the venture. Among those supporters was Henslowe, who threatened to send a burly fellow to end Kempe's dancing days forever if the money were not in his strongbox by Sunday next. The clown could not do it, and vanished again from view for a time. Then he was seen making a desperate jump from a window on London Bridge into the cold river below.

His body was not found.

He was honored by a funeral ten days later, on Shrove Tuesday, at Saint Saviour's Church. So many London citizens crowded the sanctuary that hundreds had to stand by the tombstones outside, their ears pressed to the doors to hear the organ music and the homily. Will stood with the rest, a drop in a sea of black-clad mourners. In the pause at the end of the psalm, he whispered, "They birth us astride the grave."

His mood was as dark as the cloud-clotted sky late that afternoon, as he wandered into Saint Michael's Church in Lower Wood Street and stared broodingly at the partly rotted head of King James the Fourth of Scotland, kept there in a case. After a time he left the church and walked south again, crossing the river. He pushed past parti-colored revelers making merry in Tooley Street, near the Southwark bridge-entrance where the traitors' skulls hung.

This England, he thought bitterly, looking back at the Great Gate. *This stinking privy chair, this scurvy isle, this earth of rotting skulls and home of whores, this site of godly good hypocrisy, this other Hades, demi-underworld, this cursed plot this rot this shite this England . . . No wonder poor Kempe danced out of this land.* Will thought he might leave it himself; flee to the New World, away from dead clowns and uncles and fathers and sons and silent wives and treacherous brothers and cruel lords and bishops and monarchs, away from carriages and tooth-cloths and hourglasses and mirrors. . . . He saw himself in the pine forests of the Western continent, a wild man or a trapper, cave-dwelling, writing on stone walls, the skull of a beast he'd killed beside him. . . .

He laughed suddenly and crazily. Even the drunken merrymakers looked at him askance, as he walked alone.

THAT night Ben Jonson burst through the Mermaid's door bringing a huge gust of cold wind with him. "My revenge!" he roared, waving a sheaf of papers. He lurched past the crowded tables like an ungainly bear, earning stares of vexation or wonderment. " 'Tis here! My revenge!"

Will stood. "Revenge has been much on my mind, too, friend. Guilt, and revenge."

"Guilt?" Ben said. He reached the table and sat heavily on a stool, divesting himself of his cape and holding a hand up. "Canary!" he shouted. "Now." He spread out his papers. "See this."

"Ben, I need thine assistance."

"The foul poetaster Jack Marston mocked me on stage and I'll purge him, I will, in this new play. He is an *idiot*. Here." Jonson waved a page at Will. "A fine scene, this! I've Marston puking all the foul words he invented because he could think of no others. Canst credit his folly?"

"Hm."

"Ah, thou dost it too, and I know it well."

"*You* change your own name's spelling, yet would have English stand still as gravestones."

"You make nonsense words," Ben scoffed. "*Assassinate. Addiction.*" A boy brought the wine, and Jonson poured it and swallowed. He bit into the cold fowl Will had left on the table. "What others? *Discontent. Lonely.* Stop thy mad word-minting, or I'll make thee a character."

"Thou hast already."

"Ah. I forgot me. The ten-pound gentleman with his new coat of arms in *Every Man Out!*" Jonson laughed hard, past his mouthful of fowl. He took out a knife and a pen and commenced honing the quill. "*Not without mustard*, the country gull's motto!" Another laugh. Then he frowned, remembering. "But *thou*. Thou didst sink that comedy with cursed overacting when thou didst play the part. The country accents *far* overdone. None laughed at thee. None *understood* thee. And now the play is played nowhere. Why didst thou do it, Will?"

"I cannot guess."

Jonson squinted at him blackly, and took a fierce swig of canary. "And you think I should lend my help to *your* scheme of revenge, against enemies unknown, after frotting me so roundly on the stage?"

" 'Twas payment due. Think us even, and progress."

"Pro-*gress*. *Pro*-gress. Francis Bacon's word. All think themselves God now, fit to new-create our language."

"Well, I have an affinity with my Maker. We have both seen sons buried." Ben looked full shocked at this blasphemy, but Will forestalled his outcry by pointing to the scabbard that lay wrapped in Ben's cape at the tableside. "Is thy weapon sharp, Ben?"

"Always." Ben pushed his papers and the cold capon to the side, and looked at Will. "Whom shall we thrash?"

"No one, if our luck holds. But I cannot tell; we may be beset. The rule of the world is accidental judgments, casual slaughters—"

"What mean you, madman?"

"Nothing. I go to free my uncle, and transform him to a dead clown."

"Hssst." Jonson looked quickly about them. "There is a crowd. Best we go from here." He gathered his papers and left money for the Scot, and they went out and stood at the edge of the dark street. "Now. Thine uncle? A dead clown? What mean you?"

"I have a play of an overgrown boy who says everything. He speaks quickly and much, with the tongue of an angel. His play hath too many words."

"Art mad? What's thy bibble-babble?"

"But I cannot part with a one of them, and so I need an ocular shock to balance all the chatter." Will set off down the lane with his fingers playing an imaginary flute, like the Pied Piper. "Come, my fattening friend. Go we to Southwark."

"Wait." Jonson followed. "Where *is* thine uncle?"

"At the south end of the bridge."

"Ah, no." Jonson grabbed Will's sleeve and shook his head. "So this be thy game! Nay. An evil direction, south on the bridge!"

Will looked a challenge at him. "Art coward? I never did think it."

Ben snorted. "Come." Still holding Will's arm, he led him farther down Bread Street to the red-latticed window of an alehouse. There he stripped off his glove and held his thumb to the lurid light. His once-red Tyburn *T* had hardened into a shiny pink slash of a scar. "Dost remember this?"

"Could I forget its occasion?"

"That's past. I mean to say that whate'er your mad plan with the skulls on the bridge, 'twould go hard with me were I caught. It would not be my first offense, nor my second."

"Aaaaye." Will nodded reluctantly.

" 'Sblood, if it's a skull you crave, dig one up in a churchyard. If they catch you there they'll only whip you." Ben pulled his glove back over his scar. "Only do not mistake and dig one of the graves of the mad beheader's victims. Then thou wouldst have to make do with a shinbone."

Will laughed shortly. "Thou givest good counsel, but I must have my nuncle. I will not risk thy pelt, after all. But lend me thy sword. 'Tis sharper than mine, for if quarrel arises."

Ben puffed out his cheeks and was silent for a long moment. Then he blew out his breath, and burped. "The city gates will close in half an hour," he said. "Let us cross."

Chapter Thirty-one

THE Shrovetide revelers were long gone to seek sleep in the city, but in Southwark they still wandered the streets singing catches. Will darted among them like a Spanish needle whose thread was Ben, hurrying behind saying, "Hold, Will! We'll need to wait out the hour till this crowd's abed. Or till they're full Clinked."

"Clinked!" Will laughed darkly. " 'Tis good, Ben."

"Let us hope not to be Clinked ourselves before this night's work is done."

"Never fear. We will be most inscrutably disguised."

"You are mad."

They stalled themselves at a table in the crowded Knavish Loon. There Will told the tale of his uncle Edward's hard fortune, which Ben had heard by parcels, from players' rumors, but never fully. Ben ordered canary, but Will sent it back, saying this was a time to be Lenten sober, though Ash Wednesday still lacked a quarter-hour.

"Were verse satire not banned I'd write a dark poem of thine uncle's tragedy," Jonson said, contenting himself with cider.

"There is always the wide, wide stage."

They clinked cups.

"Shall we plot the crime fully?" Will asked, after draining his mug.

Ben shook his head. "Delay lies that way. Some things you should not think about until you are doing them."

"Ah. True enough. I shall strive to remember it." Will rose. "Let's go, then. 'Tis time for night-work. To the Globe!"

Will's key opened the tiring-house door. Ten minutes after they slipped inside they emerged wearing black cloaks and dark, close-fitting doublets and hose. On his head Will wore a fool's cap stripped of its bells. He had painted his cheeks and forehead with blue wode, like a savage Irish warrior. Ben pulled a devil's mask over his face as they first sidled through the trees, then took the darkest streets to the bridge.

As was their custom, the city guards had left their station, and were playing cards twenty yards from the Great Gate. Will bade Jonson stand in the shadows and watch him; he had spent much of the year before climbing theater posts, and had the trick of it. Besides, he was smaller of stature and less like to be seen. Jonson agreed but made him trade weapons so Will had the better one, a fine sacrifice for a man so in love with his sword, and Will said so. "When I have the skull, come quick, and I will throw it to thee," Will said. "Be on the ready."

"Aye."

Will crawled up the mound of the bank to the gate and pulled himself onto a cross-bar. In less than a minute he had his hands on the steel spikes that thrust from the top. "*Paugh!* What a smell," he said under his breath. His gaze met the empty-eyed stares of English heads, each in a new stage of decay. He willed himself to think them stage properties, then suffered the distracting thought that some of them would indeed serve well as stage properties. But he shoved the idea from his mind, and steeled himself to his one purpose. Crablike, he pulled his body sidewise across the gate-top till he reached the skull he'd stared at for twelve years from the bridgeway below. He looked down at the ground. Heedless, the livery-clad guards played their game. They were singing a catch, as though Shrove Tuesday had not already passed into Lent.

"Ben!" he called in a stage whisper.

In a trice Jonson was there, holding his hands up as though he would catch a ball.

"Come, thou grinning honor." Will plucked the skull from the spike like a rose from a thornbush, and twisted toward Ben. "Here! *Ecce signum!*" He threw, and heard the *thock!* of bone on broad-cloth. The guards looked up just as he jumped from the gate-top, his parti-colored cap standing stiff in the wind.

They were chased, but both knew Southwark better than the bridge guards did, and had the start of the guards besides. They came close to capture only once, when, skidding through mud at the corner of Talbot Yard, they came face-to-face with one of the men who'd charged after them. But Will had his blade out in a moment and gave him a round stage-fight. "*Coraggio!* Hit him!" Jonson urged in his mask-muffled voice, as he cradled Edward's skull. "The *assalto!* The straight thrust! The *mountanto!*"

"I'll hit him flat! Back, villain! Thou'lt not have him this time, Gabriel Spencer!"

"Eh?" panted Jonson behind him.

The guard parried bravely, but Will's chance came when he slapped the man's arm with the flat of his sword. The surprised guard's weapon came loose and sank to its hilt in the muck. The man scrabbled for it, and Will and Ben were off pell-mell, slipping on slush mixed with dirt and horse-mire, running through a maze of streets until they had doubled back toward the river and were in sight of the Cardinal's Cap. They heard no pursuers, but still they ran the last thirty feet and slipped, spent, through the back door of the stew.

John Heminge was there, hunched over a table, playing shovelboard with Will's brother Edmund and Edmund's mistress, a girl of the place.

"Ned!" Will cried.

Startled, all three of the shovelboarders looked up.

"Look ye, Ned! I have got Uncle Edward!"

Ben, still wearing his devil's mask, pulled the skull from his cloak and waved it proudly.

"By God, what are you?!" Heminge yelled, as Edmund's girl shrieked and ran from the room. "Begone from here! Away!"

They explained themselves, though they did not get the praise they angled for, except from Edmund, who thrilled to the prank's excellence. With relish Edmund assumed the office of skull-keeper, which it followed he should be, since he now served as the Globe's props and tires man. Yet most of the players thought the theft full perverse, and certain to bring them ill luck. Their fears and Burbage's habit, displayed in days to come, of juggling the skull amongst an apple, a shoe, and an empty ale-pot made Will vow to keep the thing in his rooms, which he thereafter did, toting it back and forth in a woolen sack betwixt rehearsals of *Hamlet*.

ON the day of the first performance Will set a boy as guard over an ash-can bonfire in the cellarage. Another boy stood close to the middle-stage trap, to work a crank that would send Will up to the scaffold. Will crouched on the small elevator, his eyes rimmed red, his face powdered grey, clad in full armor, with the beaver of his helmet raised. A martial ghost was he. Only a curtain falling from stage-lip to ground separated him from the crowd in the yard, and the noise was monstrous. Then the trumpets sounded from the orchestra, and the groundlings hushed. He heard the players speaking above him. *"Go!"* he whispered. The boy turned the crank.

All went as planned for the space of ten heartbeats. But halfway out of the trap, hearing the crowd *aahhh* at the smoky haze drifting out from the cellarage, Will was knocked on the head by the loose-hinged trap-door, which swung back on top of him, clanking his beaver shut. He shoved the door open again and kept rising, but the beaver was stuck fast, and he could see nothing. Worse, he inhaled smoke from the bonfire, and when he fell onto the stage he was wheezing. He straightened at last, but only to face *away* from Horatio and the Elsinore castle guards. At the cue offered him by Horatio—*It is offended; see, it stalks away*—he began lurching blindly toward the audience, and felt himself hauled back by the guards, who thenceforth guided his traipse about the battlements with their hands.

He was partly consoled for the horror of this scene by others that went as badly, or worse. Ophelia ripped her dress and displayed her boys' hose, much to the delight of the pit. Burbage, as Hamlet, forgot lines, a thing that had never happened in anyone's memory. His speech to the traveling players was thus marred; his condemnation of clowns who *speak more than is set down for them* was mysteriously transmogrified to *Let those who play your clowns speak—let them speak—let them speak!* A yardling yelled, *Aye, let them speak instead of thee, thou bloated windbag!* Listening from the cellarage, Will buried his face in his hands.

There was more disaster. Burbage slipped and fell to the floor during his duel with William Sly, who played Laertes. Burbage had gained more than a stone since Christmas, and so Will had directed him to die over the empty throne, so the Swiss guards would not have to lift him as dead weight from the scaffold. But Burbage strained his back when he fell, and now must needs perish flat on the boards. At the end of the play the actors had to drag his guts by the legs through the curtained inner-stage entrance, in a manner which wanted dignity. John Saint Clair, who played Fortinbras, tried to fix matters, changing lines on the instant to *Come, fetch the Polish sleds, to haul him like a soldier 'cross the ice!* But Saint Clair was drowned out by audience laughter and then by the screams that the crowd let fly at the boom of the cannon on the roof, which shook the house timbers and sent thatch tumbling down on the yardlings' heads.

WILL bowed his head in a pew of Saint Saviour's Church the next Sunday. The priest chanted the liturgical oration, but Will said his own prayer in a whisper.

"That a clown's curse be lifted."
Lord, hear our prayer.

"That Hamnet Shakespeare dwell in bliss."
Lord, hear our prayer.

"That Anne Shakespeare forgive mine adultery."
Lord, hear our prayer.

"That a clown's curse be lifted."
Lord, hear our prayer.

"That Edward Arden dwell in bliss."
Lord, hear our prayer.

"That Nathan Field's new company fall flat on its arse."
Lord, hear our prayer.

"That John Shakespeare dwell in bliss."
Lord, hear our prayer.

"That Will Kempe dwell in bliss and that his curse be lifted."
Lord, hear our prayer.

Over the next weeks *Hamlet* played better, though most of the Lord Chamberlain's Men's other plays remained fraught with mishap. Still, Burbage lost flesh on a diet of watercress, leeks, and boiled eggs, and moved quicker, and once more thrived on the yells from the yard. As Hamlet he railed at the crowd, staring full at the yardlings when he pronounced them *capable of nothing but inexplicable dumb shows and noise.* Each time there would come back howls and shouts of *Whence comes thy bread and butter?* and *Off the stage, Hamlet, thou university twit!* At these jeers Dick would stride to the edge of the scaffold, raise his black velvet–clad arms, and cry, *Then prove your mettle, lordships!* He would bow with mock reverence, catching rotten pears and oranges, juggling them, then throwing them back. The groundlings adored the scene, and him.

Day after day Will hunched in his armor in the cellarage, feeling cooler and breathing easier now that he'd dispensed with the bonfire. He listened to the crowd in growing awe at the understanding they were capable of, and at their good will. Every one of them, from the onion-eating yardlings to the feather-capped lords, would forgive players anything but their contempt.

They would forgive.

FOR months after *Hamlet* was first played, London was peopled with mournful-faced, black-clad young men who walked with their hands behind their backs, glowering at passers-by and muttering *To be . . . or not to be . . .* It sent Jonson into a red wroth to see them, and to hear the play quoted on all occasions. At his own plays, audiences were content to laugh madly at the mockery of fops and whorish ladies and never take to heart his clear moral. And no youth yet had undertaken to stroll London's streets dressed as Squire Downright.

Yet the youths would be Hamlet, and lines from the play were thought wise. *This above all, to thine own self be true!* was the only phrase in taverns, streets, and houses, though the thing had been said by the biggest fool in the play and no one knew what it meant. One should drink or not drink, marry this wench or another, buy property or sell it, heed a father's advice or murder the old duffer. *This above all, to thine own self be true.*

"It is like Greek philosophy," Jonson said thoughtfully, as he munched buttered bread at the Mermaid. "Yet you know no Greek. Did you mean something?"

"Aye." Will nodded thoughtfully. "Several things."

Ben lifted a capon leg. "It hath not appeared."

NOT all in the playhouse were kind.

One day found Will seething as gay laughter spilled from a lord's room near the stage. The men staged a comedy, but its jests competed with those of the room's fine occupants. The players plowed on as best they could. There was little they could do in the moment. They could only look closely at the offending gentles as they exited and tell them, on the next occasion, that the lords' rooms were all full.

So Will watched, arms folded, when the play was done and the richly dressed men came out of their boxes, steadying the elbows of their painted mistresses. One woman's hair, black by nature, was tinted auburn. Its elaborate dressing set off the plain splendor of her straight sarcenet gown and dark velvet fur-lined cape. Will watched her for a long time as she descended the gallery stairs, her arm grasped by a giggling popinjay dressed more elaborately than she in a short, jewel-encrusted cape of peacock blue, a Spanish ruff, and a cap with three feathers. With a spasm of pity Will saw that the gallant's face was pocked and imperfectly smoothed with pinkish paste. The woman's face was pinked also, and her smile fixed; she seemed barely to attend to her companion's chatter. Even from the inner stage Will could see the darkness of her eyes.

"Dost thou haunt me, shadow of death?" he murmured.

John Lowin came behind him. "Thou'lt know that one well enough, if she dares to come back," he said slyly. "Yet I warrant thou'lt let her in her lord's room, and pay her for the privilege."

"She be not a whore," Will said sharply.

Lowin looked at him in surprise. "A jest, Will."

"Pardon."

Outside, he dusted rosin from his boot-tops and began the short walk down the street to his rooms in Green Dragon Court. When the fine coach with the pair of black horses came close behind him he did not turn. It pulled next to him then, and its door opened slightly. He had only to look up to see whom it carried and what was wanted of him, but he would not, and did not, until he heard the soft voice.

Then he gave up the walking, and stopped still. "What would you, milady, with a poor player?" he said. "Emilia, what would you?"

Chapter Thirty-two

SHE was alone in the carriage, and her face was half-veiled. Suddenly conscious of his own shoddy appearance, he put a hand to his brow and pulled his cap lower. But when he came close to the door of the coach he saw by the blurred look of her velvet eyes that she could not see him clearly. "Belladonna has not done your eyes good," he said. "Though it yet gives them their raven's beauty."

"Wilt ride with me, Will? For friendship's sake?"

He paused, debating. "I wonder that you knew me, with such sight."

She dropped her veil and he saw the remembered fullness of her lips. "I sought you in the street. Thy gait hath not changed," she said.

In the carriage she gave him to understand that the fellow she'd come with to the play was nothing and no one to her but a court *gimblet* with a taste for the plays, an under-secretary with gold pieces to *fritter,* who'd promised her a place in a lord's box. The carriage was not his, but lent her by another, one who desired to have his brave conveyance paraded about with whate'er fine women he could *muster* inside it. Her English was better, and Will listened, amused by the new terms she felt bound to bring out for his approval. She spoke fast for the space of a slow half-mile, until he asked her why he and she were speaking of nothing.

She went quiet then, and turned on him the sad night of the eyes he had praised in his poems. Their stillness drew him, and he was sorry he had not let her go on chattering her foolishness, because she was lovely still, and seemed mystic and dark, and her surface befuddled his judgment and troubled his will.

"What of your husband?" he asked her.

She laughed. "I have no husband but in name. Do you not remember?"

He looked out the window, away from her eyes. "I remember every word that passed between us."

"The words only?" Her voice was rich with suggestion.

"I forget nothing," he said carefully, taking pains not to show her his face.

"Dost thou know? I have heard thy comedies played before," she said.

He laughed briefly. " 'Tis certain you did not hear us today."

"Years ago, thy Shylock—"

"Pray don't speak of that." He shifted on the seat. "That play was not received as it was meant."

"You put me in it. A good character! The maiden flees a grim father to join the bright, civil folk."

"Ah, did I so? And did she so? Is that what you saw?" He continued to look through the small coach window.

At last heeding his discomfort, she said, "Other subjects, then."

She tapped his leg with her stiff, round fan. "Hast a mistress in London?"

"Nay, lady, I live alone, and spend my pith and marrow on my art." His thigh tingled where she'd touched it. " 'Tis a penance."

"Penance! For what, pray?"

"For . . . many things."

"For thy past? For *the expense of spirit in a waste of shame?*"

He looked at her in surprise. "Thou dost remember small things also, then."

"Should I not? I read your sonnets often."

He frowned. "I thought them in Henry's keeping."

"But some spoke of me. I took care to find and copy them out before I left Titchfield."

Will's stomach knotted.

Just then the carriage lurched into a huge rut and stopped abruptly, throwing her body against his. Instinctively he reached for her. Frozen with his hands on her shoulders, he felt his mind dart, seeking the path that would best win him his will. He chose, and was leaning to kiss her, when the carriage door was opened suddenly by a livery-clad coachman, who said, "Lady, 'tis best you and the gentleman come out here. We'll go no farther until the wheel is repaired."

They scrambled, flushed, from the coach to the uneven street. Before them lay low houses and the river. "You must boat with me to Greenwich," Emilia said. "There is my dwelling."

"Ah, lady, 'tis not fitting or wise that I go."

"But you must, else I am unaccompanied! Even when the carriage is made right, 'twill be lodged at the Bishop of Winchester's palace south of the river, here."

"The Bishop of Winchester?" He looked hard at her. "You are friends with him?"

She nodded, but evaded the question he had not fully voiced. "I must reach home by river."

Reluctantly, he went with her then on a cold boat-ride down Thames, where the chill wind came close to knocking the ardor from his liver. But it did not, quite. She lay lush and inviting against the prow, her pearl-sewn slippers, new-soiled with street mud, peeping from beneath her gown. She gave him speaking looks, and by her talk he gathered she thought he still believed she'd betrayed him long ago with Henry Wriothesley—and was content to let him believe it, meaning to stoke the flame of his desire with eight-year-old jealousy. The pettiness of her motive prompted his contempt, which mingled strangely with the pity he had always felt for her, and felt now.

He wished to feel only pity, and hated his disdain. He hated, too, that she could see how much he still desired her. But he did not fear his longing as much as he feared another thing.

"I must ask thy pardon for the bitterness of my poems," he said. "You ne'er deserved it."

She accepted his words with a nod and a smile that told him she had only been flattered by the passion the sonnets seemed to bespeak, however harshly the poems had been worded.

"I must ask also that you destroy them," he said. "For the love I bear you."

At that her smile froze. "Ne'er will I do that!"

They gazed at one another.

To offer her money would be unwise. He remembered her well enough. She was not so crass, and for him to shrink what had once stood between them to a matter of pounds and pence would only enrage her. He tried a new way. "I asked of thy husband before. Howsoever . . . out of the ordinary run thy marriage be, I am sure he would feel great pain if he found—"

She sat up impatiently in the boat, so quickly that it rocked and water sloshed over the sides, so the boatman had to let go his oars and steady it.

"I feel no guilt," she said. "I do not feel bound to so impotent a pairing."

"None could blame you, Emilia. Yet annulment is possible. With the bishop's blessing—"

The warning look on her face told him all he might have gone on to ask about the bishop's blessing. And her posture and garb told him other things: that her life at court was to her liking, and that she no longer craved marriage, if ever she had, but pleasure, and wealth, and the attentions of the great.

He understood then there was nothing he could say to get from her what he wanted. It was a blessing the carriage door had flown open when it had. Had he made love to her she would only have grown wrathful and hurt afterward, when she saw that she could not hold him. And to go with her to her rooms, to look for his poems there—the thought had been mad. The small chance of finding them could never be worth the entanglement.

And there was another thing. Though he saw clearly now that he had never loved her, the body reclining against the prow still threatened to unprovide his mind. It might not be so easy, after all, to leave her a second time.

"Did you come to flaunt thy beauty before me, lady?" he asked, truly curious. "To test my desire?"

"I *know* thy desire. I have read thy poems many times."

"I am sorry I wrote them."

"But why?"

Because I fear you will see them printed, he thought.

But he was not fool enough to say it.

THE winter of that year was the coldest anyone could remember. The Thames froze solid, and the urchins of Southwark slid on its surface with splinters of boards tied to their boots. On the north side, wealthier citizens glided or tottered on real ice-skates with carved runners or metal blades. On the eighth day of her Christmas Revels, Queen Elizabeth held an ice-party before her riverside palace at Greenwich.

Bundled in the skins of a Russian bear, the sixty-seven-year-old virgin monarch sat like a cold queen bee in a throne starred with candles, while her musicians—one of them Emilia's husband— played lute, oboe, drums, and viol before her. An ice-masque, featuring courtly poetry by Ben Jonson, was performed, and when it ended the throng of courtiers, ebbing and flowing on the hard river, formed another show for the queen. Her lords and ladies skated, danced, or merely slid before her on the ice, in warm boots and sleek fur robes, leggings, mittens, and hats. Their pearl pendants and jeweled gloves glittered in the light of a hundred torches.

There could be no boat traffic until the ice finally broke, which it did not do until close to Saint Valentine's Day. In his Southwark rooms Will heard the cracks and booms of the thawing river as he packed up his papers for his annual Lenten visit home.

But he did not go. At the last hour he was urgently summoned to a parley with the other Lord Chamberlain's sharers; requested to trot through whipping wind to the Globe.

When he arrived the others were already gathered on two benches in the lower galleries. Will listened while a lord with a soldier's beard spoke long and forcefully to their group. When the fellow was done Will picked up his cloak and said, "No."

A gabble of voices stayed his walk to the door. Burbage called for order and reminded Will that their strongbox was almost empty; they had not played for weeks because of the cold at the Globe and the still-standing edict against their fine roofed Blackfriars Playhouse. And the next closings for Lent were almost upon them, but this was *sure cash,* and a thing to be thought on.

"And thy vote is now one in eleven," Sly reminded Will.

Burbage looked at Sly angrily.

The visitor waited until quiet returned, then gazed piercingly at Will. "Only meet him, Master Shakespeare," he said. "Then make thy choice."

ROBERT Devereaux, Earl of Essex, was tall, sharp-eyed, and long-faced. He sat with straight military bearing in a camp-chair, his boots spurred as though he would presently jump a'horseback and gallop to some nearby field of conquest. His house was in the Strand. On its lower floor on his way to the stair, Will had passed through a small mob of bravos and religious zealots excitedly jabbering. This warm upstairs room had walls cluttered with maps and hanging tapestries depicting Roman battles. By Essex's elbow stood a model of an English warship, and books—stacked far more neatly than those in Will's room—lay on all sides.

Will had heard of this riverside mansion just outside the city wall, where Essex's young admirers haunted the hallways, moaning about the rotten state of England's monarchy. He had been told, indeed, that some *Hamlet*-inspired melancholics were among the crowd. But these stayed below, it seemed. In this room was none but the earl, a bushily bearded man in his prime.

None but the earl, and Henry Wriothesley.

The man who had brought Will from Burbage's house in Holywell Street now presented him to Essex, then retired from the room. Ceremonious bows were exchanged, and Will clasped hands warmly with Henry, who whispered his condolences for Hamnet's death, for he had not seen Will since before it. Henry's hair was still flowing, and as before it looked odd against his rough soldier's beard.

Essex did not dilly-dally but came straight to the point and asked Will to stage *Richard the Second* for him. Before Will could answer, Essex, transported by ambition, rose from his camp-chair and began to declaim from its now-printed script. *"The commons hath he piled with grievous taxes, and quite lost their hearts; the nobles hath he fin'd for ancient quarrels—or new ones—and quite lost their hearts.* Of course"—he said, smiling as he dropped back into his chair—"in our present day we would say not *he* but *she."*

"She whom you lately angered by striding into her privy chamber upon your return from Ireland?" Will asked. "Was't not enough, milord, that you failed to crush rebellion on that island? Had you to view Her wigless Majesty soaking her feet in salt water?"

Henry looked anxious. Essex laughed. "I cannot regret not defeating Irish Tyrone. I treated with him. He fights because he does not wish the rule of empire o'er his free people. How could I help but admire him?"

"Yes. How could you help it?" Will looked thoughtful. "Yet there is the other view. The queen paid you to—"

"Well, she pays me no more." Essex's face turned hard. "Out of her vanity she has cashiered me. The conditions she offers me are as crooked as her carcass."

"Harsh," Will said mildly.

"Aye, she is harsh, and has always been. Will you stage your play?"

"What has my *Richard the Second* to do with you, sir?"

Essex gestured impatiently. "Do not play the fool, Master Shakespeare. I have seen thy plays. *Julius Caesar."* He smiled knowingly. "And *Henry the Fourth,* another stab against tyranny. The fool Falstaff, crowned with a paper diadem in a tavern! A fitting mockery of the monarch."

"Then you make no difference between a mock monarch and a mockery of the monarch?"

"None, sir."

"Ah. Well, then. What argument dost thou see for thyself in *this* play? What canst thou hope from a wintry staging of it at the Globe?"

"*I am a subject, and I challenge law. Attorneys are denied me, and therefore personally I lay my claim to my inheritance of free descent.* That inheritance being the throne, to which my blood gives me some claim. I quote your play, Master Shakespeare."

"Yes, I know."

"That play, staged at this moment, will inflame all London against the queen's tyranny."

Will laughed. "It did not before."

"But matters have changed, Will," Henry said excitedly.

Will looked at him fondly, willing himself not to smile at the long beard of which Henry, stroking his chin, seemed so proud. He resisted an impulse to grab it and pull. The face beneath it was still a boy's. "You are ardent to be exiled a second time, Henry," he said. "Or to suffer a worse fate."

"Nay. I am ardent for justice."

Essex fished a gold timepiece from his pocket, glanced at it quickly, then snapped it shut. "The hour grows late. By God, 'tis *full* late. Late in the reign, and late in the century."

"Nay, *early* in the century," said Henry. "The new one. Time for new beginnings." He looked eagerly at Will. "Is't not so, old friend?"

Will was looking at Essex. "Sir, where got you that chronometer?"

"From one of my sea dogs, who served with me at Cádiz. He came to me here in the Strand last month. Gamaliel Ratsey. A hero of sorts."

"I see. Well. 'Tis an excellent timepiece."

"I thank you. The play, Master Shakespeare?"

"Will," Henry said. "You have wanted to *say* things in your plays. Here is something that might not only be said, but *done*."

The air in the room was tense with expectation. "It is an old play," Will finally said. "We will scarce remember it. I cannot promise it will please."

THE sharers drove a hard bargain with Essex, demanding the house receipts and forty shillings besides, but in the end they brought out moth-eaten *Richard the Second*. They presented it to an odd audience of disaffected lords and gentry in the galleries and a small knot of groundlings and two-penny patrons who braved the cold simply because they loved plays. The house was less than a third full, and weighted with men toward the stage-end, since Essex, Henry Wriothesley, and some ten other nobles had claimed space on the balcony above the scaffold. They did not behave well. When Sly, younger than Burbage and fittest now to play King Richard, emerged as if on the battlements of Pomfret Castle, Essex suddenly stood up next to him and waved to some yelling spectators below. *"Still looks he like a king!"* cried Nicholas Tooley, who played Northumberland. As Tooley said it, Essex assumed a brave martial stance, one hand on his hip and the other on his sword-belt.

Sly was furious afterwards. "God's death!" he cried. "A half-crown buys those silken apes a seat above the Heavens. It does not buy them the right to join the play! What did he want?"

"Love," said Will.

"He will not have mine. If he wishes to be a player, let him come and show us his skills."

*   *   *

THAT night Will's rooms were cold and his head ached and he lay on his bed and passed into a dream wherein he was Richard the Second and Essex was the usurper Henry Bolingbroke. They struggled against one another for a crown. Then Essex's face became Kit Marlowe's, and then it was Gilbert's, and then it was the face of the serpent on the Paradise bed, and its body slithered and coiled itself about his own, and he fought with it on a bare stage. He heard the crash of timbers, and fire crept up the curtain that hid the throne. Then the snake was gone, and flames surrounded him as he fell to the cellarage and began to dig, muttering, *Dig me a grave, a little, little grave; a little, little grave.* And the flames were at his back.

His eyes shot open, and the dream flew off in shreds. The ceiling above him looked like a blank page, and his first, hazy thought was that he should write something on it. His head cleared a little. The fire in the grate had died to embers, but he was sweating. His uncle's skull grinned at him from its place on his table. Will put a hand to his burning brow, squinting at the sickly dawn light that oozed through the shutters.

He closed his eyes again.

When he next awoke it was twilight. He was fiercely thirsty, and he needed to urinate. He stumbled dizzily to the jordan, then crouched to relight the fire. With foggy disappointment, he understood he was too ill to ride to Stratford. He heard pounding on the door below and shouting in the streets outside. *Shrovetide already?* he thought confusedly. *I'faith, the calendar is all awry.* Eventually he heard his own name being called, and realized that the door-pounding was what had awakened him. He pulled on his breeches and went to the window, and looked down on a street full of milling people. He felt dizzy again, and rubbed his forehead. "Is't thee, o my dark brother?" he moaned. "Come so untimely, on a day of feasting?"

" 'Tis *one* of thy brothers." A pair of Iberian eyes glared up at him from under a wool cap. "And if I am dark, what's that to thee? Pox, let me in!"

Sly wrapped him in a blanket and put woolen netherstocks on his feet while he told him of the event. "So they came up to the gates of Saint James's Palace with Essex in the lead, only two hundred of them. They all ran through the Strand shouting his name, thinking the downtrodden citizens would pour out behind them. But it happens we are not downtrodden enough after all. Marry, shutters closed as they ran past! I kept mine open, and I saw." He laughed hollowly. "By the time Essex reached the palace the ones behind him had looked back and seen how raggedly they were followed and had run away, all but a few. He must have known he would fail, but he was well in the brink, so he swam on. He thought he was Laertes, with the crowd behind him calling, *Choose we! Essex shall be king!*" Sly sat back, thinking. "Or Fortinbras, Norweyan conqueror."

"He thought he was Henry Bolingbroke," Will said thickly. His throat felt as though it were lined with fur.

"At any rate, he found he was plain Robert Devereaux. The queen's herald galloped afore him calling, 'Treason,' and now he's in the Tower."

"Towered. And what became of Henry Wriothesley?" Will's heart began to beat hard.

"The Tower."

Will let out his breath in a long, shuddering sigh. "I should not have . . ."

"And the Lord Chamberlain's Men are confined to London."

"We did nothing!" Will started to cough, and said roughly through his hacking, "We needed the money."

"I know what we did was nothing. But *she* takes a different view."

Sly rose and fetched Will some water from a jar.

"Ah, JesuMaryJoseph," Will said, after he drank. "The poor boy."

Sly knit his brow. "Essex is no boy."

"I meant—one of his followers."

"Think not of them, but of us. Francis Bacon will prosecute. Who will speak for us in Star Chamber? Not thee; thou canst barely talk. Perhaps I will do it."

"Nay, Sly. Not thee. Nicholas Tooley, or—"

"Someone whose eyes are blue, you mean. Who does not look like a Catholic alien or, worse yet, a Jew." Sly sat in the chair with his arms defiantly folded, glaring at Will, who was now back in bed. A part of Will's fevered brain noted that Sly's eyes were lovely, dark and deep. He looked down and coughed, and sipped water again. "Aye," he murmured.

"You are right, I suppose," Sly said, stretching his legs toward the fire.

Will hid from Sly's sudden beauty in a theatrical groan. "I am sick, brother Sly."

"*Sanchez* to thee."

"I am *sick,* thou Jewish-Spanish-English Richard the Second."

WILL was well enough that Sunday to visit the Church of Saint Anne, Blackfriars, to hear what Nathan Field's famed Puritan father would say about Essex. Yet the man preached not a word for or against the uprising, though all England's priests had been charged to read a royal document condemning rebellion, in advance of their Sunday homilies. Standing tall in his black robe and white surplice, Pastor Field only held up the queen's document by two fingers, as though it were a rotten Lenten fish, and shook it, so its royal seal danced in plain view of all. Then, as though by accident, he let it drop behind the altar, and began to read aloud the Bible text of the day.

Will judged him a man who said just what he thought.

THE men chose their own John Saint Clair to plead for them because when he was younger he had played Portia and won his case against Shylock readily on the stage. This reasoning seemed most logical to them, and served them well. Saint Clair's defense left the judges convinced that actors were such clot-headed ninnies they could not even *understand* matters of state, let alone play a reasoned part in them. The Lord Chamberlain's Men were all found guiltless in the Essex affair. Will was only a touch disappointed that he'd have no time in jail, to brag about later to Ben.

"I *am* Richard the Second! Know ye not that?" Queen Elizabeth told her councilmen, who all nodded vigorously, then shook their heads, then looked full confusedly at one another, purely baffled as to what response was wanted. "Dolts!" she said, throwing up her hands. "Leave my presence!" They scurried to obey.

On the eve of Essex's execution Will stayed in his rooms, plugging his ears against the mayhem of another Shrove Tuesday. He wrote a new letter to Henry. He had sent four already, and he did not know if a one of them had reached his friend.

Chapter Thirty-three

HE wrote to Anne that though it was now full Lent, business kept him in London and he could not come home. He thought of Gilbert's late revelation that Anne could read, a fact she had kept from him, meaning, perhaps, pleasantly to shock him one day. His fists balled tight as he remembered how his villainous brother had seen to it that it was Anne herself who was shocked. He was touched by his wife's hard-bought learning, yet dreaded the new pain it could bring if Emilia did what he feared. And well his dark lady might do it. Furred capes and pearl slippers were costly. Her fine bishop maintained her now, but might not do so forever. Her poems were a wealth in reserve. Any London printer would pay an extravagant sum for the sonnets of William Shakespeare.

It seemed strange to Will that he'd not seen her once these past eight years, not at court or at any of the lordly houses where the Lord Chamberlain's Men had been called to play. He wondered whether she had hid herself purposely from him until now. Now, had some shift in her fortunes sent her to seek him, to let him know she had power over him? He recalled how her lovely face had darkened with shamed disappointment when he'd alighted with her on the Greenwich quay only to bow courteously and say, *Lady, my business now calls me back to Southwark.* She'd been sure he would come to her rooms.

The sonnets' printing would shame Henry, too.

That is, if Henry could stay alive long enough to know of it.

MONTHS later at Candlemas, in a windy February 1602, the players stood on a scaffold in the torchlit Middle Temple of the Inns of Court, where the young lawyers lay. *"You do usurp yourself,"* said a squeak-voiced Viola to the lady Olivia. Behind a pillar, Will winced at the boy's rawness. *"For what is yours to bestow is not yours to reserve. But this is—"*

"God's judgment on a queen who'll neither provide us an heir nor let her folk choose one for themselves!" A young student of law, his robes open at the neck and his eyes bright with wine, had jumped on a table in the crowded hall. He brandished a large wooden ladle that dripped cider on the flushed, upturned faces of his fellows. "She usurps indeed!" he yelled. "Essex is dead, and who will replace him? Forward the rule of law, and not the tyranny of princes!"

The room erupted in riot. Tables crashed to the floor, and a volley of hurled biscuits, wine cups, and half-eaten mutton chops rained on the players, who all jumped from the scaffold and started crawling under benches toward the nearest door.

Will, crouched near a wall next to William Sly, grabbed Sander Cooke by the wrist as that hunched lad came sneaking along, much hampered by Lady Olivia's gown, which bunched at his knees and tore. "Get the money, Cooke," Will said.

"From *whom*, my masters?"

Will pointed to a youth in the high gallery, who was perched on a banister, wearing only a tinsel crown. As the players watched, the youth raised a horn to his lips, blew tonelessly, teetered for a moment, then jumped with a whoop into the throng below, where he was caught and paraded about like a prize-winning fish. "Him," Will said. " 'Tis he who arranged this dainty entertainment, and 'tis none of our fault that our play was cut short."

"But masters—" Sander flinched as a flying knife-blade stuck with a *thrumm* into the wall next to Will.

Will and Sly did not flinch. "I'll not stay to see the end of this night's revels," Will said. "And I'll not be robbed again, by a boy or a houseful of boys."

"Why should I—"

"Sirrah, do you qibble?" Sly broke in. "This is a piece of your apprenticeship. *Get the money.*"

JOAN'S messages with news from Anne were sparsely answered by Will, and in time they stopped coming. Busy with southern cares, Will noted the falling-off, but stashed the hurt in a cellarage of his thought. There were, after all, vexations closer to hand.

He could not gain admittance as a visitor to the Tower of London. He got no replies to his letters so he knew the earl had either not received them or was not permitted to send letters himself. But Will knew he was far from the greatest of those who wrote daily, urging their power to persuade the queen to pardon the sweet captured lord, for his youth—though he was now, in truth, nearly thirty—or, failing that, for his beauty. So Will waited, and hoped. He bided his time in his rooms, writing, or in the taverns where poets, sharers, and players did business.

*   *   *

IN the Mermaid one dark afternoon Will and Burbage spotted the target of their long-held wrath, just as they'd known they one day would. They and the rest of the brethren had never agreed what they'd do with the wretch once he jumped from his hidey-hole, and in the event, they did nothing, save try to wither him with hot stares, a mode of attack that left him looking as cheery as before. This angered them further, and so when he showed the boldness to rise from a table he'd shared with Philip Henslowe and walk at them, smiling, they found themselves full primed to spit venom in his face, each wishing himself a poisonous snake.

As *he* was.

But he looked a handsome and fresh-faced youth, now moustachioed, ear-ringed, and full nineteen. He caught the stare of the serving wench, and knew it, and dropped a coin in her cleavage as he passed her. That caused Dick to splutter and ask Will what the young jackanapes thought he *was,* to which Will replied, "You!" which caused Burbage to choke. So Dick was full red-faced by the time Nate Field reached them and bowed with the courtesy of an undersecretary before a king: velvet cap to his breast, right arm elegantly extended. The mock-courtly bow could not have been easy in the narrow space between tables, but Field brought it off full gracefully, and Will thought again, as he watched him, *Kit Marlowe.*

He and Dick stayed seated and mute. Dick *could* not speak, and Will, though impressed by Nate's audacious courtesy, was yet undisposed to give over his hot, silent glare.

Nathan shrugged, and fell into a chair. "Well, me Trojans!" His voice had matured to a mellifluous alto, near the pitch of a low-toned woman. "I have inked me a fine deal—"

"With toad Henslowe," Dick said, through a lessening cough. "We saw. With the rat from whose teeth we pulled you long ago. All for money, is't, Field? And a rat to a rat. 'Tis fitting."

"What would you, *Dick?* I run short of money."

"Could you not steal some?"

"And I crave patronage. Could *you* bethink me of a good patron?"

Various suggestions were cast at Nate, including Burbage's of the Antichrist and Will's of Sir Gamaliel Ratsey. Nate only laughed, sunk in his cocky slouch.

"Did thy new band of players not thrive, poor boy?" Burbage sneered.

Nathan took out a knife and rubbed it with his linen sleeve. Will recognized the shirt, which had once hung in the Globe's smaller tiring room. Nate said, "To speak true—"

"*Canst* thou speak true?"

"To speak true, my new company did ill on its tour of the West Country." Field frowned, recalling. "Fell on its arse, I would say."

"Then take my advice," said Will. "When you next play a play that is not *your* play, such as—shall we say—*Hamlet,* strive to play it as 'twas written, and not as you falsely remember it from hasty jotting of notes in the two-penny gallery. I saw you there, fool, in your mad stolen disguises. Well for you, that you ran from the house each time before the playing was done! Though that fact well accounts for the botch you made of the ending."

Nathan blushed faintly, but his reply was saucy. "I think I copied it fair well for my haste, and deserve your praise, friends."

"Call you us *friends?*" bellowed Burbage, and smacked the arm of his chair. His full tragic howl caused the next table's drinkers to jump, accustomed though the Mermaid denizens were to players' quarrels. "Liar and *thief!* You blamed your vice on a hapless clown."

"Oh, was he a favorite of you fellows?" Nathan widened his

green eyes, affecting an innocent stare. Burbage glared at him, while Will brooded.

Nathan dropped his eyebrows, and shrugged again. "I disliked old Kempe. Carping at me since I was a child! 'Mind the costumes, Nate Field. Stow the parts.' Marry, why should a *man* go on heeding the orders of a clown? And *you* apes! 'When thou'rt done with thy work, Nate, con a thousand lines of verse by Friday next!' "

"And Dick painted scenery and pounded boards, and I carried thatch," Will reminded him. "We all worked. We are—"

"*Brothers.*" Nate swore an oath that Will guessed he had learned on his country travels, because it concerned sheep. "Crew on a ship of fools, say rather! I *have* no brother. I am *like* no brother." He glanced at Will, who had suddenly gone very still. "Pray, why dost thou pop thine eyes at me, sir?"

"Out of guessing at last the full age of thy malice," Will said. "Six years ago you were still a child, but, it seems, you were already grown old enough in vice to steal what was then my best play."

Nathan looked a jot unnerved. Open-mouthed, Burbage shifted his gaze from Nathan to Will and back again.

Will's voice was soft. "What did you, a boy of thirteen, do with *Richard the Third,* out in the wide countryside? Pretending it was lost, and making us hunt and me sweat! I know you did not sell it, since none else has ever played it."

Burbage swore darkly.

Nathan's eyes darted furtively toward the tavern's exit. But when he spoke, it was in a cavalier manner. " 'Sblood, I threw that play from a cliff, down to Dover Beach, where I hope it molders still. I'd tired of playing Lady Anne." He rose. "And now, my fine masters, I take my leave."

"Hang thyself, Nathan," said Burbage.

He snorted. "I'll do nothing at *thy* bidding."

"You have not changed, then. Prithee, go! Come, show us thy back."

"I'll show you my *arse*, Dick Burbage. And curses on thee, Will, for rewriting *Richard Three*, so I had to keep on playing Lady Anne!"

"Ah, Nate," Will said, smiling sadly. "I fear not thy curse. A better man than thou hath cursed us already. And that one is dead, and able to haunt us much worse than thou canst."

"*I* did not kill him."

"No," said Will. "I did."

THE Tower guard wore an enormous bunch of keys at his waist, and those clanked against one another as he led the way down the stone-walled corridor. The air in the passage was not nearly as foul as that in Marshalsea Prison or the Clink, but it was fully as cold.

The turnkey did his work at the end of the hallway, then pulled open a huge door whose metal base screeched against the granite floor. He gestured Will inside, then shut the door before Will could duly observe the studious, soberly dressed gentleman who sat writing at a desk by the room's only window. The man's hair was cropped short in the Puritan style, and he wore a cloak, doublet, trunks, and hose of simple linsey-woolsey. Will raised his fist to rap against the door to call back the guard and say, *I know not this man; this is the wrong cell.* But the man looked up and said, "*There's* my poet," and Will saw, amazed, that it was Henry after all.

He embraced the earl, and began to tell of the months over which he had striven to be let in to see him. But Henry silenced him with a wave. "I had no doubt you and all my friends were doing what you could," he said. "For a year I could communicate with no one, not even Bessie. After that I could read letters but send none, and then they turned tables and let me send letters but read none." He laughed. "Can you find any sense in it?"

"Nay," Will said, staring carefully at his face. "Not a whit. Dear lad, I am full glad you shaved off that beard. But thy *hair*—"

" 'Twas unmanly."

"*Aye, by yea and no,* as it saith in Deuteronomy somewhere!" Henry laughed. "I have been reading Puritan tracts. I'truth, I think better of the smoothy-pates than once I did. They are right in saying our Reformation is something shamlike. For how is God served when the cross above the altar is taken down, only to be replaced by the royal coat of arms?"

"Thou speakest true. On the other hand, *speak lower.*"

"What will the guard do to me? Lock me in the Tower?" Henry laughed again, and touched his head. "I will grow my golden locks back, in any case. Bessie wishes it so."

Will looked about him. The small room held a rug, a desk, two chairs, and a well-stocked bookshelf. He had seen far worse prisons. Yet after only five minutes he already felt the air's dankness and the chill rising from the river straight up through the cracks in the stone floor.

" 'Tis not as bad as that," Henry said, reading Will's face. "I read and I write here. I e'en have a maidservant, though she will not let me have my way with her."

"Dost want to?"

"Nay. She is sixty. Resembles the queen."

"Ah, the queen," Will said remotely. "Idol of our love and revulsion. There can be no loneliness like hers."

Henry looked at him keenly.

Will felt a pressure against his calf, and looked down to see Henry's old cat Drake, now grown fat as a ball. "Ah. So here is why you so strangely wrote to ask me to bring you raw fish." He took an odorous package from his pocket, unwrapped its contents, and threw them to the far side of the room. "Smelt for thee, sir!" The cat bounded.

"I have your plays to read in here, Will," Henry said.

"Not the histories?"

"Those, they will not allow. The lighter works. Comedies of marriage. 'Tis good."

"Thou art happy with Bessie."

"Would I could see her! I am glad I married her and not her cousin. That was my mother's first aim. The cousin was fair enough, but the Earl of Oxford would have been my new father. A strange, violent fellow, and the author of the worst verse ever penned. I would have been expected to discuss it with him, world without end."

Will shuddered.

"But thy plays. 'Tis strange, Will! Once you spoke to me only of sons, but thy sweetest plays are all daughters now."

"I have lately discovered that girls have some merit."

"They do, sir," Henry said with spirit. "I hope one day to get one. A matched set, she and my son."

Will winced just perceptibly.

Henry looked aghast at himself, and quickly changed tacks. "Thy Rosalind, now! Like Viola, but—"

"We need not speak of *Twelfth Night,* friend, or of comedies at all." Will sighed. "In real life marriage is the beginning of troubles, not the end of them."

"Ah." Henry smiled sympathetically. "Thy tragic plays, then. I hear much. The choking of a wife for imagined adultery! Tell, *where* didst thou find a veritable Moor to play on thy stage?"

"At the dock of Saint Mary Overy. He was a sailor, cast up by the sinking of the Armada. And his *voice* ... He had, by heart, twelve books of the Quiran. A true gift for memory. Yet he did not triumph. The folk found him strange, and wanted their Burbage in blackface." Will frowned. "He was good. But no more of my plays," he said after brooding a moment. "*Thee*, Henry. Hast been given a hope of release?"

Henry's smile was rueful. "I'd have been giv'n more hope had I shown more contrition."

"Why did you not?"

The earl puffed his cheeks and blew out the air in a boyish way, thinking. "I love poetry, but 'tis not as natural with me as with thee, this practice of—"

"Ambiguities."

"Just so. I see things one way, and what I see is what men like Essex have seen. Men like Walter Raleigh, who has tasted the Tower himself on the strength of the queen's mere dislike of him, and would he had joined our rising! We all see that England needs not only a new monarch but a new *monarchy*. One that law can prevent riding roughshod o'er Parliament. One that—"

"Dear *Henry*." Will spoke low. "Quiet, pray! It may please *you* to be here, and I love you well, but I do not miss thy company so greatly that I would wish to share thy cell."

"Oh, they would give you your own!"

Will laughed softly, then said, "I *would* you could speak as you would. Today I think of a man I knew—nay, loved—who dwelt here for a time. Perhaps he lodged in this selfsame room. He did not join a mad rebellion, like thee, but he died for speaking as you just did." He paused. "I have sought to avenge him in the only way I could, to let his voice and all others' voices speak in my poetry—"

"Ah, poetry." said Henry. "We are all in love with words, are we not? But I begin to fall out of love. In here I think how our poems are a pleasurable trap, and a dream. The godly are not all fools when they condemn pretty verses. Not to *say*, but to *do*, is what—" He stopped, seeing Will's face. "Forgive me, friend. I do not speak distinctly of thy plays."

"I take no offense, Henry. But since we speak of verse, thou shouldst know a thing." He told of his meeting with Emilia, and what she'd said of his sonnets.

Henry's face grew long at the tale. "Will, she did not have them from me."

"You do not need to tell me that. She found them at Titchfield and copied them."

"Careless." Henry tapped his brow with the heel of his hand. " 'Twas full careless—"

Will touched his shoulder. "Never mind. I tell you this only so that if they are printed one day, you will not think I blessed the deed."

"I would not have. I know you better than that."

After a pause, Will spoke briskly and low. "But you did not answer what I first asked. You prate of a new monarchy that would be like Republican Rome, or Heaven. We'll not get *that* soon! The heavy-handed Scotsman is coming to rule us, and things will grow worse before they are better. Have you any hope of release from *him?*"

"I have!" Henry's face lightened. "I've had the wit to write him, of philosophy and fishing."

"What dost thou know of fishing?"

"Nothing! But he has not caught my ignorance. He answers me, with wild letters about Roman emperors and spirits and demons in the witchy wood, God be praised. If I outlast Elizabeth, I think he'll let me out just so I might persist in the chat."

Will leaned slightly forward. "Henry, I am sorry we made one with Essex's rout, and that I did not dissuade you—"

"You could not have. Peace, Will. Pray, *you* looked full pale and menacing when you entered an hour ago. Like the ghost of a ghost. What is disturbing thy sleep?"

"A . . . players' quarrel. Betrayal, hard words, and the theft of some plays. The loss of a book, long ago."

"You once told me of a book you'd lost. It seemed a petty cause for prolonged heart's agony."

"That one was a gift of my uncle's, and no small matter. But this I speak of now was a promptbook, since recovered, or at least rewritten."

Henry shook his shorn head, smiling. "The losing of books! 'Twould make an excellent dull play."

"It seems so, said thus. But there was drama enough surrounding the losses. *Lives* lost, in fact. Our dear troublemaking clown was falsely accused, and heaved from our company, which sped the decline of his fortunes. He fell out of love with the world, and he left it."

"That is sad. Yet the first mishap served you. You *did* want him gone from your plays."

Will winced as though he'd been stung.

"Forgive me," Henry said quickly. "It is cruel to speak without thinking. I've done nought but offend you today, though you have been so generous in thy love. To bring me"—he frowned, thinking—"smelt!"

The guard rapped on the door and unlocked it. Again Will heard the metallic screech, which put him in mind of racked prisoners howling. The turnkey stood framed by the doorway. "Time, sir." Behind the man's torch loomed the black passageway. Night had fallen.

Will hugged Henry hard, and said lightly, "A mirror needs no forgiveness."

Chapter Thirty-four

AT the Christmas Revels of 1602 the Lord Chamberlain called the company to play *As You Like It,* a favorite of Queen Elizabeth's. Near seventy, with a frame grown bent as a crabapple tree, she sat stiffly on her throne in the big hall, so thick-caked by her costumers, wigmakers, and face-painters that when her hands moved to clap at the play's end, she seemed a moving statue. Will pitied her trapped humanity. He played Old Adam the servant, and moved creakily himself, with his hair powdered grey.

After the playing, while the actors ate their customary meal in a separate room, he stayed behind in the place where they'd dressed, carefully rolling their part-scrolls, then making sure they were *all* safely stowed and locked in the trunk to which he wore the key.

"What signifies thy frown, Master Shakespeare?"

Will looked up from the roll of paper in his hand. A richly clad nobleman of middle height and late middle age was regarding him with brows raised. His chest swelled his brocade doublet with silver buttons, and the chain of office on his breast stood forth prominently. He held his hands clasped behind him.

"Sir Francis Bacon." Will bowed.

The man looked surprised. "We have met?"

"In a fine carriage, more than ten years past, when I'd a full skull of hair. 'Twas a brief meeting. Not a memorable occasion, from thy spypoint. Milord. As for my frown—" Will knelt to pick up the last play-scroll, scanned it, rolled it, trunked it. "I fret for the safety of my scripts. *Our* scripts, as my friends would remind me to say."

"But thy scripts are very safe here." Sir Francis gazed at him with a cat's intentness. His *esses* slurred slightly. "In Her Majesty's house."

"Of a certainty. No danger here."

"None to innocent poetry, or its perpetrators." His voice was friendly. "Wouldst share wine with me, Master Shakespeare? I've an office here in the palace, hard by this room."

Will returned his gaze until Bacon himself blinked. "Willingly," Will said then. "Though I do not drink wine."

THE room was comfortable. Its floor was polished oak overlaid with large carpets of Turkey and two plush settles that faced one another. There was a cheerful fire, and warmth kept in by heavy drawn curtains. But none of these things caught Will's interest so much as the boxes and piles of documents and books that stood against the walls, a solid border of—he guessed—contraband, running the full rectangle of the room.

"It seems a chaos," Bacon said pleasantly, locking the door. "Yet I know where everything is. And *what* it is." He crossed the room, favoring a gouty leg. Slowly he knelt, and lifted the lid of a box, from which he extracted a woman's high-heeled slipper. He unscrewed the shoe's heel and tossed it to Will. "Look inside."

Will looked. The heel was hollow.

"Keep it and use it for some play. Why should you not?" Bacon stood. "The Scottish queen used such tricks and toys to talk to her friends, during the years of her impris—*residence* in our country. The game lightened the dullness of her circumstances, and so Walsingham and I let it continue." He coughed. "As long as *she* continued."

Will dropped the shoe. "I can think of no use for it. Sir."

"Well." Bacon poured wine and handed a glass to Will, though he had not, Will was sure, forgotten Will's plea of abstinence. Will took the glass and let it stand by his elbow.

"From the look of your face," Bacon said, "your greater interest lies in the papers." He sat. "Yet the objects repay study, too. Shoes, signet rings . . . Much general truth about men can be learned from the scrutiny of small, specific things." He settled himself comfortably. "Of course, letters may be seen as *things* as well, and pondered from various angles—"

"Which you have done."

Bacon swallowed wine, nodding. "Over there"—he gestured— "is a full set of the Martin Mar-Prelate papers. The Bishop of Winchester favored burning them, as they are vile and corrosive."

Will's eyes darted to the box.

"I know you would like to read them."

"I *did* read them once, when they were freely distributed in the marketplace, for men's consideration and amusement. I recall well what they said, to the very turns of the phrases. And I wonder, if you found them dangerous—as, of a certainty, you did, to judge from thy ministers' bloody unseaming of their author from the nave to the chops—why you stow them here now."

Bacon smiled, unruffled, it appeared, by Will's failure to answer in terms befitting address of a lord. In fact, that staining of courtesy baffled and nettled him. Through his interviews with many men he had found that players—with the exception of that man Jonson—were the kings of courtliness, until they began to be whipped for denial of this crime or that. Actors were quick in the tricks of lords' habits and gestures, since they lived by mimicking, apelike, the manners of nobles—as of everyone else in the world—on the stage. Yet Master Shakespeare's bearing bespoke insult.

Bacon chose not to show that he minded. "You care little for rank," he said, smiling wider.

" 'Tis a good word, I think, and most descriptive," Will said, nodding. "*Rank.*"

Bacon laughed. "Uncontrollable word-play. But you asked a question before, and I will answer. Why do I stow vile writings here? To keep records of men's thoughts. The foul ones interest me as much as the worthy. And here I may keep those records from public circulation among the privy-whisperers. Ideas, after all, may be dangerous."

"But not to philosopher kings."

Bacon looked strangely at him. "I had heard you possessed small Latin and less Greek. Whence comes this Plato?"

Will gave a quick bark of a laugh. "My friend Ben Jonson delights in demeaning me, and he is much repeated. I *do* have small Latin, and *no* Greek, but e'en a thick Latin translation can be digested by a country clothead when there's a will to read. I know Plato." Will scanned the room, adding in low voice, "And I had me an uncle who translated Greek."

"Is't so?" Bacon said with interest. He rose and went back to the decanter. "What was his name?" he asked, pouring.

Will felt his tongue stick, and said nothing.

Bacon shrugged, and took a deep swallow. "You and Christopher Marlowe were friends," he said, returning to his settle.

"I was his friend, yes." Will regarded him without expression.

"He proved a traitor, as you know."

"Yes."

"We shared membership in a . . . group. Sir Walter Raleigh, some others whose names you, so erudite"—he tipped his glass toward Will in a mock toast—"would know. A mathematician, another poet or two. My purpose was to see that our discussions of science and philosophy did not blossom into the malignant flower of heresy, or of treachery to the Crown. The two things are, in truth, the same."

"And to thy great amazement, discussion did so malignantly flower."

"I care not for thy tone of flippancy," Bacon said, as pride of place overwhelmed him. "I was, and am, empowered to help safeguard this realm from the dangers of foreign powers, who walk with secret feet in some of our best ports, practicing daily within our borders, sowing papalist lies, and atheist anarchy—"

"If one is an atheist—and I do not say Kit Marlowe was one—does it follow that one is an anarch?"

"*Yes.*" Bacon spilled his wine on his sleeve in his emphasis, and cursed, brushing the cloth. In a milder tone, he continued, "If one cannot accept that the monarch is from God, is God's representative and insofar as we may be concerned is *God Himself* on earth, then one denies and confutes all government."

"Sir, that is not, of necessity, so. There might be a new *kind* of monarchy, its boundaries drawn by *law*—" Will stopped. Bacon was looking at him with narrowed eyes. "In theory," Will said coolly, making his player's face bland. "You spoke of Christopher Marlowe?"

"Ah, yes. He did good service to the Crown for years, working with us to study Raleigh."

Will laughed, fetching a startled look from Bacon. "Treason grows complex," he said.

"Labyrinthine. Sir Walter angered the queen on numerous occasions, arguing unwholesome freedoms of speech before both the lords and the House of Commons—"

"Our elected representatives."

"I know what the House of Commons is. Your tone is surprisingly hostile, Master Shakespeare."

"I beg pardon." In truth, Will did not know what had driven him to such unaccustomed bluntness, unless it were the ghosts of some bold-speaking friends that now seized his tongue for their own. "Say on, Sir Francis. A player studies all, and a playwright e'en more so."

"Yes. Playwrights." Bacon gulped wine hugely. "Marlowe's imaginative gift was of use in the case we formed against Sir Walter. Which is not to say Raleigh did not deserve the queen's suspicion. It is only that cases are more forcefully made with the assistance of . . . ah . . ."

"Poetry."

Bacon smiled. " 'Tis so." He rose and returned to the decanter. This time he brought it back to the settle. "Had Raleigh not pledged to find Indian gold for the queen by sailing to El Dorado, he would lodge in the Tower still." Bacon's eyes went suddenly out of focus, and he muttered a thing that sounded to Will like *Yet I'll net him.*

That Bacon was drunk, and had been already when he'd approached Will in the makeshift tiring room, did much to explain his free speaking. Will pressed him further. "Net him?"

"Net him, yes." Bacon mused. "Though my job was double."

"Double?"

"Aye." Bacon's gaze flicked across Will's face like a snake-tongue, though the lord could not see the playwright's face well, as the torches were dying. Will sat in the corner of the settle, hunched and unreal. "I listened not only to Raleigh, but to Marlowe," Bacon said. "Though in the end 'twas nothing Master Marlowe *said* that condemned him. 'Twas the play we found on his person."

Will's fingers twitched slightly. "His person?"

"My men got it off him, though he was full loath to part with it. Thou mightst say he died for it. Paid the reckoning for his sodomy and his blasphemy and his atheism and his anarchy. He met a wild justice, and it was his deserving." Bacon cocked an eyebrow, amused at a memory. "He was asked at the end to repent, and dost know what his last words were?"

Will's voice was a whisper. "His last words were . . . ?"

"He said he repented him of nothing more than that he had not killed the queen with his own hands." Bacon laughed harshly, then rose and with unsteady gait walked into a closet on the room's far side. There were sounds of rummaging, and he emerged with a bound, yellowed manuscript in hand. "This is it." He sat, flipping pages whose edges crumbled at once into dust. "*Richard Crookback.*"

Will sat on his hands.

"List," Bacon said.

> *My crooked carcass won't my aims confine.*
> *From Ireland and from Spain I'll hoist my sail.*
> *Brave continents await, whose white-trimmed shores*
> *Hem in the brown-backed hosts who'll mine my gold.*
> *From dead Plantagenets I seize my crown,*
> *On sweat of darker men I'll build my throne.*

Bacon tapped the manuscript with a long-nailed finger. "Now, that is full Marlowe, would you not say? He was your friend—"

"I was *his* friend."

Bacon nodded. "Just so. What dost thou think of those lines?"

"They're not his best. Written in haste, perhaps."

Bacon closed the bound manuscript. "My agents followed him for weeks before they trapped him. I will say that the imp fought bravely for this." He touched the manuscript again lightly. "Doubtless he meant to retool the meter—"

"*That*'s perfect."

"—before he had the vile stuff spewed all over the stage by such as—"

"Me."

"Well." Bacon coughed. "He held tight to the play, in any case, until it was ripped from his hands. And he nearly throttled one of my men before the other stabbed him in the eye."

Will blinked.

Bacon's own eyes were intermittently closing, and he leaned back in his chair. Will watched intently as the man drifted into a doze. Bacon's grip on the manuscript was relaxing. When the lord seemed to have reached deep slumber, Will reached over and tried gently to pull the book from his grasp. Then the wineglass in Bacon's other hand fell and broke on the floor, and the lord shot suddenly upright. Will snatched his hand back, and Bacon proceeded in his narrative as though there had been no interruption.

"Master Shakespeare, the queen admires your work, as do I. There are . . . odd patches . . . yet in the main thou art the good antidote to Marlowe, who sought only to sow doubt and disloyalty among common English folk by means of his tragedies."

Will was unflattered. "Say on, sir."

"Taken in total, thine history cycles encourage a healthful reverence for the Tudor kings—*and* one queen—not the bloody one—who have blessed us these past hundred years. And thy *Henry the Fifth* is a masterwork. *The mirror of all Christian kings*, as you describe him, is the perfect image of our gracious sovereign."

"I did not describe Henry the Fifth so. The Chorus in my play did."

"Is there a difference? The queen was most pleased." Bacon hummed for a moment, then began to quote.

> So work the honeybees,
> Creatures that by a rule in nature teach
> The act of order to a peopled kingdom.
> They have a king, and officers of sorts,
> Where some like magistrates correct at home,
> Others like merchants venture trade abroad,
> Others like soldiers arméd in their stings
> Make boot upon the summer's velvet buds
> Which pillage they with merry march bring home
> To the tent-royal of their emperor.

"A good memory, sir. Say on," prompted Will. "*The poor mechanic porters crowding in their heavy burdens at his narrow gate*—should say *her* gate, to be sure, since the hive's ruler is a queen. I erred there. And *the sad-eyed justice, delivering o'er to executors pale the lazy yawning drone.* Didst learn that far? Then, *the king's masons buildings roofs with stolen gold.* And—" He stopped short, suddenly frightened by his eager blitheness to prove himself, in Bacon's eyes, as *anarchic* as Marlowe.

But there was no reason to fear. Bacon was starting to drowse again, and to look through him as though he were a colorless spirit, or nothing. Will spoke loudly, in his broadest country accents. "If my play were only praise, it were shite."

"Mmm," Bacon murmured. "Thou must let others say what thy work is." He struggled to sit upright, and hooked Will briefly with his black eye. "You must not think me a fool, ignorant of thy sly stabs at the powerful. I can be merciful as well as wise. I forgave thee for attacking *me.*"

"What? How, sir?"

"In thy *Henry the Fourth.* Thy fat knave Falstaff used my name as an insult. I will ne'er forget it. *On, bacons! Avaunt, you bacons!*"

Will laughed long. Bacon joined in, though he looked a touch unsure of the nature of the jest. When their merriment died into silence, Will told him that in Warwickshire, *bacon* meant *clown.*

"Warwickshire," Bacon said, frowning thoughtfully, as though he would note well the name of the region and send spies there.

"*The devil can cite scripture for his purpose,*" Will murmured.

Bacon seemed not to heed. He was staring in a melancholy way at the yellowing manuscript in his lap. Suddenly, with a single, impetuous gesture, he tossed it into the fire. Will bolted from his chair and thrust his fingers into the flame. Bacon grabbed his arm, saying "Stop!" Will twisted from his grasp, but was too late. The old, brittle papers had flared quickly, and were now a curling yellow flame. "Art thou *mad?*" Bacon said.

"Am *I* mad?" Will cried, holding his burned fingers and staring at Bacon, then looking wildly about the room for something to ease the pain, some water. . . .

Then, unbelievably, he saw it. And the new pain of his burns was forgotten.

He'd both hoped and dreaded he might find it, if he were given the barest license to look. Now, not given license, and with hands beginning to throb, he crossed to the wall of contraband and took the small book from the stack where it lay. He opened it to its flyleaf. The inscription stood out as clearly as when first he'd read it, at bare nineteen. His uncle's name in his uncle's hand, penned with love and care, in honor of *Mary, Heaven's Queen,* to W. S.

Will held the small book up to Bacon's gaze.

Bacon struggled to focus. "That? Evidence against . . . Edward Arden. Catholic. Minor gentry . . . from . . . Kent, or Warwickshire, I believe. . . ." His eyes closed. Will slammed the testament on the arm of the settle, and the lord's lids popped open again. Bacon began to recite as though on a witness stand. "Given Walsingham by Robert Dudley, the Earl of Leicester. Given Leicester by Thomas Lucy. Local squire who intercepted it, somewhere. Meant as a gift from Arden to his mad dissident son-in-law, Wallace Somerville. The two conspired to put Scotch Mary on the throne—"

"All this I had guessed." Will stuffed the book in his sleeve. "Since the book is mine—"

"Thine?"

"Quiet thee, Lord Spider," said Will, in a voice full of hate. Bacon's eyes widened, and his fingers curled with the purpose of recording a treasonous impertinence, but his mind was full clouded and he could not remember the name of this ghostly form that stood before him. Nor could he see him well, for the torches had died and the fire was now embers. He heard the chamber door shut hard, and silence as it fell. "Our Father," he started to mumble, but before he had pled to be delivered from evil, he had fallen asleep.

WILL found his fellows at the postern gate of the palace, packing crates, arguing, worried about their playwright's disappearance. They greeted him with cries of outrage and relief. Will said he'd been wandering Purgatory, and they mocked him, rolling their eyes, well used to his whimsy.

Hearing them jest, Will imagined how quickly they'd quiet if he told them how close he'd just come to killing a man. Yet he would say nought to unnerve them. What good? He knew his flaring vengeance would be burned into ash by poetry. He pitched in with a will, hoisting the parts-trunk with blistered hands, testing its lock.

Chapter Thirty-five

THE queen's funeral procession was the largest spectacle London had ever seen. It took place in late April, and the bursting hawthorn buds, the flowering trees, and the loud birdsong played odd counterpoint to the somber robes of the fourteen hundred mourners who choked the city streets. A pageant, the funeral staged the life of the nation as Elizabeth had seen it, folk all clearly ranked, and neatly containing their passions.

Knight marshals and bell-ringers cleared the streets, and were followed by two hundred seventy-six paupers, marching four abreast. Then came the queen's laundresses, butterers, scullion cooks, and grooms, trailed by standard-bearers who bore the Crown's emblems of Dragon, Greyhound, Portcullis, and Lion. Court clerks and musicians walked in time after these, followed by law officers and Crown judges. The dour Master of the Revels marched grimly by himself. In his shadow walked London's Lord Mayor, and then came the long files of barons, earls, viscounts, and—not to be forgotten—the holy bishops of the Church of England. All came slow, and many came weeping, in their sable hoods and gowns. At the procession's end rode the queen's guard, halberds pointing downward. A murmur of awe passed through all the watchers when they saw who led the guard. For it was the estimable Sir Walter Raleigh, still handsome and green-eyed and straight-backed, and all covered in silver armor.

The survivor of his ancient enemy, he cut a fine figure at her death celebration.

In the flowering of poetic encomia for the dead queen, the absence of any poem by the playwright William Shakespeare did not go unremarked. But Will felt, upon consideration of everything, thoroughly disinclined to write one. On the day of Elizabeth's death parade he was, in fact, seated on a bench at a Southwark bear-baiting, a thing forbidden in this time of mourning but happening anyway. He was scratching his neck and watching the hounds strain at great Sackerson, boy Sackerson, the giant beast he had come to regard as a kindred spirit, hemmed in, as he was, by dog-enemies, and doomed to keep playing the game. The red-brown bear had eyes that were alternately mutely pleading and darkly furious, though they were more often furious than pleading. When Sackerson was in the ring his ferocious bellows drowned out the snarls and yaps of the curs, and he snapped their necks as they came for him, always starting with the biggest dog. He broke them all. In five years he had never lost.

Will liked him well.

After Sackerson had wreaked carnage on today's dogs, his handlers, who hated and feared him, poled him into his cage with their long sticks, standing well out of reach of his three-inch claws. *Madman,* they yelled at Will, grinning gap-toothed grins, but they did not try to stop him when he came to the cage, as he had more than once before. Will tossed the miserable bear some fish, bought at the same wharf where the previous year he'd purchased smelt for the fat cat of Henry Wriothesley—Henry, freed from the Tower the same week of Elizabeth's passing, by fiat of the new king, James. "Here, boy," Will said. Sackerson gobbled the fish as eagerly as had Drake the cat, but with a far more impressive show of teeth. Will bared his own in what he thought was a bearlike smile, and imagined that Sackerson grinned back.

The fancy heartened him. He sorely needed heartening, so foul was his mood that day. The night before, a neighbor had glanced through the windows of Will's new rooms in Silver Street, above a Huguenot wigmaker's shop. By the light of one candle, Will had been gazing intently at a lifelike plaster head, topped with hair supplied by Monsieur Mountjoy from his workplace below. The head's neck was bloody with gobs of paint and its mouth molded to mimic a look of dying agony. The startled neighbor had straight sought the thirdboroughs and told them that London's mad beheader—the monster who'd made off with pates not his own and eluded capture for more than a decade—had at last been found in Shoreditch. Marry, it must be he, the neighbor said, for this man with the gory head on his table also had at his elbow a bleached skull! The officers banged on Monsieur Mountjoy's door and made much ado, with the neighbor standing behind and crying that he feared for his life at the bloody hands of the madman. All were calmed after Will had invited them to view the head closely and showed the man that the blood on his hands was only ink. But this evidence that Will fully and finally had a mock severed head that looked *real* did little to compensate him for the loss of a half-hour's writing time, and he hated to have had to let strangers into his room. He found himself lately mistrustful of folk who might find his papers. For some years he had consigned all his promptbooks to a locked trunk in the Globe's cellarage, and worn the key always around his neck. Still he was wary of new thefts, and burdened by things he had, in the past, left lying. Left, lying.

Lying.

"THEY matter little, these play thefts, anymore," Cuthbert Burbage told him the day after the queen's funeral. "We print all thy plays now. 'Tis, at the least, a way to show them as they are meant to be—"

"You sound like Ben Jonson. They are *meant* to be played on the *stage*."

"Granted. But they will find their way onto a page, and so best to sponsor their printing ourselves."

"So you have."

"I know not why you bother locking promptbooks in Hell."

"Those are maximum scripts, and have my *directions* in them!"

Cuthbert laughed. "No one will attend to those after *thou* art gone!"

Will looked at him strangely. "Gone?"

GONE, Cuthbert had said.

Gone, like jesting Kit, who had sold his soul to the devil for money.

Alone in his rooms, Will pitied the dead man, imagining him as he'd fought the queen's agents in his life's last moments, struggling to save the last, untainted part of himself, which lived in the verse of a play.

Then he thought of Francis Bacon, his secret murders sticking on his hands. He suddenly saw the world as it looked to Bacon: a savage place, full of fleering anarchs. And he pitied Bacon, too.

He looked at his own hands, spotted with the eternal stains of glove-shop dyes.

His pied fingers tightened on the inked quill.

*   *   *

A new plague broke out. Scottish James feared it, and though he was now King of England he refused to enter the city of London. He had himself crowned at York, safely north, and waited, biding his time. In the south, parents buried their children and children their parents in their back gardens. The brothels were pulled down and the whores wandered. The theaters were closed, and the players wandered.

Come home, husband, Anne wrote in her new, childish scrawl. *Thou wilt be sicke. Marry, and wilt not, eat hollow onion filled with fig. Put posy in thy pockits, and say one of the chants. Sow thy window sills with rosemary.* He folded the letter and carried it close to his breast, and reread it so often its edges grew worn.

But he did not go home.

Nor did Edmund Shakespeare. Will's brother had caught Will's disease, which was not plague, but plays. The Lord Chamberlain's Men had at last given him stage-parts, and he devoured them fully, striving Bottom-like—though with more playing skill—to be fifty, sixty, a hundred characters. He used the enforced holiday brought by plague-closings to bolster his study, hoping and praying that William Sly or Nicholas Tooley would break a leg. The grim set of Edmund's young mouth, and the shadows under his eyes, frightened Will whenever he found his brother hunched over a scroll on the stage, or speaking brave words to a crowd of no one. He could not see that Edmund looked like him, though everyone else could.

Thomas Pope died of the plague.

John Saint Clair died of the plague.

The eight-year-old son of Ben Jonson died of the plague.

"I have no words, Ben."

The men held one another speechlessly until Ben broke the

embrace and sat back heavily in his parlor chair. "That's much feeling, from thee. I thank thee." Distractedly, Ben took a sip of Rhenish from the glass that stood on a small table by his elbow. He had grown fatter, and his too-small doublet was stretched taut over his belly. It was clear that he had not barbered himself in days. "I thank thee," he said again, in emphasis, or perhaps just forgetting he'd said it already.

He began to cry then, furious tears of shame and sorrow and guilt. The tale spilled from him. He had left his family in London before the queen's death, to be the guest of a patron in Huntingdonshire, and had not returned to the city when plague burst forth. He'd not sent for his family, thinking all would be well, and then had come the letter announcing the death of his Benjamin.

"And I must be from London when it happened!" he cried bitterly.

Will looked at him, silenced by the bottomless anguish that flowed from the man. He could do nothing but absorb it.

"He was—" Ben swallowed. "My best—piece—of poetry."

Having no apt sentences, Will asked after Ben's wife and was told that she was abed; a doctor had given her a sleeping draught.

"And nay, praise God," Ben said, seeing the question in Will's eyes. "She shows no signs of the pest."

"The Pest," Will said. "I would it were *one,* and could be slain in fair combat."

"Ah, so do I!" Half-sodden, Ben sprang up, and knocked his chair back. "Yet there is no one. No one! An invisible enemy. Ah, Will, give me someone to fight!"

LATER Will stood in the street, wondering which way to walk. Saint Giles Parish, Cripplegate, was thick with red cross–marked doors, and there seemed as many in one direction as another. He set forth randomly. Behind him a door closed, and he turned to see a man exiting Jonson's house by the side, bearing a satchel. He was short and stocky and bustling, and though Will had not seen him for years, he knew him. Tom Lodge, New World voyager and kindest of the university wits, was a doctor now, much skilled in leeching and the concoction of anodynes for pains of various sorts.

At the start of their walk, they spoke of anything but the house they'd just left. Lodge expressed sorrow for Hamnet's death, then praised Will for *As You Like It,* and Will thanked Lodge for providing that play's skeleton in a romance the doctor had written before he took up the study of medicine. After that came quiet, companionable walking, and then Lodge said it was good that Will, too, had visited the grieving, since to minister to a mind diseased was as important as treating a body.

"How could I not go?" Will said. "Ben Jonson is my friend."

"Even the best of friends may be forgiven for shunning a plague house."

Will looked at the slovenly dwellings they now were passing. He smelled the garbage that lay rotting in the gutters and heard the scurry and squeaking of rats. In this part of Cripplegate almost every other door held the red warning.

"Whence cometh the plague, think you, good doctor?" he asked.

"I know not. 'Tis a patient old evil that lies in wait for us through the years. Its seeds lie in *us,* perhaps. We may banish it for a time, but it will always come back."

"Be there men who cannot catch it, think you?"

Lodge laughed. "A fond thought. But nay. A god or a ghost or a goblin is immune. If a man does not catch it he is lucky." Lodge lifted his boot and stepped carefully over a puddle of horse-mire. "Or blessed."

"My wife sends to me of remedies. Hollow onion with fig, and posy, with"—Will smiled faintly in the darkness—"chanting. Have these things any use?"

"Nay, nor the seeds of the black peony, nor skull water. Except that countr—except that some folk believe in them, and so they may calm the mind."

"The mind diseased."

"Aye. Diseased with fear, or grief."

"Or guilt."

"Guilt? Ah, you think of Ben. Yes. That he sat not with his wife at his son's sickbed compounds the agony of his loss." Lodge sighed. "This disease is beyond my practice. This was the third set of grieving parents I visited today. I would I could have saved just one boy."

Will passed a hand over his face. "Ah," he murmured. "Yes."

"Friend Will, you—" Lodge paused, searching for tactful words. "Tell thy wife she were best not too freely to talk of the hollow onion and the chanting now. Those things have been used for long years by the country cunning women, and no harm, but now those same women risk running afoul of the Crown. Our new king is hot to hang witches."

They reached the corner of Cheapside and Ironmonger Lane. The city throngs were absent. Only belled carts could be heard creaking far up the street, along with the mournful, muffled calls of their drivers, the dead-collectors.

The two men parted ways, bidding one another good night.

WILL sat with inked quill before paper.

Will knew Ben was Ben's plague, and would stay so. He could not help him. He could only pretend to, by giving a face to the infected air. He could battle the horror, rot, and grief borne on the breeze by painting their features; by naming the hungry hell that would eat a man's children.

The plague's name was Macbeth.

He worked hard on the play through the months of the pest.

THE dead-toll dropped slowly. Below a hundred a week by September. By November, fewer than fifty. Yet the tolling of bells was still constant by day, and frequent by night, and the playhouses stayed closed.

One day he stopped at the Globe to see Edmund alone on the stage, dressed in black, his eyes sunken and bloodshot. "Ho, Ned! You look like yon skull." Will gestured at a cracked, bony sconce that lay four feet from his crouched brother.

Ned looked up from his scroll. Seeing Will, he rose, straightening his dark doublet. "Look close at it, Will. 'Tis a real one."

Will crossed to the bone and picked it up. "This is not Edward. He's well locked in my box when I'm from my room. Where got you this?"

"I dug it out of a common grave outside the London Wall."

"*Paugh!*" Will said lightly, and made a comic face. But he replaced the brittle thing on the stage full carefully, as though it were a relic. Edmund picked it up lovingly; kissed it. Will laughed. "Skullduggery and romance. You Shakespeares all are alike."

"*We* Shakespeares! Are you not one of us?" Edmund still fondled the skull, now holding it two feet from his chin with his hands, disporting himself with a sequence of horrid face-twistings. "This is well," he said through the side of his mouth. "A real skull, not plaster. You were wise, Will. 'Tis best. This one belonged to a lad or lass knocked about in life as well as in death, I would guess. It helps me to summon dark spirits from the vasty deep of my soul."

"Ah." Will nodded. "The part you rehearse mimics my play."

"And I like it well. I will know every line, and if Richard Burbage falls ill you may test my mettle in a main part. 'Tis an excellent tragedy."

" 'Tis. Master Middleton is a playwright of skill, and revenge goes well on a scaffold. But *thou* hast nought to avenge."

"What matter? I can rack memory and find something. I *play.*"

"You look grim enow for a man who merely plays!"

"*Merely* plays! *You* say that?" Edmund snorted. "To play a murderer well I must match my mind to his. *You* taught me such."

Will regarded his brother's knit brows and his sallow, wolfish face. "You are doing a good job," he said, and left him to his skull.

Chapter Thirty-six

BY mid-1604 the plague numbers had dwindled enough to quell King James's fear, and the skinny-calved royal Scotsman finally entered the city. He was welcomed by triumphal arches and banners and a half-naked Edward Alleyn, now five years retired, who could not resist the city's invitation to stand in a brief toga before the new sovereign while making a speech and waving a splendid torch.

Despite Alleyn's impressive display of arm muscles and leg, it was Will's company, not Alleyn's old one, that the new king chose to patronize once he was safely ensconced on his London throne. The Lord Chamberlain's Men became the King's Men, which pleased the players well, except insofar as the new honor required them to hire James's own private clown, Laurence Fletcher. This was an actor of no discernible skills and a hyenalike laugh. "God's *breath*," Will muttered to Sly when he first heard the frightening sound shiver the stage trees of the empty Globe. "Think you not that Kempe laughs at us thus, as he dances his way through Hell?"

Yet the money could scarcely be sneezed at.

The money, in fact, obliged Richard Burbage to accompany the new king on his annual Saint Andrew's Day hunting expedition. Within the precincts of gorgeous, well-tended Saint James's Park, King James took a piss from his horse, slobbered over his haggis, and cracked a series of colorful jests, lunging at his courtiers' codpieces to emphasize their humor. "Marry, I stayed well back from him!" said Dick. The hunting party drank much and shot nothing. On the ride back they sang Scottish wine-bibbing songs, and James passed around a bottle filled with a throat-searing liquid that felt like lye going down. A good time was had by King James and by Burbage, if not quite by all, and Will was irked that he had not been invited.

"Fear not," Burbage said, as he sat with Will in the Globe's tiring house, poking at an odd-looking wig. "You will come to the next such revels."

"Nay." Will cackled darkly. "He will have me *stocked* after he sees our new play."

Burbage looked at him. "What mean you?"

" 'Tis a moral play, and the argument doth not shine on King James." Will was flipping freshly made promptbook pages with zest. "I am glad King James in his mercy has freed my dear friend from the Tower. I am glad he showers us with gold. Yet I feel impelled to show our new patron a mirror in which he may see his bloody, doglike pedigree." He looked aggressively at Burbage. "Else is art tongue-tied by authority!"

Burbage sighed.

"For kings rule by murder, do they not?" Will began to shout. "Not by law or consent, but by murder. Murder of men. Murder of *boys. Macduff's* son. *Siward's* son. One boy, Fleance, is saved from Macbeth. But how is *Fleance's* seed, which is the seed of

James, to come to the throne without *more* killing? And so it is proven. Our kings are not gifts from God. A lawless tribe are they! 'Tis a bloody register, our royal history, in Scotland as in England, world without end, blood, blood, blood, *blood, blood*—"

"Aye, Will," Burbage said absently, turning the strange wig to gaze at it from a new angle. "But King James will see nothing of that in thy play. He'll like the witches. Marry, see this, Will! Thy Monsieur Mountjoy made it at my behest." He reached his hand inside the wig and tugged at something inside the scalp. Immediately the ends of the wig stuck up rigidly, like porcupine quills. Burbage pulled the thing over his head and widened his eyes in horror. *"Why do I yield to that suggestion whose horrid image doth unfix my hair?"*

Will slammed the promptbook shut. "Burn it. In the ash-can below! Come. We will go together."

"Perhaps th'art right." Burbage removed the wig and looked at it fondly. "But I cannot bear to part with it yet. My da would have liked it. And old Kempe."

"Speak *not* of Kempe." Will frowned. "Tell me instead why you no longer fear the heresy and dissent I sow in my plays. You feared it full well, once."

"I know, but nothing ever happens. No one can tell what you—"

"They will *hear* this time, and *see* a truth that men have died or risked death to proclaim! In this play is a mirror, an *actual* mirror, and though its message be darkly couched in metaphor—"

"Darkly couched is good. Good for me. And good for you, too, Will, unless you honestly crave your fat friend's martyrdom."

MARTYRDOM was, perhaps, too strong a word for the new circumstances of Ben Jonson, lately seen battling his grief by haunting the city clad in a garish kilt and engaging in gross behaviors, such as tossing ale in folks' faces and gargling wine. All these outrages he was wont to make good by some reference— spoken in a fair Scots burr—to *customs of the court at Edinburgh*. These activities had seemed, to Burbage, unwise from the outset. But worse had been Jonson's insistence on wearing his kilt right onto the scaffold of the Blackfriars Theater while one of his plays was in process. Blackfriars, owned but still unopened by the King's Men, was rented to a boys' acting company. This innocent group had been glad to stage a comedy cowritten by Ben and his erstwhile enemy, now temporary friend, Jack Marston. Yet they had not expected Ben to wander on stage in the midst of it, towering over them, toting a bagpipe, flapping his tartan, pointing to his *thairty-pound knights* in the audience, and making crude jests about haggis.

The crowd had gone near mad with laughter.

Ben's cell in Fleet Prison was more comfortable than his old lodgings in the Newgate jail. Paying a visit, Will found that in the Fleet Ben had a table to write on. And write Ben had. As before, papers were everywhere. Jonson had been alternating letters to King James, full of servile abasement and apology, with jeering missives to his partner Jack Marston, foul fox, who'd fled London and capture. The Marston letters were spiced with saucy epithets like *shotten sheep* and *Iceland dog*. Ben had also written all his lordly friends, none of whom lacked power. Will undertook to deliver some of the letters himself.

In the end it was nothing Ben said to King James that got him out. It was his poems to the earls of Suffolk, Salisbury, Montgomery, and Pembroke, and to Lucy, Countess of Bedford. These so sweetly balanced a merry wit with a fine, slavish fawning that all those addressed in them felt compelled to plead with the king on Ben's behalf.

"I will do you one better," Will vowed the night of Jonson's release, as he bought the rumpled, unshaven fellow a drink at the Mermaid Tavern. "I *will* do you one better. Thou'lt see!"

"*THE* pox!" Will hissed at Burbage the next Saturday at White-hall. "I *knew* Condell should not have worn that peaked hat!"

Their new queen, who sat by her husband's side on a dais in the middle of the hall, was the only member of the audience not tittering. Her sable man's-hat, of the latest fashion, was almost identical to that of Condell's First Witch, who now cavorted with the other hags on the makeshift stage. The queen's brow under her stylish hat-brim was creased with a furious scowl. Will offered Condell a different hat before his next entrance. Yet this hat resembled another watching lady's, and it soon became clear that the fine audience thought they were watching a satirical attack on new clothing styles at court. "*Pox!*" Will muttered again, and sent all the witches out completely hatless for their cauldron scene. But since Condell, Heminge, and Tooley had no witch-wigs—the hats had been meant as alternatives—the men now resembled some of the heavily rouged and powdered male courtiers. Mocking laughter, as well as some disgruntled muttering, swelled again.

"It is nothing," Will said to Sander Cooke, now a husky eighteen, who watched with him, big-eyed, from behind a curtain. "Hand me the mirror now. This shall be the great scene. *Now.* Walk!"

Sander and Will were dressed in white robes as the seventh and eighth phantasmal Stuart monarchs, poised to frighten Macbeth in the witches' cavern. Will had been practicing for days, holding his large mirror at the perfect angle to reflect the face of King James, who he knew would be seated some thirty feet in front of and three feet above him. What he had not foreseen was the slotting of their play in midafternoon, a result of the over-crowding of the Christmas playing schedule. Now, as they walked with the dazzling afternoon sun slanting through the high window, Will's mirror sent the sun's rays right into King James's eyes. The king's hands shot up in front of his face as he cried, "The devil! Why doth that ghost-mon blind me? Make him stop!" Will tried to shift the glass, but succeeded only in making things worse, by blinding the queen and, next, a whole row of Scottish courtiers. In the ensuing hubbub Burbage's line *Thy crown does sear my eye-balls!* went unheard. This was as well in the circumstances, Will thought, as he flipped the mirror and got off the floor as quick as he could. In the neighbor room he disguised himself as the Scottish thane Monteith, elfing his hair into twine-bound knots as he vowed through clenched teeth, "The play *will* go on. The play *will* go on."

The babble in the hall died down and all went well until Mac-beth slew the English youth Siward, played by Cooke.

"Dost thou see, fine king?" Will whispered, looking through the curtain's spyhole past Sander's prone body, collapsed on the floor, at James, who stared raptly at all. "Dost thou *see* the cost of thy greed for power? Dost thou—" He frowned suddenly, and pulled Nicholas Tooley to his side. "How does Sander turn white as he lies there?" he asked. Sander was barely breathing. His corslet of light chain mail had come loose, and from his arm, pressed tight under his doublet, something dark was seeping.

John Heminge joined Will and Tooley. "He is meant to be gone before Macduff kills Macbeth," Heminge whispered. "He is—"

"That is not pig's blood," said Will. "Pull him *off!*"

Burbage, his sword raised against that of Sly's Macduff as they launched their final combat, looked strangely at Heminge crawling past him whispering, "Pardon, lads!" The two swordsmen had to foot it neatly to avoid tripping over him, and Sly muttered through the edge of his mouth, "Get *off!*" It was not the time to explain, so Heminge ignored the fighters and grabbed at Cooke's legs and began to pull. But Cooke would not *be* pulled. He smashed a mailed boot on Heminge's hand and would not give him purchase. By this time Burbage had fast-footed it off the stage and Sly had returned swinging Monsieur Mountjoy the wigmaker's horrible plaster head, a good thing, since that monstrosity drew all the watchers' gazes and enabled Will to join Heminge in pulling Cooke behind the curtain by main force.

"Quick! A surgeon!" Will said to one of the boys, who left running. "How could Dick's sword not have been bated?" He held a rag against Sander's side to stanch the blood flow.

"A pox and a murrain on thee both!" Sander swore weakly. His face bore a look of manly rage. "Coming on when you had no cue! You are Kempes, both of you!" He gasped, and took a sip of the water Tooley was holding to his lips. Then he swore again, and said, "Ye had almost ruined our play!"

SANDER Cooke recovered, in time. When his scar healed he showed it to women and told them he'd won it at Cádiz with Essex.

And Burbage was proved right. King James loved *Macbeth* and found in it the most extreme forms of compliment, so much that he began to order it played for him three times a year. These occasions were more dreadful than dull to the King's Men, since at least one thing went horribly wrong with the staging every time.

Yet James never noticed, or else did not mind.

He commanded a Saint Martin's Day performance of *Macbeth*

for November 1605, and weeks ahead of the date, the Revels Master called for special rehearsals at his palace near Westminster. Grumbling, the players practiced by torchlight, until the moon through the window rode high.

The first night, weary from hours of reciting and swording, Will left for home alone. Dick would not come with him; he was angry because Will had tempered a mix of goat's blood and draper's dye that would not leave the skin for all leaching and had administered it to Dick's hands before informing him of its full properties. "This is well for our tragedy, but must I walk as guilt-stained as damned Macbeth for my life long?" Dick complained. "Find me a remedy, and then we will speak!" Will assured him lye would work, and was hurt when Dick only swore at him in reply. Now he trod the dark streets in solitude, feeling lonely and disgraced.

As he skirted a building, he heard muted voices and an odd grating sound coming through the edifice's open cellarage. Cautiously, he stooped and stuck his head through the opening. In the candlelit cellar, several sweaty men were using shovels and picks to enlarge a hole in a river-rotted wall. "Mother of Christ, this shale's hard!" gasped one. Will could see that the man was holding his spade wrong and adding hours to his labor. But he withdrew his head and continued his walk, thinking it best, after all, not to meddle.

DURING the players' last bow on Saint Martin's Day, the King's Men were joined by a member of King James's privy council. Deftly inserting himself between Burbage and Will, the man grasped their arms and called for silence. He thanked them loudly and full courteously for the allegory they had shown this estimable audience. The play was, he announced, a clear representation of the abhorrent treason done earlier this month, when papalist devil Guy Fawkes, hellishly tunneling below ground with his heretical accomplices, came near to blowing up the Houses of Parliament whilst the king sat in attendance. "Yet there's more—"

"There's *nae* more," Will said, falling unthinking into the lord's accents, and trying to disengage his arm. But the fellow held it firmly.

"These foul would-be regicides, so clearly figured in the monstrous Macbeth, have been seized, alongside others guilty of the crime of companioning them. And as this day's entertainment has also shown, God's wrath shall behead all such men's witchlike, jesuitical, equivocating schemes, once a righteous English chastisement has opened their lips to confession!"

"WHAT made you of *that?*" the actors buzzed on the barge floating homeward. "Will? What made you of—"

"Speak *not* to me." Will sat at the prow with his head in his hands. "I have nought to say about anything." Then he found, suddenly, that he *had* a thing to say. He looked up. "God's *death!*" he howled. "All London knows that this play had been written a *year* ago! Nay, two!" He pounded his hands on the barge-boards. "Men are tortured and they call on my play! James hangs women as witches and points to my play! I meant it to be *banned*—"

"Can you not see that it *does not matter!*" Burbage shouted at him waving hands still blistered by lye and soap-in-water. "Things do not happen because *you* wrote a *play*. Every man sees what he wants to see! And 'tis not only you up there. Who is't you think *you* be?"

"No one," Will groaned, dropping his head into his hands once more.

Chapter Thirty-seven

SOON after, Uncle Edward's skull spoke to Will from the hallowed spot on his writing table where for years he had kept it whenever he wrote. It was past the witching hour when it happened, and his simple room was beautiful, its surfaces lit by wintry moonlight that poured through his unshuttered window. The skull was luminous, except for its shadowy eye sockets. From his bed across the room he saw it move its nerveless jaw.

It said, *Seek grace through horror. Speak what you feel, not what you ought to say.*

He was sure he was dreaming.

A freezing wind blew him downhill to the river, where the boats were still running despite the ice on the float. He tightened his cloak about him and crossed in a wherry to Southwark. There he disembarked and walked the streets near where he'd lived before he'd removed himself from the daily sight of whores, wretched

and beautiful, whose images haunted his sleep at night. He had
sought them now and again, for pleasure on hazard, and at times
found himself in strange beds when the sun came up. On such
mornings he would look at a woman's dark eyes that had seemed,
by the light of moon and candle, invitingly calm and infinite, and
would see only plain, tired Englishness. Pitying the hearts behind
those eyes, pitying himself, guilty and fearful and ashamed, he
would pay over his coin and flee. Then he would spend days
drinking boiled water and cider and pissing madly, racing from
jordan to table to playhouse and back, all a-tremble and watching
himself for signs of the pox. For years he'd been lucky as Oedipus,
but his self-disgust grew, and more and more he craved the life
of a monk in a cell.

He would do purer penance.

Today he averted his eyes from the rebuilt stews and stopped
his ears against the women's song. He passed the old madhouse
and a new bear-pit, and a low house whose sign said LAZARUS
NEWMAN, ASTROLOGOMAGE. ALCHEMY, FORTUNES TOLD, AND INTER-
COURSE WITH SPIRITS.

THE sharers, once more eleven in number, sat on stools or
crowded together on trunks and a settle at the Southwark home
of John Heminge. Other players sprawled on cushions on the floor
or leaned against walls. Three boys lay on Heminge's rug, awaiting
their scripts with expressions ranging from mild excitement to
deep lethargy. Will had gone home to Stratford for Christmas.
There Gilbert had shunned him, and his mother, now high in
years, had called him Edmund. Anne had been distant and more
than a touch marble-cold, though he'd twice or thrice succeeded
in thawing her for an hour or so. Susanna had spent her time
swapping eyes with a young, odd-brained local doctor who visited
her in their parlor. Only Judith had sat with him, from time to

time speaking with voice soft and low, but mostly listening, quiet and shiny-eyed, as he read to her from the play whose parts he now passed to the waiting actors.

There were quarrels, as usual, when the parts were received.

Willie Ostler spoke with surprising boldness for a boy so new in his apprenticeship, saying the part of Cordelia was nothing, my masters, nothing, nothing, nothing, and he wanted more lines. "Fie!" said Heminge's wife, who was pouring the ale. "That one's as bad as Nate Field."

"I think, Mistress Heminge," Will said, "it partakes of the wildest fantasy, the assertion that any young boy, however peevish a brat, could match his black heart with the awesome badness of Master Nathan Field. As for you, sirrah—" He looked hard at Willie Ostler. "The part of Cordelia is not to be explained or justified to such as you. It is to be read, understood, and played on the wide, wide stage. Else"—he pointed to the Heminges' back door—"there lies your way."

Willie Ostler subsided into quiet grumbling.

"Will." Engrossed in his part, Robert Armin spoke with his eyes on the paper.

"Robert."

"Believe me, *I* take no offense at small parts. Not in tragedy. I play the fool, and have my chance in the lighter plays. This is—I had expected—"

"Yes?"

"But this! That you would grant a jester license and scope . . ."

"Say't, Robert!"

But Armin, mouthing lines, had already forgotten Will.

Will smiled, and turned to Burbage. "There you have it, Dick. My part of our bargain."

"What?" Dick's scroll lay before him on a table. His face looked whitish and strange.

"Our bargain. Dost remember? Once I promised to write you the greatest tragic part ever played on any of the world's stages if you only spoke some paltry lines from my *Richard the Third*."

"I said those lines because I sounded good saying them, and not for any faith in *your* bargains." Burbage spoke slowly, as though in a dream.

"Yet see how God has not forgotten thee, in despite of thy faithlessness! I never promise but I mean to pay. What sayest thou?"

"That I cannot do this."

The room fell quickly silent.

All those assembled knew Richard Burbage could memorize five hundred new lines of dialogue in a morning. He could improvise in iambic pentameter when the boys forgot their lines, and do it so the audience never noticed a gap. One long-ago day in the old Theater, the stage balcony had collapsed, dropping Burbage to the floor in the midst of a speech. He'd continued his monologue in the air and landed on his feet without once breaking the blank verse. Then he'd played on through three fight scenes, and not until ten minutes after Kempe's closing jig had he confessed to the men his ankle was sprained.

Dick was a player's player. He was word made flesh, come to dwell among them. Not even Will knew what it might mean when Dick said he could not do a part.

Armin broke the silence. "What, now, Dick!"

Burbage seemed to awaken from his trance. "What I mean, to be sure," he said, "is that if any man could play this part I could play this part, but no man could play this part, so I cannot."

"The man's lines are fewer than Hamlet's!" Will cried.

"Measure not the *number*. What of the *volume*? What didst thou think? That I should be a *horn*? A trumpeting *elephant*?"

"Ah, this is *nothing*, Dick. In the beginning are the words. They will speak spirit into you. Marry, you *know* this!"

"Mystical Shakespeare nonsense, when you give me direction to YELL AT THE TOPS OF MY LUNGS FOR FIVE ACTS RUN-NING—"

Mistress Heminge shrieked and a glass shattered.

" 'Tis well, Dick!" Will said in excitement. "Only three hours more of it, and thou shalt have been Lear!"

THE language itself changed Burbage's mind, as it always did.

"*How shall your houseless heads and unfed sides, your looped and windowed raggedness, defend you from seasons such as these?*" he would cry suddenly, turning to Will as they walked, blown by brisk March winds, through Fleet Street or Cheapside. "*That* trembles on the brink of music, friend!" His voice startled flocks of pigeons and pedestrians. At home in Holywell Street, Dick practiced cursing in his garden, till his wife grew tired of his railing and told him to stop.

"A good brother and a bad one," said Edmund, smiling at Will. He shook his scroll. "Marry, what might *that* mean?"

"Be glad that you may play the good one, though thou'rt named for the bad," Will said.

"Is't not that the bad one is named for me?"

"Ah—did you come first? I suppose that you did."

"I would rather play the bad brother. He will be the interesting one."

"Nay, he *is not.*" Will looked unaccountably angry. "You've not read thy part. And thou shouldst be grateful to play either one, over Sly or Tooley. I argued hard for thee."

"I *am* grateful," Edmund said, scanning his part-scroll with greedy eyes. Behind him, his mistress moved slowly to the window of their Southwark parlor and gazed listlessly out. She was heavy with child. "I *am* grateful," Edmund said.

*   *   *

BURBAGE, now besotted with the part of Lear, agreed with the other sharers to help finance a wind-machine for the storm of act three. They placed the huge crank-driven fan in the opening of the cellarage trap. Sly turned it, while two men rolled cannonballs in the upper back galleries and eight players below raised a ruckus, banging pots and shaking sheets of metal.

The first time they used it in rehearsal, it blew Burbage's white wig off.

Practice must then be halted for general laughter, and then started again, then halted a second time after Dick yelled *Blow, winds, and crack your cheeks!* and was met with a volley of farting sounds, offered by the boys. Three of the newer players then fretted over the difficulty of recapturing a thing they called "tragic mood," and proposed communal retirement to the Knavish Loon for refreshment of spirits for the morrow. Burbage, sounding much like his father in days of yore, heaped scorn on these men for their effete modern whining, then looked darkly at Will. Will spread his hands as if to say *What, Dick?* But Dick had turned back to the play, and practice continued, as it did the next day and the next, until all was as ready as ever it would be for performance.

"WOULD we might have real thunder!" John Lowin said fretfully, looking up at the clear spring sky. "Christopher Marlowe could summon thunder whenever *Faustus* was played at the old Rose."

"Because he had a pact with the devil," Will said mildly, jotting notes in the promptbook. "*You* will have to make do with God."

THE thing came off so well Will nearly concluded Kempe's curse had failed, for once. But that was before, having grown fretful at

Edmund's absence from their after-play celebration at the Knavish Loon, he met his brother at his home.

Edmund opened the door in the same trunks and cotton shirt he'd worn on the stage. They were full rumpled, as was his hair. He was hollow-eyed, and looked almost as old as Will, though he was, in fact, sixteen years younger. His common room smelled of blood and sweat, and was dark from the cloths that hung over the windows.

"What is't, Edmund?" Will asked, though he feared he could guess.

"Born dead." Edmund sat in his chair. Will stayed standing. Behind him he could just see the bed in the other room, and a still form lying there.

"And she . . . ?" he asked with dread.

"Alice is sleeping. The baby was buried this morn."

"This *morn*? But why did you not—marry, *I* could have played your part, Ned! I know it cannot have been money—"

"Of a certainty, no." Edmund looked coldly at his brother. "You give me enough."

"You need not play tomorrow," Will said, looking at him with horrified sadness. "I *forbid* you to play tomorrow. Stay here with thine Alice—"

"I am a man, and you will forbid me nothing." Edmund looked at Will fiercely. "I will see you tomorrow at the play."

That was the beginning of it. The end came the following February.

IN 1606 the men at last opened their roofed playhouse, Blackfriars. Now they could play indoors on cold days and, on warm and fine ones, could offer two plays a day, one at the Globe in the afternoon and the other to the fine folk indoor, at night. Those who dwelt near Blackfriars hated them, but the wealthy flocked to the theater and paid angels, not pennies, for seats. So the men did not care, and were richer than ever before.

The players liked gold, and in time it seemed a small matter, if crowds would come, to hire more actors and play plays simultaneously, one each at Blackfriars and the Globe in the afternoons, and now a *third* play at Blackfriars after the sun set. When the Thames froze solid in late January, folk could save a penny and walk across water to the playhouse. Over they came on that broad thoroughfare, by the hundreds, to see the players declaiming with their breath hanging frosty in the air before them. When the men played *As You Like It* the branches of the frozen ash trees, a fair model of the Arden Forest, bent low over the stage as though freighted with crystal. The men lit braziers in the tiring rooms and stomped and danced backstage to keep their bloods flowing. The vendors in the open yard sold hot chestnuts. In the Woolery at Christmastide, Will had stitched and dyed gloves that looked— from a fair enough distance—like the skin of bare hands, and those they all wore now while performing.

Yet Edmund Shakespeare would be damned if he would give up a smidgin of the *real* in his playing. He would not wear a suit of moleskin as *King Lear*'s mad Tom O'Bedlam. A clout of rags would serve his turn, since that was what Tom O'Bedlam wore. Grave dishonesty it would be, Edmund said, to play him other than as he was written. He would not refuse to *feel* the chill the poor Bedlamite felt, if he was to play the fellow. It was full February, and the water was frozen on the Thames. And though no one knew it, Edmund was full feverish already.

NED lay babbling in his bed and his lover wept and held him close. A surgeon came, grim and dignified in his coif and cap. He cast Edmund's water, bled him with leeches on hips and arms, and spooned into his mouth extract of codfish oil mixed with powdered swordfish blades and angelica root. All this Edmund promptly spewed on the surgeon's gown.

The surgeon said it was time for a priest.

One of the players in the room went to fetch one. As they waited, Will knelt by Edmund's bed. But he could think of no final blessing to say save *Poor Tom, poor Tom, poor Tom.*

Chapter Thirty-eight

ANOTHER year passed.

The King's Men were playing at Whitehall Palace, though Will was not. His parts had grown ever smaller as he'd grown more steeped in the role of watcher-through-eyehole, striving to see that all went as planned, and more often to guess why it hadn't. In *Twelfth Night* tonight he took no part at all.

Standing just outside the doorway to the large chamber, he could see at the rear of the watching crowd of courtiers old Francis Bacon, still proud in his place earned by statecraft and earnest support of King James's accession. By his side was a painted woman, whose loveliness was marred by the pains she'd taken to hide her years, with tint-pot and pencil and white fuchsia that masked the real qualities of her skin. She was one of a score of painted dolls who sat by the painted men of the court in the hall, with King James and his queen in the center.

"*Lechery!*" said John Lowin. He was Sir Toby Belch, and

lurched drunkenly about the floor not twenty feet from Will. *"I defy lechery."* Laughter swelled at Sir Toby. Will noted it and was pleased, though he was not watching Lowin, but Bacon, as that lord leaned close to the woman and whispered a thing in her ear.

Will's lip twisted in revulsion, but he could not take his eyes away from the pair. Absently, he scratched his neck.

"What's a drunken man like, fool?" Willie Ostler spoke as Olivia.

Robert Armin jingled his belled jester's staff. *"Like a drown'd man, a fool, and a madman."*

AFTER performances players were amply provided with meals in the kitchens, but were never invited to dine or sup with the elegant folk of the court. Now, packing their gear at the end of the hall, they watched as the lords and ladies together rose and charged the banquet tables in the room beyond, vying frantically for the stuffed capons, mince pies, towering cakes, and sugared candies and sweetmeats that lay on the board.

Through the wide doorway the players stared, enthralled, as a servant opened a pie filled with live blackbirds. The birds, terrified, flew out of the pie and winged about the windowless banquet room, putting out candles with the rush of their feathers. The ladies shrieked in wild pleasure, and it seemed to the players that a mad game of blindman's buff began. Within the minute came fresh entertainment: a thundering crash, followed by a many-throated groan. The table had fallen to the floor under the press of crowding people. By the torchlight that lit the edges of the banquet room Will could see a bevy of gorgeously clad nobles kneeling, grabbing food off the carpet. One man lurched back, bottle in hand, into the main hall where the players were, and vomited on James's now-empty throne. Then he wandered out again.

Stepping inside the hall, Will saw some of the older players pull back the boys, who thought in the dark they might vie with the highborn for cake. Then he felt his shoulder touched from behind, and turned. Henry Wriothesley stood smiling, blue-eyed and handsome as ever, his blond locks regrown and reaching below his shoulders. Along with the players, he was laughing at the scene in the other room. He proposed that he join Will at his meal in the kitchens below.

"Let us shog!" called Sly to Will, as Sly held tight to a struggling Willie Ostler. "We are done here."

"Aye!" Will agreed, and turned with Henry, saying in a lower voice, "They are all whores," meaning the men as well as the women. But the painted lady to whom Sir Francis Bacon had whispered during the play had not gone into the banquet room, and as Will said *all whores* she was approaching. Without meaning to, he hooked her gaze and stared at her as he walked past. Her belladonnaed eyes looked back at him with vengeful fury. He did not stop. With Henry's hand still on his shoulder he left the hall and descended the back stairwell, mechanically following his brothers, the players.

Yet he felt her dark stare on his back.

THE sonnets were published in a small quarto volume with his name displayed prominently on the cover. The printer Rich Field, his old friend, had refused to touch them, but of course another man did, and it was much to that other man's profit, so rapidly did this new book find buyers. The mysterious dedication to W. H., *the only begetter of these sonnets,* Will took to be Emilia's carping allusion to *William and Henry,* two friends as one, with her, the third subject of the poems, left out of friendship's circle. As, from start to finish, she had been.

He took it all as his due.

Though it was full playing season, and plays were wanted, he took his horse from the mews and left London, covering the distance to Stratford in a day and a half. Even so he arrived too late. He saw his sonnets in the window of a bookshop in Stratford High Street.

A miracle of modern commerce.

New Place was quiet when he came through the door. It was Sunday afternoon, and his wife and daughters were from home, it seemed. Visiting? He cringed at the thought. Hiding, perhaps, in Henley Street? His eye caught a movement in the garden outside, and he crossed to look. There was Gilbert, walking with garden shears, clipping at hedges and branches. His brother turned and met his gaze.

"I reckon you think this my doing, somehow," Gilbert said, laying the shears on the broad cutting block in the kitchen.

"A foolish thought. It could not have been."

Gilbert sat down, his face guarded. "Brother," he said, "when I heard of thy poems in the marketplace—"

"From whom?"

"A friend. Not Anne. I left work and I bought out the lot. I burned them."

Will was silent a moment, nodding at his brother. Then he said, "Too late, to be sure."

"To be sure. She had seen them already. A well-meaning neighbor." He laughed brusquely.

"As well meaning as you when you showed her the poem *you* found."

"I am sorry for it now."

ANNE saw the brothers sitting together when she entered. Susanna was with her, and smiled with pleasure and surprise to see her father. But she sensed right away that something was deeply amiss. A look from her mother sent her out of the kitchen and into the parlor beyond. Another look, and Susanna closed the door.

Anne crossed to the larder and took out a wad of dough. She laid it on the table before the men and began beating it with her hands. Gilbert rose. "I'll take my leave," he said roughly, and took the shears. The door closed hard behind him.

"I am keeping this knowledge from thy daughters, but of course they will know," Anne said, now shaping the dough with vigorous movements. "They will know."

Will still sat, his mouth covered, willing her to look at his eyes. He thought if she did, her hard surface might crack and out would spill lively anger, or grief, or anything. But she did not look at him, and her voice remained cold.

"You will know that I did not mean their printing," Will said. "Had I had any means to stop it I would have."

"I would not have thought you *such* a fool."

He did not know whether she meant she had not thought him fool enough to feel the feelings the sonnets spoke of, or to do the things the sonnets recounted, or simply to make it possible that others might read them. It did not matter. All of it was folly enough.

She suddenly stopped her kneading and looked full at him. "Marry, I am not such an idiot that I thought you faithful."

"Anne—"

"I have known of your mistress well enough!"

" 'Twas long past. You must know that too."

She shrugged. "I am not a fool, so speak not thy bibble-babble to me. I care not what you do in your city. But to shame me, and Susanna, and Judith—"

"Ah, God! I know all this."

"Dost think, silly man, 'tis a merry thing to sit in a church pew and watch the neighbors point?"

"Nay, nay!" Will rose and tried to approach her, but she repulsed his hands with a furious shrug. He stood close to her. "Come to London now, then. Come all. Let us live together at last! I will buy us a house e'en grander than this, I will—"

"*Dolt!* I should leave my home and my life to escape the shame of a thing *you* did? And folk can read in London, I trow! More so than here!"

"Annie, sonnets are mere games of words. They are out of the fashion now, besides."

"William *Shakespeare's* sonnets are not out of the fashion!"

"Well. Sonnets are taken lightly by readers—"

"Not by me."

"I grant it. But to others' minds—"

"*Better* minds?"

"Pray, let me *speak*. I say to *others'* minds, they are a kind of play. Folk know this—"

"Not in *Stratford!*"

"No." Will swallowed. "But London differs from Stratford. This is why, if we remove to the city, my love—"

"*Call you me 'love'?*"

"I do, my sweet love, and now *list*. We—"

Anne hurled her ball of dough on the table, where it instantly flattened. She put her hands on her hips. "I have listened long enough, you cream-faced folly-pated black-hearted son of a *glover*. I have listened, and I have *read*. I have read not just one but *all* of thy poems, though some of thy twists of words full baffled me. In the end, God forgive me, I can say one thing only. And that is that I know not *what* you are!"

His face crumpled then like the face of a wounded child. He

felt a pressure behind his eyes, and tilted his head back, blinking quickly. "No, Nanny," he said pleadingly. "Say not that!"

She turned from him, showing a back as straight as a statue's. She said nothing more to him for the week he remained at New Place.

But she watched from the upper window, standing before their great bed, as he rode with his traveling pack down the road to Clopton Bridge. Susanna came up behind her and laid a hand on her shoulder.

In a low, soft voice, Anne said, "Susanna, I fear he will die there."

BACK in London Will kept to himself for weeks, avoiding the society of men, trying not to hear his sonnets praised by anyone. His playhouse brethren knew him well enough to see what had happened to him was terrible. So they spoke, in his presence, of other matters, of which there were always many to be discussed: things like the pulley and rope Burbage had installed in the roof of Blackfriars, so play-gods and goddesses could be lowered to the ground. Will thought it a dangerous notion, but his vote was but one in eleven, and so he spilled his voice for nothing.

When he saw Jonson in the Mermaid one day he knew he could not avoid speech. So he took a new tack, launching the talk in the direction of Ben's plays and Ben's plays and Ben's plays, and Ben's poetry, and far away from the dangerous shoals of his own. Ben helped him in this endeavor, as Will had guessed he would. Ben was fat as a pig now, and full outlandish, wearing a jeweled turban borrowed from the tiring house at Philip Henslowe's new Fortune Theater. He was hosting a group of six poets mostly unknown to Will. They feasted on a dozen capons, fifty quail eggs, five eels in aspic, a barrel of roast chickpeas, and ten kinds of bread, and washed it all down with French, Italian, and Spanish wines.

Will ate little, and drank cider.

By his elbow sat a slim fellow, dapper in his frayed gentility. His cuffs, torn but patched by some loving wife, made Will think of his own threadbare wear when he'd first come to London, twenty years in the past.

"Master Shakespeare," this man said kindly, "I find thy *King Lear* the finest thing written."

"Written? Is't so?" Will said sadly. "I thank thee."

The man began to recite.

> *Come, let's away to prison;*
> *We two will sing like birds in a cage.*
> *When thou dost ask me blessing, I'll kneel down*
> *And ask of thee forgiveness.*

Will looked at him with interest. "A fair memory, and a knack for the rhythm. Hast an interest in playing?"

The man laughed. "*That* would cook my fortunes. Nay, though I thank thee. I still have hopes to thrive at James's court, though my star doth not presently shine."

"The court," Will said, struggling to mask his disdain. "God speed you there. I do not doubt you are a man of letters."

"Nothing to vie with thine accomplishment, but I pray that God may one day speak through me." He shook Will's hand. "Forgive me. Jack Donne is my name. My wife, Anne—"

"My wife is Anne, too."

"*What's in a name?* Annes differ mightily."

Will laughed. "So they may."

"I meant to say that my wife and I enjoy thy plays together.

An occasion for harmony between us. Time and space disappear. London might melt into Thames and the empire fall; we would not know it. A transcendence of our two-ness, when we read thy poetry as one."

Will gave a short, hard laugh. "I am glad to hear that my poetry may bring a man's wife closer to him. As for my own house, my poetry hath divided it."

Donne made a sympathetic noise and regarded him soberly, while Will wondered what it was in the man's countenance that tempted his confidences. The corners of his mouth felt weighted, and again he felt the odd pressure behind his eyes. He blinked rapidly.

"What is the matter?" Donne asked him.

At the table across from them Ben was making good on a bet to swallow ten quail eggs whole and deliver an improvised couplet on the virtues of each. He had just downed the eighth with a half-bottle of Rhenish, and most of the table was cheering, but several dedicated versemen were scoffing that the last eggy Alexandrine was lame, 'twas full runny and half-cooked, and Ben must do another.

Half-watching, half-hearing, Will considered Donne's question. Through his mind paraded a series of scenes in no clear order, all colored by moods ranging from tragic to merely sad. He saw and heard the Globe audience yelling jeers at scarred Gabriel Spencer, who stood before them as Shylock the Jew, displaying his human hands. Then he saw a woman hanging dead in the yard of the Clink below a sign that read THIS BE A WITCH! He saw Anne's hard look as she pounded her dough, and the black, tear-filled eyes of Emilia. He saw Henry's wounded face as it had been when they stood by his *faux* moat at Titchfield Manor. And then he heard Kempe's desperate curse as it rang from the Globe's rafters, and saw the mottled, angry face of the clown.

He closed his eyes then, and straightaway knew he should not have, because there behind his lids floated the grim, sallow intensity of Edmund's eyes as they devoured a part-scroll. Then, worst of all horrors, came the wide, blue, loving gaze of his son. Hamnet was always there, in the place behind Will's eyes. The boy sat hugging his knees, which were knobby and scabbed and imperfectly covered by hose torn from tree-climbing and fighting with sticks, and he barely breathed in his excitement as he listened to Will recite the fairy queen's rhymes.

Hamnet is not, Will thought, squeezing his eyelids tight. *Edmund is not. Kempe, corpsed. Anne, frozen.*

Hamnet is not.

He opened his eyes and looked down at his dyed, hangman's hands. "I fear," he said slowly, "that I have done harm."

Now Ben was juggling the remaining quail eggs, skillfully, given his advanced state of inebriation, and chucking every third one into a watcher's mouth as the table roared.

"Perhaps I might do something good," Will said. He gave Donne a look of shy pleading, as though the man were a priestly confessor.

"What?" Donne asked gently.

"I would like, perhaps, to save a boy." Will smiled sadly. "A *real* boy. But it seems I can do nothing that has not to do with a play."

"Ah," Donne said. "Well, a play is a way." He leaned toward Will and touched his arm lightly. "Why not choose a boy, and save him how you can?"

Chapter Thirty-nine

ANNE lay in the Paradise bed below the carving of the snake. Her body stiffened whenever she thought of her husband, which was more often than she liked. Will lay on a straw mattress in Silver Street, suffering its scratchy ticking. He thought of Anne and of many other things too, as he dreamed a new play. The space between London and Stratford did not melt, and their twoness was not transcended. Will wrote.

> *Let Rome in Tiber melt, and the wide arch*
> *Of the rangéd empire fall!*

He stood before the door of a house in Golding Lane, hard by Henslowe's Fortune Theater. He had come without the leave of his fellows, who owned ten-elevenths of the promptbook he was holding in his hand. He knocked hard, and kept knocking for a full five minutes. At last the door was pulled roughly open. A tousled head stuck itself out at him, spouting a string of oaths.

"Cannot you tell when a man's not at home, knave?"

"I can tell when a lazy *boy* of a player is still abed at noon from his late-night carouse."

"Ah. Master *William* Shakespeare." The young Adonis narrowed his green eyes into a squint and looked Will up and down. "You are losing your hair." The lad himself had a thick head of golden-brown thatch, for all he was scraggle-bearded. His chest was bare, and he was wearing a pair of outlandish baggy Arabian breeches and felt slippers with curling tips. His gold ear-ring glinted in the mid-day sun. "Do you crave audience with me?" he said scratching his chest. "What hast thou in thy hand?"

At the young man's side a girl appeared. She was sleepy-eyed, and loosely garbed, and as she moved to embrace the fellow's waist her robe fell open to reveal a shapely breast. Will's eyes flicked toward it, but he willed them to return to the young man's face and said, "Send thy . . . lady away, so please you, and let me in."

"Go, sweet duck. To the kitchen. Eggs and butter."

The girl disappeared.

The door opened. "In, then. See how a *new* Burbage lives."

HE sat with a baggy-breeched leg thrown over the arm of a tin throne, *borrowed,* he said, from the Fortune's property room. He had first, with a mock bow, offered the throne to Will, but Will said drily that a playhouse plank was good enough for him, and would Master Field had *borrowed* one of those for his humbler guests! Then he sat on a stool and said what he had come to say.

As he did so, Nathan Field's eyes gradually lost their sly squint and went wide and then wider. When he spoke at last, however, his tone was still mocking, and colored by a pale shading of contempt. "I play *man's* parts now."

Will laughed.

Nathan sat up straight, brows knitted, and clutched the arms of his throne. "Why dost thou laugh?"

"A *man* does not have to prove he is one. 'Tis full evident. Not so with you."

Nathan frowned more deeply. "Have done with your insults."

"Good, then. I have done." Will rose. "And I bid you—"

"Wait." Nathan jumped to his feet. "Let's see the play."

"Why? 'Tis, as I said, a woman's part it offers thee. I grant thee, she is almost a goddess, and speaks all air and fire, but a woman's tires she will wear, and of course no son of a Puritan pastor would want to court his da-da's continued disdain by—"

"*Show* me the thing!"

Will raised his eyebrows.

"So please you, Master Shakespeare, I would—peruse the part."

Will waited, brows arched, saying nothing.

"I would—consider it." Nathan looked suddenly befuddled. Fear flickered on his face, then confusion. "What is the good of it, at any rate? None of your King's Men would share their stage with me."

"I would not go so far as to say they like you. Yet the play comes before all else. You know that well. You might help us solve this thing. Augustine Phillips is too old. Willie Ostler's voice is a tin whistle, and Sander Cooke has gone all *bass!*" He laughed. "Shouldst hear the fellow, Nate!"

"I do." Nathan laughed too, suddenly. "I . . . go to your plays."

"Ah." Will nodded soberly. "So."

He spent a moment trying to engage Nate's eyes in a level and serious cross-gazing, but Nate had gone shifty again and was darting looks out the window, and at Will's scuffed boots, and then back, as though drawn by a lodestone, to the promptbook in Will's hand. Without wanting to, Will suddenly saw the loveliness of his face and his form. His mind fled the apprehension as though it had touched a live coal, and then Nate was a youth again, angry and sullen and proud. Will pitied him as a father pities his children.

"Sirrah Nate," he said, as briskly as he could to hide his emotion, "the truth of it is, we have no one to play her. Yet we must begin practice tomorrow morn, at eight of the clock." He placed the book flat on his hand like a serving platter, and extended it to Field. "Our one copy."

Field stared at him, then looked back at the book again. "A fine trust *you* show," he said. He jerked his head in the direction of the room beyond. From its precincts drifted the sounds of a girl's humming and the shaking of a pan over a fire. "She trusts me, too. Can you credit it?"

"More pity to her," Will said, smiling wryly. "Women are . . . Though I grow old, I have not yet mastered the way of them. Be as you please with women. But if you wish it, I think I can lead you to begin to earn back the trust of men."

Nathan laughed harshly, and sat back in his throne. He looked at the book now in his hand, but he did not open it. "Why would you wish to do that?" he asked.

Will thought. "Partly," he said after a moment, "as you remind me of a lost friend who, had he lived, might someday have wished to redeem *my* trust."

"A player?"

"A poet."

Nathan yawned.

Will smiled. "And partly because you are still, for all your bold postures, a boy to me."

*   *   *

AT eight of the clock the next morning the Globe stage was quiet, though all of the players were gathered there. Upon his arrival, Will had told them what he had done. Burbage had let fly a horrible howl and flown at him, until eight hands restrained Dick and pulled his fingers from their poet's windpipe. Now half the men paced and muttered their lines while the others sat silently, staring at nothing. Will, ostracized, sat on the stage balcony with a scroll, correcting the lines of Enobarbus, Mark Antony's lieutenant. They had their parts, but no promptbook.

And no Cleopatra.

The bells of Saint Paul's chimed eight, and the wind brought their pealing faint across the river. The pacing, muttering, and staring continued, intensified. At a quarter past the hour Burbage tossed to his feet a tin goblet, which bounced on the scaffold. He looked up at Will threateningly. "Well, my fine friend, we may see our new play at the Fortune next week, I warrant. What do you think he got for it? As much as we paid you?"

"More, I hope," Will said mildly. He scratched through a line. " 'Twas *worth* more."

This was too much for Burbage. With a new and louder yell, he made for the ash tree on his left, meaning to scale the balcony with intentions that in no wise matched those of gentle Romeo. Sly went to give him a leg up. But the hubbub was instantly quelled by a loud whistle that sounded from the far wall of the playhouse behind them.

Everyone turned.

Nathan Field was advancing toward them between the empty, planked rows, clad in illegal cloth-of-gold and bearing a well-thumbed promptbook. "Eight of the clock's a poxy hour, Trojans!" he yawned, in a voice that carried well.

*   *   *

WILL began to think it possible that ashy phoenixes could rise. Stones had been known to walk, and the fury of wives, sometimes, to abate. In loving arms even a statue could come to life. New Place was a cold place, and had been for years. But even there, hate might one day be thrown away.

This thing seemed more likely to him when he was in London.

So it was in the great city he spent most of his months and mused on Time, even as it passed and lined Anne's face and made his hair greyer. He thought of the things Time ruined and the things it might restore. He considered the matter continually, sometimes alone, sometimes at plays, sometimes at taverns or ordinaries.

He pondered the riddle of Time as, on his way to the Globe, he passed the rector of Saint Olave's, Silver Street, who stopped and said, "Master Shakespeare, you have not been to church these two Sundays past."

"That house you worship in is too narrow for me," he said, without breaking stride, but he smiled when the pastor said to his back, " 'Tis bigger on the inside."

The Globe, his topless tower, was bigger on the inside too. He spent the bulk of his time there now, writing, his papers spread on the tiring-room floor. He labored to make verse grow like a rooted tree from the soil.

Sometimes he wandered next door to the bear-pit.

ON an oddly springlike evening one late February, Will sat, half-present, at another of Ben's festive tutorials at the Mermaid Tavern.

Jonson, now girthed like a bear, sat surrounded by young poets, wine, and a great deal of food. He had lately been rusticated—*expelled, like a fart, into the country,* said he—for complaining loudly at Whitehall about the rudeness of the court audience, who had laughed during one of his masques, and missed its moral. Now he was back in the city, and celebrating his return with a broiled sturgeon and a chicken pie.

He welcomed Will and called him a King's Ninny and bid him sit down and learn to be wise. Then he waved a drumstick at the front of the tavern, saying, "*Exemplum primus.* Regard yon stuffed man!" Will looked, as did the rest of the gathered group. Proudly exiting the place was a man clad in velvet trunks, watered silk stockings, and a fine cobweb collar, all wrapped in an intricately cut Spanish cape. He wore an ostrich-plumed hat and high-heeled shoes with roses on their tips.

"God'a'mercy, the poor fellow wants to be loved," said Will.

"How can you know it?" a young poet asked, with interest.

Will shrugged. "By imagination I insinuate myself into his place."

Ben laughed. "I'd like to see *you* in such gear."

"I shall ransack our tiring house, and you will."

"But let us discuss thy plays, Will!" Ben said. "*Hamlet* is great."

"And yet . . ."

"And yet, certain flaws mar its plot."

"Ah."

"Why is't that Hamlet finds he has his father's signet ring in his purse, when he has been hastily hustled to a ship, under arrest? Is it by magic?"

"I suppose so."

"And he says he has been in *continual practice* fencing when Laertes was in France, but he has not been. All we have seen him do is screech and mope."

"Then Hamlet lies."

"Established. Now, why does Gertrude not pull Ophelia out of the—"

"Nay, Father Ben, another play!" said a young man to Ben's left. "*Julius Caesar*. Master Shakespeare, why is't, therein, that Brutus seems to know of his wife's death, but when he is told of it again he treats the news as fresh?"

"I know't! I know't!" said another man, waving his hand in the air.

"Master Beaumont, I call on you," said Ben, pointing a capon wing.

The young man lowered his hand. "Marry, 'tis this! Republican Romans must *always* be told twice that wives are dead. 'Tis the same for Enobarbus in *Antony and Cleopatra*. *Fulvia is dead,* and then, *Eh?,* and again, *Fulvia is dead,* and then, *What?,* and then—"

"*This* is no answer!" thundered Ben, slamming his fist on the table. "It merely compounds the problem! To the very *bottom* of the class, Master Bibble-Babble Beaumont. And study thy Plutarch, *in the Latin,* before thou darest to speak again in my august presence!"

Master Beaumont took issue with the phrasing of this reprimand, and a group discussion ensued. So hot and lively was it that none noticed Will as he rose, pocketed the remaining sturgeon, and slipped from the room, bound to Southwark to see a furry friend.

HE spent the night in Othello's bed in the Globe's cellarage, with a candle. He rose early in the morning to walk past the Clink and the stews and the house of Lazarus Newman, Astrologomage, and from thence down to the river. A week earlier the ice had cracked on the Thames, to the undoing of three gallants who the day before had dared one another to race from the north to the south bank, and had fallen through somewhere in the middle, leaving nothing but plumed caps to mark their passing. *Sic transit gloria,* Will thought, remembering the colorful feathers afloat on the grey water. He thought of poor dead Kempe, and chuckled with morbid hilarity.

Then he hustled back to the Globe.

"YOU are mad," said Burbage, without anger or surprise. He kept his eyes trained on Will as he said to Heminge, "John, we have rope in the back for binding."

"You are a merry man, sir," Will said. "Yet this can be done. I am fast friends with this bear. I feed him daily—"

"Bedlam bound. Real horses for Macbeth and Banquo—this was a feat! But *this* plan be lunatic. Let us get on with real business."

"*Real* business. Yes. The Admiral's Men fire real cannons in their war plays. We, too. Why shall we not employ a real bear?"

Ten pairs of eyes looked doubtfully at Will. Finally Henry Condell spoke, patiently and slowly, as though addressing a young child, or an idiot. "Because a cannon, howe'er so real, won't run mad about the stage and savage us with its teeth."

"Now, that is a thing to be thought on. And yet such a quibble—"

"What wouldst thou think, then, once poor Augustine's arm had been bitten off by a bear?" said Burbage.

"My arm?" Augustine Phillips looked alarmed. "Why shall it be *my* arm?"

"It need not be his arm," Will said. "Indeed, it shall be *my* arm. I will play Antigonus in this winter's tale. *I* will be chased by the bear. Come, listen." He leaned forward, intense in his purpose. "This boy is an old boy, and we can get him for shillings. He's little to be feared, with a muzzle as grey as Antigonus's pate. And the boy loves me! He'll willingly follow me off stage, and no damage done. I've a simple plan that will make all go right."

"*Simple* is well worded," Burbage said. "I love you as a brother, but you are a dolt, and I swear by Hell's vasty deep and all the spirits that ever were that you shall not persuade me to *this!*"

THEY housed Sackerson the bear in his cage until the day of performance.

The morn of the chosen day found Burbage and Sly stripping boards from the rear tiring-house wall, muttering charms and prayers, widening the passage for the beast's eventual entrance. The gamekeeper they'd hired followed Will's instructions and fed Sackerson no breakfast.

At a quarter to one Will left Condell and Heminge battling with five men from the audience who had roped a pickpocket to one of the stage trees and were pelting him with fruit. Grabbing the hand of Willie Ostler, he led the boy through the back door of the tiring house to the trees behind, where the players often changed clothes in summer. "Sit," he said. "Only mar not thy gown."

Ostler sat, looking quizzical.

Will stood before him like a pedagogue. "You'll not play women's roles much longer, so attend well. Make this thy great one."

"Of a certainty, master—"

"No. Think. *Make this thy great one.*"

The boy looked at him, shaken by the roughness of his tone. "Aye," he said. "Sir."

"Now listen. I ne'er wrote anything harder for a boy. Not for Sander Cooke. Not for Nathan Field. And you know not that, you'll make a botch of it." He crouched and stared straight into Ostler's eyes. "As thou standst on the block in the last scene, th'art a statue. A real statue. Frozen in place, made in memory of a dead woman. And how wilt thou pose? Tall-standing, with thy hands raised, so." Will showed him, then spoke, holding the position.

"Thus for eight minutes, looking straight ahead, not moving at all. A fly will buzz by thy head. Thine arse will itch without mercy. But thou'rt a stone statue. Not acting. *Being.* Stone. *Dost hear me?*" Will curled his hands into fists and looked at the boy fiercely.

Ostler drew himself up in fear, nodding vigorously. "Aye, sir!"

"I wonder if thou dost. Yestermorn in rehearsal thy finger curled, and thine eyes moved halfway through the scene, following Master Burbage across the stage." Will crouched again, looking levelly at the boy. "Will that happen today?"

"No, sir."

"How not?"

The lad thought. Then he said, "I will fix my eyes on the thatch at the far end of the roof. The ragged part, that Master Burbage says he will repair."

"Good lad! And when wilt thou start to move?"

This time the boy's answer was prompt. "Music."

"Yes. When it strikes, then you walk. One hand lowered to thy skirt, the other out, palm outstretched, toward thy waiting husband." Will rose and dusted his old man's robe. "Your husband wronged you long ago. Your son perished because of him, and your daughter was lost for years. You died of grief and loneliness and longing. But the man has done penance, and now you must live again, and show him that you forgive him."

He heard teeth chattering, and looked suddenly down. Willie Ostler had turned pale and was shaking.

"Ah, do not fret, lad," Will said in a kinder voice. "We chose you because we knew you could do it." He pulled the boy up and clapped him hard on the back.

"Then I shall do it, sir," Willie said, gritting his teeth.

OSTLER was not what Nate Field had been, but he did what he had been asked. When the play was over the actors received such applause Will thought all his trouble well spent; even his mad race from the playhouse, necessitated by the hungry rage and quick-flying feet of Sackerson. To his disappointment, friend Sackerson had wished to feast on playwright's flesh rather than on the three paltry fish Will had kept hid in a kerchief and then dangled before the beast from back of the right-hand stage door, after his own hasty exit from the scaffold.

Like Sackerson, Will was fast for his years, and his sense of direction was sure. He made straight for the tallest elms on the rivershore, in transit passing John Lowin, who was standing outside answering nature's call. Lowin looked up in surprise at the roaring, and needlessly yelled to Will, *The bear is chasing thee!* Will did not even deign to wave at him, but pressed on, and jumped for a tree, the bear at his heels. When he reached its top he saw, through the Globe's open roof, that the play was still going on. And why should they have stopped it, to be sure? Shrieks had rung out in the audience, but the scare proved momentary. The beast was gone and Will's part was done.

It was a long time before his brethren came to his rescue with pistols and poles. There had been an ovation, and second bows to make, after all. By the time the hunting party arrived Will was already on the ground. Sackerson, haply, had wandered off down the bankside, seeking fresher fish. Will thought he could guess the bear's general location from the howls of scattering anglers and boatmen, but when he turned in dread to view the carnage, he saw Sackerson mildly reaching into the river and skillfully grabbing a carp, and then another. The bear munched contentedly, and left the humans alone.

After a while he disappeared into the woods.

The crowd of players and pedestrians and fishermen gathered near Will, waving weapons and ropes and nets and babbling excitedly. In time the bravest or rashest fellows broke off to search for Sackerson, while some others stayed to rehearse the wild scene in conversation and turn it into a tale. A few men struck out along the bankside paths, headed for the Dark Angel or the Cardinal's Cap or the Knavish Loon for a tankard. Will and Burbage sat down by the lucky elm to discuss alternative bears for Friday's performance. They argued for at least an hour.

Beside them the Thames ran past, on its way to the sea.

JUDITH knocked on Anne's door, then listened with her ear against the wood. She heard the clack of the shuttle and came in without waiting to be asked. Her mother sat by the window, working her loom and humming.

"Mama," she said. "Have you come no farther on that blanket?"

"I made a botch of a patch and I must redo it. I have bought wool enow. Bought some, sold some, bought more, carded it, sold that, and made a fine profit, I shall say."

"Why waste your time weaving and unweaving?" Judith held the scribal copy of her father's new play before her mother's face. "Why did you not go to London to see this play?"

"London? Not I, in London. *You* go." Anne frowned slightly. "I have read it, and think the play foolish enough."

"*Foolish!* Mama, can you see nothing?" Gently, Judith placed the play on her parents' bed, and touched its cover. "The rhythm . . . ," she murmured, as though to herself. "It still beats, underneath. But 'tis—broken. Wandering. As though a man were lost in a wood. . . ." She looked sharply at her mother, who was still industriously working the shuttle. "Mama," she said sternly, "if thou dost not relent, thou provest thyself the most marble-hard of mates!"

"*You.*" Anne stopped the shuttle and rose to her feet. She pointed accusingly at Judith. "*You!* I have told you there are things you are not to meddle with! This is one of them."

"I will meddle as I please in what concerns my heart."

"*Your* heart!" Anne raised her hand. "You anger me!"

"Madam, I am a woman grown and you may put down your hand."

"*What!*" Anne stayed still where she was, her hand high. Her body was frozen in rage, though her face was lively, and she spoke quickly. "*Audacious minx!* Let me say *this*, then! If you think *your* frenzy can change twenty-three years of that shag-eared man's neglect—"

"Neglect!" Judith gestured widely at the lead-paned windows, the Turkey rug, the damask curtains. "Does this spell *neglect*, madam?"

"Madam me no more madams, saucy girl! Neglect is just what it spells. I have a husband's money instead of a husband, and do not think that I haven't *added* to that store of wealth! You know little of the case, and care less. *He* hath thy worship; thy fine father, who hath betrayed and bewhored me and abandoned the three of you, to where we have lost—"

"*Can't you see he cannot stop writing it?*" Judith cried. "Not *any* of it!" She sank to the bed, wild-eyed and teary, and hugged the small book to her chest. "Mama, his plays are full of murdered boys and guilty fathers, and lost uncles and treacherous brothers, and absent mothers—his own, I trow! And innocent, suffering *wives!*" She wiped the tears from her cheeks with both hands, but more came, and her voice broke. "Mama! Ah, Mama! I tried to be a boy for him but I am not and I could not. Susanna said you feared he would die in London, and he *will*. Can you not see he will never come back here until you *forgive him?*"

Anne lowered her hand to her side and sat slowly back in her chair. She began again to work the loom. "Daughter," she said gently, "I thank thee for thy counsel. But leave me now. I've much to do here."

Judith threw herself full length on her mother's bed and gave vent to huge, howling sobs. Her weeping sounded heartfelt, yet, to her mother's ear, a touch theatrical as well. Anne worked her shuttle, listening. After a few minutes she drew a napkin from her bodice with one hand and extended it to her daughter, bidding her stop her nose, so please you.

Judith did so, and quieted. Then she rose and kissed Anne on the top of the head. Taking the play with her, she left, and softly closed the door.

Anne stopped weaving then and covered her mouth with her hands. For a long time she gazed through the window at her single proud ash tree, a seedling blown in from the wood, now grown into tall, full-leaved beauty at the base of her garden.

Chapter Forty

IN late summer at Greenwich Palace the King's Men performed Will's new play, *Cymbeline*. Henry Wriothesley was in attendance with his fair wife, who seemed much entranced with the players. When the play was done Henry left his Bessie to bat eyes at William Sly as that handsome fellow packed up the properties. Henry and Will walked through the crowded hall, and Henry named for Will the visiting dignitaries and the new English and Scottish lords and their wives. Will's eye was caught by a lady with hair of pure, straight black, wound in intricate coils on her head. She was dressed in a fashionable gown of blue satin stitched with Dresden lace at cuffs and collars, whose white contrasted markedly with her skin, which was berry-brown. Her face was not lovely by English standards, but the glow of her dark eyes was like nothing he had ever seen. She stood straight and walked with a free, boyish stride that put him in mind of his youngest daughter. Yet, unlike his Judith, she seemed to carry a stillness within her.

Her eyes showed it. As she went she gazed about her as though she had sprung, a goddess full grown, into a world that was brave and new but that she somehow surpassed, and looked down on with amusement. A tall, bearded man held her arm protectively. The pair passed within five feet of Will, and when the woman felt his eyes on her she stopped for a moment, and looked at him questioningly. He smiled and bowed, and she smiled and passed on.

He felt his knees weaken.

His fit did not disturb him. At nearly fifty, he knew it was not her he desired, but rather some far, trackless wild, blank as a fresh scroll, clean as a swept stage, and silent, silent, silent. To that undiscovered country her black eyes promised passage.

Or so it seemed.

He watched as the tall man led her through the doorway, then turned to his friend. "Dost know *her* name?" he asked.

"A very strange name," Henry said. "Pocahontas."

Pocahontas. He said the name under his breath for days as he walked about, as though it were a wizardly spell. He caressed its trochaic rhythms as he wrote in the evenings.

Po-ca. Haunt us.

THE King's Men took *Cymbeline* to Blackfriars soon after its palace success, but after the head of the majestic plaster eagle ridden by the man who played Jupiter broke off before a crowded house, with bird and player in full flight, Will began to eschew the roofed playhouse. John Heminge, standing horrified below, had tried to save the botched scene with the improvised line, *"His royal bird discards his head in rev'rence!"* but no one heard. The audience were hooting and roaring so none of the lines were audible. Will thought the play a ruined piece of work, though the crowd had enjoyed themselves. He was not cheered by Burbage's counsel that the audience would take the play *they* wanted, so better to smile and play it as it fell out.

The next day he tried to lose himself in his own Globe's audience, but he could not; he was known and clapped on the back, and still he came home cross with jealousy. The play had been Jonson's *Epicoene,* and what vexed him was a particular scene that had taken a thing from *Twelfth Night,* but Ben had done it wittier, *so* much wittier. And how they all had laughed! Groundlings and foplings and wenches, doubled over and wheezing ten times as much as they ever had for Will's scripted jests, but it mattered not, it mattered not, it mattered not.

"Straw, straw, straw," Will said to himself. "It is all straw, and I will leave it."

I T had been strangely warm all fall, and on the morning of November second Will wore only a shirt and light woolen breeches as he pulled his chair back and bound the finished script of a play. He put on a summer cap as he left to carry the foul-papers down to the bridge.

Birds cawed on the bankside, then rose to fly south. A falcon wheeled high over the river, plunged low out of sight, then soared up higher than before, carrying in its claws what looked to Will like a pen or an arrow, but was probably only a stick. He crossed the river, carrying a marigold to lay on his brother's tomb. When he came to Saint Saviour's Church he went first into the dark, cool nave and sat in a pew for a time. Then he came out again and entered the graveyard. He began to walk toward Edmund's stone, past the sexton, who was digging a new grave. Then he stopped, stiff with disbelief.

His uncle Edward Arden knelt by Edmund's stone with his

eyes closed, crossing himself. Beside him lay a book. He was dressed in riding boots and a grey worsted cloak, and looked to have ridden right out of the Warwickshire fields.

Behind Will, the sexton's shovel arced and dove. He heard the spade crunch into gravelly soil. Feeling hot eyes on him, the man at Edmund's grave looked up. When he did so, Will breathed again.

It was not Edward, of course.

It was Edward's son, Adam, the lawyer.

Will gave his flower to Edmund, and the cousins, who had not seen each other for many years, sat by the river and spoke of law and kings and plays. Will took out the Catholic spiritual testament he carried on a scratchy cord around his neck along with the key to the trunk full of his promptbooks that lay in the Globe's cellarage. He told Adam where he had gotten the testament, where he had lost it and found it again, and the bad purpose for which it had been used. Adam clapped his shoulder and said he had known. He had seen the book piled with the rest of the "evidence" they'd used to convict his father more than twenty-five years agone. All who scanned it even then could see that the inscribed praise of *Mary* on the inner leaf was praise for the Virgin, and not for the Catholic queen whose son now ruled them all.

"But that did not matter to them," Adam said. "They wished to kill a traitor and this, thy lost book, like everything else in their mock of a courtroom, was a prop. If you carry that thing as a penance, throw it in the river."

Will put the little book back inside his collar.

"Marry, you are proud, are you not?" said Adam.

"I am not proud," said Will. He threw a pebble in the river and watched it sink. "I have just been meditating that my plays are all straw and had best be burned."

"Oh, la. Why?"

"They have done little good in the world. This was plain from the start."

"Then why didst thou keep on writing them?"

"For money and because I could not help it."

"Excellent reasons, both." Adam smiled.

"But I had wanted to say what I *thought*."

"The trouble is, you think everything."

"Yes. . . ."

"Which is the same as to say you think nothing."

"I think thy judgment harsh."

"But at the same time you think it is *not* harsh, am I right?"

"Yes . . . No! I mean—"

"I *know* what you mean."

"No one else does."

"Look." Adam pulled a paper from a pocket of his gown. "A pencil?" Will took one from his hat. Adam sketched something quickly, then held it before Will. "A game I play with my grandchildren. What seest thou? A horse or a tree?"

"A horse *and* a tree. See, here is the—"

"Marry, *get* thy hand off it. I know where the horse and the tree are; I drew the thing!" Adam folded the paper and stored it in his purse. "My meaning is that everyone else sees one or the other."

Will's eyes widened. "Is't so?"

"Yes! And you, poor man, see all, and would say all." He laughed—a short, harsh bark, like Edward's. "So you walked into London with your thousand truths, and out they all came on the stage. Yet thy plays did not wrest the world to *thy* will, and so all's for nought! Fie, fie, cousin. An ass plods into Jerusalem bearing a god. The ass is blessed, but is not itself a god."

Will's ears bristled. "I cannot fathom thy meaning, but I know when I am mocked. In any case, I am what I am."

"What words! You *do* think yourself God!"

"God! If only you knew. I look at myself in the glass and I see—nothing, no one; or a shape of death or a ghost or a yale—"

"A what?"

"A yale. A furry beast with two heads who lives in the Arden Forest."

Adam regarded him soberly. "And you think you are one."

"At times, yes, I do, sir."

"Well, my father was right to try to keep you entrapped in the confines of his library." Adam glanced at his timepiece, and rose. "It pleases thy fancy to think all these things, I am sure!"

Will reddened. "It doth. And yet I believe them, too."

"I know." Adam looked at him kindly. "Come to supper of an evening, Will. Thou hast never met my wife."

Will stood himself, bowed, and thanked him graciously. Then he gestured at the book Adam carried. "So you read that."

Adam glanced at it. "Aye! Hast thou?"

"I await the translation." Will's voice was rueful.

" 'Tis a most entertaining story. Its hero dwells in a dream of the past and fights windmills." Adam frowned. "The author was jailed, I do think. . . ."

Adam took a boat to the river's north side, and Will walked west. His cousin's avuncular manner had left him passing melancholy. Reaching the Globe, he stood at its main entrance, beneath the painted, hanging sign of Hercules holding up the world. He shared the demigod's look of tired valor.

The sun told him he was early for the sharers' meeting, so he took a turn past Bedlam, then down Rotherhithe Street. He circled past the stews, and stopped before a low house. For the thousandth time he read its sign.

LAZARUS NEWMAN, ASTROLOGOMAGE. ALCHEMY,
FORTUNES TOLD, AND INTERCOURSE WITH SPIRITS

"Knave," he mused aloud. "Trafficker in grief and false hope. The dead are dead."

A curtain moved in the window, and he glanced at it. He saw the flash of a pale, bearded face, and then a hand pulling shut the drape.

On instinct, he rapped on the door.

After a minute it opened.

A man with a lengthy red beard stood before him, clad in a dusty purple robe and a soft cap embroidered with signs of the zodiac; mathematical symbols; and geometrical shapes, circles and pentangles and parabolae stood on end. He wore spectacles of dark glass. "Yes?" he said. His voice was high-pitched, and it cracked.

"Doctor Newman," Will said, and bowed. "I have come to purchase thy services."

The astrologomage gestured toward a stool by a table. He took a place across from the playwright. Will glanced about the room, which was crowded with books and papers, and whose walls were hung with drawings of the planets. On a table in a recessed alcove stood beakers filled with odd-colored liquids. A compass lay on a round table in the middle of the floor. Heavy velvet curtains shrouded the windows. A candle burned in each corner, and a fifth one stood at the center of the round table.

"Thy name, and thine errand?" the man asked Will.

"If you know fortunes, sir, you should tell *me*."

Doctor Newman stared at him for a moment. "I will gaze within," he then said, "at the cosmic speculum." He leaned back in his chair and stared skyward, stroking his beard with a finger on which a stone of green shone dully. Slowly, with an air of discovery, he announced, "Thy name is *William Shagsbeard*—nay, *Shaxper*—nay, now it comes full clearly—*Shakes—Shakes—*"

This was too much. "Poxy knave of a *Kempe!*" Will leaned over the table and tugged hard at the man's beard, which came off easily in his hand. "I *knew* it was thee! What a frail ruse is here, thou patched foot-twinkler! That any rogue figure-caster in Southwark would not know my face at once! 'Tis *etched* in the quartos, by the love of God!" He grabbed the clown's spectacles, and Kempe half-rose and struggled to push him back. Kempe's chair slid back and turned over.

"Leave be!" the clown said.

"No! *Off* with these! *Off* with them! *Out* on thy vile occupation! Th'art meant to be dead!"

"*I'm not dead!*"

Will suddenly let him go. Kempe lost his footing for a moment, but nimbly regained it. "Are you *mad?*" he shrieked at Will. "Leave go my robe!"

For Will had sunk to his knees and was embracing him, hugging him as tightly as he could, feeling the pressure again on the back of his eyes, though he'd not yield to it, never yield to it, for what was the good of tears? So he only heaved a dry sob and said, "Kempe! Kempe!"

THE story was tangled, and the clown—dragged by Will to the Globe tiring house—seemed to change it a little each time he told it. The players transformed it themselves in their own telling, so in the end no one was sure what was fact and what fancy. Yet the main thing that seemed indisputably to have happened was that Kempe, upon returning bruised and crestfallen from Switzerland where the Reformers had thrown hard bread at him, had removed to Oxford, and declared himself an astrologer. There he had earned, he said, shillings by the shovelful, awing his clients with mystical phrases learned from his almanacs and Marlowe's *Doctor Faustus* and the old Robert Greene play *Friar Bacon and Friar Bungay*. At length, however, he ran across the hard problem that none of his predictions ever came true. So he made them come true. He would prophesy that a starving student would find a bag of gold under this tree or that if he dug by the light of a new moon, and then he would bury the gold there himself.

"That was stupid, Kempe," Burbage said.

"You speak true, as I found in time."

After three months Kempe was so entirely ruined he'd no recourse but to announce, in a public lecture at Queen's College, that on his next journey south he would fall to his death from London Bridge. He collected the money from wagers made in advance, then removed to the city and, in front of witnesses, jumped into the river—spoiling a costly outfit, which was much to be lamented. "And the wet fur lining—faith, 'twere as if a man would swim with lead fins!" He nearly froze to death in the drink, but managed to pull himself covertly to shore and, what was more, to steal new clothes from the Rose Theater's tiring house. A new name followed, and—

"Enough," said Burbage. "We have abased ourselves, telling thee the truths we discovered after thy leaving, and crawling to kiss thy feet. We have undertaken to repay thy clients in Oxford who will now be seen to have won their bet. We have restored thy lost share. And we shall be heartily sorry and thy slaves forever, but thou must do a thing for us."

"And this thing is?" said Kempe. He was trying on new watered silks in the large tiring room, where the sharers crowded against the walls.

"Remove thy foul curse! Marry, since you left us, props destroy themselves, men are stabbed, trap-doors fall on our heads, bears chase us, and the *audience*—God's death! When I played Hector in *Troilus and Cressida,* a butcher leapt on stage, thinking me unfairly matched with Achilles, and went after Sly with a razor strop!"

"Marry, this is mere *life*," Kempe said. "Can you not accustom yourself to it? Now, this cap goes well—"

"Please, Kempe!" begged Burbage.

"What a gaggle of superstitious geese are ye!" Kempe frowned at himself in the glass, debating the relative merits of orange tawny and peacock blue. "T'faith, it stuns me I had none of you as clients in my sorcerer's den. My curse was the taunt rhetorical. I meant nothing by it but insult, and am not to blame for your mishaps." He laughed. "Besides, you had full many difficulties *before* I gave you my malediction. Dost remember the Richardless *Richard the Third*, in Hastings?"

Will was seated on the stage, already writing a new fool into his new play. He could hear Robert Armin courteously informing Kempe—who had stood off from him on their introduction—how much he had admired the playing of Bottom in *A Midsummer Night's Dream*. He'd seen Kempe, in fact, four times in the part! The other sharers were muttering and shifting their feet. Kempe was fully cheered by Armin's flattery, but still could not be persuaded even to pretend to unsay his curse.

IN the weeks that followed all was a frenzy of practice and practice and practice and visiting, because Will's daughter Susanna and her doctor husband came to London to see him. They did not bring him his wife, but they brought him his granddaughter. So Will alternated dandling and cosseting the babe with his frenzied part-changes and mad counseling of players to do this or that. His heart sailed high on the billows, though at times it crashed down too.

At night he slept deeply, and sometimes he dreamed himself on a ship, looking up at a sky. Grey clouds rolled back and the water was bathed in sunlight, and blessings on blessings danced in the air above him. But then he awoke, and knew himself a dark thing, malignant, deformed, and misshapen. And he cried to dream again.

*   *   *

STANDING on the scuffed boards of the Globe's inner stage, Will blinked in the late-fall sun. He narrowed his eyes and peeped out at the noisy crowd. Silk-clad gallants in the house's top tier, wool-wearing merchants and wives in the middle. In the yard, blue-capped apprentices, prostitutes, roaring boys. Dark-clad Dutch businessmen, Portuguese hidalgos in bright colors, winking French courtiers. Beggarmen left legless by Spanish cannon, and a sprinkling of old North Africans, unmoored decades past by the Armada's wreck. White faces, dark faces, howling or frowning or smiling. Everyone in the world.

Nothing that is human is foreign to me.

Someone rolled a cannonball down the rear upper-gallery floor, and wet sailors ran, yelling, past Will and onto the stage. The play had begun. Gripping his staff, he strained to look into the pit, where the groundlings shouted and shoved. The staff felt alive, as though it would straight turn snake, and twist and hiss in his hand. He was Moses and Merlin and Prospero, the wizard of this magic island.

And for once he would speak from center stage.

They were a Trinity of fools, Kemp, Armin, and Fletcher, as Stephano, Trinculo, and Caliban. The crowd nearly roared the thatch off the roof when Kempe first swaggered on singing loudly, *I shall no more to sea, to sea; here shall I die ashore.* Willie Ostler skidded barefoot across the wet stage as Ariel, but the slide made him faster, and faster, and faster, and soon nearly all was over and there was only one thing left to do.

Will stood on the stage alone.

He had lost his wizard's staff in the tiring-house chaos, and in its place he now bore a broken oar, its paddle intact but its handle short, split in the playing of the rough first scene. "What is't, a winnowing fan?" came a shout, from some gallery wit who knew his Homer. Will tried not to smile.

He said goodbye.

Then he begged their pardon, and asked for release.

They blessed him with their hands and their throats, yelling, cheering, pounding their palms together. The noise went on and on. After his fifteenth bow he looked nervously to his left, and saw Burbage, King of Naples, standing grinning under his gilt crown, and Kempe and Armin, both outlandish in motley, and Laurence Fletcher, still crouched in Caliban's posture but smiling, his face smirched with monstrous umber. *Ah. Not all for me,* Will thought, in some relief.

He looked to the far side of the scaffold, and saw Sly and Phillips and Tooley and Lowin and Heminge and Condell and Willie Ostler and the other boys. Then he saw Cuthbert Burbage walk out from the inner stage, and then Sander Cooke, now a burly man, and could it be *Nathan Field* coming on? Incredibly, it was. The saucy, green-eyed rogue was striding cockily as though he owned the Globe stage, though he darted a quick sheepish eye at Kempe. And why was Ben Jonson standing there? More folk crowded onto the stage as Will turned slowly, letting his gaze pass over them as though they were a wonder, and he a visitor from some far place. More men and boys joined the half-circle, and finally it struck him that they were not walking forward to bow to the clapping audience, but standing back, and clapping and clapping themselves.

It was all for him after all.

He had thought applause would free him, but it held him fast. Twenty minutes passed and still it went on. Dinner engagements beckoned and court cases pressed and church bells rang for evening services, but not one man, woman, or child left the playhouse. At long last the noise ebbed into silence, but the folk stood there still, before and behind, waiting, as though Will should give them something: money, or food, or a rhymed couplet. So he walked to the uttermost edge of the stage and then stopped, and racked his brain, which had gone as quiet as the house. He felt dizzy, and thought he stood at the edge of a flat earth, and that if he took one step more he would fall silently forever. He steadied himself with his oar.

But there, on the hard lip of the world, he found nothing to say.

Chapter Forty-one

BACK in Stratford he spent his days strolling his garden and the fields, walking past the stumps of Maypoles hacked low by order of the Puritan town council. He idled.

He read letters from Burbage, which told him Nathan Field had rejoined the King's Men as a sharer, was playing men's parts to stupendous applause, was called a second Burbage. That Nate's new best friend was Will Kempe, the clown, who to all appearances was growing younger. That Edward Alleyn, in deathless vanity, had left London and founded a school which he had named the College of God's Gift. Will learned Ben Jonson had made himself a laughingstock by printing his plays in a volume with a Latin title, and by claiming that neither public *nor* private playhouse audiences were wise enough to understand them. And he read that a bear had been sighted west of the Severn, in Wales, wandering the foothills of mountains where bears had not been for centuries. Some thought the beast a spirit, and left him votive offerings in the hollows of trees. Others thought him King Arthur come back to life. Very few thought him only a bear.

Burbage wrote that the London beheader had finally been caught. All London had been shocked to find that the monster was, in fact, Edward DeVere, seventeenth earl of Oxford. Under questioning, that lord confessed to a long life of spirit-trafficking and demonic possession, and to a score of killings that included the never-before-solved murder of Lord Strange, the Admiral's Men's old patron. Lord Strange had fallen prey to Oxford's wrath when he'd refused to allow the playing at the Rose of one of Oxford's comedies, calling the thing "trash and folly." Now in the Tower, Oxford had repented of his crimes. Since he was fast friends with King James, who shared many of his interests, there was high hope of his pardoning.

CHANGING leaves, not saints' days, now marked the passage of time.

Stratford passed a law banning plays.

The town council asked the Shakespeares to offer lodging and board to a visiting Puritan pastor. The godly man was preaching as he traveled the Midlands, seeking followers to join his flock and set sail to Holland, and perhaps, from thence, to the New World itself. Will gladly agreed to play the host.

"Samuel Godwin is my name," said the tall-hatted man who came to the door, clutching his battered traveling case. He was dressed in black, but his face was merry. "Thou lookst strangely," he said to Will. "Dost know me, brother?"

"Marry, I do!" Will said, and pulled him into the house, closing the door hard. "Once I looked for you through the lanes and alleys of Southwark and Shoreditch, and nary a man had heard of you!"

"Do you mistake me for another?"

"Perhaps you think growing from boy to man and changing

your name make a fine disguise. But I am a man who does not forget things, and I know the scamp who pushed me onto a scaffold with Edward Alleyn in the Stratford Guildhall years ago, before I was halfway ready. Yes, I know thee, Felix Culpeper."

"That was *thee?*" the pastor said, and laughed loud and long.

He told Will he'd worn a dozen names both before and after that day in 1588, and that he'd left Kempe's and Alleyn's company later that summer, and joined another. For years he'd wandered the roads, playing. He had grown to a man and made one of Nathan Field's first company, and at twenty-five had played in *Hamlet* in the city of Rye—

"Not *my Hamlet!*" said Will.

"Nay. Some botched version of Field's own, I think 'twas. In any case as I knelt on the scaffold as Claudius, trying to pray—"

"Claudius! At twenty-five!"

"I was acting!" cried the fellow. "Ah, but pardon my wrath, brother. As I say, as I knelt on the scaffold and tried to pray, my blood ran suddenly cold. I said my lines." The pastor closed his eyes and recited. *"What's prayer but for to prop us up so we don't fall?"*

"Ah, God, I ne'er wrote *that.*"

The pastor opened his eyes and looked at Will sternly. "Brother, thou takest the Lord's name in vain."

"Forgive me. Say on. Claudius, blood running cold."

"God suddenly spoke to me then as I knelt. I saw myself, wallowing in sin, slogging from town to town, polluting my body with drink and lechery. I fell out daily with my fellows, did all things ill, and poisoned my soul with petty hate. Brother William, at that moment I rose and walked off the scaffold."

"Ah, no!"

"I did it, brother. God had called me, like he called Samuel before me. And so I changed my name."

"Again."

"For the last time, brother."

"Did thy fellows forgive thee?"

"I asked them to. I got three kicks in the breech-pants, and a punch in the eye from young Nate Field. With that for my pay I left Rye and began the Walk Unscripted." He pinned Will with a zealous eye. "I have never looked back."

THAT night Will lay in the Paradise bed while Anne slept huddled far on its western edge. He stared at the ceiling and dreamed a waking dream. In it he joined Godwin's group of pilgrims on a Southwark wharf, and set sail with them for the open sea, meaning to cross unpathed waters to undreamed shores. Yet a storm blew from nowhere and tossed the ship. The company knelt and prayed, and each member offered to die if he or she were the sinner God sought in His wrath. Will was standing behind the mast, jotting with ink on the mainsail, when the men and women all rose as one and pointed at him, and then they advanced on him and tossed him overboard. He sank willingly, like a stone. Eons passed, and certain fathoms deep, at the oozy sea-bottom, tiny fish swam through the sockets of his briny skull, and the ocean shaped his moldering bones into something rich and strange.

He opened his lids, frightened by himself and his fancy. Anne breathed in the bed beside him. He reached to touch her shoulder, but before he reached her he pulled his hand back, and touched the carved headboard instead.

ANNE'S back was to him. Her arms moved vigorously as she scrubbed plates.

"Tell our daughters I will come at Lent, as always," he said hollowly. "I will visit the child. And Judith may come when she wishes. I'll rent rooms for myself, and I've bought the gatehouse by Blackfriars. There will be space enough for many visitors."

"Will you write more plays?"

"If I can. If I cannot I will see things well done at the Globe."

"Traipsing about like a ghost?"

He was quiet for a moment. Then he said, "I would that you . . ."

Her arms stopped scrubbing, and she waited.

He sighed. "Nothing." He rose and went out to his horse, which was harnessed to a post in the street. She followed, drying her hands with a dishclout. He kissed her hand formally, and bowed with a flourish that made her smile faintly and drew stares from the Stratford passers-by.

They had never been to the court, or on a stage.

After Will rode away Anne went back into the house and cleaned every room. Then she took each garment from its chest or trunk and shook and refolded and replaced it. As she shook out one of her old aprons a sprig of dried honeysuckle fell from its pocket. She held the sprig to her face and breathed its faint odor.

Then she rose quickly, went to the barn, and saddled her mare.

I T was June, near Pentecost, and the city was hot.

He stood on Maiden Lane, while past him rumbled carts bearing carrots, corn, nails, paper, and glass. Each thing seemed both itself and a symbol of something invisible.

He closed his eyes.

The sun beat on his head, and he sweated. He took off his hat and mopped his high forehead. It was late afternoon and the day's play was over. There was no one in the Globe, and Will was both glad and sorry about it. His key still opened the lock to the tiring house. He went down to the cellarage with a torch and opened the trunk that held his promptbooks. For hours he turned their pages. He read till his brain was filled with the clamor of Cleopatra and Juliet's Nurse and Richard the Third and Coriolanus and Rosalind and Hamlet, Hamlet, Hamlet. At last he closed the books and the trunk and his eyes and pressed his hands to his ears, seeking silence.

Then he rose and walked about Hell with his dwindling torch.

Around him lay toys and trifles and amulets, the scattered properties of the playhouse world. He gazed at the broken bed of Othello and the throne of Richard the Third and the ghastly severed head of Macbeth. Next to that head he saw Burbage's horrible fright wig lying in the mix of ashes and hazelnuts that covered the earth. The wig's wire-hairs still pointed upward like porcupine quills. Will picked it up. "I had told Dick to burn this," he muttered, throwing the wig in the ash-can that stood between the trunks of the stage trees. He lit the thing with his torch, and it blazed up merrily, and stank.

He wandered about for another half-hour, then climbed back up the ladder to the trap in the stage.

He always remembered everything. So it must have been advancing age, or some darker purpose lurking below his clear thought, that made him forget to douse the embers.

HE was stretched on the south bank by Saint Saviour's Church the next day, patting a cat and thinking of nothing, when he smelled the smoke. They had been playing *Henry the Eighth* at the Globe; between the usual crowd noise and the play's thundering cannons the sounds had bespoken no mishap to him. But then the sweetly harsh odor of the smolder came, and he heard the cry of *Buckets! Buckets!* He looked, and saw the pillar of cloud rising from the thatch.

He jumped up and ran.

Miraculously, all the crowd and the actors had already poured safely out. The one injured person was a man whose breeches had sparked, but he'd quenched the hot with the last of his bottle of ale and was now cavorting half-naked at Thames-side, loudly telling the tale. Will raced past him and the players, who stared at him goggle-eyed—they had not known he was in London. Burbage, still crowned as king, clutched the sharers' strongbox as though it held the wealth of a monastery, but he reached his free hand out for Will, yelling, "Stop, fool! There's no saving *things!*" Will shook him off and ran into the tiring house, chanting something that sounded like *Burned with my gold about me! Burned with my gold about me!* Nathan Field tried to follow, but Sly tackled him and held him back, for the walls were ablaze. Tongues of flame crept up the green stems of the stage trees, and the thatch was an unbroken wheel of fire. As Sly grappled with Field and the men shouted and the smoke poured from the house none noticed the smaller figure that did dart in after Will.

THE panel between the stage and rear rooms had collapsed.

The smoke was thick, and Will covered his mouth with his sleeve. A beam fell and grazed his shoulder. He stumbled and fell into another splintered beam, and blood sprang from his cheek. The air was acrid, and his eyes stung, but he pushed on, and in a moment he stood on the scaffold. Above him the painted balcony was burning, its sun, moon, stars, and planets blackening into ash. He dropped to his knees and felt for the handle of the cellarage trap. The metal was hot and seared his hands, but he bit his lip and pulled the door open roughly and quickly. Then he dropped to the bottom.

Hell was murky, but his feet knew the way.

Coughing, he found his promptbook trunk and knelt by it. He did not try to lift or even to open it. He hugged it. Then he laid his head on top of it, and was still.

But then he felt hands at his waist, pulling him. He turned and pushed the fool back, trying to say *Get away, poxy meddler! Save thyself and get out!* But the smoke burned his throat and he could only cough. The hands returned, grabbing frantically at him, and in desperation he understood he would have to die trying to save this idiot, this well-meaning dwarf or boy. He grabbed the fool by the legs and waist and stumbled back to the ladder. Together they went up, him pushing the other all the way until by miracle they reached the far end of the stage. It had not yet all burned, though the boards were buckling and the soles of his feet felt the heat through his boots. He saw nothing but smoke, but he stumbled on into the uttermost back of what had been the tiring house. He and his burden fell over the red-hot grunsel-edge of the door-frame to the ground outside. To their right a wall collapsed, and they rolled away from it and down the hill, with arms and legs entangled. A crash shattered the air, and Will looked back to see the balcony, now a mass of flaming timbers, fallen through the stage. By themselves stood the ash trees, their bark blackened but their green wood strong. They shook their leaved heads proudly above the wreck of the playhouse.

I T was Anne who pinned him to earth.

He lay limp with shock. She jumped up to her feet, still coughing, and grabbed his wrists to pull him upright. His breeches and shirt and her smock were scorched and torn, and both their faces were covered with cinders. "To the river! Come!" she urged frantically, and he let her pull him downhill, past the useless brigade tossing leather buckets, and the more useless afternoon gawkers, until they slid on the muddy bankside and fell face-first into the shallows.

The water shocked Will awake. He righted himself, and pulled Anne up, too, crying out with the pain it caused him. He was cut on his shoulders and his cheek was well gouged, but Anne saw right away that the burns on his fingers were the worst of his wounds. She pulled off her hood and tore it in two and drenched the two parts, and with them bound his hands. He stood immobile as she worked, his hands palm up, staring at her.

"I came," she panted. "I came to London by myself and God help me, I straightway was lost and I did not know where anything was! I knew not how to find you—" Here she started to sob. "This will hurt, but needs doing, Will! I knew not where you were, so I came down to the river and I saw the playhouse roofs. Then I knew what to do. I took a boat to the Globe. I saw it burn—"

"Why did you not *leave* me?" he said fiercely. "I am *no one* without it!"

"List, you!" She grabbed his shoulders and gave them a shake. "You are not *no one!* You are married and your name is *Will!*"

He held his jaw rigid. "Yet you cannot forgive me for the other one, or for—"

"Hsst! I forgive you for her, and for him. And for accusing me, which was not all unmerited. Though *mostly* it was," she added quickly.

He blinked rapidly. "And for Hamnet?"

"God's death, I *forgive* you for Hamnet, and you will forgive me. It was long ago and broke both our hearts. Let it be!"

"And if I do not *ask* to be forgiven?"

She gazed at his set, wounded face. Then she took his chin in her hands. "God hath time to pick such nits. *I* do not." She dropped her arms to his waist and pinched him. " 'Sblood, will you *wake?* This week of mad journeying will cost me—cost *us*— days of sheep-shearing, since those quack-brains I hired from Shottery can do nothing without my oversight. Twenty pound lost, I would think! And the garden's fair *choked* with weeds that thy brother'll not come to the end of alone; not him, stopping to pull on an ale-pot every five feet. The beans'll not thrive *this* summer; I'll be egg-fried if they do, with butter, Will. They'll be full botched. Botched!"

She placed his hurt hands gently at her back. Then she hugged him hard as he stood there, stiff as a statue, sopping wet.

In her arms he became human, and wept.

ACKNOWLEDGMENTS

The list would be long if I set down the names of all the biographers, theater historians, and other scholars and authors, as well as the actors and directors, whose talents helped shape my vision of Shakespeare whether those people knew of it or not. I do want specifically to acknowledge the beautiful poem "Instructions to an Actor," by Edwin Morgan, which inspired one passage of dialogue in this book; and to thank those few who read and liked this novel in its original, twelve-hundred-page incarnation. Without their encouragement the manuscript would have lain in a dark drawer forever. Thank you, David Daniell, Tom Lucking, Amy Silver, Michèle Sterlin, Curran and Emmy Tiffany, and Amanda Tiffany.

I'm also grateful to my agent, Carolyn French, my editor, Allison McCabe, and copyeditor Sheila Moody for their hard work and keen eyes.

No words of mine are fit to frame the thanks I owe William Shakespeare. But those who cannot heave their hearts into their mouths are grateful nonetheless.